I0746285

Praises for Memories of Lucinda Eco

With all the haunting beauty of a dusty desert road, *Memories of Lucinda Eco* sweeps the reader into a magic-infused Baja California filled with equal parts curses, friendship, brujos, and love. Perfect for young adults and adults who feel young, Barnes' fiction is filled with with powerful lyricism, understated sophistication, and jarring discovery.

— Kevin J. Anderson, New York Times
bestselling coauthor of *Dune: House
Atreides*

With thrilling world-building, bold writing, and a heroine to root for, *Memories of Lucinda Eco* has all the elements I'm looking for in a fantasy.

— Lauren Kate, New York Times bestselling
author of the *Fallen* series

From the first page, author Scott T. Barnes draws us into the tender, heartfelt relationship between Lucinda and Abuelita. This exciting, suspenseful, and moving adventure follows Lucinda's determined attempt to save Abuelita, to always do better, and to make her grandmother proud. Filled with heart, *Memories of Lucinda Eco* shows us what love of family, friends, and community can achieve. A beautiful book.

— Jeanne Cavelos, bestselling author of *The
Passing of the Techno-Mages*

The novel is a spellbinding blend of magic and mystery, alive with tension, laughs, and real emotional resonance.

— BookLife Review, editor's pick

A resonant and unsettling fantasy steeped in small-town Mexican culture.

— Kirkus Reviews

Readers will quickly warm to Lucinda's courage and kindness, leavened with a streak of teenage sass. Her bond with Eva, whose fashionista propensities complement Lucinda's down-to-earth style, is heartwarmingly rendered.

— BlueInk Review

In Scott T. Barnes's powerful fantasy novel *Memories of Lucinda Eco*, a teenager encounters dark magic and fights to protect her family and friends by realizing her bruja powers.

— Foreword Reviews

Memories of Lucinda Eco is an exciting blend of mystery and the mystic, set in the deserts and villages of Baja California. Scott T. Barnes is able to bring to life characters both young and old, good and evil. It is well worth a read.

— Robert W. Enstrom, author of *Encounter Program* and *Beta Colony*

A complex hands-across-time story of magical rescue, from grandmother to granddaughter and back again, set in the Baja California landscape of lizards and arroyos, manzanita and mezcal.

— Donna Glee Williams, author of *The Night Field*, *Dreamers*, and *The Braided Path*

Scott T. Barnes weaves a multidimensional multilayered tapestry of contrasting realities and beliefs that envelopes a rainbow of characters (and the reader) as they navigate encounters with divergent dogmas, perceptions and worldly circumstances. *Memories* opens our eyes to the magic of life, love and the conflicts that shape our realities (real and perceived), while explaining the unexplainable.

— Bob Sojka, author of "Between the Zeros and Ones" in the acclaimed 2022 anthology *Neosapiens*.

Barnes's writing is lyrical and compelling in his exquisitely jarring world of fierce brujas and magical allies. The term "brutally beautiful" kept coming to me as I read.

— Jessica Guernsey, author of "The Gingerbread Contract" and other short stories

Memories of Lucinda Eco had me from the opening scene. The magical realism of Mexico, so integrated into the daily lives of the characters, was fascinating, and I felt like I knew the characters intimately. A great read that kept me guessing until the end.

— R.A. Johnson, pan-genrist author

Memories of Lucinda Eco takes us to the dusty town of Punta Colonet in Baja California. Fifteen-year-old Lucinda, trying to unravel the witch's curse that threatens her beloved grandmother's mind and life, is sucked into the Beyond and a world of *brujería* so vividly rendered I almost feel I'm becoming a *bruja* myself...

— Candyce Byrne, editor *Cosmic Muse*; co-editor NewMyths magazine

Memories of Lucinda Eco is delightful. Barnes deftly transports the reader through time, place, and other-worldly dimensions, all while weaving in elements of magic, danger, and teenage angst. Come for the promise of adventure; stay for the loving bond between our willful heroine and her audacious abuela.

— Angelica Duardo, singer, songwriter

A magical journey of a young witch discovering her heritage and the path into the Beyond, a lost realm of beauty and wonder that once connected us all to the spirit world. Scott T. Barnes' imagery of the Beyond is unforgettable, and the concept that the lure to repossess its full knowledge and power can lead to overwhelming, corrupting greed is an intriguing warning for all young witches to learn.

— Susan Shell Winston, editor NewMyths magazine, author of *Singer of Norgondy*

Memories of Lucinda Eco

Scott T. Barnes

Memories of Lucinda Eco

Scott T. Barnes

Published by New Myths Publishing
Copyright © 2024 by Scott T. Barnes
All Rights Reserved
www.newmythspublishing.com

978-1-939354-23-5 ebook
978-1-939354-24-2 hardcover
978-1-939354-26-6 paperback
978-1-939354-25-9 audio

Cover copyright © Scott T. Barnes
Cover art by Tom Tolman
Cover design by The Book Break team

Dedicated to my three allies, my wife Grace, my daughters Elizabeth and Kaylynn. I love you all.

ONE

PRESENT DAY, PUNTA COLONET, BAJA CALIFORNIA NORTH

The parade route led from the Chaparral Hills into the brick-and-adobe town of Punta Colonet, past the municipal building, and into the dusty baseball field. Tractors, pickup trucks, decorated flatbeds, and horse-riding vaqueros passed by, kicking up fine particles of dust. None of the streets here were paved, except the toll road. The crowd had grown and grown, and so had Lucinda's anticipation.

Lucinda and her grandmother stood in the portico of the municipal building. The eves kept off the worst of the sun, and the cement walkway elevated them enough to see reasonably well. The high school soccer team was just passing, their star players holding onto the roll bar of a Toyota pickup and whooping. As if their one-and-seven record was something to whoop about.

Lucinda reached down and entwined her fingers with her grandmother's. She could feel the soft, wrinkled skin of grandmother's fingertips, the calluses on her palm, and the old woman's hidden strength. At fifteen years old, Lucinda had never been allowed to stay at the parade until the end. Until they burned the witch in effigy.

Anticipation made her palms slick ... not to mention her armpits.

She tried to ignore those.

The hum of twin propeller motors came to them at the exact moment the sun ducked beneath the ridgeline. Orange and red streaks bled across the western sky, and the mood along the parade route shifted. Lucinda felt the change as a tingle in the nape of her neck.

The last of the young children were whisked away home. Teenagers reluctantly looked at their watches, stood on tiptoe to try to catch a glimpse of the gigantic, papier-mâché witch, and departed more slowly.

The town made ready to honor its martyr.

Dark-clad people began to emerge from the alleys, from the empty field by the tire store. They climbed iron bars over windows and perched on rooftops like twilight crows. They thronged the street. Porch lights clicked on overhead. By the time the propeller plane rolled into view — driving, not flying — the shift was complete.

Painted on the side of the airplane was *Flying Samaritans*, which everyone knew by sight if not by pronunciation, for the Flying Samaritans ran a free medical clinic here in Punta Colonet. This was the last float that children were allowed to see. White Christmas lights decorated the fuselage. Lucinda thought the twinkling lights looked like slag from the foundry she'd visited once in Monterey.

Abuelita's firm hand squeeze told Lucinda that yes, they really were going to stay together until the end, until the little Baja California community re-enacted the witch's execution.

Lucinda had only just celebrated her quiñceanera two months ago. Most of her friends didn't get to stay late until they turned eighteen, but Abuelita had insisted Lucinda was ready at fifteen. And not much could stand in Abuelita's way once she made up her mind. Not even Mamá.

Lucinda swallowed her burbling claustrophobia with a gulp of Strawberry Fanta. "Come on, Abuelita, all I can see are hair and armpits. And hairy armpits. I want to see Eva's costume."

"We'll see Eva at the bonfire," Grandmother Herminia replied with a game smile, "which will be much easier to get to from back here. We'll be ahead of the crowd."

Nevertheless, she allowed Lucinda to drag her forward between rough, campesino cotton, slick silk, and the ruffled shoulders of traditional dresses — the women typically perfumed by half an aerosol of floral hair spray. The crowd seemed to part before them and Lucinda blessed their good fortune, and then began to wonder why this was so easy, and about the time she started to get nervous they stumbled into an opening. A circle of men drinking. There was a large blue ice chest, empty Corona bottles littering the ground, and the thick smell of Marlboro cigarettes.

And El Jaguar, the local gang boss, lounged in their center. He was eerily thin, his wrists hardly larger than garden hoses, decked out in a tan leather vest, collared shirt, and bolo tie. El Jaguar sat with one leg over the arm of a folding chair — the only chair Lucinda had seen along the route — and no one stood between him and the road. No one dared.

A fierce-looking Rottweiler panted beneath the chair.

El Jaguar's head swiveled and locked on them. The shadow from his oft-broken nose slid across his face like a knife. It felt as if they had just stepped into a fight circle.

Lucinda immediately thought *"The Witch!"* For El Jaguar styled himself as *El Brujo*, and the havoc he left in his wake gave credence to the claim.

He inclined a bottle of Corona toward them. "Herminia García, and her granddaughter, how pleasant. Watch with us."

In the distance, a mariachi band began a dirge. The trumpet shuddered on the high notes as if unaccustomed to playing such sadness.

"The torch bearers are coming, and our family is waiting for us," Abuelita lied, smoothly. "We must cross the street while no one is coming."

"Surely, you can spare a moment," El Jaguar said. "You will not find a better spot to view the parade anywhere."

Then a strange thing happened. The colorful, perfumed throng seemed to get pulled away, as sets get drawn behind the leg drapes of a theater by hidden means. Lucinda and El Jaguar were alone on the empty parade route, she straightening up from her stumble, he bouncing one foot casually against the side of the folding chair. Lucinda didn't quite believe what she was seeing. She wondered if she had in fact tripped and hit her head on the ground and this was all a hallucination....

El Jaguar's swinging foot slowly came to rest, and he grinned with half of his mouth. "My angel, how you have grown."

Why would she hallucinate about El Jaguar? Why not Jin from BTS?

No, something was wrong here; something worse than a bump on the head. She didn't like the way the hoodlum leered at her, at her chest in particular. She'd worn a floppy blue tee-shirt deliberately as she wasn't entirely comfortable with her curves. Lucinda had been a late bloomer — and often wished she hadn't bloomed at all! A loose T-shirt and jeans, who would remark her?

Who but, of course, the local gang boss.

"Do you like our private hideaway?" he asked.

"Where are we?" Lucinda nervously inquired, her mouth getting dry. Oh, this was bad. This was really, really bad.

"I could show you such things, my angel. Such things as you have never seen."

A sense of dread descended over Lucinda's head, her shoulders, her back. She didn't know whether to run, scream, or kick the man and hope his aluminum chair collapsed into a heap.

But run where? They seemed to be all alone—

A tug on Lucinda's hand returned the mob, the smells, the noise. It was the tug of Abuelita's hand on Lucinda's own that brought them back, as if they had simply popped out of the theater's wings. El Jaguar's thugs chuckled at something, an inside joke or, more likely, the stupid look Lucinda must have been wearing.

How could she have slipped into such a rotten hallucination?

Her cheeks warmed as if twin rays of sunlight beamed down on them. Embarrassment mingled with trepidation. Doubt mixed with certainty. *Something* had happened, something not entirely normal.

She wondered if El Jaguar — *the Witch!* — had used some power. Hypnosis, or a darker magic. El Jaguar bragged about his magic, and the priest was afraid of him. He forced the locals to pay protection money or he'd put a curse on them. Most often his thugs would simply beat them up. But there were unexplainable illnesses, people dropping dead on the street, and worse. Mothers threatened disobedient children with El Jaguar's curse.

El Jaguar leaned over and poked a finger in Abuelita's side. The old woman scowled.

"You've been widowed five years and you still don't find me attractive, grandmother? I must be truly ugly."

"Not ugly, just unpleasant," Abuelita replied. "And drunk."

The man pulled from his bottle of Corona. The henchmen were smoking, but Lucinda no longer smelled tobacco. Instead, there was the overwhelming cinnamon of churros.

"Surely you'll let me get to know your granddaughter better," he said, an ugly, frightening mirror to what the hallucination had uttered. "She has come of age — you're letting her stay at the Parade of Heroes after dark. That means she's ready to discover all kinds of things."

Lucinda's heart couldn't have beaten faster if she had sprinted three hundred yards.

"Con permiso," Abuelita insisted. "Our family is waiting."

As they started to move El Jaguar grabbed Lucinda's arm. His brown, bloodshot eyes were as hard as scratched glass. "A family? What do I care about your family? I had to build a family from nothing. From the dust of nothing."

It wasn't right for him to grab her arm like that. His hand, it was like...

...like a vulture's claw. She shouldn't let him touch her.

That churro cinnamon, so thick in the air, spicing this world with the next. She could almost feel the world tremble. She didn't want to go back to that scary place where the two of them were alone. She wouldn't let that happen. She wouldn't!

The beer in El Jaguar's lap.

She couldn't look at El Jaguar without feeling that this world was about to disappear ... but she could look at that beer. That disgusting, bitter, bubbly yuck. Her dad had once caught her sipping on his beer a few years back and he'd forced her to drink the whole thing so that she'd never be tempted again. She hated it. Disgusting! Just remembering that — and the headache the next day — made her temples throb and her tongue dry out. She focused her attention on that feeling. The struggle and outrage, the touch of El Jaguar's fingers and thumb around her triceps, the sweaty stickiness of his skin against hers — it all had to come out. Lucinda's muscles began to tremble, and amazingly the beer seemed to respond. Foam rushed out. The bubbles increased in size and intensity.

"Well, then," she said, pouring all her derision into that beer, "that's your problem."

Lucinda held out her Fanta bottle and struck the top of the Corona. The foam became an outrageous spray, blasting El Jaguar in the face, the hair, the chest. He yelped, nearly toppled over in his chair. The gross smell of hops covered the cinnamon.

Lucinda jerked her arm free.

"Little Chicken, *now*," Abuelita said, using Lucinda's pet name.

They hurried across the road just in front of the mariachis. Lucinda half-expected El Jaguar to follow, but he was too busy wiping beer off his face and out of his hair. The Rottweiler lapped at the growing puddle.

Grandmother Herminia pulled up directly opposite the gangsters, straightened her shoulders, and smoothed her dress with dignity.

"Why don't they put him in prison?" Lucinda said, proud that her voice didn't tremble. On her own she would have kept going, but she wanted to be brave for Abuelita.

"El Jaguar is a feature of Punta Colonet," Abuelita said, "like the mole under your eye. Now that you are of age you will simply have to get used to him."

"I don't want to get used to him." She didn't particularly like to be reminded about her mole, either. "I hope he drinks himself to an early grave. Like — tomorrow!"

The mariachis passed, their wide-brimmed, black hats blocking El Jaguar from sight. The torch bearers followed. Six cones of flickering fire. One of them would be Lucinda's bestie Eva, behind one of the porcelain death masks, but Lucinda couldn't concentrate enough to figure out which one. Too many uncertainties swirled around in her brain.

"Abuelita, does El Jaguar control minds? For a second I felt as if he had taken me to another place. It was like we were all alone on the parade route, just me and El Jaguar." Lucinda couldn't tell what grandmother Herminia was thinking; Abuelita's wrinkled and usually expressive face remained carefully neutral. "He claims he has all kinds of powers. He claims he is a witch, or warlock. I'm surprised to see him here, at the burning."

"Did he say anything to you?"

Abuelita didn't even question this "other place," which was more than a little disconcerting. "I, um, I don't remember exactly. He didn't make any sense." In truth, Lucinda did not want to think about it. She knew all too well what he wanted — even if she hadn't understood the words.

Abuelita crinkled her eyes. "El Jaguar has a twisted spirit. He comes to the parade to show he is not afraid to see the people burn the make-believe witch." She worried the inside of her lip with her teeth, seeking the right words. "If El Jaguar could control minds, you wouldn't know it. He could make you bark like a seal, or stand on your head, rub your belly, and say the alphabet backwards. A twisted spirit, that is more insidious. Let him know you are not afraid, but do not confront him. He is as unstable as he is dangerous. As much child as man. It is a great sadness. You know, he was orphaned twice over."

"That doesn't excuse him being a bully," Lucinda said.

"No, that doesn't excuse."

Lucinda wondered how you could possibly be orphaned twice over — did his foster parents die also? More likely they dropped him off by the road and kept driving until the gas ran out.

She didn't get a chance to ask for clarification. In the west, where the sun had so recently fallen, the witch bobbed as if floating on top of the crowd. It was a giant, papier-mâché head, fully ten feet tall, with bright red lips and horns poking through black, paper hair.

"Little Chicken, did you smell the cinnamon around El Jaguar?" Abuelita asked.

"You mean the churros?"

"Yes, the churros around El Jaguar."

"And?" Lucinda prodded. "Does this have something to do with the way the beer foamed?"

"Later, after the parade."

Does this have something to do with why we came here? Lucinda wanted to ask. There seemed a great deal left unsaid. Why *had* Abuelita pressed her mom on this point? But she knew enough not to ask. The old woman spoke in her own time or not at all.

Full dark, the martyr walked before the witch, a girl hiding her face behind the white mask. She was a real girl, petite like Lucinda, not a papier-mâché puppet. A pigtailed, twelve-year-old wearing a school uniform in an older style, longer skirts and knee-high socks. The witch's last victim.

Outrage at the young woman's murder caused the town to rise up against the witch. This, the girl-martyr, was Punta Colonet's greatest hero.

With solemn steps, the schoolgirl passed, followed by the witch. Lucinda could see now that it wasn't just a floating head. It had a body of sorts, bedsheet sized clothes hanging off a metal frame. People wearing black pushed the wheeled contraption forward. The crowd closed in behind.

Lucinda stood on tiptoe. Across the street, the folding chair was abandoned. Lucinda could not spot the hoodlum or his men anywhere.

They cut through the park, ignoring the men perched on the jungle gym like animals. There was something infernal about this night. The white paint on the pepper tree trunks seemed to glow. Lucinda began to wonder if coming had been a good idea. Not just because of El Jaguar, but the whole thing. This was supposed to be the Parade of Heroes; it felt more like a night of devils. It felt icky just being there, like that time she and her mother had gotten lost in Ensenada and wound up in the red-light district. Lucinda remembered a scantily clad prostitute, leaning back with one foot against the door frame of a bar. Smoke curled between her fingers from the stub of a cigarette. There was a giant hole in the thigh of her fishnet stocking.

"Hey, hija," the prostitute had called to Lucinda. She pointed at her own eyes, then at Lucinda's. Not so much to say she was watching, but more to warn, "Not much separating me from you."

In the center of the dirt lot that served as parking for the baseball field (also dirt), hay bales had been piled in a semi-circle, and the torch bearers took up position around these. Punta Colonet wasn't a fancy town with street lights. The six torches were practically the only illumination. That and the ubiquitous cell phone screens. Occasionally a firework popped off, dazzling eyes and ringing ears.

The rest of the floats had disappeared. The schoolgirl martyr walked once around the bales of hay, and the witch rolled into the center. The head was transferred to a wooden scaffolding, the metal-frame body wheeled away.

Standing on tiptoes, Lucinda could pick out Eva: the torchbearer with platform shoes. Eva always wore a fashion signature of some kind. She was chosen for the role because her family founded the Rattlesnake Thespians. She tried to wave and catch Eva's attention, but there were just too many people around.

Someone, probably a politician or something, started talking through a static-filled speaker. Lucinda strained to hear. Presumably he would tell the story of the witch and his victims. Or some version of the story, anyway.

El Jaguar appeared between Lucinda and her grandmother, his nose practically against Lucinda's neck. "You smell so familiar," he said. "Like a cologne my father used to use. Only, I had no father."

"Santiago! Your manners," Abuelita said.

He appeared to shrink, just a bit, at the use of his real name. "I don't answer to that."

Lucinda said, "Leave me alone, *Santiago*."

"It is a lonely life, the life of the witch," he said. "One must always watch his back. Listen to the whispers."

He twined Lucinda's black hair around his finger. It was not particularly long hair, bobbed off the shoulder in what she considered a K-pop style, and El Jaguar's knuckles wound closer and closer to her skull. With each twist, the roots hurt more.

In the dense crowd, no one would hear them. No one would even notice them. You could get trampled, your blood could spill like sticky Strawberry Fanta, and no one would notice until they swept up the trash the next day. All eyes focused on the papier-mâché witch and the torchbearers setting the hay bales alight as the staticky voice droned on. Flames licked up the witch's shoulders. Infernal light colored the people of Punta Colonet into red, chattering demons.

"Let's get out of here, Abuelita," Lucinda said. She was nervous, more than nervous; it was a struggle to get the words out. "Santiago doesn't know how to be a gentleman." If she had her Fanta she would have whacked the hoodlum with the bottle, but she had discarded it in a trash barrel at the park. She felt in her pockets, though she already knew she had nothing to use as a weapon. No pocket knife, not even a sharp stick. How far would this brute be willing to go in public?

Or would he simply magic her to that place with no one around, that empty parade route....

She couldn't turn her head. Her eyes scanned for a police officer. Better yet, one of the blue jumpsuit-clad military police. With a machine gun.

All she discovered were the bared teeth of El Jaguar's Rottweiler.

"You smell it too, don't you Lucinda?" El Jaguar said. "The sweet spice of magic? It can take you to such places. Such places." He repeated the final words, drawing the 's' out into a serpent's hiss.

A thrill passed through Lucinda's mind. *Magic? Spice?* Abuelita had asked about that churro smell too....

"Enough!" Abuelita said, and yanked on El Jaguar. He tripped to his knees. With his hand still wrapped around Lucinda's hair, her head jerked sideways.

Lucinda grabbed the hand, the fingers that were balled tightly around her hair. She couldn't find purchase on any finger except the pinkie. The smallest digit. That one she took in her fist and twisted toward the ground with all of her might. El Jaguar screeched like a cornered possum, a sound like vocal chords tearing. Cinnamon billowed across the gathering.

Lucinda wouldn't let go for anything. She twisted, and twisted some more, holding the digit tight so it wouldn't slip free. Outrage exploded inside her again.

The Rottweiler leaped. Not high, and not far. For it didn't have to go far to chomp on Lucinda. It sank its teeth into her left thigh and crunched down to the bone.

The pain nearly made her pass out. Nearly, but not quite. Lucinda released the pinkie, fell back, and landed with legs splayed, the dog between them, attacking her thigh, rooting with its blunt teeth for her femur. She was sure the bone would burst against the relentless, crushing bite.

In the background, against the swaying people, Grandmother Herminia fought with El Jaguar. Lucinda was losing consciousness. She wasn't sure of what she saw. Not sure at all. It didn't look like two people fighting, but rather like a puma fighting a scarecrow man with an oft-broken nose.

The puma, her Abuelita?

Scarecrow man, El Jaguar?

She heard a crackle of bone. Scarecrow man fell. And the puma lifted the Rottweiler by the scruff of the neck, shook it, discarded it.

A blurry, pain-filled nightmare.

Nothing she was sure of. Nothing real.

Abuelita now, a kindly grandmother again. But what was she doing? She was licking her hand and smearing saliva through the hole in Lucinda's jeans, directly into the wound. Abuelita's long gray hair spilled over everything, a soothing cascade.

Lucinda couldn't be sure, but it looked like Abuelita's torso was bare.

This couldn't be real. It couldn't.

"Am I dead?" Lucinda asked, her consciousness slipping away. "Where am I?"

"Home soon, Little Chicken," replied Abuelita. "You will be home soon."

Two

1967, Outside Santa Rosalía, Baja
California South

Herminia Carrillo (Lucinda's grandmother) — age 17

From the backseat of the Jeepster Hurricane — a topless, cherry-red beauty — Herminia Carrillo pressed her body against the wind and squinted her eyes. She was trying to recognize landmarks from her trip here many years before, but the high-desert landscape blurred together after a while. Boulders, dust, cactus, canyons and washes, red skinned manzanita, cactus, stone, dust, washes and canyons.... It all started to look alike. Especially on a bumpy, dirt road after a few hairpin turns that turned the stomach into milk cake.

Herminia's black hair whipped around her head like an out-of-control eggbeater while the neckline of her yellow dress buzzed pleasantly against her collar bones.

There were four: Curtis, the driver, a B-list Hollywood actor; Brennan, his handsome friend; Sybil, a hippie who had temporarily hitched her star to Curtis; and Herminia. Herminia had offered to guide the Americans into the mountains to see pictographs in order to relieve the monotony of making beds at the Loma Linda Resort.

Working as a maid — boring!

Guiding would-be stars into the mountains to see cave paintings — *mucho mejor.*

Would her American guests be angry if she failed to locate the cave?

Herminia doubted it. They were happy enough with the wind and the roar of the four-cylinder engine. But Herminia would be angry with herself. A day wasted. A fee unearned. Moreover, she really wanted to revisit the pictographs. As vibrant as any in the world, or so her father said.

They were close. She was certain the hidden path could be no more than a few miles distant. Or had they passed it already?

She had that same tingle in her wrists as last time, when she had visited with her father. A physical reaction to being so close to the — yes — holy site. She thought of it that way, at least. Holy to her ancestors, the Cochimí Indians.

Of course, she and her father had come here by mule. Four days camping in the mountains, just the two of them. And those paintings! Although it had been years, those pictographs found their way into her thoughts day after day, her dreams night after night. Colors as vibrant as any dragonfly. Herds of deer and bison, stalking wildcats, even sea life. And the hunters—

A brown form leaped into the dirt road, stared at the oncoming Jeepster Hurricane, and froze. A buck mule deer.

Herminia sucked in her breath, braced herself against the seat in front.

Curtis braked. The Jeep skidded sideways, threw Herminia against the door, threw Sybil sideways onto her lap, threw dirt and gravel twenty feet into the air.

But too late.

There was a dull thud as the deer hit the bumper. Herminia felt it distinctly, as if the animal's soul had passed through her fingertips roughly. The buck stuck there, head lying on the hood, body plastered to the grill.

Herminia had trouble swallowing. Her tongue wanted to hide in the back of her throat. Dust billowed around them.

The Jeep finally stopped and the buck rolled off the hood onto the dirt road. Its head flopped in an unnatural angle.

With shaky legs, they all climbed out and stood around the animal. Blood trickled from its nostrils. A long, oval-shaped ear fluttered once.

"Is it dead?" Sybil asked.

"As good as," Curtis answered, pushing on the back of its head with his leather shoe. "Its neck is broken."

The deer blinked.

Pity for the poor animal moistened Herminia's eyes.

Curtis reached for its legs to pull it off the road, and Sybil wailed, "You're going to hurt it."

"Too late for that."

"But it's still alive."

The buck had two-point antlers covered with velvet. Herminia lay her palm against its neck. She could feel a weak pulse. Since childhood she had fished the Gulf of California with her parents. Her skin was dark brown because of it. The muscles beneath her yellow dress were lean, the palms of her hands and feet calloused. She understood about hunting for food. Some animals had to die so that others could live. Accidents like this.... Mourning was fine, but it was better to make the best of unfortunate circumstances.

"We can only do one thing," Herminia said. "Put it out of its misery."

No one said anything.

"Care to help me?"

Sybil sobbed once or twice and climbed back into the backseat of the Jeep. Curtis put up his hands — *no*.

"I, uh, I'll check to see if there's a gun in the glove box," Brennan said.

Herminia closed her eyes and prayed to God that the deer find peace. She didn't know if heaven was for animals or not, but she prayed that the buck would be allowed in.

"No gun. I say we just leave it," Brennan said.

Herminia stroked the buck's muzzle. "I'm sorry my friend. I'm sorry we hit you, and I'm sorry we don't have a better way to stop your suffering." She slid her hand to her ankle where she kept a diving knife, unsnapped the scabbard, and drew the six-inch blade. A swift stroke severed the carotid arteries. She wiped the knife on the buck's fur, finishing the job with a sand scrub, and returned it to her ankle scabbard.

Once the blood drained completely, Herminia lifted the buck over her shoulders, carried it to the back of the Jeep, and set it into the trunk.

"It'd be a crime to waste the noble animal," she said.

Sybil stared at her with forehead-wide eyes.

Readying herself to vault into the backseat, Herminia noticed something about this place. Was it the feminine swell of the hillside? The way a jumble of boulders resembled a gigantic rabbit? The stunted pine tree or the bleached white of the alluvial sand?

No. None of that recalled anything. The hillside could have been any of a hundred along this road. So what—?

And then she realized: The tingle in her wrists had disappeared.

Strange that the buck had jumped out at just the right place. They might have driven several miles before she realized they had missed it. It was almost as if the deer had wanted them to stop here. Almost as if it had sacrificed itself....

What a crazy thought.

The men started to climb inside the Jeep, but Herminia stopped them. "We walk from here. Take your packs and all the water you have. We can refill it at the cave."

"I don't see the trail," Brennan said.

"There is no trail. Only my memory."

Herminia shrugged on a canteen and a small pack.

Sybil slid from the Jeep and stumbled into Herminia's arms. A blond with a long, freckled face, Herminia thought of Sybil as a classic hippie. With a little more ambition, she could have made surfer.

Sybil held Herminia close and pressed her mouth to Herminia's ear. "My Mexican guide, you are so frigging sexy."

Herminia parted her generous lips in a smile.

———

For the first hour they waded through waist-high chaparral, making forward progress by sheer leg strength. There were no signs that anything of interest lay beyond. Whatever trail Herminia had taken with her father had grown shut.

Of the complex smells, Herminia picked out her favorite: sage. She veered that way and ran her hands along the long, stiff, blue-white stalks to get the oil on her hands. Now and then they caught sight of El Boleo Copper Mine, a giant pit, golden and pink in the distance. Not so much an open wound as a reveal of the mountain's hidden beauty. An earthen sunset. They had driven past it on the way here. Without the copper ore, there would be no roads into Santa Rosalía's mountains, only mule trails leading to farms and bootleg stills.

Beyond the brushy hill they dropped into a dry, boulder-strewn arroyo. Herminia checked everyone's clothes for ticks, and they set off again. The scratches on her legs hurt a bit, but she'd had far worse from reefs and falls on ships.

Ships ... the thought gave Herminia pause. Her parents worked as fishermen on Hotel Loma Linda's pangas. She hadn't spoken to them for nearly three months, ever since she declared she wasn't going to follow in their footsteps. As much as Herminia loved the sea, her future lay elsewhere. Where was an open question, but certainly not on the deck of a little panga helping tourists pull in fish they hadn't caught. Cleaning the fish. Preparing the fish and defending them from seabirds. Patting the women on the back as they sicked over the rail.

Herminia was 17; she could make her own destiny!

Sybil linked her arm through Herminia's. "Hey, you in there?"

"Just thinking."

"Groovy." Sybil pulled Herminia close and whispered in her ear. "What do you think of the men, hmm? Better than strawberry paletas?"

Herminia threw back her head and laughed. Sybil cracked her up like no one she had ever met.

"Come on, which one do you like?"

"Both," Herminia said, to tease.

"You can't have both. Do you think this is a Grateful Dead concert? I don't even have any weed."

Herminia shrugged. "What do we need men for? The mountains

aren't enough? Look how beautiful they are. The mountains can be our lovers, like in the poems."

The air was hot and clean and spare. It was all uphill from here. Even Sybil fell silent against the heat and fatigue. More than once Herminia bruised her sandaled feet on water-worn stones.

An hour in and they stopped to catch their breath. They sat with their backs against the shady side of a boulder. Their legs, sticking straight out, roasted in the sun.

"Almost there," Herminia said, passing Sybil a canteen.

Sybil brushed the blonde hair from her eyes and drank deeply. "These better be some cave paintings to hike all the way out here."

"Just some finger-painted animals," Curtis said. "I've seen Indian paintings all over the southwest. They are all basically the same."

"So why did you want to come out here, if you know everything?" Sybil said.

"Fishing's no good."

Curtis would be surprised at these pictographs, Herminia knew. More vibrant, more graphic than anywhere in Baja, or so her dad told her. As quick and vivid in her memory as the buck deer she'd had to put down.

Herminia had only ever seen the one site, but someday she hoped to do a pilgrimage to all the painted caves in Baja. After all, she was part Cochimí, and she wanted to see what her ancestors had been up to before the Spanish arrived.

A sound that didn't belong in the mountains intruded on Herminia's thoughts, insistent, regular. Sybil was saying something about bleaching her eyebrows. The men were complaining about the heat. Herminia shushed them with a finger to her lips.

The Americans quieted.

She'd give that to them. As fishermen, they knew how to be quiet. The rustle of clothing died.

Gradually animal sounds replaced the human noises. A woodpecker pounded on old wood. A flying beetle, iridescent green, cruised overhead, as loud as it was awkward. A claw scratched against stone, over and over again. A claw or a fingernail.

Repetitive and regular.

Scratching.

Out of place among the chaos of nature.

Still with a finger to her lips, Herminia began tracking. The Americans followed.

The noise came from a jumble of rocks at the western edge of the wash. More precisely, from a lizard scratching against a line where two boulders came together. It looked like a recent landslide. Perhaps the slide had trapped the lizard's mate.

The lizard turned its head and fixed Herminia with a stare.

It was a typical desert iguana, taupe-color skin, pentagonal, gray patterns across its back, about twenty inches nose to tail. But its face looked swollen. The eyes — something was wrong with its eyes.

The lizard scurried over. Herminia knelt and it scampered into her outstretched hand. Its claws made painful white dimples on her forearm.

The Americans gathered around.

Xs crisscrossed the eyes, and Herminia thought with horror: *Someone stitched its eyes closed.*

"My God!" Curtis said, coming forward. "Barbarians."

"Who could have done this?" Brennan asked.

Herminia didn't want to frighten her guests. Nor did she want to lie to them.

Was it a warning: NO TRESPASSING! *Or something more sinister — something to do with visions and sight? Something to do with brujos.*

She stroked the lizard's rough back, tried to find a reassuring answer. "The Catholic Church never fully supplanted the old religions here. Occasionally, even today, people make appeals to the old gods, or seek to contact powers beyond this world. It is sad, but at times animals suffer for human superstition."

The lizard didn't seem to be suffering. It acted quite content under the stroking of Herminia's finger.

"This can't have happened long ago," said Curtis. "The lizard would starve without its eyes. No way to see and catch insects. Or find water for that matter. Must have been done within two or three days."

Good observation. Though Herminia wasn't entirely sure the lizard was helpless as all that, not after it had run so deftly into her hand.

"Does this have anything to do with the pictographs?" Sybil asked.

Herminia said, "The way the eyes are sewn shut I would guess they were trying to create a second sight, see into the spirit world. Probably some superstitious campesino was trying to communicate with their ancestors, or with the animal spirits depicted in the caves."

"Can't they just take LSD," Brennan said, "like any normal person? Timothy Leary should take up a teaching position in Baja."

"Do we turn around?" Sybil asked.

Curtis cleared his throat. "I say we take a vote. Who is in favor of going forward?"

The men raised their hands.

Sybil said, "I vote with Herminia. She's our guide; her vote should count for more than ours."

Herminia placed the lizard on the ground. It scurried straight to the line where the boulders met and began digging again. Completely futile. And beautiful at the same time. No way could this desert iguana move those boulders.

Herminia wanted to help it dig, find out what might be under that scree pile.

Another mutilated lizard?

A body?

She inhaled through her nose the mountain potpourri: sagebrush, mountain mahogany, manzanita, sand and dry air. Human body odor.

No noxious odors.

Nothing to indicate decomposition.

The cave was so close. Brilliant paintings of hunters and game, arrows and bows, eagles, coyotes, so much more. It resonated in Herminia's mind like a task left undone. And the Americans had paid her fifty American dollars to guide them. A month's wages.

"You wanted an adventure," Herminia said, and gestured to the iguana. "What is this? We go on."

Probably the cave had been carved by water in the distant past, and over time the stream, which only flowed after a rain, had dug away the canyon. So now you had to ascend three or four hundred feet to get to the entrance. It wasn't particularly steep. The scent of wood smoke grew as they neared the top.

They came across a little camp on the level area just outside the cave. A circle of rocks contained dying embers and a blue enamelware coffeepot placed directly on the coals. Two flannel shirts, recently washed and wrinkled, lay drying across the branches of a mesquite tree. Wedged between two boulders was a twenty-five gallon metal barrel with a spigot, presumably for water.

A portly man wearing jeans and a flannel shirt reclined in the shade, a straw cowboy hat pulled over his face. He peeked from under the brim as they approached. Herminia recognized his features as Cochimí. He was perhaps thirty years old. He didn't appear to be armed.

"Buenos dias, los norteamericanos." The Cochimí's voice was high pitched, and he lisped through broken front teeth. He didn't smile, and he didn't frown. His face had the relaxed composure of complete authority.

Despite the heat, a chill spider ran down Herminia's spine.

"Is this the cave?" Curtis asked, pointing to a slit in the mountain. "Are the cave paintings inside?"

"Sí."

"Can we go in?" Sybil asked.

The Cochimí nodded.

From his pack, Brennan pulled out a silver flashlight. The Americans moved to the entrance.

Herminia hung back. This man — there was something about him. At the Loma Linda Hotel she had met actors and musicians with charisma to burn. Although not always handsome, they secreted a sort of aura that made people admire them, follow them — men and women alike. It was not just their self-confidence. It was a chemical thing, engendering a reaction you couldn't control.

Curtis had a bit of it. That's why Sybil was so willing to hitch herself to Curtis's star. Nevertheless, Herminia had never felt anything so strong as the aura around this Cochimí.

"Your name?"

"Herminia. Herminia Carrillo."

"Herminia Carrillo," the Cochimí lisped. "The cave has marked you. You have been here before."

She nodded.

"You feel the pull of the Beyond calling you back."

Whatever he meant, she refused to answer.

With his slovenly looks and broken teeth, the man was unattractive in the extreme. And that lisping, girly voice! He used strange expressions in order to create an aura of mystery—Herminia could see through that simple trick.

Beyond.

Marked.

Calling you back.

Circus tricks.

So where did his charisma come from?

Herminia squatted, pulled her yellow dress over her knees, and wrapped her arms around them. "I came here because the Americans paid me to bring them."

"Curious how things work," said the Cochimí. "Let me guess: they paid you an exorbitant sum; enough that, if you chose to stay here for a few weeks, you would have plenty of money."

"Everyone knows that Americans are rich." Herminia didn't like how close he was to the truth. Probably he was just fishing, trying to figure out if she had money or not.

"And then," he continued, "on the road here, something made you stop at just the right place, despite the fact that the path has become choked with brush since your last visit. Some sign, perhaps?"

Herminia sucked in her breath. That buck throwing itself in front of their Jeep. Did this man have something to do with it? Or was it a lucky guess?

The Cochimí removed the hat from his head and examined the weave of the straw, picking at it with dirty, broken nails and frowning. "These things work out in the end, if your ally wills it."

"I don't have any allies," Herminia replied. "I have been making it on my own since I was fourteen." *A little exaggeration never hurt anyone,* she thought. Herminia had been living with her parents until a few months ago.

"Tell me what I am thinking," she said.

The Cochimí laughed, making her feel stupid. "I am not a mind reader."

"What are you, then?"

"Perhaps I am your master." He said the word gently, implying *master* as a music conductor, rather than the word's more sinister connotation. Or so Herminia supposed. "Go on inside, your friends will need you in there. You can come back to me after they leave."

"What?"

"Go." He pointed his straw hat at the cave entrance, and, slightly disoriented, as if awakening from a brief nap, Herminia was surprised to realize the Americans had already gone inside.

The first paintings had faded so badly from the sun that they were hard to discern. About twenty feet in, the original, vibrant oranges became apparent. Natives with bows and arrows hunted mule deer across the walls and ceiling. The hunt finally successful, vermilion blood splattered along a natural crack. Other animals began to appear. Varmints, birds, predators. Bushes, trees, grass, even flowers. The painters used natural features to give the art three dimensions. A colorful stone embedded in the wall became an eyeball. A rough patch was scrub brush, or the back of a mangy coyote. The hues remained every bit as brilliant as what the local weavers used for their blankets and sarapes to this day.

Herminia ran her hands along the sandstone walls. The silica was so fine you could file your fingernails with it. The cave flew straight in, throat-like. Herminia recalled her father pointing out the various features ... back when they still got along. She wanted to savor every minute here, this beautiful conjuncture of memory and sensation.

A pad-pad of footfalls approached swiftly from the deep. Sybil emerged into the light, her expression going from fear to relief upon seeing Herminia.

"Oh, it's you," Sybil said. "You were taking so long...."

"Do you want to go outside?" Herminia asked, concerned for her friend.

"And be alone with that Indian? No way."

The two fell into step together. Yes, Herminia thought, she was starting to think of Sybil as a friend. Sybil was funny and nice, and smarter than she let on. More than that, they shared the same fundamental problem — not having found their place in the world.

"How are the men doing?" Herminia asked.

"They can't stop talking about the 'vibrant colors' and 'unusual creatures.' Why don't they just shut up and enjoy it?" Sybil giggled. "I should put that on a T-shirt: 'Just shut up and enjoy it.'"

She sidled up and pressed herself to Herminia's side. Her body was soft, her bare forearms cold. "This place is starting to give me the creeps. Starting with that creepy Indian outside. He was a shaman, wasn't he? I'll bet he sewed that poor lizard's eyes closed. He'd cut our hearts out and eat them if he could."

"Human sacrifice died with the Spanish conquest," Herminia replied, defensively. She didn't like outsiders criticizing her culture. Why did Americans always harp on the excesses of the Mayans and Aztecs ... and Toltecs and Olmecs ... and.... well, okay, human sacrifice was pretty common to mainland México, but that was a long way from Baja.

Though Sybil was probably right. The Cochimí probably *had* mutilated the lizard. No one else lived around these parts. But for what reason? She found the thought both frightening and intriguing. What could he possibly have hoped to accomplish by blinding the lizard? Would he actually consider doing the same to a human if it served his purposes?

She patted Sybil's hand in what she hoped was a reassuring gesture.

The cave took a gentle bend and they could no longer see the exit. The way ahead appeared to go on forever, a tunnel to the valley of shadows. With each step, their eyes failed to adjust as fast as the darkness strengthened, until they had to put their hands to either side to keep from hitting the walls. Sybil stumbled twice, and then it was Herminia's turn. Their heads scraped the ceiling now and again. The way became rougher. If Herminia hadn't visited here before she would have stopped, for she knew that caves often turned into cenotes — open wells a hundred feet or more straight down. Water filled or not it didn't matter since there was no escape once you fell.

Shouts came from deeper in: curses in English. Curtis and Brennan, worried, almost panicked.

Sybil stopped moving.

"We have to help them," Herminia said. Sybil didn't budge. Nor would she release her grip on Herminia's arm. "*I* have to help them. You stay here, Sybil. If I don't come back soon, go outside and get the Cochimí to help."

"I'm ... I'm not leaving you," Sybil breathed.

"You need to let me go."

"I'm not going to that ... that shaman for help."

"Then come on."

They stumbled forward, Herminia cursing the poverty that had kept her from purchasing a flashlight for this trip. She had forgotten how deep and dark the cave was, and she hadn't planned on getting separated from the Americans. If she or Sybil broke a leg now they would need rescuing as well....

Around a bend they found the others, wraiths peering down on a macabre tableau. The flashlight shone on a pale, male face, a face disfigured from scrapes and seeping blood. Herminia's pulse raced. She stared for a second before realizing—

The Americans were okay. Her charges were okay.

"Who is it?" Sybil asked.

"We found him lying here," Brennan replied.

The man wore long pants and a white, cotton shirt rolled up at the sleeves. Scrapes covered his face and forehead, arms and hands, as if he had thrashed wildly against the stone before succumbing to whatever malady brought him down.

Now he lay still. In the dim light-pool of the flashlight, his skin appeared pallid and feverish. Though he must be around Herminia's age — seventeen or eighteen — his face carried an equal measure of innocent boyishness and aged sorrow.

"If that Indian did this," Curtis said, "I'm going to kill him."

"Stop it!" Sybil said. "He had some sort of fit or something. These are abrasions, not bruises from a beating." Sybil knelt, put her palm on the young man's forehead, and pulled back an eyelid, revealing an unfocused, hazel iris. She then took the man's wrist and felt for a pulse. Herminia was surprised at the confidence with which Sybil did this, as if she had worked in a doctor's office or something. Very different from her reaction to the deer. "Well, it's beating," Sybil announced. "It won't get any better here. We need to carry him outside."

Handing Herminia the flashlight, Brennan took the man's armpits and Curtis the feet. As they started to move, the flashlight played against the wall, to the painting of a sailfish. Herminia recalled it perfectly from her previous visit — it had been her favorite feature. The fish had been done in black outline. The brain of the sailfish had been solid white, as was its bill; its eye was vibrant blue, its sail and fins red. The rest of the body had been left as natural sandstone.

The sailfish was no longer discernible. The paint had been spread across the stone, as if someone had poured turpentine across the pictograph and half-scrubbed it away. The resulting smear was triangular with a white, eye-like blob in one corner. The eye had zigzag lines across it. It looked very much like the blind desert iguana's head.

Outside, they lay the unconscious man on the ground.

"What happened to him?" Curtis asked, while the others checked for a snake or spider bite.

"His ally willed it so," said the Cochimí, pouring himself a cup of coffee.

"What? What's wrong with you, man? This boy is sick. He needs a doctor." Curtis pushed up his sleeves, as if he wanted to fight.

The Cochimí dismissed this with a wave. "Take him. He is lost to me."

A seagull landed on a nearby mesquite and squawked at them. Seagulls had no business this far from the sea — Herminia wondered if it was the Cochimí's ally.

Look at you, she thought dismissively, *thinking with the charlatan's own vocabulary. Don't let him get to you.*

Keeping an eye on the bird, Herminia helped rig up a stretcher using dead manzanita branches, shoelaces and belts. They even took the two shirts the Cochimí had laid out to dry, and a blanket Sybil had brought to picnic on.

"The unconscious one, what happened to him?" Herminia asked.

"Do not concern yourself with Faustino," the Cochimí said, watching the preparations with amusement.

"What should we tell the doctors? We are not going to just let him die."

"Faustino Arce is lost in the Beyond. Unless he can find his way back, there is nothing you or I can do."

"Ready," came a voice, as if from far away.

"Take his place, Herminia," the shaman said. "Come back to me, come back to the cave and I will teach you. You are almost there — your awareness is already halfway into the Beyond."

"Herminia, are you coming? Herminia?"

"I need to go," Herminia said, blinking heavily.

It seemed that the shaman whispered a word in her ear, a word that sounded like a serpent's rendition of *apprentissss*, though she would have sworn his lips didn't move.

Herminia backed away, stumbling in the process.

They descended the arroyo with all haste, dragging the stretcher on the soft sand, carrying it over the rough bits. Even Sybil and Herminia took turns dragging and carrying. Curtis muttered about the barbarism of Indians and Mexicans, and Brennan kept glancing sideways at Herminia.

It didn't take long for their muscles to ache. Faustino never made a sound, even when the stretcher bounced over rocks the size of bowling balls.

When she wasn't carrying, Herminia hung back with Sybil so as to avoid the grumbling and glances.

"What did he mean, 'apprentice?'" Sybil asked. "Do you think he gave the boy peyote for some kind of ritual or something?"

So, she hadn't imagined that after all. Herminia hadn't been sure. "Faustino doesn't look drugged. I've seen people overdose at Loma Linda. It usually involves a lot of vomiting and rolling of eyes. Very smelly."

"The seagull was the shaman's familiar, wasn't it?"

Herminia shrugged.

Sybil said, "I might put on a ditsy act, but I'm not stupid. That Cochimí — Indian or whatever — he's got his eye on you." She placed her hand on Herminia's shoulder and pulled her to a standstill. "Don't trust him. I'm begging you."

"What? I— Trust him?"

"There's something not right about him. Listen, there's a lot of this going on at UC Berkeley, people talk a lot about free love and enlightenment and spiritual awakening — and then drug you with LSD. You wake up naked on a park bench wondering what happened. Don't trust him. Don't eat or drink anything he gives you."

"The shaman said that Faustino is lost in the Beyond," Herminia said, anxious to change the subject. "'Unless he can find his way back there is nothing you or I can do.' I wonder what he means."

"Ladies," came Brennan's voice from up ahead. "Everything okay?"

"Yes," Sybil said. "Just relieving ourselves."

"We've found shade. We're taking a break. Our lizard friend has been waiting for us."

"Be right there." Sybil let go of Herminia's arm. "Listen, Herminia, you are an amazing woman. You have been good to us. If you ever need anything, I think I'll hang around Santa Rosalía for a while. It's a special place. Look me up."

Did the American think Herminia was going to stay in the mountains? Become some sort of cave woman? What was wrong with these people?

Herminia made to say as much, but the words caught in her throat.

What *was* she going to do?

Apprentissss.

The $50 Curtis had paid her now seemed a paltry sum. She'd burn through that in a week or two, and she'd be back to making beds again. Might as well be old and gray for all the freedom that gave you. This Jeep ride into the mountains was the most freedom she'd ever have. Once they dropped Faustino at the hospital it was all over.

Maybe becoming a cave woman wasn't such a bad plan.

She chuckled a little to herself at the notion. But still. What if the Cochimí really were a shaman?

What if he could teach her?

They rejoined the men. Sybil splashed some water on Faustino's forehead. She tried to get him to drink, but his throat wouldn't swallow.

It was the same place they had rested before. The blind lizard continued worrying against the rock. Nails scratch-scratching, regular as a heartbeat. The lizard gave Herminia a reproachful look.

Herminia moved to the scree pile, put her ear near the stone, and heard something scratching from inside. Something trapped on the other side, trying to claw its way out.

She thought of that sailfish pictograph, how it had been smeared across the stone, how the smear looked so much like this blind lizard.

Herminia moved the blind lizard to the side and dug her fingers around the stone, pulled, dug around the edges, and pulled again. Soon her fingers were raw and the muscle fibers in her back felt like they would separate. It was like trying to free an anchor from a particularly stubborn kelp holdfast.

Finally the rocks shifted. Not much. Just enough to create a gap. A face poked out. Another lizard. But the opening was too small for it to escape.

The top stone wobbled.

"Curtis, Brennan, come on, help me," Herminia shouted.

"What? We need to get this boy to help," Curtis said.

"There's a lizard trapped in here."

"Stop fooling around with lizards."

Herminia leaned back on her haunches. "I— I think this is important."

Sybil joined her. Brennan came soon after, and then Curtis, declaring, "Everyone on this mountain has gone insane." But he lent his strength, and the rocks tumbled to the side.

The second lizard emerged and nodded to Herminia, as if thanking her. Its mouth and ear holes were sewn shut. The reptiles scurried over to Faustino and climbed onto his chest, one blind and one deaf-mute. Faustino stirred and groaned, but did not open his eyes. His color improved immediately, from pale to sunburned pink.

"You're all insane," Curtis said, staring at the miraculous improvement.

"There must be a doctor associated with El Boleo mine," Herminia said. "We can stop there. If there is no doctor, we'll take him to Santa Rosalía."

"And then to the nearest bar," said Brennan, "I'm badly in need of a Corona."

They ported Faustino on their shoulders through the waist-high brush of the final hill. Herminia felt sure he would pull through now that his lizard was free. The reptiles perched on Faustino's chest like lookouts on a crow's nest. Once the red Jeepster was in sight, they jumped to the ground and disappeared.

The buck in the Jeepster's trunk watched them approach with glassy eyes, and recalled to Herminia the shaman saying that these things worked out in the end. This deer had made sure they had stopped at the right place. It had all but offered itself as a sacrifice.

An offering, from apprentice to master.

Nighttime, the moon gave the world a sepia sheen. The hour of rattlesnakes in these mountains. Herminia made noise to warn wild animals of her approach, and set each foot carefully to avoid twisting her back or ankle, for she carried a heavy weight.

She paused when she smelled the mesquite fire. A dollop of pitch popped. A cricket chirped.

What made her return? Was there some sorcery in the shaman's words?

She could turn back now. No matter what had compelled her to this point, she retained the freedom to choose. Forward to another world, a world of crazy vocabulary. *Beyond* and *allies* and lizard magic.

Back to Santa Rosalía and bed-making.

Or a reconciliation with her parents, listen to their "told you so's," hang her head a few days, and ask for forgiveness.

They might actually give it.

A good life — fisherman. In most respects, a life beyond what she should expect on this Earth.

Herminia shifted the buck's weight on her shoulders. A trickle of sweat ran down her side beneath the yellow cotton dress.

Her decision had affirmed to Curtis that all Mexicans are crazy.

Brennan had solemnly shaken her hand.

Sybil had given her a hug. "Take care, you hear? Don't forget to look me up in Santa Rosalía." A slip of Southern accent had come through, and Herminia wondered where exactly Sybil had been born, and if she were embarrassed of her roots.

Herminia advanced.

Now she could see the glow over a silhouette of stone and brush.

Now she could see the outline of the shaman.

She stepped into the circle of light and set the deer at the shaman's feet. Despite her exhaustion, Herminia took the knife from her ankle sheath and began skinning the animal. She did not think this man would appreciate any excuses for physical weakness, and she wanted very much to impress him.

The shaman eyed her curiously. "Why did you free the lizard?"

She did not ask how he knew. The shaman must know many things. "Faustino was going to die."

"So his ally willed it."

"Who is his ally?"

The shaman scooted over a bucket full of damp corn husks — all prepared for her and the buck. As Herminia cut chunks of meat from the deer's bone, the shaman wrapped them in the corn husks and lay them in the coals. Over the gamey smell of raw venison Herminia smelled the shaman's male body odor.

"Did I meet his ally?" Herminia pressed. "Was that the lizard?"

The shaman said, "Faustino will be back, once the doctors treat him. He will be back and he won't thank you."

Herminia finished butchering the deer. Several times the shaman added wood to the fire to make enough coals to roast all the meat.

"Is it the way of a shaman to never answer a question directly?" Herminia asked.

"Now you have laid down a challenge, Herminia Carrillo. To never answer you directly." The shaman laughed, and the way the sound hissed through his broken teeth wasn't entirely pleasant. He wrapped the final piece of venison in corn husks and set it onto the fire. With a stick, he pushed coals over the top. Then he scrubbed the blood from his fingers with sand. "Tomorrow we find out if you are apprentice material.

"Tomorrow you enter the cave on my terms."

THREE
PRESENT DAY, PUNTA COLONET

The family gathered in the little house as families do after great, tragic events: funerals, miscarriages, announcements of marriage into drug families, or the cancellation of a favorite telenovela. They arrived throughout the July morning: the brothers and sisters from Los Estados Unidos, the aunt that had gathered them through the long process of Family Sponsored Visas, some relatives who lived near the little house in Punta Colonet, Mamá and Papá. Others. They had brought their smells with them. Shoe polish. Hair polish. Sweat from the road, or fruity perfume to cover the sweat from the road.

To Lucinda, these brothers, her sister, the cousins; this crowd felt as alien as the Sunday crowd leaving an unfamiliar church. Friendly, well dressed in black and white, carrying Italian-made purses, and alien.

Her mother had sulked Lucinda from the stove, and now Lucinda leaned against the frame of the living room window. That was about all her mother did these days — sulk. Wasn't that *her* job as a teenager? The two had hardly spoken since the parade, other than Mamá telling Lucinda it was all her fault. Whatever *it* was. ("Oh sure," Lucinda had replied. "It's my fault El Jaguar is a perverted psychopath. It's my fault he hung around the parade to molest teenage girls and old women."

Well, what was she expected to say? She was still sore from the dog bite, and tired. And, truth be told, terrified.)

Lucinda's hands itched to grind up some chilis in the mortar or stir the mole bubbling on the back burner. The distinct scent of drying tomatoes colored the air; it was starting to stick to the sides. Soon, the mole would burn.

Across the Transpeninsular Highway, behind broken glass-topped walls and a screen of guard dogs, another family gathered in a similar fashion for a similar reason. El Jaguar's great, armored hacienda was visible from Lucinda's perch, partly obstructed by the sloped roof of the hair salon and Flying Samaritan clinic, which shared the same building. One by one the long, black cars discharged their well-dressed passengers. Ten cars and counting.

If Lucinda had had binoculars, she would have tried to discern their faces. Angry, resigned, impassive ... relieved?

The loaded pistol had discharged; the burning fuse had ignited the firecracker.

Boom. El Jaguar was dead.

Grandmother Herminia had killed him.

Today the District Attorney would decide whether to file murder charges.

Talk of witches and magic swirled in Lucinda's imagination. That infernal night. The burning effigy. The puma fighting the scarecrow.

Lucinda's jeans had an enchilada-sized hole right in the groin. And yet the bite had left only the smallest of scars.

She remembered Abuelita licking her hand, smearing saliva on the wound.

Abuelita refused to talk about it. "I don't remember much," she said, to all of Lucinda's questions. "The fight passed in a blur. The bite must not have been deep, Little Chicken." Abuelita had poked her hand through the hole and made funny shapes with her fingers. "These cheap, Chinese knockoff jeans, they tear like paper."

Lucinda hated to be lied to.

Mamá called Lucinda's talk nonsense. 'No one believes in witches or monsters. Why do you watch this nonsense on TV? I'm telling your father to get rid of that idiot box.' (Mamá never would — she liked her telenovelas too much.)

Didn't the whole town believe in witches? Wasn't that what the Parade of Heroes was all about?

"Is that your friend Mateo?" Abuelita asked from behind. "With the binoculars?"

Lucinda squinted. Behind the glint from broken glass-topped walls, the sun bounced off twin lenses in an open window in El Jaguar's hacienda. "I ... don't know. He's not a friend. We're just in the same class together."

Was that Mateo, El Jaguar's 15-year-old son? Should she be concerned? Come fall, they would be forced to share a classroom, a playground, a teacher, and friends. That's the way it was in a small town with one high school: everyone forced together like beans in a pressure cooker.

Abuelita put an arm around Lucinda. "Come here and sit down."

People were sitting everywhere: on orange plastic Fanta crates, on the green throw, on the three wooden chairs and the faux leather recliner that was Papá's pride. Everywhere but Abuelita's marriage trunk: a carved, wooden chest along the north wall. No one sat on that, or even looked at it for very long.

The old woman steered Lucinda to the marriage trunk with an arm as firm as a goat's hind leg. She wore a long shirt of white, green and red (México's colors) and a frilly white blouse, in stark contrast to the somber colors of the rest of the family.

That morning, against her mother's wishes, Lucinda had dressed in her favorite scoop necked tee (purple-gray, horizontal stripes) and blue jeans — not the holey one. She, too, refused to dress for mourning.

"The worst part is the waiting," said Abuelita. "So let's play a game. Let's pretend we are all at a baile. Who do you think is a good dancer?"

The question caught Lucinda off guard. That was one of the reasons she adored Abuelita — the old woman was always catching people off guard with her off-the-wall ideas, usually phrased as a question.

Lucinda tipped her jaw at her brother Enrique. He was the oldest. His hair was slicked back with some kind of gel or oil, his white collars starched and pressed, his mustache trimmed. He had danced with her second at her quinceañera, right after Papá.

"Two left feet," Grandmother Herminia said. "Did you know that at your sister's wedding he stepped on her feet so hard she barked like a harbor seal?" Abuelita mimicked the sound convincingly.

Not only was this a complete fabrication, but Enrique would be mortified to hear it. Lucinda laughed aloud. "Did Tina lay an egg?"

"She laid all the money people paid to dance with her. A wad so fat your mother thought it was a pasilla chili and tried to cook it."

And so it went, Abuelita making up stories about the dancing abilities of various family members, sometimes exaggerating their skill and clumsiness, and always coming up with just the opposite of what anyone would have thought.

Lucinda felt better there on the marriage trunk with Abuelita. She realized her shoulders were up by her ears, and rolled them a couple of times to relax them. That was probably the only lesson she retained from her brief stint at salsa class at the community center, but it was a good one. Relax: shoulders away from ears.

Aunt María, who was actually Lucinda's great aunt — grandpa's sister — knelt down and put both her hands on Lucinda's knees. She was the one Lucinda and Abuelita had decided would dance like a knight in a rusty suit of armor — trying to escape from quicksand.

"I have been talking with your mother," Great Aunt María Torres said, adjusting the stylish, red-rimmed glasses on her nose. "If things are too difficult at school, you can come live with us. Until you graduate high school."

"I don't want to go anywhere."

Mamá had agreed to what?

Mamá bent to take something out of the oven, pointing her sizable bottom at Lucinda instead of catching her eye. This didn't reassure Lucinda at all. Mamá was always deciding things like Lucinda was only a kid, and getting Mamá to change her mind was like dragging a burro through a patch of cactus — by the tail.

"Of course," Aunt María said, "but if you have to. If school gets, well—"

"Words aren't Chicklets to be mashed between your teeth," Abuelita said. "Swallow or spit."

"Things could get ugly," Auntie said. "Doña Herminia may not always be here to protect you. You know, with her powers."

Abuelita pursed her lips and wrinkled her nose as if Auntie had done something terribly uncouth, such as passing gas during confession.

Lucinda stuck her hands between her knees and squeezed her legs together. Abuelita had categorically denied that anything unexplainable had happened at the Parade of Heroes. El Jaguar had attacked them with his dog. People had pulled the hoodlum off Abuelita, and the dog off Lucinda. El Jaguar fell and broke his neck.

Nothing to see.

Happens every day.

Her parents believed it. The police believed it. Lucinda had almost persuaded herself as well.

And now Aunt María had to bring up *Abuelita's powers*. What was she talking about?

She definitely was having a talk with Abuelita as soon as Aunt María was out of earshot.

Aunt María seemed to be waiting for an answer, so Lucinda said, "Thank you, Auntie. I will think about it. But there's something you should know..." She tried to think of the worst thing. "...I smoke. A lot."

Aunt María patted her leg. "Perfecto. I smoke too."

"In bed," Lucinda added. "Terrible. I drop the ashes all over the pillow. Mamá says I'm going to burn the house down one of these days."

"Me too. Just last week I fell asleep on the couch. The butt dropped from between my fingers and burned a hole through the cushion clear to the floor! I stuffed it with tissue so my husband wouldn't notice.

"We'll have so much fun, Lucinda. Our town has a good school, and we can take the bus to the cinema. Six stops only. I was not able to have any children; I'll spoil you like a high-bred Chihuahua." She leaned forward to whisper. "My husband is usually drunk, so you don't have to listen to him, except his snores. He might even move in with his mistress if you come to live with us. If we are lucky."

And with a wink, Aunt María spun off.

"And I thought El Jaguar was a nightmare!" Lucinda whispered to her grandmother.

But the old woman, her eyes staring straight ahead, held up a finger, demanding silence with her rigid pose. Conversation died around them. Everyone listened.

At first, they heard nothing. Then came, very faintly at first, the sound of rubber pressing against packed dirt. The hum of a well-tuned automobile.

"That would be the courier," Abuelita said.

It could have been any car going to any of a dozen houses on this road. Or someone lost, or someone going to one of the crossroads higher up.

No one doubted Abuelita.

A knock.

Papá opened the door to reveal a man wearing a uniform, fist raised to knock a second time. Lucinda wasn't sure if pesos changed hands or not; she wasn't familiar with this sort of thing, or if he was a postman or some other courier man. The uniform didn't give much of a clue, somewhere between slate green and algae blue, with a badge or name tag on one breast or the other, or maybe it was just a rectangular patch indicating the brand of clothing. He brought with him the sweet smell of cinnamon, and a slipperiness to the air, as if you were looking through sunglasses smudged by greasy fingerprints. It was hard to be certain if the courier were tall or short, handsome or plain, or if his mustache ended straight like a smile or curled like the blades of scissors.

Lucinda's sister Tina took one look and added a snort of mescal to her Tecate, topped it with a squeeze of lime, and chugged deeply.

By the time Lucinda looked back to the front door, the courier had faded outside. Papá emerged from a rectangle of light, letter in hand. The envelope's perimeter had slanted, red bars. It looked tremendously important. He tore it open with impatient fingers. Strangely, a little down feather floated to the ground, the kind they use to stuff pillows.

"Listen, Little Chicken," Abuelita said, urgently, "I haven't always told you the whole truth. Whatever happens, I—"

"Did you smell that? The cinnamon?" Lucinda's throat clenched;

she could barely get the words out. It reminded her of El Jaguar in the worst way.

"Sí. Things could get very bad, Little Chicken."

"Abuelita, I know you love me. Tell me something I can use."

Abuelita said, "Inside this trunk there is a mortar and pestle. They need something only you can bring." She poked Lucinda's chest. "You and your ally. You like cooking, no?"

"My ally? Who is my ally?"

From across the room, her father said, "Listen, here is the important part:

"After a careful review, the office of the District Attorney of the County of Ensenada has determined that Herminia Carrillo Eco acted in self-defense. Case AH 38517 is closed barring new evidence to the contrary."

The room erupted in cheers.

Lucinda wanted to stand and join in celebration. Perhaps they could discover which speculation about her family's dancing was not so far from the mark. Perhaps Tina really did dance like a penguin over hot coals. Perhaps Pepe really could stand on his head, twirl, and drink horchata from a straw at the same time.

She wanted to jump and shout and whoop with the others, do some crazy dance Abuelita would talk about at another party, but she couldn't do any of those things. Something dragged her toward the floor. Some weight lay over her; a heavy, floppy weight that seemed to cling to her. They tumbled off the marriage chest and onto the cement floor, Lucinda and the weight. She squirmed and kicked to get free. It was some person, she realized before long, and she didn't find it the least bit funny.

Finally, she freed herself and rose to her knees.

The person just lay there, face first. Gray hair, a strong back, arms and legs bent in ways they shouldn't.

Abuelita.

Lucinda wasn't the screaming type. Her heart pounded, but she didn't scream.

Reaching from behind, she felt the pulse in Abuelita's jugular. Strong, regular. She licked her finger and put it under Abuelita's nose.

Yes, breath caressed her wet finger, in, out.

"Hey, Papá!" she yelled.

He didn't hear.

"Papá!"

Still nothing.

A thrown tennis shoe got his attention, and Papá's shout got them all scrambling.

Papá took charge, rolling grandmother Herminia over, checking her vitals, deciding whose car to use to take her to the nearest hospital in Ensenada.

Backing up, Lucinda's heel stumbled into the marriage chest and for the briefest instant, as brief as the green flash of the sea, a pleasant face beamed at her. A young, brown-skinned woman in the backseat of a Jeep. Bench seats. A red Jeep with white trim. Wind whipped the young woman's black hair, dust billowed as from a windstorm.

It wasn't just any young woman. It was Abuelita.

Grandmother Herminia, many years ago. Her wide, beautiful eyes bulged with alarm. A brown form bounded into the road before them, a buck mule deer. The Jeep skidded sideways, throwing gravel and sand high into the air....

Lucinda blinked.

As quick as that, the vision disappeared. Lucinda was back in the little house, in the little town. Abuelita was being carried outside.

Four

1967, MOUNTAINS OUTSIDE SANTA ROSALÍA,
BAJA CALIFORNIA SOUTH

The first wink of sunlight woke Herminia from where she had slept on her side. She pulled her shoulder and hips out of the hollow they had dug in the sand. Her bed had been rather comfortable, actually. The sand held the sun's heat far into the night, and cooled in conjunction with the mind slowing into dream. The mountain air — that was a different story. Even in the summer it could be cold against bare skin, and the shaman hadn't offered any blankets.

Herminia smiled. She liked a certain amount of discomfort — it made the body feel alive. She stood in one swift motion, and swayed hips and feet to a cha-cha in her head. Some people were yawners and stretchers, others were grumblers and coffee-ers, Herminia was a cha-cha-er. The rolling, Cuban rhythm woke the whole body into a nice, smooth glide.

The music in Herminia's head stopped abruptly, interrupted by the sound of a car door slamming. They were way too far from the road, weren't they?

She tied the straps on her sandals, checked her ankle knife (still in place), shouldered her small pack, and followed the sound. Over the rocky knoll that housed the cave entrance she discovered the shaman rummaging in the bed of a boxy, white Chevrolet pickup. It was parked at the head of two weed-free ruts that might generously be called a road. The shaman wore his trademark flannel shirt and jeans.

"Ah, Herminia. I must run into town to drop off the excess venison. If it doesn't spoil first, the ants will get it."

"You've got to be kidding!" she exclaimed, stalking up to the shaman. "You had this pickup and you didn't even offer to take Faustino Arce to the hospital?"

"His ally willed it," the shaman said, shrugging.

Herminia pointed a shaking finger at him, then at the ruts that must lead to the mine road. Everything up here did, eventually. The refreshing morning air had turned sour. "You are going to answer some questions for me."

The shaman gave a mocking bow. "You may call me Don Esteban. Don Estaban Ríos, if you must, but Don Esteban will do."

"Who was Faustino Arce to you, Don Esteban?" She put as much sarcasm into the honorific *Don* as possible.

"But you already know this. Faustino was my apprentice. That is why you are here — to take his place."

"Take his place! Faustino's not even gone and you're looking for a replacement. You said it yourself — he will be back."

Don Esteban smiled his broken-teeth smile.

"Why the hell should I take his place? I will end up lying on the floor of the cave like some coyote leavings, and no Americans to take me to safety."

"Exactly right — if your ally wills it," Don Esteban said. "On the other hand, you could end up a bruja. Not some psychic charlatan, but someone who can fold reality, transform into the animal of your choosing, explore the fathoms of the mind, or cleanse a broken spirit. Someone who can travel from here to Florida faster than a dream. Someone who can navigate the Beyond, the realm that lies parallel to and just outside of this one." It was clear from Don Esteban's inflection that he considered 'navigating the Beyond' more important than all the other things he had listed. Whatever that meant. "With even one ally," the shaman continued, "your powers would be beyond imagination. This I can show you. This I can teach you. The cave awaits, Herminia Carrillo, if only you will answer its call."

"This is crazy," Herminia repeated. "You are a cold-hearted son of a snake."

"Again, you already know this."

Herminia dropped her accusing finger. She trembled from adrenalin. The shaman was right, she had learned nothing from her angry questions. Nothing much — she had already known the shaman was cold, had already guessed that Faustino was his prior apprentice. *Current* apprentice, if he had survived.

She wouldn't take Faustino's place, whatever Don Esteban thought. If Faustino wanted back, she wouldn't stand in his way. This much she decided.

Don Esteban began removing some things from behind the seat of his pickup.

Herminia breathed deeply, willed herself to calm. "Why did Faustino's ally reject him?"

"Why does the wind blow from the north today and from the south tomorrow? Scientists try to explain this with pressure systems and solar flares. They see no further than the tips of their noses. What the wind knows is that the system is out of balance. Only by moving from here to there can balance be restored."

"So balance is what is needed in the universe?" Herminia guessed.

"Of course not. It means weathermen are idiots," Don Esteban said sagely, as though some great insight had been imparted.

She thought this might be a joke, but couldn't be sure.

It was hard to remain angry at the portly Cochimí. All parts of him — body, face, and mind — exuded reasonableness. Especially since he hadn't done anything *to* her — not directly. In fact, he was offering to teach her.

He handed Herminia three objects: a sketchpad, a pestle, and a mortar. "Come. You have passed the first test — you did not run away screaming. Your lessons can begin."

Myriad thoughts formed and dissolved in Herminia's mind, but none formed a coherent question. She followed.

"All of the ink used in the caves was created by natives from materials nearby," the shaman explained, picking a fruit from an elephant tree — a tree about six feet tall that grew from bloated trunks that spread from the earth like a giant's gnarled, arthritic fingers. Purple juice smudged Don Esteban's fingertips. "Guided by their allies, they experimented to form the perfect colors for their drawings. Before I can consider you as an apprentice, you must first copy every drawing in the cave with your own, homemade inks."

"Did the Cochimí paint these?" Herminia asked.

"We do not actually know who painted here: the Cochimí or a tribe that came before. It does not really matter. In that sense, we are all Cochimí."

Another enigma.

Herminia picked her own fruit from the brittle elephant tree. About the size of a grape, the fruit was hard as a Juniper berry. She dug her fingernail into its skin to see the purple flesh underneath, and was surprised to discover a single, yellow seed. "I have never made ink before."

"Nor had the people who first came here. Open yourself to the materials. Give yourself to the mortar and pestle. Feel the drawings with your eyes."

"Where do I find the materials? Where do I start looking?"

"Your ally will help you," the shaman grinned, "or he will not."

Whenever Don Esteban smiled, Herminia had the vague feeling he was mocking, and it annoyed her. She hefted the mortar in her hand. About the size of half a coconut, the mortar was made of black basalt, with three legs and the face of a wild boar, and of course a hollow bowl in which to grind things. A standard, generic design one could purchase at any cooking or tourist shop. It had a comfortable weight. The stubby pestle, also of black basalt, fit her hand nicely.

"*She* will help me," Herminia corrected, rolling the pestle around in her hand. "My ally is a female."

The shaman laughed.

They meandered all over the area. Don Esteban would point out various plants and animals. He had a keen eye, often spotting things Herminia would have walked right by: a splash of color from a flower, a pack rat hidden beneath a mesquite tree, a horned toad, a vein of diatomaceous earth. He possessed a naturalist's knowledge of local flora and fauna.

The sun beamed down at 10 o'clock when their footsteps brought them back to the cave. The interior temperature was pleasant, the air dry and fresh.

Close to the entrance, faded, orange, bow-wielding natives hunted deer, arrows flying. Deeper in, the paintings became more interesting. Less damaged by the sun and elements, Herminia could see that the orange color had probably been red originally. Here, the natives and animals were made with two colors: red and black, their bodies neatly divided in two.

Why would that be? Were they trying to depict some sort of duality?

The artists improved also, though Don Esteban said that the drawings had been done over hundreds, possibly thousands of years. The color palette increased. A blue river separated a man and a fox. A crow observed Herminia with eerie, yellow eyes. White war paint decorated the faces of warriors.

They stopped walking about five hundred feet in, well before the place Faustino had fallen. The dim sunlight from the entrance barely illuminated the passage. Herminia's eyes couldn't adjust any further — she would need a flashlight to explore beyond, let alone copy any paintings.

She didn't tell Don Esteban about the flashlight in her pack. It felt right to keep some secrets, since the shaman was being so enigmatic. The flashlight had been a goodbye gift from Sybil and Brennan. (Curtis had been in favor of forcing Herminia to ride back down to Santa Rosalía, under Brennan's bottom if necessary — for her own good.)

Herminia felt something in these caves, a tingle in the bones. The sort of feeling you get when you feel someone staring at you before you actually spot them.

She wondered: *Who drew this? What did they understand of the world? Of beyond the world?*

Had Faustino Arce stood here as she did now?

Don Esteban said, "I do not know why Faustino's ally rejected him, in that sense. It will not be the same reason your allies reject you."

"Allies, plural?"

Don Esteban appeared to be waging some sort of internal struggle on whether or not to answer. Finally, he said, "It is beneficial to figure things out for yourself. And potentially quite harmful to gain knowledge before you are ready. Nevertheless, I will tell you this: every human has three allies. No more, and no less. The allies reside in the Beyond. If someone can travel to the Beyond, there is a chance he or she will encounter their ally and bond — as I have. That is the work we will do here, to teach you to travel to the Beyond. Safely. So that you do not end up like Faustino."

These were strange turns of phrase. *Beyond. Ally. Bond.* And Don Esteban's use of singular and plural made no sense. Every human had three allies, plural, but the brujo would bond with his ally, singular. Herminia knew she was pushing the man's patience, but decided to risk another question. "Did Faustino have the training I will receive?"

"Sí. And more, for he has studied under me for several years. This is why I know it is his ally's will that he fail."

Years! No way was Herminia going to be a cave-woman for several years. She'd have to figure out a fixed time frame and stick to it. If she didn't see progress in, say, a week, she'd be out of here.

"Are the allies, like, animal familiars?"

"No, Herminia Carrillo. We brujos eat animal familiars for breakfast." Don Esteban put up his hands. "Enough talk. Examine the drawings. Begin near the entrance where the light is good. Figure out what you need for ink and make it. If it is not just right, do it again. I don't expect it to be right the first time. Oh, and remember, you can't be sure until the ink is dry. The hue changes as the ink dries."

They left the cave, and Don Esteban retrieved a copy of El Universal newspaper from the front seat of the pickup. He discarded all the pages but the racetrack results, and began studying them intently.

Herminia squinted at the nameplate. Strangely, the paper was dated May 18, 1967. That very same day. Herminia couldn't imagine how Don Esteban had received today's newspaper here in the mountains. Even if the El Boleo mine had a subscription, how could Don Esteban have gone there and back without her knowing it?

"I thought you were leaving," she said, hoping that by watching and listening she could spy out where that road led.

"Mind your paint," he answered, "and I'll mind mine."

. . .

Herminia made multiple attempts to duplicate the red ink. Guessing that the orange color came from clay (there was a lot of it nearby), she experimented by mixing water and clay, and painting with a fingertip.

Her initial drawings would have embarrassed a preschooler. Page after page in her sketch book was filled with disappointing tests.

Sometimes Don Esteban would peer over her shoulder, grunt, and go back to his track sheet. Later in the day, he fired up the Chevy and drove away.

That was a relief.

The Chevy's engine seemed to be traveling downhill until eventually it could no longer be heard. Just as she had suspected — it intersected the mine road at some point.

Herminia stretched and took stock of the situation. The concoction (it couldn't rightly be called "paint") was too runny. It was too orange. It faded terribly on paper — what would it do on sandstone? It might not even stick.

Congratulations, apprentice, you've made dirty water.

In frustration, Herminia picked up a stone and heaved it as far as it would go, startling a covey of quail. They took off with humming wings and chirping beaks.

Use your head, Herminia thought. *Stop searching around and* think. *What do I know that is red?*

Blood, of course.

Iron.

That's what makes blood red. Maybe that's why clay is orange, too.

So why wasn't clay a brilliant red, like blood?

She spun a hunk of clay in her hand, thinking. *There must be other stuff in here that isn't red. How to get rid of it? How to bring out the iron?*

She sat for a very long time studying the clay, trying to figure out how to purify it. Purify. What else needs to be purified ... besides Sybil's reputation?

That brought a laugh.

But seriously. Pigment isn't the only thing that needs to be purified. So does copper. They don't dig up pesos at El Boleo mine; they dig up ore. And the ore needs to be smelted. They apply heat — far more heat that Herminia could ever produce, but perhaps a little would suffice. Heat ... hmm. It wouldn't hurt to try.

A search of camp yielded a frying pan. Herminia stoked the fire and warmed small chunks of clay. Little by little the clay turned a deep, satisfying red. It took the rest of the daylight hours to make enough to fill the bowl of the mortar. The fired clay ground into a fine, beautiful powder.

Don Esteban did not return that night, but even alone on an empty belly (he had taken *all* the venison), Herminia slept content in the day's work.

The next day she started thinking about the liquid component of the paint. Water wouldn't do it — too runny. Oil might, but how could she possibly make oil? She had a vague idea that refining oil from things — olives and corn and whatnot — involved a lot of pressing and processing a large volume of stuff. She didn't have either tools or stuff. Some sea creatures had oil, but she wasn't going to harpoon a whale just to make some paint!

She skinned a few layers from the elephant tree, just in case, but came away with water-laden wood. Water, not oil.

Napping didn't help. Nor did feeling sorry for herself. (Her tummy was empty, after all.)

Walking in wider and wider circles brought her to a trickling stream and natural pool in a deep canyon. She waded in ... and noticed someone watching her from the pool's edge. The blind lizard. She was convinced — utterly convinced — that it knew perfectly well who she was, where she was, and what she was doing.

"Are you really blind, my friend?" she asked.

The lizard did a mini push-up.

"Ah well, God made us all beautiful, eh?" Herminia removed her dress and threw it up onto the rocks, laughing as the lizard scampered away.

A glorious swim later, Herminia felt more human, less irritated with herself and the shaman. She even scrubbed her dress in the rolling stream below the pool. On the next trip to Santa Rosalía she would buy some soap, she decided.

The blind lizard waited on the flattest, most comfortable rock. There Herminia reclined, enjoying the sun on her bare skin, while the dress dried nearby.

"How is your master doing?" she asked. "Faustino Arce, isn't that it? Are you in communication with him?"

The lizard did a push-up.

She sat up, ready to race over and cover herself ... then admonished herself — *tonta*. This is a lizard! And a blind lizard to boot. And then another thought hit her: perhaps the shaman can watch through the lizards' eyes....

Well, she decided, what of it? American girls showed as much skin at the beach every day of the week. She adjusted her bra, reclined again and dozed.

Returning to the camp some time later, her belly slightly tender from too much sun, Herminia startled the covey of quail again. *If only I had a net, or a gun,* she thought, *I could have delicious quail for dinner. What do you think, Lemon, would you like that? Perhaps I can brain a quail with a well-thrown stone.*

The blind lizard padded beside her. She'd decided to name it after a blues musician. One of Loma Linda's guests had left a record collection that the maids played over and over, and Herminia particularly liked the soulful guitar of Blind Lemon Jefferson.

Her stomach growled. *Man, she was hungry!*

Herminia stopped walking.

That was the second time the covey of quail had startled from that mesquite tree. Why had they returned to the same place?

She backtracked, dropped to her knees, and crawled under. The tree's stiff, poky branches concealed a half dozen nests, and within the nests, several dozen delicious-looking eggs. Tiny, dappled, bite-size ovals.

She offered an egg to Lemon, which the lizard ate with great gusto.

Herminia was too hungry to bother with cooking. She popped open the eggs, one after another, and sucked them dry. One, two, three...

They were tiny quail eggs, after all. Not like chicken eggs. This would barely count as a meal.

...four, five, six.

The white stuck to her fingers and dripped down her chin.

It wasn't very enjoyable. No salt, no lime juice, no hot sauce. And even without spice, an egg tastes better cooked than raw, so when the worst of her hunger pains had faded, using a nest as a basket, Herminia carried the rest of the eggs back to camp.

As she wiped the clay particles from the frying pan preparing to fry some tiny eggs, her mind turned back to paint. She seemed no closer to creating the liquid part of paint than yesterday. Water wasn't working. Oil wasn't available. What could combine with the red pigment to create a substance that would stick to paper and sandstone?

The pigment needed a binder.

Herminia didn't cook much, and she certainly didn't bake. Basically, if the food needed more preparation than heat and chilies it was more than she wanted to invest. But she knew a little through observation.

Bakers used eggs as a binder, didn't they? Maybe they could work for paint.

The egg whites seemed like the best bet, but after several tries all she managed to do was create a sticky, slimy mess. But the yolks....

After much experimenting, a few expletives, and a few thrown stones, Herminia discovered that the yolks could be removed intact, and passed hand to hand, back and forth, until the skin dried. She soon mastered the technique of drying the yolk skin, piercing it, and dumping its contents into the mortar. Add a little water and red color, and the concoction made a passable red paint.

More than passable — brilliant!

Herminia marveled at how much she had accomplished. In two days, with no instruction from that slovenly shaman, she had manufactured her own paint. No doubt this paint, if applied to the bare stone inside the cave, would last generations.

Herminia had some natural skill at drawing but no training apart from one semester of art at middle school taught by the PE teacher — a man so fat he couldn't cross the school parking lot without sitting down.

She had to practice the shapes over and over to even approximate the simplest of cave paintings. Though it was doubtful that the shaman expected artistic genius; he must intend it as some kind of lesson in discipline. Mindless, reptilian repetition, recalling all the worst teachers she'd had over the years.

Copy this sentence twenty times: *I will not chew Chiclets in class. I will not chew Chiclets....*

She'd had to come up with multiple pigments: black (charcoal), blue (wild berries), yellow (elephant tree seeds), white (diatomaceous earth). But boredom and frustration were growing. The cave descended beyond sight. Her back ached. She hadn't eaten much. (She *had* discovered one package of the roasted venison in the coals — thank God).

Worst of all, she hadn't changed her underwear in four days. Diaper rash was a serious concern.

That's when I'll leave, she decided, rubbing her lower back from the strain of sitting cross legged too long. *One outbreak of red pimples where you shouldn't have red pimples and I'm out of here.*

"Why do you hesitate?"

What—?

Don Esteban's voice had come from deeper inside the cave. Footfalls approached from the dark. Moments later Don Esteban arrived, dressed as slovenly as ever, carrying a grocery bag. His pants sagged worse than a plumber's.

Herminia stared at him incredulously. "Did you just go shopping in there? I didn't hear your pickup."

Don Esteban removed a carton of eggs from the grocery bag, handed it to her. "This will help. Making egg tempera from quail eggs can't be easy."

He held out his hand, and Herminia gave him the sketch pad. He flipped to the beginning and went page by page. "These drawings are like the people outside. They are two-dimensional. They have no depth."

Herminia understood that by "people outside" he meant the people in Santa Rosalía — and the rest of the world. People who had not discovered the caves and trained with the shaman.

Don Esteban studied a drawing of the blue river separating the man and the fox. "It is not their fault, any more than it is a dog's fault that it cannot speak, or an insect's fault that it cannot feel love. They have no access to the Beyond. Nothing but flesh and memory." He wrapped his heart and his head when he said "flesh" and "memory."

"Would they be more than people if they were trained?" Herminia asked. "Would they be superheroes or something?"

"No and no. They would no longer be less than people."

Less than people? Was she a less-than-person when she had arrived? She felt vaguely insulted. And what about that other apprentice, Faustino, the one Don Esteban had left for dead? Had Faustino also been a less-than-person?

The shaman returned the sketch pad. "Still, the question. Why do you hesitate? Why have you not copied the crow pictograph?"

Herminia looked again. Twilight-deep inside the cave, this image was by far the strangest she had run across. It seemed to show a crow that had swallowed a man, or perhaps a man turning into a crow, for the man-shape was inside the bird, and the bird's open beak pointed up to the ceiling. She'd been sitting here for a good half hour and hadn't drawn a line. Just looking at it made the nape of her neck tingle. She wanted to shiver in the worst way.

"These drawings are more intricate than I had supposed." Herminia pointed to the five fingers on the man's hand, to the feathers on the wings, and to the crow's eyes. "Deliberate contouring. Layering of different thicknesses. There — a white glint in the left eye I hadn't noticed before. Perhaps a child would have fingers delicate enough to do that, but a fisher-woman."

Herminia dipped the calloused pad of her index in the yellow paint and wiped it on her sketch pad in an artistic swipe, leaving a lemon-colored apostrophe. "That's my best."

Stretching out her well-tanned legs, Herminia slid her hand down her ankle and loosened her dagger. She was flexible enough to reach it easily. Don Esteban's eyes followed the length of her leg.

So, he was a man after all.

She pulled a lock of hair over her shoulder, and with a swift cut severed several inches.

"I'm going to borrow some of your fishing line," she announced, "just as soon as I carve a handle. I will need to fashion a brush to paint this properly. And then I am going to town. Give me a ride?"

"Use your thumb," he replied.

Loma Linda resort had fired Herminia. Fortunately, her friend Rosa warned her before she had the humiliation of facing the brute of a manager. The man was capable of suggesting some disgusting way of earning her job back — and Herminia might have had to reply with a kick to his vanity.

"I saved your things," Rosa said, leading Herminia down a slate-paved path to the Honeymoon Cottage. "You can stay here tonight if you don't turn the light on, but tomorrow it's booked."

"You're a good friend, Rosa."

It was a beautiful suite, half-moon love seats, down comforters, curtains, and white accents everywhere, gold-colored fixtures. They changed the white roses daily. Herminia took one from a crystal vase and inhaled its domesticated loveliness.

Her clothes were laid out on the bed next to her green duffel bag, pressed and folded neatly. There were definitely benefits to being friends with the maids. Rosa had even brought the maids' record player and their meager record collection. She selected the *Blind Lemon Jefferson Volume I* and put it on.

"How was it?" Rosa asked, sitting on the bed.

Herminia sat next to her. They were friends, but not really close. They'd known each other only three months, since Herminia had moved here. Like many of the maids, Rosa simultaneously dreamed of being swept off her feet by one of the rich beautiful guests, and believed it impossible for someone of her humble birth.

Herminia preferred to believe that anything was possible, even in México.

"It was wonderful," Herminia said.

"Are you moving to the United States? I knew you had fallen for one of those norteamericanos guapos. Tell me, do they really have hairy chests....?"

Herminia hugged Rosa and laughed. "No. I am not going there. I found a sort of teacher in the mountains."

Rosa narrowed her eyes. "Are you pregnant? It's too early to be sure, but there are—"

"No! Nothing like that. I haven't even kissed anyone."

Herminia took a deep breath. How could you explain to someone who hadn't been to the caves, seen the lizards, the pictographs, the shaman ... someone who hadn't lived what you had lived? "Do you know what it is like to fall in love? To be so full of hope that you almost explode, and so full of dread that you almost want to sabotage the relationship yourself so that your heart doesn't get broken?"

Rosa nodded. "You met someone else? Someone besides this movie star and his friend?"

"Yes, Rosa. And I am excited — and afraid."

"Is he handsome?"

"No, he is very ugly. He has broken front teeth, and a big belly, and he sleeps on the ground. But he does own an old pickup truck."

Rosa laughed. "Perfect! — if you hate your parents."

"Oh, Rosa, what am I doing? It just feels right, you know? You won't believe this, but he is really just a teacher, not a boyfriend. I am going to learn what I can from him, and then I will decide what to do. Maybe I will come back here and make beds."

"You are not telling me everything, Herminia."

"It is nothing dangerous, or wrong, I swear—" Herminia stopped herself there, not at all sure this was true, and she had never knowingly lied to a friend. She put her hands behind her on the bed and let her head lie back. From the ceiling hung an elegant chandelier, sparking from the sun's dying rays, fireflies in daylight. Scratchy blues licks serenaded them to soulful contemplation.

"We are young, we can fall in love and get our hearts broken," Rosa said, wisely. "Otherwise, what will we have to look back on?"

"Yes!" Herminia exclaimed. "Yes, exactly."

Herminia bought sturdy flip-flops, long pants and a flannel shirt in case it got cold, a bathing suit — in case the shaman joined her at the canyon pool, and extra batteries for the flashlight.

Now, with all her worldly possessions in the duffel bag over her shoulder, Herminia entered the hospital.

"Yes?" the receptionist said.

"Herminia Carrillo for Faustino Arce."

The receptionist scanned a list on a clipboard.

"He was brought in five days ago," Herminia said. "He may have checked out."

The receptionist's finger found a line that seemed to satisfy her. "And you are—?"

"Herminia Carrillo."

"Sister? Wife?"

"A friend."

The nurse looked up with a bored expression. "Only close relatives may visit patients without their express permission. I could give him your name. Miss—?"

"Carrillo. Herminia Carrillo." Herminia memorized Faustino's room number before the receptionist covered it with her forearm.

Room 212.

"I was just up there," said the receptionist. "Mister Arce is resting now. But I will give him your name when he wakes up."

Herminia smiled her warmest smile. "No need. I will look him up when he gets out. Soon, I hope."

It was an easy thing to buy a pack of Pall Mall cigarettes and wait by the hospital's rear entrance. She leaned strategically against the wall of the building, one foot against the bricks so that her bare knee showed. Within a few minutes, two doctors emerged, and Herminia shared a smoke with them. The biggest challenge was not to cough, and to hold the cigarette between her first and second fingers as if she'd been doing it for years.

When they went back inside the doctors held the door for her. They didn't even blink at the duffel bag, probably supposing she was carrying in her scrubs.

Upstairs, room 212. It was not a room at all, but a separation of curtains with a number embroidered on the bottom. The curtain swished against Herminia's bare ankles after she closed it behind her.

Faustino was propped up on pillows. His wrist was taped as if he'd recently had an IV drip. He regarded her quizzically.

She scanned his chart ... found the medical-speak totally incomprehensible.

"Well?" Faustino asked, eyeing the duffel bag. "Should I be alarmed?"

"You are going to die a very painful death," Herminia said, tisking.

He chuckled. "I mean you."

"Do girls scare you?"

"Depends on which girl."

She arched an eyebrow.

"I think you have the wrong patient. Beautiful women don't visit me."

Faustino had the lean, light-skinned look of the mountain folk — the mostly European descent *gente de razón* of southern Baja: strong, yellowish teeth; straight, short hair; muscular, beanpole arms beneath the blue cotton gown. His name, Arce, was a proud, local name.

From the rucksack, Herminia removed the sketchpad and handed it to him.

Faustino flipped through, slowed to examine the river separating man and fox, and stopped on the crow-man.

He rolled away a little and handed the sketchpad back to her. This slight movement obviously cost him much energy. "You must be his darling."

She sat on the edge of the bed, sensing that this made Faustino uneasy. Herminia liked using her femininity to make men uneasy. It made up for the other, annoying things that came with being seventeen. Particularly the fiery loneliness. She let her hand fall on the sheet, not quite touching Faustino's leg. Maybe this would shake him up enough to talk.

"When will he show me magic? When I am with him it's like— I can feel—" She found it impossible to describe the supernatural feeling she got from the shaman, but she sensed that Faustino understood. "Tell me, what can he actually do?"

Faustino tapped the crow image. "This does not exist in the cave. I, too, was assigned the task to make paint and copy the drawings. You won't find this on my sketchpad anywhere. It exists only in the Beyond. Have you shown it to him?"

Herminia nodded.

"Then we are late. Too late." He rubbed his finger nervously on the bed sheet. He muttered, "You should have let me die."

What did one say to that? Couldn't Faustino see how glorious life was? How beautiful the scent of roses? How magnificent the flight of hummingbirds? How precious the softness of skin? No, in such a mood the darkness of the mind blinded him.

"He said you have been his apprentice for several years. You must have learned many things. What can you tell me? What do I need to know?"

"It is beneficial to figure things out for yourself," Faustino said.

Herminia pretended to pout. "It's not nice to throw the shaman's words back at me. Okay then, what happened to you in there? Why were you hurt?"

Faustino gazed through the wall, at a memory perhaps, or a possible future. "I was traveling through a cave. Not the one you know, with the pictographs, but one that lies parallel to that one."

"In the Beyond."

"Yes."

"What is this *Beyond*?"

"The Beyond is different for everyone. You can think of it as a sort of parallel universe. But it is malleable. It changes according to your will."

"Is it a dream world?"

"No. And yes. The Beyond can be every bit as real as a dream, and it can change as fast. The key difference is this: if you die in the Beyond, you die for real. If you are injured in the Beyond, you are injured here, though it may not show in the same way. Rather than an injury to your flesh, the injury is to your soul or spirit. I do not know for sure. That is what happened to me."

"Are there demons there?"

He adjusted his sheet, probably not aware that he pulled it higher on his chest. "The demons you bring with you, and other things more dangerous still. Take my advice and run away as quickly as you can. Never come back. Never visit the cave again."

The curtain drew back. The receptionist frowned in.

Faustino gestured angrily at Herminia. "Who is this person? She keeps bothering me."

His way of protecting her — an invitation to flee? Herminia didn't know how to take his outburst.

The receptionist handed each of them a scrap of paper. "I am to give you this."

"Who sent this?" Faustino said.

"I— I don't remember," the receptionist said.

The scrap of paper held an address, a date and time: tomorrow at one p.m. Although there was no signature, she knew it came from the shaman. He wasn't going to let her flee that easily. Nor did she want to.

Her heart beating hard from Faustino's unexpected turn of mood, Herminia stuffed the sketchpad back into her duffel bag and shouldered it. "I'll be seeing you, Faustino Arce," Herminia said, as the receptionist hustled her downstairs.

FIVE

PRESENT DAY, PUNTA COLONET, BAJA CALIFORNIA NORTH

Something was missing. Lucinda was sure of it.

The sounds of Mamá banging around, getting ready for work, had pulled Lucinda from a slippery dream. She rubbed the crumbs from her eyes, trying to recall it.

Curiosity. Curious. Following cinnamon footprints. (Cinnamon color? Cinnamon smell? She no longer remembered.) The maker of the footprints stretched from shadow to shadow, always out of reach. The man knew—

Lucinda lifted her torso to one elbow and blinked in the dim light of her bedroom. Lucinda was scrunched on half of the twin mattress; the other half was empty. Abuelita was gone. Her comforting smell remained, fading slowly — as homey to Lucinda as the smell of fresh-baked bread.

The empty sheets caused Lucinda to catch her breath. Abuelita hadn't been the same since the day the District Attorney's letter came. Her memory had been erased. Wiped clean. Oh, she could speak and eat and tell the days of the week, but she no longer remembered her family, her past. She barely remembered her own name.

Had the empty sheets caused Lucinda's feeling?

Not likely. The old woman had always been an early riser.

Memories.

Had the cinnamon man said that word?

Memories. Yes, Lucinda was pretty sure that was it.

The dream had carried with it the feeling that something was missing, that something had disappeared. Lucinda had screamed through her dream searching for that missing something, and awakening hadn't lessened the feeling any.

Under her pillow Lucinda kept her Hello Kitty watch. The strap was barely long enough to fit on her wrist anymore, but she hadn't been able to convince her parents to buy her another. She pressed the light button: 7:15 a.m. Traffic rumbled outside.

Dressed in a gray camo Pink pajama tank and shorts (a quinceañera gift from her sister Tina), Lucinda padded out to the living area. Sitting at the dining table, a bowl of coffee in her hand, Abuelita acknowledged Lucinda with a wink.

"Morning, Abuelita," Lucinda said.

"Good morning, jovencita," Abuelita replied.

So, nothing had changed. The old woman didn't remember Lucinda's name. *What she wouldn't give to have Abuelita call her* Little Chicken *once more.*

A stroke the doctors had called it. *As if.*

She just didn't believe it. El Jaguar's family had everything to do with it, or let the devil take her. The timing was a dead giveaway. The timing and that uncanny courier. No one could remember what he looked like, or even if it had been a man or a woman. Slippery, just like Lucinda's dream.

Lucinda heated up some goat milk on the gas stove.

Mamá bustled from her bedroom dressed in work clothes and comfortable flats.

"You're late," Lucinda said, cheerily, pouring the steaming milk into a bowl, alongside a bowl of Corn Pops cereal (which she ate dry). Papá had returned to the U.S. during the night — no wonder Mamá was running late. They had probably stayed up late watching TV and talking. Fortunately, Lucinda was a deep sleeper and didn't have to listen to her parents complain about her all the time.

Lucinda took the bowls of milk and cereal and went to the marriage trunk where she normally sat to eat breakfast—

A rectangular film of dust on the floor showed that the trunk had been removed during the night.

"Now hija, before you say anything—"

Abuelita's mortar and pestle had been in the trunk. The last thing Abuelita had told her before the curse struck was to use that mortar and pestle.

Lucinda hadn't gotten around to it.

Nine days had passed since the district attorney's letter — because Lucinda was waiting for Abuelita to return from the hospital, waiting to see how she was.

Waiting because she had been afraid. A little.

She should have used the mortar and pestle while she'd had the chance!

"Where?" That was all Lucinda was able to articulate.

"We sold it."

Mamá's body half faced her, and half faced the door. Her tongue worked nervously behind closed lips.

"You're lying," Lucinda said.

"No, Hija. Your grandmother is very sick. The bills are expensive. We sold her things, her goat—"

"Patti? You sold Patti? Abuelita loved that goat!"

"Patti? Who is Patti?" Abuelita asked, setting down her bowl of coffee.

"Hija, you are going to upset grandmother Herminia."

"She should be upset — at you!" In Lucinda's hand was possibly the last bowl of Patti's milk she would ever drink. Stubborn, lovable Patti. She felt guilty for drinking the last of it. Guilty and empty and angry all at once.

Abuelita glared from Mamá to Lucinda. "Who is Patti, and who should I be upset with?"

"Never mind, Mother," Mamá said, and then to Lucinda, "Your grandmother had a stroke. We have to prepare for a long convalescence. Many bills to pay. I may have to take time off work."

"Who bought them?" Lucinda asked. Start with what was important, step by step; she *had* to get the mortar and pestle back.

After a moment's hesitation, Mamá replied, "Sergio Barril."

Sergio Barril was a nice, middle-aged man who had a small herd of goats on the far side of the arroyo. His wife sold goat's milk door to door. Lucinda and her friends knew them well. The answer half relieved her — at least Patti would be well-treated. She might even be able to visit the goat from time to time. Señor Barril might very well have bought the goat.

She thought of the trunk and objects inside it.

The trunk: made of wood, very solid, carvings of sea turtles and sailfish alternated on the four corners. It was so cleverly made you couldn't run a fingernail inside the seams.

The mortar: squat and stout, the black stone repeated the sailfish — sea turtle motif. One of each animal was carved onto the bowl's rim, along with the face of a fierce cat. An ocelot, according to Abuelita. Most mortars sported a single face of a bull or pig. Not Abuelita's. It was a unique piece.

The pair gave off a sort of feeling, the way an old TV set that isn't properly grounded gives off static if you touch the screen, except a static of the mind rather than of the body. They made most people nervous. Very few people would even consider buying the trunk or mortar set, despite their artistic qualities. In fact, Lucinda didn't know of any in Punta Colonet, excepting perhaps El Jaguar's family.

There were a few other knickknacks in the trunk that Lucinda had never paid much attention to: some old clothes, a broken carving of a turtle, some papers and envelopes with antique-looking stamps.

Lucinda stared at Mamá, analyzing the way she stood, chin raised, defiant, the way her hands gripped her black purse with white fingers.

"No, he didn't. Sergio Barril never would have bought the trunk. He keeps bread on a shelf over the door to ward off demonic spirits, and a glass of water over the fridge to absorb evil energies. He hands out bunches of grapes at New Year's Eve, because everyone knows that if you eat twelve grapes just before midnight you will secure for yourself twelve months of happiness." Lucinda spoke louder and faster as she wound up her argument. "He was afraid to sweep around me because everyone knows if a broom crosses a single woman's feet she will never have babies. Señor Barril is *way* too superstitious to go anywhere near that trunk."

Mamá took a can of Illy espresso from the refrigerator and dropped it in her purse. "I don't have time for this. I'll have to drink my lunch as it is, getting to work at this hour." Meaning canned espresso for lunch.

"I need the mortar and pestle back," Lucinda said, hoping to salvage something before Mamá fled to the cannery. If given enough time, Mamá's resolve would stiffen. "Abuelita told me to use the mortar. Those were her last words before she was cursed. If I have to, I will talk to Papá. He wouldn't stand for this."

"My God, this is what we were afraid of. Your grandmother was not cursed. The doctors say she suffered a stroke. Don't call your father. He has enough to worry about with his greenhouses."

"I will. Papá would never have agreed to whatever it is you did."

"Hija, this was his idea."

That stopped Lucinda cold. Papá left all of the domestic issues to Mamá. Partly because he was never home, and partly because that allowed him to play the good cop if something did escalate to his attention.

Mamá bit her lip. "We are trying to protect you, Hija. That is why we sold it."

"Ah, ha," said Abuelita. "Sounds sensible to me. I don't know what all the fuss is about." She turned back on her seat and blew into her black coffee, staring in fascination at the ripples her breath caused.

The last thing — the last fully coherent thing — Abuelita had told Lucinda was to use the mortar and pestle. Would that even be possible now? What had her grandmother intended for her to do?

"I am going to go right over to Señor Barril's and buy it back," Lucinda threatened.

"You will not. With what money?"

"I am going right over there to talk with him. He will give it back to me — or I will work it off. What does he want with a mortar and pestle?"

Mamá stared at Lucinda for several seconds. Then she zipped her black purse closed. "You do what you need to do."

Lucinda watched her mother's back until the door closed, blocking the line of sight. By Mamá's demeanor, Lucinda was sure of two things:

One, Señor Barril did not buy the mortar and pestle. Patti, yes. Mortar and pestle, no.

Two, Lucinda would never see that trunk again.

No, Mamá had found some definitive way of getting rid of the trunk and the mortar and pestle, and Lucinda had a suspicion it had to do with Papá heading north, across the long, empty desert, into the U.S. Mamá had said the whole thing had been Papá's idea. Which meant either the mortar and pestle had been sold across the border to some no-name antique store, or it was buried in the desert.

Gone. Definitively gone.

Sunday, July 21. Four days had passed since Abuelita had returned from the hospital, and still no improvement. The old woman vacillated from being in a state of hopeless confusion, to thinking Lucinda and her family were guests in the Loma Linda hotel, a resort in the south of Baja. Apparently, this is where Abuelita made beds when she was a teenager.

Time for action.

Virtually everyone in Punta Colonet would be going to church — including El Jaguar's family. After that, half the town would go home to watch soccer, and the other half would head to the cemetery to visit departed loved ones. That's what Lucinda would do on a normal Sunday, walk up the hill to the cemetery with the family to visit her departed grandfather.

Mamá was having trouble getting Abuelita dressed for church. The old woman kept trying to look for her car keys — even though she hadn't owned a car in twenty years.

Perfect.

Hollering that she would see them at church, Lucinda sprinted out the door, down the hill, and up the Transpeninsular Highway to her favorite breakfast spot. Javier's was a little white cart with a built-in cold box, a blender, and a bucket to rinse glasses. An orange extension cord ran from the blender into the window of the window/glass shop — a good Samaritan who let Javier make a living off his electricity.

Lucinda's white Sunday dress blew gaily around her legs as she ran. She waved at a gorgeous girl in a fashionable off-the-shoulder dress, floppy hat, and faux Louis Vuitton purse by the cart.

Eva Navarro, waiting for her, as planned.

The two girls hugged, which they always did if they hadn't seen each other in more than a few hours.

"Banana smoothie," Eva said to Javier.

The restaurateur was probably in his forties, with a thin mustache and several missing teeth.

"Orange juice," Lucinda said.

That's all you could get here: o.j. or smoothies. Why you would want anything more before lunch, Lucinda had no idea.

Each girl carefully stacked three ten-peso coins on the cart.

"Are those Steve Madden?" Eva asked. "Nice."

Pleased that Eva recognized the brand, Lucinda put her leg forward to show her new black booties. "Tina brought them for me from the U.S. She got the size right this time."

"So," said Eva, her green eyes sparkling, "I hear your grandmother has been cursed."

"Sí— What?"

"Everyone is talking about it. I hear your dad took her to the hospital because she had a curse, and now she can't even remember her own name. It is like El Jaguar cursed her before he died. 'If you kill me, you won't remember it.'" Eva let out a fake, evil laugh. "Everyone is talking about it," she added.

"I hate small towns," Lucinda said, scrunching her eyebrows together. Here she thought she was such a good detective, but everyone in town had guessed the same thing.

"Well, is it true?"

"My parents think so. They won't admit it — they say Abuelita had a stroke."

"No way," Eva said. "My uncle had a stroke. Half of his mouth stopped working. He smiled like this." She lifted half her lip in a snarly grin.

"Exacto. You know it." Lucinda had done a little research. Strokes could do a lot of things besides paralysis, but she didn't mention this.

She knew Abuelita had been cursed, and she needed Eva's help. No need to complicate things. "Let me tell you everything."

Lucinda started by describing the attack at the parade and continued step by step, how Abuelita might have been jailed for murder, how the family waited for the letter from the district attorney, how the courier came and the letter absolved Abuelita and everything should have been a celebration ... but instead Abuelita collapsed. Then Abuelita returned from the hospital without memories. Cursed. And finally there was her parents' removal of the marriage trunk.

Eva's eyes kept getting bigger and bigger. "So your parents disposed of the trunk in the desert like a drug cartel getting rid of a body? Far out!"

"Orange juice," Javier said.

Lucinda received the glass, and rotated it so that the previous drinker's lipstick didn't touch her mouth.

"Abuelita's marriage trunk," she agreed. "It was Abuelita's prize possession. She didn't let anyone open it on pain of death. It had some carvings on the corners, sailfish and turtles and stuff, but she loved that thing."

The orange juice tasted divine, sweet and tart and refreshing, just the right amount of pulp to whoosh around her cheeks.

Lucinda loved O.J. almost as much as she loved the trunk. The smooth cedar had made her feel safe. She would sit on it and watch television, eschewing the wooden chairs and even Papá's recliner. As a child, Lucinda had once climbed inside and fallen asleep. She'd had the best dreams ever — flying with her favorite doll at her side, skimming over trees, piercing fuzzy clouds, eating ice cream and never spilling on her clothes despite the wind and the loop-de-loops.

Church bells began ringing the nine o'clock hour; deep-throated gongs that spoke directly to your bones. They were answered by a tinny recording of bells (the Methodist church), then more bells from across the dry riverbed. The town of Punta Colonet boasted four churches in all.

Mamá and Abuelita would be arriving any minute.

"What was in the marriage trunk?" Eva asked.

"A mortar and pestle."

Eva's grin fell. "A mortar and pestle?"

"Yeah. I know. Weird, isn't it?"

"Were they, like, a family heirloom?"

Lucinda worried her lip. "Abuelita told me I had to use them. She said something about me bringing something to it, me and my ally. I don't know what she was talking about."

"Witchy stuff," Eva remarked. "Is your grandmother a witch?"

"Of course not!" Lucinda was distinctly aware that Javier was listening.

"Did you ever ask her?"

"No. Why should I? There are lots of uses for a mortar and pestle — chilis, salsa, spices to grind."

"Your smoothie," Javier said. He handed Eva the drink, and an extra banana with a shy smile.

With any other fifteen-year-old, this would have been creepy, but this was a standard reaction to Eva. Anything less would have been creepy.

Eva tossed her luxurious, blond hair and returned her own banana-winning smile.

She handed the banana to Lucinda.

Javier didn't notice. He seemed to have forgotten how to blink.

"Listen, Eva, I need to ask you a favor before my mom gets here," Lucinda said.

"Cool. Secrets. I love it."

"This one can't get out to anyone."

"Is it about the curse?"

"Sí."

The girls downed the last of their breakfast. Lucinda then took Eva's arm and steered her away from the cart. The Camino Hacia Dios church was a few blocks south and up the hill, on the same side of the Trans Highway as Lucinda's house. The girls spotted Lucinda's mother and Abuelita walking ahead of them.

"Mateo," Lucinda said.

"Mateo? El Jaguar's son?"

"The one and only. I need you to get close to him. Find out if he knows who did this. And how to reverse the curse. Mainly how to reverse it." *And how to make sure it never happens again.* Lucinda didn't say that last part, mainly because she didn't have any idea how to do that. "Mateo must know something," Lucinda added. "The day Abuelita was cursed I caught him staring at our house through binoculars … like he was waiting for something to happen."

"Hmm," Eva mumbled. Not very reassuring. The cloud that rolled across her green eyes was less so.

"Come on, you're my BFF, right?"

Eva stopped and put her hands on Lucinda's shoulders. There it was again — that cloud in Eva's usually vivacious greenies. "No can do. This is your plan. You need to execute."

Lucinda's heart sank. Her star forward just quit the field. "But you're so good at this."

"At pretending to be interested in somebody?"

Lucinda felt her cheeks redden. "Bueno— I wouldn't put it that way. I would say something about your Shakespearian acting abilities."

Eva laughed. "My point, exactly. If you are ever going to join the Rattlesnake Thespians, you need the practice."

"My parents will never let me join," Lucinda pouted.

Eva's family had a theater company called the Rattlesnake Thespians. They put on plays all over town — and sometimes even in Ensenada. They got to stay out late, and make people laugh and cry and forget about their miseries. Someday the Thespians might even be famous.

"My parents say actors are a lousy influence," Lucinda confessed in a low voice. "It's a wonder they even let me talk to you."

"If you reverse your grandmother's curse, they'll have to give you a chance."

"That would make it worse. My parents are scared of doing anything."

"And you aren't? Listen, Lucy, it's normal to be scared of El Jaguar's family."

Lucinda shrugged, trying not to show the butterflies in her belly. "It's only Mateo."

"Exactly. And you, my BFF, are going to wrap Mateo around your little finger. Your grandmother's curse will be reversed in no time."

The girls linked arms again, just as they reached Mamá and Abuelita.

"Well, hello, Eva," Mamá said.

"Hello Mrs. Eco, hello Señora Herminia," Eva said.

Mamá cast a disapproving eye at Eva's bare shoulders. Abuelita looked around to see who Eva was talking to.

"Will you be joining us this morning?" Mamá asked.

"Thank you, Mrs. Eco, but I will sit with my parents. In the back."

"Oh, are they up at this hour?"

"They haven't gone to bed yet," Eva answered, with a wink at Lucinda. "You know us theater-types."

Mamá sort of growled in reply.

Six

1967, Santa Rosalía, Baja California
South

Herminia folded up the piece of paper that the clinic's receptionist had given her and put it in her pocket. She had exchanged the yellow dress for khaki pants and a sleeveless, white shirt with embroidered butterflies that showed her midriff if she stretched. The address on the paper was several blocks inland from the wharf, and as she drew closer she became more aware of the slap-slap of her flip flops against the dirt road.

The address was a little house that served meals out of its living room. No sign indicated that it was a restaurant other than the wide-open front door and the wooden tables and chairs — the tables sporting red-checkered tablecloths.

Two couples occupied one of the tables, their knees nearly touching underneath. Don Esteban and Faustino occupied another. A closed door led to the bedroom-bathroom. Off limits to customers — except for children. Through a swinging blue door was the kitchen, and with the señora going to and fro with dishes, glasses, and food, this door swung back and forth with the regularity of hips swaying to a salsa beat, pulsing forth a delightful seafood aroma.

Faustino caught Herminia's eye for a second, then dropped his gaze to the tablecloth. Herminia remembered his advice to flee as far and as fast as she could, and wondered again how genuine it was. Was Faustino concerned for her safety, or was he simply trying to get rid of a rival?

A boy of around eight handed Herminia a well-stained paper with a single word and its English translation: *langostino — lobster*, and several drink items with prices scratched off and elevated.

Herminia strode to Don Esteban's table, pulled out the chair and sat.

"Order up," the shaman told Herminia jovially. "You are paying."

Faustino lifted a Coca-Cola in her direction. Some color had returned to his cheeks, though his movements appeared feeble.

Herminia ordered an Orange Fanta, wondering if she dared splurge on lobster. Her money wouldn't last long if she had to pay for Don Esteban all the time.

"One of my favorite spots," the shaman said. "Summer or winter, the best seafood on the coast. I don't know how they do it. I worried when grandmother died a few years back, but thankfully the señora took notes. The lobster is every bit as good." At the word *notes*, he tapped his head, as if saying the notes were taken mentally and not with pen and paper.

Don Esteban was unusually chatty, and their conversation proceeded almost as among equals, though Herminia was ever aware that he was the master, she the junior apprentice. The shaman might cut her some slack since she had no experience, but their relative positions were obvious from the body language if not the words. The shaman was completely at ease, while Herminia couldn't entirely suppress a twitch when initiating movement.

Faustino's position was less clear. He avoided talking to Herminia directly, though he cast surreptitious glances at her whenever he thought she wasn't watching. In the macho culture of Santa Rosalía, she found Faustino's apparent bashfulness ... well ... charming was a good word for it.

Herminia suppressed a smile, and decided to avoid over-analyzing.

The food was served — lobster for all. The sea breeze drifted through the open window. A peek-a-boo ocean view was afforded between a car mechanic's garage and a stand of palm trees. A lamp sat in the window, unlit now. If the husband were out to sea, it would be lit at night, a little beacon, a wish.

White movement caught Herminia's eye. A seagull in the open doorway. The seagull hopped inside, flapped its wings and landed on their table. Herminia immediately remembered the seagull she and Sybil had remarked at the pictograph cave, the one Sybil thought was the shaman's familiar.

"*Vete!*" the serving boy shouted, waving a menu at the bird.

The seagull spread its wings in return, looking much larger now.

The boy shrank away, uncertain, and held the menu like a shield.

Two steps later the bird had a corn tortilla in its beak. It crouched at the edge of the table, then paused. Don Esteban had caught its eyes.

The seagull lurched sideways, as if suddenly drunk, and dropped the tortilla on Don Esteban's plate. Followed with a peck to the lobster tail, a tearing of white meat, and this dropped clumsily onto the tortilla. Conversation at the adjoining table died. The seagull tried with its beak to roll the tortilla into something resembling a taco. Then it jumped to Faustino's shoulder, pooped, and flew out the door.

The guests at the nearby table laughed.

Herminia grinned, but a cold feeling crept from her belly outward. Had she really just seen the seagull make a taco for Don Esteban?

The serving boy ran from the room, chattering wildly, and from behind the swinging kitchen door came loud scolding. Evidently the señora thought he had an overactive imagination.

Faustino wiped the blob of white from his shoulder with an embroidered handkerchief. A muscle in his jaw quivered.

Conversation resumed quickly at the other table, the guests rationalizing the impossible as easily as a desert traveler would rationalize a mirage.

At the shaman's table the three were more subdued. Even now, after such a display, Herminia almost succeeded in telling herself all of this could be explained rationally.

A tame bird. Perhaps the restaurant owner had trained a seagull to come in and put on a show.

No, the excited boy and the exasperated señora still going at it in the kitchen belied that.

Isn't this what she wanted — to learn real magic from a real shaman?

A part of Herminia was horrified. Controlling another's mind as easily as that? Think of the evil that could be done! You could force someone to love you. You could force them to rob a bank, jump off a cliff, or kill. An equally excited part of her leapt at the possibilities: riding dolphins as easily as horses; training birds to be your eyes and ears while hunting, or coaxing fish into telling you the best places to lay your lines....

The shaman watched the emotions war across Herminia's face with amusement.

Brujo, Herminia decided. Shaman was such a nice word. Don Esteban was a brujo — a witch — pure and simple. Best to remember that.

Finally, Herminia asked, "How did you make it do that?"

"I did not make it do anything," the brujo replied. "The seagull wanted to do it."

Faustino snorted. "It wanted to poop on my shoulder?"

"Seagulls delight in pooping on humans. I simply nudged it in a specific direction." Don Esteban took a bite of his taco and chewed thoughtfully. "I have no power of compulsion. The seagull you just met is my ally, not my servant. Most of the time he dwells in the Beyond."

Don Esteban held up three fingers, and ticked off one by one: "There are three branches of magic: Spiritual, Mental, and Physical. All this you will learn in time, Herminia — if you become my apprentice. Spirit magic deals with the Beyond, that world that lies beyond this one. A witch such as myself with Spirit magic — that is, with a Spirit ally — cannot make a normal seagull do anything. A witch with a Mental ally, on the other hand, could force the seagull to pluck its own feathers and dance over hot coals until it burned to death."

"Compulsion sounds evil!" Herminia said. "It sounds like slavery, or worse. You are robbing the person of free will."

"Evil, good, what is that to a witch? You do not know what you are talking about, so I will not hold it against you," replied the brujo. "No more than I would hold it against a dog that just learned to stand on his hind feet and recite poetry, if he still bent to sniff the rear of a regular dog on occasion."

Herminia drank some Fanta to hide the reddening of her cheeks. She considered throwing the soda in the brujo's face.

Faustino had the good taste to look offended.

"We are, all of us, animals in the flesh," Don Esteban continued in the same condescending monotone. "Ever since God separated Adam and Eve from their allies, we humans have had to live as animals."

"We sniff each other's rears," Faustino said, sarcastically.

"Without question. This one has been with me long enough to understand at least this much. Brujos look to elevate ourselves to the potential that was lost when humans were expelled from the Garden of Eden. Many cultures have sought this original power. The most obvious benefit is life without end. No death, no disease. The Nazis called it the Übermensch. They made many mistakes. You cannot grow beyond an animal by becoming more animal. You must have an ally. And to find your ally, you must travel Beyond."

"Faustino says I have already traveled Beyond," Herminia said.

The brujo said, "There are two reasons I brought you two here, besides the fine lobster. The first is that Faustino is too weak to hitchhike to the cave — I will give you both a ride. The second is that before we continue your training, I must get your assurance on something. No matter what happens. No matter what you see or think you see, no matter what danger you are in, you must pledge never to help each other."

"No problem," Faustino responded, immediately.

"Even if Herminia is unconscious on the floor of the cave, you will not stir."

"No."

Just like that.

Did Faustino answer this in an attempt to protect Herminia? Was he giving her an opportunity to flee and not look back?

"Compassion is a great weakness," the brujo said. "You must pledge to accept the will of your ally, whether you understand it or not. Accept it — and do not question."

"Fine," Faustino said. "She agrees."

Herminia stared at the young man. She didn't like anyone telling the world what she did and didn't agree to.

For some reason, Herminia recalled the loyalty the blind and mute lizards had shown Faustino, the way they rode his chest through the sea of chaparral when the Americans carried him to the Jeepster. Animals often had better intuition than humans. They often knew who was a good person and who was wicked.

The lizards had shown loyalty to Faustino. That was a good sign.

On the other hand, Faustino was rude. He seemed to suffer on-again, off-again moods.

That was a bad sign. Trouble in the mountains, for sure. It would be like a pressure cooker up there; camping, obeying the brujo, getting sunburned during the day and cold at night, with no proper toilets or showers or anything, persevering in whatever tasks the witch assigned.

Faustino fiddled with his Coke bottle, wiping sweat off the glass with his fingers, his eyes avoiding contact.

Unable to see into Faustino's motives ... or his character, Herminia realized her answer did not depend on Faustino at all.

Could she leave Faustino to die on the cave floor if her ally willed it?

Slowly, she nodded.

"Now for the formalities." Don Esteban stabbed his thumb with the tines of his lobster fork. A great spurt of blood ran down his wrist, and he made a smear of it on the checkered tablecloth. He showed no emotion whatsoever at this, no sign of pain.

He lifted his chin at Herminia. "Your turn."

The fork looked dull as a coin. Herminia examined the restaurant knife. Not much better. But she had the diving knife. Its thin blade made a slick, almost pain-free cut on her right thumb, and Herminia dribbled her blood with El Brujo's on the tablecloth.

"Press your thumb to seal it."

Faustino's head turned away; his eyes drew closed.

I'm doing this thing, Herminia thought, her belly clenching. *I'm becoming a bruja.*

She pressed her right thumb to the blood. A wave-like feeling passed down her body, from the crown of her head to her sandaled feet, as if she had passed through an electrified membrane.

The restaurant's señora swung around with a second Orange Fanta for Herminia, even though she hadn't ordered one. "Are the seagulls bothering you?" she asked. "I can close the window."

"No, it's all right," El Brujo responded, setting his napkin over the smear of blood to conceal it. "There won't be any more problems with animals."

SEVEN

PRESENT DAY, PUNTA COLONET, BAJA CALIFORNIA NORTH

Camino Hacia Dios church was built of simple materials: plain cement blocks for the first four feet or so, and board and bat above. The best thing about it was the air conditioning unit attached to its side. Attendance had soared when Father Ramón had it installed the previous summer, turning mass from a penance into an absolution.

Eva pointed to a Rottweiler huddling in the condenser's meager shade: the Morales clan was here.

Lucinda breathed in deeply and exhaled strongly before following her mother and Abuelita inside, trying to steel herself for what was to come. This would be her first encounter with any of El Jaguar's family since that fateful parade. Now that Eva had refused the job of speaking with Mateo, Lucinda's confidence vacillated on a thin line. Why did her friend have to flake out on her? Eva was so much better at this sort of thing than Lucinda — and they both knew it. Lucinda's strategy of pumping Mateo Morales for information might just fail because Eva wanted to make some kind of stupid point about *doing things yourself*.

Awesome timing, Eva. Thanks a bunch.

Long, narrow windows in the shape of the cross welcomed sunlight above the double entrance door. The smell of burning candles and incense filled their lungs. The four women dipped their fingers into the holy water font, and Lucinda tried to push the anger from her face before making the sign of the cross over her heart.

No organ pipes or anything fancy like that soared overhead; no ornate silver altars or gigantic gilded crosses like you might find in Taxco, just a cobweb-infested ceiling badly in need of dusting. Everything in Camino Hacia Dios was plain and functional. Communion was served from folding tables draped with a white cloth. The priest, Father Ramón, spoke from behind a wooden podium that doubled as a music stand.

Lucinda liked it like that: simple and functional. No gilding to God's message.

It took a few seconds for their eyes to adjust to the dim interior. The church was about three-quarters full with people drifting in, promising a full house. Two rows of choir boys assembled to the left of the vestibule. Father Ramón stood near the rear door.

The Morales clan had the front right pew all to itself: Mrs. Morales, Mateo, and two heavies flanking them. The rest of the bench was empty.

No possibility of approaching Mateo here.

Lucinda bit her lip, wondering when she would get an opportunity.

They moved to the right-hand side of the church, to the altar of San Cristóbal, patron saint of travelers. Mamá donated a ten-peso coin and took one of the beeswax candles. Holding Abuelita's hand in her own, Mamá whispered a prayer for Don Pedro García, Lucinda's grandfather, that he arrive safely in heaven (he passed on eight years ago, but Mamá always said the same prayer), and for Papá, that he arrive safely in the United States, and lit the candle from a candle stub already burning.

Lucinda added a prayer in her mind: that God restore Abuelita's mind — or show Lucinda how to reverse the curse. Because everyone knew God sometimes worked miracles, and sometimes chose to work through people.

As they turned from the altar, an older man wearing a brightly colored sarape stepped up to Abuelita. The man had a narrow face, cleft chin, and a pencil mustache long gone gray. A sunflower smiled from his shirt buttonhole.

"Doña Carrillo," he said, bowing to Abuelita. "How marvelous to see you."

Abuelita nodded without recognition. "How good, nice to see you also."

Mamá extended her hand. "This is my mother. She was called Doña Herminia Carrillo many years ago. Her family name is García now, although her husband passed away some time ago. And I am Magdalena Eco. This is mi hija, Lucinda. Lucinda Eco."

Inwardly, Lucinda cringed. Had it come to that, that Abuelita could not even answer for herself? Trying to keep her face neutral, Lucinda curtsied. That's what you did with older gentlemen who called people Don and Doña.

With a slight glance at Lucinda, the older gentleman remarked, "You are as beautiful as your grandmother when she was your age." His eyes resumed their scrutiny of Abuelita.

"You must have known my mother from long ago, if you still call her by her maiden name." There entered into Mamá's voice a strange hitch, as if she were now talking to a policeman, and was afraid she might have to offer a mordida. "We don't see many friends from her previous life."

"I don't suppose so." The gentleman's voice had a tenor's richness. He was striking, really, in the fashionably outdated sarape, skinny pants, cowboy boots. The string tie with a silver horse-head fastener shone with warm, reflected candlelight.

Lucinda could not recall ever having met this gentleman before. She wondered if he and Abuelita had been friends way back when ... or something more.

Abuelita asked Mamá. "Do I need to tip him? What is he standing here for?"

"No, of course not." Mamá reddened.

Lucinda reddened.

Eva giggled behind her hand.

"Thank you for your service — whatever you did. *Con permiso,*" Abuelita said, as if the man had driven her here in a taxi or carried her luggage or something. She scooted past the gentleman and took a seat in a middle pew.

The gentleman cleared his throat. "Dementia, the curse of the old. Has Herminia been like this long? Without memories?"

First *Doña Carrillo* and now *Herminia,* which must be very familiar for the older gentleman. Maybe he and Abuelita *had* been more than friends. Lucinda became very intrigued with the possibility. A sheen of water brimmed the man's eyes, as if he were devastated with the thought of Abuelita's infirmity.

"Not long," Mamá said. "It happened very suddenly."

"Friday before last," Lucinda found herself saying. Normally she wouldn't open up like this to a stranger; the man's sadness was contagious. Her tear ducts threatened to flow.

"Suddenly, all at once?" he asked.

"Sí," replied Mamá, "all at once."

The man slipped the sunflower from his buttonhole. "In that case, Doña Eco, Lucinda, my sincere condolences. My very sincere condolences." He followed Abuelita, handed her the sunflower, and exited through the rear door with a swift stride.

"That was awesome," Eva said. "Your grandmother has an admirer."

Lucinda had trouble swallowing. She didn't know whether to find the incident touching, funny, or sad. Mamá was right, they hardly knew anything about Abuelita's past, and now this older gentleman shows up out of nowhere and recognizes Abuelita. A few days too late.

The gentleman didn't just recognize Abuelita, Lucinda thought, it was more like he had been waiting for her. He called her 'Herminia' at the end, as if they had been close friends. Or more than friends.

The choir began singing.

Eva's parents waved from a middle pew, and Eva went to join them. As always, Eva's parents wore bright colors — blues and reds today, Mrs. Navarro only slightly more flamboyant than her husband. Eva's bare shoulders looked perfectly tame next to their macaw-shaming outfits.

Lucinda and Mamá filed in beside Abuelita.

For an hour and a half, Lucinda lost herself in the mass. She loved the ritual of it all: the singing, the sermon, the sweet-smelling incense, the cardboard-tasting wafers of communion. As often happened, she felt that Father Ramón (and God through Father Ramón) was speaking directly to her. A little white board on a tripod summarized the theme of the week's sermon:

The Lord has his way in the whirlwind and in the storm, and the clouds are the dust of his feet.

Nahum 1:3

Without Father Ramón's interpretation, Lucinda wouldn't have understood the passage at all. The priest explained it meant that you had to trust God to bring good out of chaos, crops from violent rains, prosperity from suffering.

Lucinda grew a frown as the sermon progressed.

Trust God.

What did that even mean?

Well, yes, with Abuelita they were going through quite a storm. Any street charlatan or market haggler could have told her that — she didn't need Father Ramón and his fancy Latin. Why couldn't the sermon have told her what to do? *Trust God.* As in, do nothing? Hope for the best?

The Lord has his way in the whirlwind.... That didn't seem very helpful just now. And who cares if the clouds are the dust of his feet? Is this just a fancy way of saying God walked in heaven? Everyone knew that. Lucinda's frustration grew by the minute.

After the service, Eva met her at the exit. Mamá said she had someone to talk to and followed the great flow of patrons headed to the parking lot where horchata and cantaloupe water awaited. Others started directly up the hill to the cemetery to visit their deceased relatives before the heat of midday.

The two girls and Abuelita went the opposite way.

"Did you enjoy the service, grandmother?" Eva asked, politely.

Abuelita shrugged. "Why do we have to listen to the entire timeshare pitch just for the free drinks? They know we can't afford to buy."

"Stop laughing," Lucinda said to Eva, knowing it wasn't her friend's fault that Abuelita's answers were so random, but still feeling defensive.

The old woman started humming. Still holding the sunflower the gentleman had handed her, Abuelita began plucking petals from it one by one, marking their path with yellow.

On the low side of the church, they saw Mateo squatting on his heels next to the Rottweiler, drawing in the hard-packed earth with a stick.

That dog, just like El Jaguar's dog. Purple gums, scary teeth. A hundred pounds at least. Lucinda's thigh quivered with remembered pain.

The Rottweiler yawned.

Lucinda stepped on a loose rock; her ankle buckled. She had to grab Abuelita's shoulder for support.

Mateo squinted up at them.

He looked as awkward as ever: rumpled clothes, hair parted haphazardly, a boy with few friends and social skills, and a family everyone avoided. He couldn't possibly have cursed her grandmother, could he?

No, Lucinda decided right then and there. Mateo couldn't be a brujo. But he might know something. He might just.

Lucinda cleared her throat. "Mateo, this might sound strange — but then again for you nothing is strange. I mean your father is El Jaguar." At this Mateo's head twitched on its neck. "I mean, your father called himself El Jaguar. They say he talked to voices and that he could make himself into many people with different personalities."

"Did you come here to apologize? That is not such a clever trick."

This irritated Lucinda, and she had trouble keeping her voice even. She knew she should have started with small talk ... but how do you do small talk with such a weirdo? Eva might have figured something out, but Lucinda — not her thing.

"Mateo, my grandmother, she had a stroke. The same day we got the letter from the district attorney that said there would be no charges filed. The same minute my father read the words. I can't believe that was a coincidence. I think there was a curse, a spell of some kind. The stroke has robbed Abuelita of her memories."

"A blocked artery to the brain," said Mateo. "A stroke, the fifth-most common cause of death. The first-most common cause is heart disease. The second is diabetes—"

Lucinda tried to remain patient. "I saw you staring at our house with your binoculars. And I saw other things. At the Parade of Heroes I saw my Abuelita fighting El Jaguar. I was there, right next to them. Only it wasn't my Abuelita and El Jaguar, it was a puma and a scarecrow."

She remembered it vividly. El Jaguar taking her to that strange place — hypnotizing her or something — offering to show her *such things*. Calling her *my angel*.

Disgusting!

The puma. The scarecrow. The Rotteweiler that bit her thigh.

Oh, she remembered it all right.

And Abuelita licking her hand and applying saliva to the wound — the wound that disappeared without a trace. As if by magic.

"You can see many strange things in Punta Colonet," Mateo said, and lay his arm across the dog's broad black back. "This is Satélite. He is eight months old and weighs eighty pounds. He will keep growing until he is three. The only thing El Jaguar ever gave me."

Lucinda wished Eva would chime in, but her friend seemed incapable of speech. Eva simply shifted her purse strap on her shoulder; her posture was one big question mark.

"Mateo—"

The skin around Mateo's temples drew taught. "Your grandmother was right to kill El Jaguar. That is what my mother says, and I agree. She says El Jaguar was a bad man and the federales hauled him away once and he came back. He tried to kill your grandmother and she killed him, and we are glad for it. El Jaguar was a bad man. He hurt me."

Lucinda had never heard that Mateo's father hurt him, and she realized that there were many things she did not know about Mateo. How strange that he kept saying *El Jaguar* and not Papá or father or something.

Almost as if referring to a stranger. Or a non-human.

Almost as if Mateo hated his own father.

Satélite wiggled under Mateo's arm, and Mateo began stroking the dog without looking at it, his gaze far away. Lucinda found she wanted to trust this awkward lad. They had been in school together for years now — there was only one public school in Punta Colonet after all — and Mateo had never caused any trouble. He was a quiet person whom everyone ignored. He might have attracted the attention of bullies, but no one wanted to mess with his father. So he passed from grade to grade, invisible.

Lucinda wanted to believe he had nothing to do with Abuelita's curse, though she wouldn't completely let her guard down. "Mateo, I'm going to tell you something because I trust you. I don't think you had anything to do with this. Just between you and me, okay?" Boys always liked it when you shared something secret with them. Especially awkward, unpopular boys. She felt bad for using him, but she had to get at the truth. "We were in our house — but you know this. You were staring with binoculars, yes?" He nodded, not meeting her eyes. "Just the instant Papá read the letter from the district attorney, Abuelita fell down right on top of me, dragged me to the floor. The strangest thing was that I touched her marriage trunk, an old wooden trunk we've had from forever with some fish carved into the wood, and I had a vision. It popped right into my head. You know what I saw?"

"No." His hand had stopped moving.

"A woman, maybe seventeen or eighteen, in the back of a red Jeep. I saw it clear as the nose on Satélite's face. A woman leaning against the wind, black hair flying around a brown face, and the Jeep skidding sideways to try to avoid hitting a deer. I don't think they made it..." This brought an unexpected gush of emotion; tears threatened to sabotage Lucinda's discourse. "It was like I had a vision of some kind. I think it was related to Abuelita losing her memories. I think ... I think the woman in the Jeep was Abuelita."

"You can see many strange things in Punta Colonet," Mateo said again, like an automaton.

Just then, Abuelita bent over to retrieve something from the ground. She straightened with a bright purple something pinched between index and thumb. "Look at what I found." Abuelita plopped it in Lucinda's outstretched hand.

It was, on closer inspection, a kernel of corn, the hard, decorative variety that is no good to eat. Lucinda rolled the kernel around in her hand. It had the shape of a human heart, and its purple hue had depth, the way that the best nail polish had depth. Lucinda wondered how it had gotten embedded in the sunflower.

Mateo rose from his haunches and peered at the corn kernel, forehead creased. "Where did you get this?"

"It dropped from the sunflower," Abuelita said. "Isn't it pretty?"

"Where did you get the sunflower?"

"A gentleman gave it to us," Lucinda said. "I've never seen him before."

"Where? When?"

"Just now. In church."

"Your grandmother's been cursed," Mateo said, backing away from them.

"That's what I've been trying to say..." Lucinda said, but stopped talking as Mateo sprinted around the far side of the church, Satélite snapping playfully at his heels.

The three women stared after him.

Finally, Abuelita said, "The dog was all right, but what a strange boy. Why would someone draw so many skulls?"

Indeed, human skulls formed a semi-circle around the condenser where Mateo had been knifing the dirt with his stick.

Between Lucinda's fingers, the maize kernel softened and turned to powder that rained to the earth in a purple cascade. Astonished, Lucinda held up her hand to examine it. Purple dust coated her index and thumb as if she had pressed them to an ink pad.

EIGHT

1967, MOUNTAINS OUTSIDE SANTA ROSALÍA, BAJA CALIFORNIA SOUTH

Herminia scrambled over the granite boulder. Her sandals were tied to the belt at her waist; her bare feet, toughened by years on the panga, could find purchase where no leather soles could. She grunted against the burning in her thighs. A grunt was a good sound. A natural sound, and she didn't feel less feminine for grunting if the occasion warranted it.

And it certainly did. The two apprentices, Herminia and Faustino, had been hiking, climbing, crawling, whatever it took, over the tortured crags of the high desert for hours. The altitude made breathing a chore. The dry air that burned the lungs, the heat radiating off the rocks that attacked the feet, the glare that stabbed at the eyes.

They needed to find a specific species of lizard to help them safely travel in the Beyond. Strangely (strange to Herminia — as normal as ice cream to the brujo), Don Esteban said their allies would test them; make it difficult to find the desert iguanas they needed. Even though a bruja's whole purpose was to meet and bond with her ally.

How frustrating! Almost like trying to meet the right man.

Normally, the forearm-sized desert iguanas were all over the high desert. You could hardly throw a rock without hitting one. Today, nothing. The brujo was right. Neither she nor Faustino had seen nor heard any lizards since they started hiking before dawn. Even the rattlesnakes were in hiding.

Cresting the boulder, Herminia's sharp eyes caught a slight difference in the landscape. Something alive. Herminia sat on her heels and drew her arms around her knees, staring at the color contrasts, the different textures. Her dry breath hurt her nostrils, as if they were about to crack into a nosebleed.

If it hadn't done a push-up, she might have missed it. In the shade of an agave squatted the lizard. Its rough brown texture blended almost perfectly with the high desert.

Herminia stuck her tongue at it.

It replied in kind.

She wondered if the lizards sensed heat through their tongues the way rattlesnakes did. Or if it was provoking her.

From behind, Herminia could hear Faustino struggling to catch up. He was rather weak for a mountain born. (Faustino grew up another twenty miles into the hills — she'd learned much about his background in the past few weeks.) It wasn't just the recovery from the hospital stay. His mannerisms bespoke a familiarity with physical weakness. Climbing up here, Faustino spent much time seeking out the easiest path with his eyeballs and his shoes — even though he wasn't patient by nature. He wore leather gloves rather than using bare hands. He figured out clever ways to avoid exerting his muscles.

Faustino would have to go around this boulder, not over it, Herminia knew. He would make it, he always seemed to, but he would never make it in time. Either Herminia would have caught the desert iguana, or it would be long gone and she wouldn't tell Faustino about her failure.

She stuck her tongue out again.

Sweat trickled between her breasts, making her aware of the cord she had braided at the brujo's direction. The fibers came from the blue-green leaves of the sisal plant, sort of a larger version of the agave before her now, a succulent with sword-like leaves poking out from a central hub. Herminia had stripped the sword-leaves of their fibers and woven the thin, twine-like cord herself. Then she crisscrossed it over her shoulders, behind her back and over her chest, all at the brujo's precise direction.

Ritual and handcraft seemed very important to being a brujo.

Herminia had caught Faustino staring as she tied it off by her armpit. The binding pressed tightly against her breasts like the underwire of a bra — she could see he appreciated it, and she'd flashed a mischievous smile to tease him.

The pressure of the cord didn't feel sensual now. All day it had chafed, and the sweat-soaked creases were beginning to sting.

"Come over here, little friend." Herminia undid the knot and unwrapped the cord from around her shoulders. She had mixed feelings about this whole thing. She knew what the brujo would make her do to the lizard, and she could think of no way of doing it that would not hurt the animal.

Sew its eyes shut: that could only be called torture.

She hated the idea. On the panga she had always killed the fish with a quick blow of the cudgel. Quick, painless. She didn't let the tourists do it. They thought they were being merciful with light blows. The opposite was true: one quick, heavy snap. No pain for the fish.

Sew the eyes shut....

She tried not to think about it. If the brujo said it was required, what could she do?

Faustino called her name from down below. He was closer than she had supposed.

"Up here," she replied. "I have found a lizard."

"A desert iguana?"

"Come and find out."

Herminia extended her right hand and wiggled her fingers.

The lizard's face was green-brown and triangular. Starting at the neck, it had a mostly black body with light spots. The pattern reversed around its hips, where the body became light and the spots black. A thin, white line ran down the entire back. Herminia had never taken the time to examine a desert iguana in such detail before, and she found it beautiful.

The lizard began to walk toward her.

Herminia heard Faustino's shoes struggling to find purchase on the granite. So he decided not to go around; he went over. She frowned. Faustino's clumsy approach would scare the lizard, sure as anything. Unless it was really as the brujo said. Unless the desert iguanas would really give themselves to you.

Herminia fastened a little lasso in her cord. Not a very useful knot on a fishing boat, but one she had memorized nonetheless, trading the knowledge of the clinch knot for the lasso with a vaquero from — of all places — Hawaii.

"Come here, my sweet friend. I would very much like to catch two lizards today, and I have only a few hours until it is dark. Which one do you want to be? The mouth-and-ears sewn shut, or the eyes sewn shut?"

Herminia winked at the lizard through the lasso.

One step at a time it came, twisting a little with each step as lizards do, first to the right, then to the left, making crescent moons with their bodies.

"I think you shall be the eyes, as you were the first. You will forgive me? Please."

Now clear of the protection of the agave, the high desert shadows that fell across the lizard's face came into sharper contrast. There was something wrong, too many shadows. Herminia could see it now. Some deformity of the face.

Herminia's heart began to thud. Faustino had nearly crested the boulder. There was no way she could hide this thing. It was hers and hers alone. Her ally had brought it to her. Faustino would see it and she was stuck with it, deformed or no.

What was wrong with it?

The glare from the sun on the bleached rocks made seeing details particularly difficult.

Slowly, deliberately, the desert iguana put both clawed forefeet on top of Herminia's right foot. Swallowing against a dry mouth, Herminia scooped it gently in her arms. This lizard had suffered, and it would suffer more. She wished she could return it to the safety of the agave.

Too late.

Faustino stepped beside her. Between pants, he said, "I'm about done with this. We could have waited in camp if the ally is going to bring the lizards to us. This suffering is just to make Don Esteban laugh." Faustino wiped his arm across his forehead to clear the sweat from his eyes. "Well, is it a big one?"

Now Herminia could see that the lizard didn't suffer from any natural deformity. Her ally had directed it to her. But it couldn't be hers: this lizard already had been used as a guide.

With a sickening feeling in her gut, Herminia held out the lizard to Faustino.

"Here," she said. "This one is yours. I call him Lemon."

Herminia strode into the circle of firelight and dropped the flashlight at Don Esteban's feet, not bothering to turn it off. Placing herself opposite Faustino, she sat heavily on the sand, her legs splayed toward the fire. Her thighs were golden in the firelight, and muscle-sore from the miles they had hiked. Her mouth still felt dry from mild dehydration.

The brujo was busy carving a piece of manzanita wood. Herminia couldn't yet tell what form it was going to take, though it appeared to be some kind of animal. Faustino was equally busy using safety scissors to cut free the old threads that held Lemon's eyes shut. Once he had finished, he plucked the loose threads out of the scars. And then immediately replaced this with new thread, knotting the eyelid shut after each turn.

Awaiting its turn, the deaf-mute lizard clung to Faustino's pantleg. They had agreed to call that one Jefferson. That was the only thing they had agreed to the whole afternoon.

Faustino glanced up at Herminia and grinned.

Herminia pushed her dress down to be sure Faustino couldn't see more than she wanted him to.

"You can't go into the cave without a lizard guide," El Brujo said, not looking up from his wood carving.

"I was just in the cave," Herminia replied, unable to keep the irritation from her voice. "There is nothing there that wasn't there when the sun was up."

"Be grateful your ally willed it so," El Brujo replied.

"Which ally?" Herminia snapped.

"The one who hasn't yet rejected you."

Herminia grunted, leaned forward, turned off the flashlight. "I will go in without a guide. I am not afraid." She almost believed this. The mesquite smoke curling from the fire was sweet and heady. It emboldened her. She became keenly aware of the warm pulse of the fire on her bare soles, the daytime warmth flowing from the sand onto the back of her legs, and the nighttime cold creeping into her dress' neckline and down her back.

El Brujo's knife whittled across the wood, making a fox's head suddenly recognizable. "You have no ally, Herminia. Faustino might survive without a lizard guide; he has an ally of sorts, though it remains to be seen if that ally wants to bond with him or abandon him in the Beyond."

"I found both lizard guides, if that is what these are," Herminia said. "*Pobrecitos!* It is cruel what you have us do to them."

"Not cruel. Necessary," Don Esteban corrected, unperturbed. "As a fisherman, you must have hooked countless fish. Pulled the sharp wires through their lips, yanked them from the water they need to breathe, and then killed them."

"Only what I needed to survive."

Don Esteban's eyes flicked up. Though they were not hard eyes — they were small and somewhat sunken in the puffy flesh of his face — those black eyes took on a keen edge.

"Survive and make money," Herminia allowed.

After a moment, Don Esteban's eyes left hers, and his knife renewed its cutting. "Of course. They are only animals. Their suffering is of no consequence to the fisherman. And the apprentice does what he must in order to become a brujo. Without an ally, you would not survive in the Beyond for long, Herminia. Your intent is too haphazard, too loose. You feel sorry for the poor lizards; you feel nothing for fish. You want to be a bruja; you want to be a free spirit. Your mind wavers like a palm frond in the wind. Only with the help of your ally can you master the Beyond enough to survive. But if you do not have an ally, you must use a substitute. These lizards serve that purpose. They help you focus your intent with reptilian-like single-mindedness, so you do not become distracted and die."

"But why blind them? Why sew their mouths and ear holes shut?"

"You see how they survive quite well like that, hmm? To answer your question, with their eyes sewn shut they can see clearly in the Beyond. With their mouth sewn shut, they can communicate with the brujo. With muted ears they do not become overwhelmed with the auditory chaos the Beyond might throw at them. They are more in the Beyond than here, in that sense. They eat, drink, sleep in the Beyond. They come to this world only when they hear the call from their brujo. It is strange to me that Faustino's lizards came when you called. Or maybe they came when Faustino called, and you simply got to them before he did. Faustino is lazy on his feet, no?"

At this, Faustino pulled the knot on Jefferson's mouth particularly tight.

"That is so unfair!" Herminia said.

"*No importa* what is fair or unfair. Your allies will choose whether you become a bruja or no. That is the way. But I will not send you carelessly into the Beyond without lizard guides."

"Then you take me, Don Esteban," Herminia said. "Hold my hand. I won't let go, I promise. Show me the Beyond."

"If your ally wanted you to go to the Beyond, you would have found your own desert iguanas," Don Esteban replied. "You are not ready."

"But I *did* find—"

"I will take Herminia," Faustino said, and he smiled. "If she promises to hold my hand and not let go."

"Hold your own hands," Herminia said. In the fire's warmth, the soles of her feet had begun to sweat. She pulled them under herself, crisscross.

It was so unfair that Faustino would get to travel to the Beyond and she had to stay here — even though she had found both lizards. She sensed her chance at becoming a bruja slipping away.

Herminia didn't plan on staying in the mountains much longer. Painting and making paint, braiding cord, chasing lizards across the desert, camping. It had some appeal, sure, but the excitement was wearing a little thin. If she didn't get a taste of Don Esteban's magic, she was heading home. Tomorrow, if necessary.

Yes, tomorrow. If she didn't go Beyond this very same evening, she would hitchhike to Santa Rosalía tomorrow and never look back.

Don Esteban set a mortar and pestle before Faustino. They were made of basalt, like the one Herminia had been using to mix paint. The pestle had no special design. The mortar had three legs and a face on all three sides.

Alongside the mortar El Brujo placed two glass jars.

"As before," El Brujo said, reminding them both that Faustino had been an apprentice long before Herminia.

Faustino unscrewed the lid on the first jar and poured some maize kernels from it into the mortar's empty bowl.

"Since I am not allowed into the Beyond, at least tell me what Faustino is doing." And then Herminia raised her hand, so that her words would not be taken too literally. "I see what he is doing. Tell me what it *does*."

Faustino began smashing the kernels into bits he could grind more easily.

Don Esteban said, "He is preparing himself for a journey into the Beyond, the world that lies parallel to this one. The mortar, the pestle, the paste, these do not take you. Your ally takes you into the Beyond. This ritual Faustino is performing helps you access your ally's power. Before you have bonded with your ally, there is no other way into the Beyond. Once you have bonded, this becomes unnecessary. Convenient, but unnecessary."

Herminia reached forward and, ignoring Faustino's scowl, rotated the mortar beneath his pestle. Like most mortars, this one had three legs. Unlike standard mortars, which usually had one face, this one had three. On one side was the head of an owl. On another was the head of a crow. The third sported a lump of stone that had not been shaped.

"Three faces on the mortar, like the three allies," Herminia commented.

"Very good. You listened. Faustino was here for a year before he heard that simple truth." The grinding became noticeably rougher, which seemed to amuse El Brujo. "Every human has three allies: Mental, Physical, Spiritual. These are not separate entities. Or they were not in the beginning, when Adam and Eve inhabited Paradise. However, Adam's original sin got mankind thrown out of Paradise — and God stripped mankind of his power and split his power into three parts.

Your ally hears you from the Beyond because it is not separate from you at all — it *is* you. The ally takes the form of an animal — which has led to all kinds of misunderstandings. We brujos do not seek to become animals, nor do we worship animals. We seek to bond with our allies to become more human."

"An owl and a crow," Herminia remarked of Faustino's mortar.

"Faustino's Spiritual ally — the screech owl, and his Physical ally — the crow. Both have greeted my apprentice. Both rejected him." Herminia got the feeling that the only reason El Brujo was speaking so plainly was that it irritated Faustino. He seemed to delight in pitting his apprentices against each other. "The crow trapped Faustino's lizard and left him to die. Fortunately for Faustino, you happened along at just the right time."

Herminia had to admit, Faustino was great fun to tease — he took everything so seriously. Even now he ground his teeth with nearly the same force as the pestle ground the corn into meal.

"The picture on my sketch pad," Herminia said, "the crow-man. That doesn't exist in the cave's pictographs. Faustino said that I drew that in the Beyond." *A crow-man. Did I see something of Faustino in the Beyond? Or was it coincidence?*

"Some people are more aware of the Beyond than others. They are closer to their allies than average. They may occasionally have visions, or see ghosts, or even have small powers, such as the ability to cure warts. Such people are suitable for apprenticeship."

Faustino's maize had become a fine powder. He took a dollop of lard from the second jar and began mixing it into the cornmeal. If it weren't for the backdrop of the brujo, the cave, and the campfire, the resulting masa-like paste would have looked mundane in the extreme.

"What Don Esteban is saying," Faustino said, "is that this is my last chance. If I fail to bond with my Mental ally, I cannot become a brujo. I will be sent away."

At the mention of Mental ally, Herminia recalled Don Esteban's horrible description:

A witch with a Mental ally, on the other hand, could force the seagull to pluck its own feathers and dance over hot coals until it burned to death.

She wasn't sure if she was more concerned about this being Faustino's final chance, or about what he might be able to do if he did bond with his Mental ally. Would he be tempted to use *compulsion*? Should she be afraid of him?

There must be some positive things about having a Mental ally, right?

Right?

"If Faustino fails a third time, he will have bigger worries than being sent away," Don Esteban said. "Enough talk. The cave is impatient."

Faustino cleaned the mortar with his finger and licked every last bit from his finger. Lemon and Jefferson scampered to his shoulders, one on each side. Taking the flashlight, he and Don Esteban entered the cave.

As soon as they were out of sight, Herminia sniffed the mortar. She smelled nothing besides corn.

Faustino had done a good job of cleaning the stone bowl, but he had neglected the rod-like pestle. A fair amount of masa clung to its tip, and Herminia scraped that into a ball and popped it into her mouth. It had a taste of mealy corn and lard, and didn't make her woozy or anything else that would indicate some kind of drug.

She didn't think the brujo would drug them, but it paid to be careful.

On silent, bare feet, Herminia followed the others inside. The air felt moist, as if instead of a cave, they were entering the mountain's throat. There was virtually no light, but the tunnel had a smooth floor and few turns for the first 500 feet — and these Herminia had memorized. So what if she scraped an elbow or bonked her head — Herminia wanted to travel Beyond.

She walked quickly. She wanted to see firsthand what sort of spells the others might cast ... and duplicate them if she could. El Brujo would probably be very angry if he caught her.... No, he probably would shrug his shoulders and leave her to her fate. If she managed to make the magic work, travel to the Beyond, well, what could he say to that? It would be her ally's will.

She'd like to throw that line back in his face.

It wasn't long before she caught sight of the flashlight's yellow glow. As Faustino's hand trembled, the flashlight, too, trembled. He was alone. This didn't surprise Herminia much. El Brujo had always been able to disappear in the cave. Whether he went Beyond, or knew of some hidden side tunnels, she neither knew nor cared at this point. Herminia's excitement — and frustration at not being included — had been building like steam in a pressure cooker. She sprinted the final three paces and took Faustino's free hand.

"Yi!" he screeched, nearly jumping through the roof. "What are you doing here?

"Making sure my desert iguanas are safe. Little darlings," Herminia cooed, rubbing Jefferson on the top of the head.

"You shouldn't be here. Don Esteban told you not to come."

"He had a change of heart."

"You're lying."

"Does it look like I'm lying?" She squinted away from the light Faustino swung in her face. "Don Esteban helped me make masa paste. How else do you think I could have come here alone, without a light?"

"Can you see in the dark?" Faustino asked, bitterly. One of his favorite moods. "Have you progressed so far already?"

A gust of wind blew from deep inside, a rich, moist wind, carrying the scent of the sea. The desert iguanas strained toward it.

Reassured by the familiar scent, the fisherman's daughter pulled Faustino forward, guessing that they must have discovered Don Esteban's secret path to the coast ... or to the Beyond. "Come on," Herminia said, stepping briskly, "I hope you know how to swim. I have missed the Gulf of California."

NINE

PRESENT DAY, PUNTA COLONET, BAJA CALIFORNIA NORTH

The bright orange five-gallon bucket brimmed with water. Lucinda stuck her hand in. Still warm. About elbow deep, her fingers encountered the rough shells of clams, regular in their striations. As she rolled them between her fingers they made the sound of rocks grinding together, simultaneously muffled and amplified by the water. The smell of the ocean waifed up.

Lucinda brightened. She loved cooking, loved the smell of it, the texture of it, the taste of it. On Canal 11, *Graciela Montaño* explained how to plate chiles en nogada (large posada chilis stuffed with meat, fruits, and way more spices than Lucinda used). Just background noise; Lucinda had seen that episode more times than she could remember.

Clams were Papá's favorite. Too bad he wouldn't be around to taste them. Managing the greenhouse in Fallbrook, California, took all of his time and energy, and Punta Colonet to Fallbrook was a long, long drive. Papá only came home at Christmas and Easter. And for special occasions, such as to read the D.A.'s letter exonerating Abuelita.

Or to bury Abuelita's trunk in the desert, Lucinda thought, trying and failing to banish the irritating recollection.

From the refrigerator, Lucinda brought out what she needed:

onion, garlic, cloves, cilantro. As she worked, she worked to dismiss her fears.

Of course Abuelita had had a stroke.

A stroke. Of course it was. This is the most logical thing. The fifth-most common cause of death in the world. So common.

That was the problem; Lucinda could not bear that grandmother Herminia would die of anything common. Only something heroic could take Abuelita down.

Mamá rushed out of her room and unplugged her phone from the charger. She had already been to the open-air market and back, and now was late for work. As always on market day.

Perfect. Lucinda had already sent a text message to Eva — and erased it.

"Good, you found the clams."

"Yes, Mamá."

"They'll be better if you cook them right before dinner."

"Yes, Mamá."

Lucinda continued cooking. She wanted something to do *now*. Sleep hadn't come until after midnight. Too much thinking.

Now was a good time to pester Mamá, when she was in a rush and couldn't obfuscate.

"Me and Eva saw Mateo at the church."

Mamá checked inside her red, faux Louis Vuitton purse to be sure her bus pass and work ID were there. "You stay away from that family. They are grieving."

"It was an accident. I didn't mean to see him." Lucinda dropped a handful of sesame seeds into the family mortar and began to grind. The heavy, stone bowl was made of dark basalt, with a bull's head carved on the rim, and three legs. The pestle was half as long as Lucinda's forearm. As the seeds broke down, their nutty oils danced with the clam water smell in the kitchen air, a meeting of land and sea. "Mateo said something odd," Lucinda added.

"The Morales clan doesn't need any reminders that the Ecos live just across the highway."

"Oh sure, I'll just pretend I don't see one of my classmates."

In the other room, Abuelita began humming.

"School doesn't start for another month and a half, so there is no need to see him." Mamá held up a single finger. "I know you are getting at something, *hija mía*. Because I am in a good mood, I will let you ask one question."

A tingle went up Lucinda's spine. "One thing? About anything?" Mamá never gave open-ended promises like this.

Mamá's eyes glittered. "Sí. Anything. *Que quieres saber?* Something about boys? About life? This is your chance."

This was almost like— Almost like magic. Maybe something was in the air. What should she ask?

"Ten seconds," Mamá said, "I'm late for work."

"What? That's not fair."

"Eight, seven—"

"You can't just add a rule!"

"Six, five—"

What should she ask? Lucinda already knew more about boys than she ever wanted to know — the internet assured her of that. Grandmother was a lot more important. The curse. Magic.

"Are there any other witches in El Jaguar's family?" Lucinda blurted, with one second to go.

About a dozen emotions flashed across Mamá's face. Some of them looked spontaneous and uncontrolled. Others she seemed to be selecting from, as if deciding what camouflage to wear. She settled on amusement.

"Well, I guess I've taught you the facts of life well enough if that's your question."

"Don't change the subject. You promised."

"Hija, brujos don't run in families. Witches don't exist. Get that thought out of your mind."

"But El Jaguar—"

"El Jaguar used people's fear to frighten them. You are spending too much time with that girl, Eva, and her make-believe. What does she have you playing this time, *A Midsummer Blah-Blah?*"

"*Midsummer Night's Dream,*" Lucinda said. "That was last year, and you wouldn't let me perform."

"Nor this year. In fact—"

Mamá didn't get a chance to say what her "In fact—" was. Probably some new restriction Lucinda would have to ignore. But at that moment Abuelita exited the bedroom, belting a pink bathrobe, and dropping white hair all over the floor. Little mounds of hair rested on the shoulders of her robe, dunes pushed there by the wind. Right on the crown of her skull a purple, spider-like splotch stretched towards the old woman's ears, neck, forehead.

Lucinda rushed forward, hands outstretched. The skin on Abuelita's skull was powder dry and flaking. The center was hot to the touch. "Abuelita's sick. We have to do something."

Mamá hadn't moved or blinked. "She's just losing her hair. Lots of people do."

"She's not just sick. She's been cursed. Abuelita, are you okay? How do you feel?"

"I've been waiting and waiting for room service. This isn't much of a hotel." Abuelita shuffled to the window and pulled the curtain back. Abuelita never shuffled. Walked, strode, danced, even sprinted, but never shuffled.

A seagull hopped on the windowsill on the other side.

"What happened to the ocean?" Abuelita asked, tapping on the glass. "Is it low tide?"

The seagull tapped the glass in return.

Mamá began shaking her head. "If grandmother isn't better soon we'll take her to the Flying Samaritans. They will fly into town next weekend. That's good. They aren't from around here."

"We should take her to the hospital. Now!"

"We don't have any money. They won't do any good, the doctors. Just wasted money." Mamá started backing out of the house. "Hija, you are not to do anything to attract attention. Understand? Do not take grandmother to the hospital. Do not call a doctor. Do not go near the Morales' house or talk to that Mateo boy. For anything."

"Mamá, what are you afraid of?"

Mamá refused to answer.

. . .

A Sharpie, an old tennis ball, a piece of paper. That's all Lucinda needed to replace a cell phone. *Mi ventana,* she wrote on the tennis ball. *My window.*

On the paper she wrote, *Air C., 11 AM. Call Eva,* and posted it in the window facing Mateo's. Then she cruised down the hill, across the road, behind the hair salon/clinic building, to the tall, glass-shard topped wall. An easy lob and the ball landed inside Mateo's yard. Immediately, a dog fight erupted on the other side.

No doubt Mateo would come to investigate. The only worry was whether the dogs would leave enough of the ball to piece the message back together.

She returned home and made a quick breakfast taco with beans and cheese for Abuelita. The spider-splotch on Abuelita's head looked no worse, though certainly no better. On sudden inspiration, Lucinda outlined the illness with a Sharpie.

"What are you doing?" the old woman asked.

"Giving you a — um, sunscreen." Lucinda had almost said, 'a tattoo,' but that might have alarmed Abuelita. "You don't want to get burned. This will protect you."

"It tickles my head. Don't you have that kind that smells like coconut?"

At the appropriate time, Lucinda coaxed Abuelita down for a nap and headed to the church. Mateo and Eva were huddled in the meager shade by the air condenser unit, along with Satélite.

Lucinda hesitated to approach the dog, but it did nothing more threatening than to lick her proffered hand and pant amiably.

Mateo held out the drool-soaked remains of a tennis ball. It was split into three parts. Most of *ventana* had been chewed off.

"You need to get yourself a cell phone," he said.

"Not everyone is rich." Lucinda took the soggy, tennis ball remains and put them in her rucksack, trying not to feel too defensive. Her parents did very well for her family. They didn't need cell phones to be happy. Besides, Mamá already had one.

There was an awkward silence as everyone rocked on their heels.

Mateo fished inside his baggy, shorts pockets and took out two more tennis balls. With a sheepish grin, he said, "For next time."

"Two?"

He shrugged. "In case you have more to say."

"What about me?" Eva gave a false pout.

"I'd have to carry a yoga ball for all you have to say," Mateo said, and everyone laughed.

Light beat down from the white sun, and up from the tan earth. They squinted around for a more comfortable place, cooler and away from eavesdroppers.

"We can go to my family's mausoleum," Mateo suggested. "It is cooler there."

A slight tingle went down Lucinda's spine. She touched Eva's bare arm.

Eva looked fabulous in one of those cold shoulder top shirts, black, with white stretch jeans — something Lara Croft might wear to a board meeting.

Lucinda had thrown on the same jeans as yesterday (she only had two) and a pink tee. No makeup.

"It's okay, I go there all the time," Mateo said, slipping his heavy backpack over his shoulders. "The grave diggers are my friends."

"Creepy," Eva said, catching Lucinda's eyes.

Lucinda didn't want her friends to think she was afraid. She was, a little, but she didn't want them to know. "Better than out here," she said. "I've got questions for you about Abuelita being cursed. You were right, Mateo, Abuelita lost all her hair, or most of it. And a weird thing is growing on her head."

As they walked, she described Abuelita's illness. The way the purple-y, bruise-y spider-splotch was hotter than the surrounding skin, almost as if it were alive.

Mateo didn't look surprised.

Lucinda wasn't sure what that meant, and she was determined to find out.

The night of the parade, Abuelita had transformed into a puma to protect her. Lucinda was more and more certain that is what happened. Not an illusion. Not hysteria and Strawberry Fanta and bad lighting. To protect Lucinda, Abuelita had really transformed.

Which meant that Abuelita was a witch. Just like El Jaguar.

What other secrets had the old woman harbored?

A clump of forget-me-nots had sprouted just outside the wall that surrounded the cemetery. Considering it a good omen, Lucinda picked two (leaving the rest for other mourners) and headed to her family plot.

In the Punta Colonet cemetery, most of the graves were dirt marked with simple headstones. Some, like Lucinda's family plot, were flat cement slabs with name plates attached as needed. At the high end of the cemetery stood a row of mausoleums, grim generals surveying parade soldiers.

The Eco plot was on the low end among plenty of empty dirt plots and unmarked cement slabs anticipating late arrivals.

Lucinda lay her flowers across grandfather's tomb. Don Pedro García had died February 26, 2011, but Lucinda remembered him well. He was gentle and strong, quiet of voice.

How much did he know about Abuelita? Was he a witch also?

So many questions. She said a quick prayer for his soul.

"Um, Lucy, have a look at this." Eva was toeing some shards of glass that glinted in the midday sun.

Lucinda said, "It looks like someone left a glass vase. The wind blew and it broke. We should clean it up."

The vase had fallen between the Eco tomb and an unmarked slab. She wondered which of her relatives had left the flowers.

"My friends will clean it up," Mateo said, indicating two men lounging in the shade of the cemetery's only tree. "That's their job, when they aren't digging."

"Not that," Eva said, "the flowers. Isn't that the same kind of sunflower Mustache Man gave your grandmother? He must have left them."

Three very dried sunflowers lay among the broken glass.

Sunflowers weren't a common flower to leave for the departed, and to find them here, on Don Pedro García's tomb! It was too much of a coincidence. Why would anyone ... why would Mustache Man ... leave flowers for her grandfather? And then Lucinda's knees grew weak. "I don't think this is for my grandfather," Lucinda said, "I think Mustache Man left these in anticipation of Abuelita dying."

"Don't touch them," Mateo warned. "They might also contain a blood curse."

"Blood curse?" Eva said, wrinkling her pretty nose.

"I'll explain in El Jaguar's mausoleum. Not here. Too many ears."

Lucinda glanced around. A few people wandered among the graves, none of them less than fifty years old. Three teens here on a weekday were sure to attract attention, particularly if they were talking and not laying flowers or cleaning a grave site.

"Let's go," Lucinda said.

She needed explanations.

As Lucinda and her friends headed uphill, the gravediggers hailed Mateo, and Mateo went to talk with them. When he caught up with the girls, Mateo said, "They will take care of everything. I told them not to touch the flowers, but to bury them in the deepest hole. They understood. They know enough of El Jaguar to be careful."

Mateo led the girls to his family mausoleum, located in the cemetery's highest, furthest corner. Built of rough cut, white stone, squat like a horned toad, the tomb looked unfinished. Raw. You had to descend three steps to get to the iron door. Chiseled above it was the family name: Morales.

"So, how do we get in?" Eva asked.

Mateo slipped a bronze chain from around his neck. On the end of the chain was an ornamental key of black metal, its head fashioned into the head of a cat with open maw. A jaguar, Lucinda presumed.

The lock opened silently. An oil can stood just inside the door, and Mateo oiled both lock and hinges. He locked the door behind them.

A brief staircase dropped them into the tomb proper. Vertical windows pierced the north and south walls.

"If you stand in the shadows, no one passing by can see you," Mateo said.

"Neat," Eva replied, rubbing her bare shoulders.

The air was a good 10 degrees cooler than outside, and the creepiness subtracted another 10 degrees.

The Morales mausoleum was nearly as big as Lucinda's bedroom. A marble sarcophagus took up most of the space, with a walkway around all four sides. Yellow veins crisscrossed the polished stone. It looked outrageously expensive, like something for the king of Spain.

On the left, near the head, a single inscription read:

Santiago Morales
   3/7/1960-6/6/2019

Below that, a bas-relief figure of a Jaguar such as one would find in the old Mayan pyramids. Lucinda had seen pictures in her history book of such pyramids, with names like Chichén Izá or Tikal, where blood-soaked shamans cut still-beating hearts from human sacrifices.

That thought brought a queasy feeling to her tummy.

Mateo retrieved a plastic bowl from the shadows and filled it with water for Satélite from a canteen in his pack. The dog lapped up a good amount, then laid down and closed its eyes.

Lucinda felt better with Satélite lying down, ignoring her. She wondered if she ever would be comfortable around dogs again. Her eyes strayed from the Rottweiler to the sarcophagus. She ran her finger along the groove of the S in Santiago. Her finger came back clean.

Santiago Morales.

Beneath this slab lay the remains of El Jaguar.

The only other time Lucinda had heard the man's real name was from Abuelita. He had always been El Jaguar to Lucinda — and to everyone else, a mythic beast roving the streets of Punta Colonet. A night avenger. Dark. Violent and glowering.

His business: extortion.

The nightmare memory tried to force its way out: the Parade of Heroes; El Jaguar's touch on her arm; the cinnamon slipperiness of his powers taking her ... somewhere ... with just the two of them alone on the parade grounds....

Lucinda swallowed with a loud gulp, deliberately making her throat contract. That slight pain helped clear her mind. Helped clear the desire to vomit from her belly. Though not entirely.

There was something missing in this mausoleum. It was a big, expensive place. A family tomb. And yet....

"Where are the other names?" Lucinda asked.

Mateo patted the right side of the sarcophagus. "Mother here, Magdalena Morales. I don't have any brothers or sisters. My father had no family. My mother's family lives somewhere in Chihuahua or Sonora, I can never remember. We do not visit them." He looked into Lucinda's eyes. "But I will never rest here. Never. I will build my own tomb, and it won't even have a window in this direction."

I had to build a family from nothing. From the dust of nothing. El Jaguar's words came to Lucinda clear as the day he said them.

A light blazed. "Selfie!" Eva said, leaning between Lucinda and Mateo.

When the white cleared from her vision, Lucinda saw the funniest shot on the cell phone: Lucinda half-frightened, half-surprised; Mateo intense, almost angry; and Eva grinning as if accepting an Oscar. As different as the see-no-evil, hear-no-evil, speak-no-evil monkeys.

"This place is perfect," Eva said. "A creepy tomb, the mark of El Jaguar." She put her arm around Mateo and snapped a selfie. "Me and a strange boy."

Ducking from under Eva's arm, Mateo emptied his backpack onto the marble slab. A canteen. Two doggie bones. A mortar and pestle. Indicating these last two, Mateo said, "These belonged to El Jaguar. He used them in his incantations. If we are going to reverse your grandmother's curse, we will have to learn how to use them."

Reverse the curse. Lucinda had not really considered reversing the curse herself. Discovering what happened — yes. Finding the culprit and forcing them to reverse it, or finding someone else to help — absolutely. But reversing it herself....

The thought was appealing. Far-fetched, but appealing.

"Okay," Lucinda said, grabbing the pestle and rolling it around in her hand. This pestle was shorter and fatter than the one in her kitchen. Made of dark, speckled stone, one end was smaller than the other and obviously meant to be used as the grinding end.

Most mortars were shallow bowls on three legs. On one end would be an animal face, usually a bull or a pig, making them look like stubby, three-legged animals. Abuelita's mortar actually had three faces spaced equally around the rim: a sailfish, a sea turtle, and an ocelot.

El Jaguar's mortar had the usual single face — but neither a pig nor a bull. Its face was a cat, very much like the ocelot on Abuelita's mortar. Lucinda didn't like that at all. She didn't like that it came from El Jaguar, and she didn't like that its designs had something in common with Abuelita's. Maybe all witches had ocelot faces on their mortars. She ran her thumb over the image, trying to remember if it was exactly the same as, or just similar to, grandmother's ocelot. She couldn't be sure. Her parents just *had* to bury Abuelita's trunk in the desert! Thanks to them, she would never know for sure.

Thanks to them, she had to touch El Jaguar's contaminated things.

Trying to keep her voice even, Lucinda said, "Mateo, you said Abuelita was poisoned, and she wakes up this morning with a spider splotch on her head and hair snowing down on her shoulders."

"Snowing?" Eva asked.

"Exactly like snowing."

"Did you bring the kernel of corn?" Mateo asked.

"No. It turned to dust right after you ran away."

"Dust the color of blood?"

Holding her hand up to the light, Lucinda showed the red stain on her fingertips. "Washing doesn't remove it, not even with lime juice."

One eye set slightly higher than the other, his head cocked to the side, Mateo gazed not so much at Lucinda's fingers as beyond them, beyond her. Not a sound nor a whisper of breeze penetrated the mausoleum's stone walls. Even Eva respected the silence. Her hand with the cell phone hung limply at her side.

"Blood magic," Mateo said, in a whisper. "When the curse is activated, the carrier disintegrates."

"Holy guacamole," Eva said.

Mateo smiled, a great big grin that touched his whole face. "I know something you don't know. This is a good thing."

For some reason, this infuriated Lucinda. Maybe it was pent-up emotional strain. Maybe it was the creepy tomb. A feeling of frustration, a feeling of outrage welled up from her feet, up her thighs, through her ribs, into the palms of her hands. Her face flushed.

"What?" she shouted, "What is so funny about blood magic?"

Without even thinking, she shoved Mateo. The strength of her emotions gave strength to her arms. Mateo sailed backward, tripped over his feet, landed on his back, balled up, and covered his head with his arms.

"Uncalled for," Eva said, her eyes as wide as an owl's.

Mateo waited for another blow to fall.

And waited.

And waited.

Lucinda was panting. Adrenaline coursed through her body. She was afraid she'd broken him. It had felt like that day at the Parade of Heroes, when she'd made El Jaguar's beer create foam before she'd even touched it. But El Jaguar had been casting some sort of spell. Mateo was just being Mateo.

"We're not going to kick you," Eva said, biting her lip and waited for a cue from Lucinda.

"We might," Lucinda panted, "unless you tell us exactly, and I mean exactly, what you mean by 'blood magic.' And 'your grand-mother was cursed.' And anything else that might help. Or so help me, I'll kick you until I have to buy a new pair of shoes." She didn't mean that. He looked so pathetic, frightened as a doe in the crosshairs of a rifle scope, that she wanted to reach down and help him up.

Besides, she couldn't afford a new pair of shoes.

"Magic is real," he began.

Eva kicked him lightly in the rear. "We got that, genius."

Mateo scrambled to his feet. He was about as tall as Eva — three or four inches taller than Lucinda. With his slouch and knock-kneed walk, Lucinda had never noticed his height. And yet he had crumpled like a corn-husk doll when she pushed him.

What could have made him like that?

El Jaguar, of course.

What kind of abuse had El Jaguar inflicted on Mateo, his own son? Lucinda could hardly imagine — and didn't want to try.

Mateo brushed imaginary dust from his clothes, not meeting their eyes. "Blood magic is a powerful kind of curse. It requires the victim's blood, which you can get by force or whatever. Doesn't matter. El Jaguar couldn't do it."

"Wait, what? He couldn't do it? Why not?"

Blood magic requires blood. Lucinda filed that away for future consideration. *Whoever did this had access to Abuelita's blood.*

"Mostly this was all a big secret. I mean, real magic. But when El Jaguar was drinking, he liked to brag. One time, when he was really drunk, he said there were different kinds of magic: Spirit Magic, Physical Magic, and Mental Magic. A witch can only do one. El Jaguar's kind was Spirit Magic."

Lucinda leaned against the sarcophagus. She could never forget that cinnamon magic, slipping in and perverting her ... her spirit.

Mateo continued, "El Jaguar's curses were a slow, feather curse. They sapped the will. It made people like, well, like the dust that puffs from a carpet when you hang it over a wall and whack it with a broom. Nothing to them. No depth, no will to go on. No soul, maybe. I'm not sure. It took longer, and was more terrible, than blood magic. And nothing you could do to help them. The victims wasted away like heroin addicts.

"You remember the pharmacist? He wouldn't sell El Jaguar what he wanted. People thought the pharmacist was addicted to his own pain killers, but it was El Jaguar that killed him." Mateo shook his head, remembering. "This blood and maize, this is fast. Physical Magic. It doesn't attack the spirit, or the mind, it attacks the body. It is ugly but painless. El Jaguar would trade for some, when he wanted to do things quick."

"Wait. There are other witches?" Eva asked. "Spirit, Physical and Mental? And they have a market day or something? 'Curses, twenty percent off if you buy three!'"

"El Jaguar used blood maize on the puppies that wouldn't be trained. They lost their fur, like you describe, a patch growing until they were completely bare. A dog looks ridiculous without fur. It made El Jaguar laugh. And he didn't want to keep feeding them." Mateo said this with far more regret than when he mentioned the pharmacist. "And then the puppies died. He made me bury them. That was one of my jobs — to bury the unwanted puppies."

"My God," was all Eva could say. "Lucy, your grandmother deserves a medal for killing him."

Lucinda grabbed the pestle and began slapping it against her other palm. "So El Jaguar didn't make this, this blood curse?"

Mateo shrugged. "El Jaguar is dead. He makes nothing now, except nightmares. Those were a specialty. A Physical Witch made the blood maize, and unless we can reverse it, your grandmother is going to die. Doctors, normal medicine, they can do nothing. One cycle of the moon, that's all she has. I would say she is going to a better place, except she was a witch, wasn't she?"

"What? No, of course not." Lucinda didn't believe the words. They just came, an automatic response. "Eva, take pictures of all these, just in case. It might be important later." She knew she was being bossy and didn't care. Not for this.

Eva photographed the mortar and pestle from multiple angles. And Satélite. And the sarcophagus.

When their eyes recovered from the flashes, Lucinda said, "Okay, maybe." She held up her finger. "I said MAYBE Abuelita was a witch. A good witch, like Glinda or Dumbledore. Just before the letter came from the District Attorney, Abuelita told me that there were things in her marriage trunk that could protect me. She didn't get a chance to explain more. There were people around. The courier came. I couldn't see him very well. It was like he was slippery."

That word again. *Slippery.*

Mateo sniffed.

"And then Abuelita fell down on top of me. And her memory was gone. Bang. Just like that."

"Girlfriend, that's clear as coffee. Care to pontificate with a little less opacity ... as a theater critic would put it?" Eva grinned at her million-peso words.

"One: inside Abuelita's trunk were a mortar and pestle, very much like this one. Two: Abuelita said that the contents of her trunk could protect me. That I should *use* the mortar and pestle. That means they must have some power over the curse, no? Three: Mateo is right. Since we don't have Abuelita's things, we will have to use El Jaguar's mortar and pestle and see what happens. Let's just hope that El Jaguar hasn't tainted these things in some way."

"Chill," said Eva, always game to go where Lucinda led.

"First, Mateo, I need to know if I can trust you. Why are you helping us? Why are you helping me?" *Abuelita killed your father, after all*, she thought, *even though you refuse to call him that.*

Mateo's fingers made little circles on the palms of his hands. He seemed unable — or unwilling — to respond.

"Like, not very convincing," Eva said.

"And the reason is...?" Lucinda prompted.

"I, ah, I would like to reverse some of the harm El Jaguar did. Not because it was ill. I mean, that is one reason. But mainly because I would like to beat him. One time, I would like to destroy one of his plots. Though I am not sure that your grandmother losing her memory is such a bad thing ... but this blood curse, and the puppies, and it makes me so angry. And ... well ... two girls are talking to me, no? That is something."

Eva burst out laughing.

Mateo shrugged. "Well, you trust me or you do not. Your choice. Your choice but my mortar and pestle. What do we have to grind?"

Too bad Lucinda hadn't brought any sesame seeds. Those had such an earthy smell. So grounded. So healthy. Slippery, Spirit magic wouldn't have a chance against that.

A thorough investigation of their pockets came up empty. Lucinda was starting to think they would have to dig for some earthworms to grind when Eva discovered a sugar-free mint in her purse. Eva removed a hair from it and handed it over.

"Any last-minute advice?" Lucinda asked Mateo.

"Plan your grandmother's funeral," he offered, without emotion. "The odds of this working are about as high as the odds you two will talk to me once the school year starts."

Eva touched Mateo's wrist gently. "Listen, Mateo, I promise you that I'm telling the whole truth ... and that Lucy agrees with me without reservation: Self-pity isn't attractive. Remember."

Turning the mortar so the cat faced her, Lucinda said, "I want to find out who cursed Abuelita. Show me a face. Give me a name." She felt a little bit ridiculous.

Eva said, "You have to believe it. Put yourself in the role of a bruja. It's called Method Acting. Stand in the posture of a witch. Wear the face of a witch. Think the thoughts of a witch."

Lucinda rounded her back, scrunched up her nose, and thought about toads and spiders. She crushed the candy with little circles of the pestle. A pleasant, minty aroma began to waif up.

That was the only result, other than a slow disintegration of the candy.

"You look like a hunchback with constipation," Eva said.

Mateo began scratching Satélite's ears. The dog's tail thumped the concrete floor.

Soon the mortar was filled with fine, white powder.

"What am I supposed to do?" Lucinda asked. "Cackle?"

Eva said, "How about you try lipstick?"

"I never wear lipstick."

"Well, let's try some. Too bad I didn't bring Purple Noon."

With a very professional hand, Eva applied Burberry Kisses to Lucinda's lips — and touched up her own. "There, now you are not you. You are a witch. A real one, not a cartoon witch. A witch who can grind up potions in a mortar and pestle and divine who cursed her grandmother.

For a charm of powerful trouble,
Like a hell-broth boil and bubble."

"Maybe you should do it. You're the actress."

"Shh," Eva replied. "Think of something real. Be something real."

What is real about Lucinda Eco? Lucinda wondered. *She's not a woman, not a full one, anyway, and she's definitely not a little girl. She's never had a boyfriend. She doesn't have a job, or a cell phone, or an email account, or more than two pairs of jeans.*

Lucinda took a deep breath, knowing that only one or two of those things really mattered. The pestle wore the mint into the smooth basalt of the mortar.

When she was allowed to go to the Parade of Heroes, Lucinda thought she might get a clue to her — what? Identity? Purpose? Inner Self? By being allowed to see the witch's effigy burn, Lucinda expected to pass the divide between girlhood and womanhood. She would be an adult at last.

Instead, everything went sideways. El Jaguar tried to violate her, and Abuelita became a puma.

Her grandmother. A puma.

A bruja.

Yes.

I am Lucinda Eco, Abuelita's Little Chicken. That's real. I am the Little Chicken witch. And I like to cook. This is like cooking, like grinding those sesame seeds this morning, the way the clams clinked in the seawater.

What if Graciela Montaño were a witch? Lucinda imagined her favorite TV chef with long, blackened teeth, purple fingernails tipped with red, one eye plucked out.

No, that's back to the cartoon brujas. Graciela Montaño with a mortar and pestle. Blood leaking from a wound in her palm where she cut herself, dripping into the mint in the mortar. She felt nothing but the beginnings of a cramp in her hand from gripping the pestle too hard.

"What are you thinking about?"

"Eh? Graciela Montaño, the chef. "

Mateo scoffed. "An actress for something real? That's like thinking about dirt to try to get clean. 'Impostor' is an actress' middle name."

Eva added something, Mateo replied, but Lucinda didn't catch any more. They were right, of course, she needed to get real, get her feet on the ground: like a Little Chicken, like Abuelita.

A breeze ruffled Lucinda's black hair. Satélite growled.

Of course, with her feet so firmly planted on the ground, Abuelita could both defy the gang boss and show him grace, joke about her relatives' facility at dancing while loving them with all her heart, and pull magic from, ah, from somewhere to become a puma while remaining completely, unalterably a woman. Abuelita had earned every blemish on that beautiful face, every crinkle around her eyes; marks of experience, they symbolized that Dios had done well with her.

Lucinda tried to draw strength from her connection to Abuelita. She pictured the older woman's straight, grinning teeth; the muscles in her neck as she threw back her head and laughed; the collar bones pointing toward strong shoulders; the woman's supple back; her shapely calves that men still tried to ogle beneath her long dresses, those strong, sand-gripping toes, and most of all, the fierceness that lay underneath it all like a spring-loaded chassis. The older woman's café-colored eyes hung before Lucinda's imagination now, twinkling, mischievous. One of them winked...

The tomb's oppressive walls seemed to flip away. Lucinda and her friends stood in a garden. Well, Lucinda and Eva stood. Mateo tripped face-first onto a patch of green plants. Eva began babbling, something about "I can't believe it" and "Santa Madre de Dios, what have we done?" Satélite tried to bark in all four directions at once.

The sun shone directly overhead. Unlike Punta Colonet with its dry heat, here the air was armpit humid.

Too stunned to be frightened, Lucinda bent over and plucked one of the bumpy leaves from the green plants. She crushed it, and brought it to her nose. "Mint, we're in an herb garden." The mint's aroma, sharp and soothing and refreshingly familiar, helped untie the knots in her intestines.

They'd done it. They'd managed the same trick by which El Jaguar had taken Lucinda to the empty parade route. She felt strangely elated and numb, like an athlete who won a race without realizing he'd passed the leaders.

"Why aren't you freaking out right now, girlfriend?"

Lucinda extended a hand and helped Mateo to his feet. He seemed only a little dazed, not much worse than per usual, and suffered only minor scratches on his face from the plants.

"You good?"

"Yes," he wiped his sleeve across his nose. "Yes, okay."

Lucinda turned to Eva. "Take off your shoes. No questions, just do it. There, you feel the dirt under your toes?" Holding her sandals in one hand (were those Valentino Garavani's?) Eva nodded uncertainly. "Grounded, like Abuelita. It works."

Dirt paths framed rectangular patches of herbs and colorful chilies. A whitewashed building surrounded the herb garden. Pillars held up a balcony that ran around three sides, and windows and doorways frowned down at them from the second floor. On the fourth single-story side, an archway led from the herb garden through the building to what appeared to be another larger garden.

The upstairs rooms had numbers on the doors: *204, 206, 208....* One of the downstairs doors was labeled *Laundry*.

A voice asked, "Who are you?"

It was an odd voice, strained as if by distance or years of cigarette smoke.

Satélite growled, low and menacing.

Mateo said, "Sich legen!" and the dog lay flat.

A young woman sat crisscross on a cement bench. She had dark, mestizo features. A white, chiffon dress smoothed over her knees. Her back was straight, her eyes bright, her eyebrows strong.

"How did you get here?" This time the voice matched the body. A confident, young woman's voice. A little afraid. She uncrossed her legs and stood. "Where are your lizard guides?"

"I'm Mateo," he blurted, obviously smitten by the dark-skinned beauty.

Eva shushed him.

Stunned, Lucinda dropped the crushed mint leaf from between her fingers. She was sure the woman hadn't been there when they had first arrived.

"Mint," Lucinda explained.

Lucinda could hardly believe it. Had they come to the past? Were they in a different dimension? The woman was the spitting image of Abuelita fifty years ago.

"It is very dangerous to travel without lizard guides. You never know where you might end up. One stray thought, and all could be lost." The woman's head cocked to the side. "I feel like I know you."

"I'm Lucinda, this is Mateo, and this is ... our friend." One of them, at least, could remain anonymous, just in case something bad happened.

The young woman bent to pet Satélite.

The dog sniffed her bare feet with suspicion. Its hackles lifted.

The young woman could be Grandmother Herminia. She *could.* That would make the most sense. By crushing the mint candy, they had gone ... somewhere. Abuelita's past? Her mind?

"What's your name?" Lucinda took another step.

"I— I don't remember." The woman tugged on a lock of hair, frowning. "I'm the guardian of this place, I think. I've been waiting for someone to eat the herbs so I could tell them not to." She laughed a throaty laugh, just like Abuelita's. "I don't know who I offended to get this peach of a job. You are the first visitors I have ever had."

Some movement caught their attention. Through the archway, a little dust devil spun into view. The garden on the far side of the archway appeared to be larger than this one. Lucinda could see rose bushes and trees, and in the distance, light reflecting off a rectangular mirror pool. A second dust devil whirled into view, then a third. They whirled about randomly...or not quite, as they seemed to avoid contact with one another without trying to.

"I've been watching them all morning." Young Abuelita meant the dust devils, indicating them with a gesture. "They never come beyond the opening."

"No wind," Mateo observed. "How are they blowing?"

"No dust," Eva added, slipping her white sandals back on. White, like her jeans, of course.

As they approached the archway, the weather on the far side began to get cloudy. Mist rose from the ground. Electricity made Lucinda's arm hairs rise. She was afraid to touch anything lest she discharge a gigantic spark. She was even afraid to take Eva's proffered hand.

"I feel like those dust devils are a part of me." The young woman's head turned sharply toward Lucinda. Her eyebrows drew together. "Do you know it, my name? I can't remember."

Lucinda's throat was dry. "I remember. Your name is Herminia. Herminia Carrillo." She hesitated to use Abuelita's married name — this version of Herminia came from long before she met grandfather. *Young Abuelita*, Lucinda thought, *this is Young Abuelita.*

Eva hissed air between her teeth. Clearly she didn't trust the woman yet.

Young Abuelita took another step forward and thunder rumbled, vibrating their diaphragms. A blood-red cardinal exploded from a rosemary bush and flew between them. Its wing actually clipped Lucinda's face as it passed.

The soft wing-tip feathers slapped through Lucinda's jaw as if they had been made of carbon steel. Purple spots hovered in front of her eyes, her teeth hurt, her lats clenched, stretched, strengthened, offsetting a corresponding build in her pecks. Sensation rippled up and down her body. Lucinda's nose suddenly identified all kinds of odors: cinnamon, vanilla, mint, three different rose varieties, wet and dry soil, the dry husk of a deceased trapdoor spider, the aroma mob from Herminia, Eva, Mateo, and her own body — including feet Lucinda hadn't scrubbed quite vigorously enough the previous evening.

The red cardinal landed on the wall opposite the archway and whistled seven short notes. Lucinda located it without turning, knew exactly where it was. She rubbed her eyes, trying to rid them of the spots, trying to understand what had happened.

Someone placed an alien hand on her shoulder. "Are you all right?" Young Abuelita asked.

Lucinda's friends hadn't noticed her distress, but Young Abuelita had, of course. They had always had a certain connection.

"I don't know," Lucinda answered, honestly. "A passing spell, I guess. I'm feeling better already." Not just better, she felt strong enough to pick up Young Abuelita with one hand.

Weird.

Another rumble of thunder salted their hair with cement dust from the archway overhead.

"Stay back," Mateo warned Young Abuelita. "This area is charged against you, I think. Charged against you specifically."

The dark-skinned woman retreated a couple of steps and Lucinda's hair relaxed against her arm. The static dissipated. Beyond the arch, a dust devil passed and flipped the mist away.

Once more they were staring at a bright, sunny garden. The red cardinal whistled gaily.

"Is it always like that?" Eva breathed.

"Sometimes there is also lightning. I cannot leave, unless I learn how to climb these walls. The doors are locked, and the windows can't break." Young Abuelita squatted on her heels, completely natural, and pointed at the nearest dust devil. "That one is always near the entrance. It looks like a happy one."

Indeed, if a dust devil can be said to be happy, this one was happy. It had a jaunty curve, a playful bounce to its funnel. It smelled of pine trees and spring mornings.

"Is it safe to go through the door without a — what did you call it — a lizard guide?" Lucinda asked. She wondered what in the world that could be. So many things she didn't know.

Young Abuelita shrugged. "For you, I think, it is safe. You made it this far."

Lucinda took a deep breath. Her newfound strength — her cardinal's strength — gave her confidence. "Come on." She stepped onto the brick walkway leading through the arch. The dust devil bounced a few inches off the ground, as if encouraging her to continue.

Lucinda took another step. Eva linked arms with her on the right; Mateo joined on the left and put a tentative hand on Lucinda's shoulder. Satélite scrambled between their legs.

Once through the arch, Lucinda could see that this garden, too, was surrounded by a high wall. The far end was five hundred feet away, perhaps more. Many paths lay before her, and a mirror pool. She had never visited such a garden.

Lucinda's fingertips made contact with the dust devil. At first she felt a sucking feeling, similar to when you touch the water going down a drain, how it wants to suck you down also. She pushed her fingertips in just a bit farther. A strong wind whipped her hair. The pull ... the whirling suction grabbed hold of her belly, her chest, her hips. Her shoes lifted, lost contact with the ground; she felt light as a feather; helpless as a kitten in the hands of a man.

The dust devil yanked the three friends inside.

Lucinda's body bulged in unfamiliar places. Her eyebrows arched and thickened. Her nose flattened. Her lips grew fuller. She wanted to panic, but her body was too busy fitting into this new shape to dump adrenaline. It wasn't exactly that Lucinda was changing; it felt more like someone poured liquid Lucinda into an already-existing mold.

This new body bounced and vibrated in the back seat of a Jeepster Hurricane. A beautiful, red Jeep with white trim that practically screamed ADVENTURE. The Jeep fishtailed; a blond woman sitting across on the bench seat squealed as a bandanna tore from her hair and sailed into the air.

Lucinda recalled the blond woman's name: Sybil. Sybil Kersey. An American.

And now the final change occurred. Lucinda's mind dropped fully into the memory. That's what the whirlwind was: one of Abuelita's memories. Lucinda no longer thought of herself as Lucinda. She had become Herminia Carrillo.

Not Abuelita.

Certainly not.

She was Herminia Carrillo. Young, vivacious. Sexy, even.

In the prime of life.

They roared up a straight stretch. A brown form leaped into the dirt road, stared at the oncoming Jeepster Hurricane, and froze. A buck mule deer.

Herminia sucked in her breath, braced herself against the seat in front.

The Jeep, a topless, cherry-red beauty, skidded sideways, threw Herminia against the door, threw Sybil sideways onto her lap, threw dirt and gravel twenty feet into the air.

But too late.

There was a dull thud as the deer hit the bumper. Herminia felt the thud distinctly, as if the animal's soul had passed through her fingertips roughly....

Ten

1967, Beyond

Herminia shimmied through the narrow opening, losing a button in the process. "Pass me the flashlight," she told Faustino. "It will be easier if you have both hands free."

That wasn't exactly true. Herminia's confidence had faltered for some reason, though she couldn't put her finger on why. Perhaps it was because the sea breeze seemed to be coming from everywhere and nowhere at once, as if little fans were hidden in all the cracks and crevices. Though only shoulder-length, her hair was all a-tangle, unsure of which way to blow. She wanted to hold the light to reassure herself. The cave felt different somehow. She had expected it would, else all this had been a sham; she had expected it wouldn't, doubting Don Esteban still.

How could this brujo Don Esteban — only a few years older than she was — guide them to some mythical *Beyond*? She wanted to believe and she wanted to laugh out loud.

She definitely didn't want to be duped.

The masa paste had left grit between her teeth, and with the grit the pleasant burning sensation of chilies on her tongue and gums.

She shone the light ahead. Debris choked the way forward. The ceiling was uneven, at times low enough to knock her forehead, at times rising out of sight in what might be separate passages. The walls were rough and unpainted.

Except there.

On a smooth section of the wall, her light found another, colorful painting. This one took her breath away. "Faustino, you have to see this."

Herminia could hear Faustino struggling through the narrow opening, labored breath, fabric tearing as it caught somewhere.

Finally he joined her. "This cave goes on and on. I have never—"

And then he saw the painting.

It was by far the most vibrant, most colorful pictograph she had ever seen. It had multiple tints of green, red, brown, blue, black, white, yellow. And it depicted something Herminia had seen before. The Garden of Eden.

Two native figures drawn with black and red paint, a male and female, Adam and Eve. With an extended hand, the Cochimí Adam had just reached a fruit dangling from a tree. To his right, Eve watched expectantly, to his left, an evil-looking snake coiled around one of the strange fruits. In a triangular pattern beneath the Adam figure were three animals: an owl, a coyote, and a raven. A blue wave connected each of these three animals to Adam.

Allies, thought Herminia. *Adam with his three allies.*

A jagged, violent break severed the waves from Adam and his allies.

"We've found it," Faustino said. "In three years of trying I have never come so far. Look, these are the three allies of original man: an owl, the Spiritual ally; a coyote, the Physical ally, and a raven, the Mental ally."

This reminded Herminia of a conversation.

The three of them had been sitting around the swimming hole: Herminia, Faustino, Don Esteban. Herminia had brought her half-formed mortar in order to work on it, but the sun had been too warm, and the water too inviting. It sat next to her like an accusation.

What are you doing here?

Why are you wasting your life?

Why don't you reconcile with your parents?

Herminia, comfortable in her wet, one-piece bathing suit, tipped the mortar on its side.

"How do we get there? How do we get Beyond?" Herminia had asked. "I have been through the cave. It is a dead end."

"So you say. If I were to explain everything I know about the Beyond — and there is probably much I do not know," Don Esteban said, flicking water at a passing dragonfly, "you would be too terrified to continue."

"Stop with the questions, woman," Faustino groaned, and plopped his shirt over his face.

The sun was beginning to turn Faustino's skin red, and Herminia hoped he'd get a painful sunburn.

"Who are the allies?" Herminia asked. "And why did Faustino's ally want him dead?"

El Brujo held up both hands. "You will have enough questions when you make your first trip to the Beyond."

"I have questions now."

"For now, close your eyes and imagine that you are this pool. Imagine that you feel the rough walls, and the water striders on your surface."

Herminia closed her eyes, breathed deeply, centered her mind on the calm waters of the spring-fed pool. She breathed in the scent of wet sandstone, slowed her heartbeat, became the pool in her mind. When she was nearly there, Don Esteban cannonballed into the water, startling her. He grunted and shook, and threw himself about like an animal. His fat body was a lot more agile in water than on land.

Faustino laughed.

Herminia had come to interpret this sort of thing as Don Esteban's sense of humor. She tossed the brujo's shoes into the pool for revenge, but he didn't seem to care. She wasn't sure when exactly she had fallen asleep, for in her imagination Don Esteban's face flattened, he grew feathers, he became an owl and emerged from the pool, spread his wings and took flight on silent wings.

An owl. Just like the figure in this painting.

"Brave girl," Faustino said, tracing the outline of the painting with his fingers. "Always wanting to be first. I thought we were going to hold hands."

Herminia wasn't sure if he was being sarcastic or if he genuinely wanted to hold hands. Either way, he'd have to work on his manners before she agreed to that. She asked, "Do you think the masa paste contained drugs?"

Faustino shrugged, and a weird, skeletal shadow shrugged on the ceiling.

"Do you smell the sea?" he asked.

"Yes."

"Is there a breeze coming from the back, where the cave should end?"

This was so obvious ... but she understood. If they both felt the same thing, how could it be a hallucination?

She nodded.

"And the pink elephant in the corner, is it dancing on the mushroom?"

Herminia grinned in spite of herself. The knot in her stomach unwound a bit. Faustino could be funny — when he wasn't practicing bitter or sullen.

"Yes, poorly," she said.

"No coordination at all," Faustino agreed. "It dances like a gringo." Faustino put extra derisiveness into that word *gringo*. He held special hatred for Americans — and wanted everyone to know it. It had something to do with El Boleo mine, which Herminia found hard to understand. The mine brought prosperity to Santa Rosalía. And problems, yes. The sort of problems you got when hundreds of men lived and worked away from their families: drinking and prostitution, mostly. But that wasn't specifically an American problem. It was a sign of how much men needed women to keep them in check — not that they'd ever admit it.

"Faustino, I have been through these caves many times. They dead end, somewhere behind us." She pointed back the way they had come. "I would have sworn on the Virgen María that this branch of the cave did not exist. Likewise, I have never seen this pictograph before."

"The answer, Herminia, is that Don Esteban lies to us. He acts like we have never been to the Beyond before, that we can only get here on his specific instruction, but we have. *You* have—I knew when you showed me the sketch pad when I lay in the hospital in Santa Rosalía. The painting of the man inside the crow does not exist in this world. When you copied it, you already were in the Beyond."

"So what is the Beyond?"

"Ah, I do not think even Don Esteban could answer that. We can refer to it as a dream world. A spirit world, if that sounds more UC Berkeley. That is who you hang out with, right? Norteamericanos from Berkeley."

"Hollywood, for your information. I haven't seen them since the day they rescued you. What's it to you?"

"Nothing. Nothing at all. They are all the same, *los gringos*. Each as greedy as the other."

Herminia moved to examine the pictograph more closely and her footstep felt sluggish, heavy. She stumbled and dropped the flashlight. It winked out; they were now in total blackness.

Something cold tickled her ankle.

Water.

Had they descended below the water table, or stumbled upon an underground river? Her mind tried to make sense of the situation. Conceivably a thunderstorm could have dropped rain high in the mountains, water that came here through hidden ways, and would disappear the same way.

That made sense. Water probably created this cave, after all.

"Don't move," she said. "We need to remember which way is the exit."

"What is it? What happened?" Faustino said. "Herminia! Herminia, I hope you find your ally soon or we are in deep trouble."

The water was rising fast. It passed Herminia's calf and sloshed above her knees, weighing down the hem of her dress.

"Take my hand, please," Faustino said. "Please. I don't want to be lost."

She groped around but felt nothing. Panic rose in her throat. "Over here," she said, talking so the sound of her voice would guide Faustino. "Take a step this way. A baby step. Don't fall or break anything. We will get out of here together."

"There is no getting out of here, not without an ally."

Cold water climbed Herminia's sensitive thighs. A minute more and it would soak her underwear. The horrible possibility that they would drown here, high in the desert mountains, seemed impossibly real.

"What about your lizard guides? Can they show us the way?"

She heard the distinctive metal whisk of a lighter opening, the snick of a flint, and a bright flame illuminated the cave. Of course, Faustino would have a shiny gold Zippo. Faustino's eyes were wide and haunted. The shoulders of his shirt were bare. No lizards.

"They have deserted us," he whispered.

At that moment their feet dropped into nothing. They sank as fast as they could panic. Faustino flailed. Herminia put her forearm before her face to protect it, but hit nothing. She took a deep breath as water closed over her head like a liquid door slamming shut.

The Zippo — dead.

This pool was genuinely deep. Though she reached with her toes (her sandals having come off in the fall), Herminia could not feel the floor, the walls — nothing. A fluttery feeling stimulated the nape of her neck.

She tried to take it all in, tried to process logically. Her chest began to feel pressure to breathe, despite the knowledge that this would kill her.

Another thirty seconds. I can hold my breath that long. Another minute, perhaps, since my life depends on it. A minute, come on, Herminia, think.

She wanted to swim — to swim, and to breathe, but where?

Not logic. This is not a place of logic. What was that word? Don Esteban had used it. The lizards were there to— Something about focus, or sharpen.

In any normal circumstance, she could have recalled it in a second, but with the darkness closing in, the cold water enveloping her. So difficult to think. No matter how much she wanted to, thinking—

That's it. Intent.

This is a place of intent.

She opened her eyes, or perhaps she only blinked. Light seemed to be coming from everywhere at once.

Light?

Light!

Herminia didn't think she was dreaming. This felt far too real to be a dream. The cold water felt wet, drained the heat of her body, plastered the dress to her legs, impeding her movement. The flashlight shorted out, spun in place, as if of the same buoyancy as the water. She kicked it. It spun more quickly, like a child's toy. She felt no up, no down. An air bubble released from her mouth drifted away like an empty snow globe.

Something brushed her foot. She recognized the stiff-flexible texture of a fish's dorsal fin, saw a sailfish glide underneath her and turn a lazy circle.

A strange feeling passed over her, from the top of her head to her toes. It felt nearly identical to the apprentice bond El Brujo had placed on her in the lobster cafe, like passing through a static-charged, electric membrane. This time, much like when you open your eyes after a paralysis dream and realize that you can move at will, the membrane brought with it a sense of total awakening.

Herminia did not feel her ally, any more than she felt her spleen, but she knew they had bonded. What she felt was a heightened sense of smell, of taste, of hearing, of vision, of balance, of touch. A heightened sense of being.

She laughed out loud and turned to share her happiness with Faustino and saw him kicking frantically up, a trail of bubbles leaving his jeans. *Don Esteban would be pleased*, she thought, the conversation from the lobster cafe coming back to her. *We are certainly not helping each other.*

Faustino's panic stirred her own fear. At this moment she realized that she couldn't breathe underwater — was she breathing before? — and she held her breath. In one direction was the sea floor, deep brown; in the other, blue sky and a rough-hewn square floating on the surface. Herminia frog-kicked toward the square, following Faustino, though with measured strokes to conserve energy. It looked like a long way to the surface (the light came only from this direction now), and the real distance was greater than she thought. To get some relief from the burning sensation in her lungs, she used the diver's trick of releasing air a little at a time, then a little more, then more than she could have imagined, until her lungs were completely empty, and only with great force of will did she resist the urge to inhale.

She thrust her head into a calm sea and inhaled in great gasps. Blue sky overhead. A few wispy clouds. The square was a raft of logs lashed together. Gasping, with grunts and curses, Faustino pulled himself aboard. The craft wobbled mightily. The logs comprising it measured about six inches in diameter.

A sailfish jumped over Herminia. Her ally — it must be! It was as large as she was, with a blue and yellow back and a sliver belly. Water dribbled across Herminia's forehead as the sailfish passed overhead. Herminia had always considered sailfish good luck, though she had pulled many aboard the pangas for tourists.

Herminia free-stroked to the raft and climbed aboard. Faustino lay on his back, his legs pulled up so they wouldn't dangle in the water. With both of them aboard, the raft lay low in the water. When the swells rolled underneath they broke on its edge with a plop.

Faustino managed to lift his head and croak, "What the hell are you doing?"

Herminia twisted the water from her hair, letting it splash on her bare thighs. All this was pretty disconcerting, all right; she could forgive Faustino's change of humor. Her white bra was completely visible through the dress' yellow material. She considered removing both to shock Faustino, but decided that wouldn't be prudent. Faustino was tough to read; no telling how he would react.

For whatever reason, the fear Herminia had felt as she pitched into the dark had disappeared, to be replaced by a strong sense of tranquility.

Of belonging.

Of curiosity.

"We are safe, Faustino. We have a raft and good weather. Let us see what comes, hmm? We made it. We made it to the Beyond!"

It would have been more fun to be here with the Americans who drove her into the mountains, she thought. *They would be more interesting than this moody Faustino. Particularly that handsome Brennan. Or Sybil Kersey — that woman was a riot!*

It was just a passing fancy, but a pleasant one. Herminia tilted her head to the sun, enjoying the heat on her face and neck.

"Take us back." Faustino climbed to his knees, setting the raft to rocking. "I said, take us back!"

"Calm down, Faustino. I'm not doing anything."

The sailfish jumped in a smooth arch, slicing back into the water the way a needle pierces flesh.

Faustino crawled closer. His teeth ground audibly, as if trying to pulverize each other.

"Faustino! What are you doing? You are going to flood us."

Herminia could dive overboard and swim away if she had to; Faustino was a weak swimmer, but she doesn't want to give up the raft. How long could she actually tread water in this endless sea? A few hours? No, she had to get Faustino to calm down. "The raft will tip over if you come closer. There is already too much weight on one side."

Knee after knee he continued. Herminia backed until her toes fell over the lip of the raft and caressed the ocean.

The sailfish jumped again, sleek and deadly, clearing the water by a good six feet.

Faustino lunged. The shift in weight didn't upset the raft. The raft didn't pitch at all — it collapsed into driftwood as if the bindings had dissolved. This time the water went in Herminia's nose, salty and uncomfortable.

Faustino splashed around like mad.

A white ghost charged, the sailfish, aiming to skewer Faustino with its bill.

"Back!" Herminia wished with all her might. "Take us back, please."

Dry land, in the dark. Herminia's clothes were soaked. She sat there, trying to make sense of what happened.

Next to her, she heard Faustino vomiting.

It must be drugs in the masa paste, she thought, but didn't believe it. She had tried marijuana once (it made her want to sleep), and alcohol, of course (it made her want to dance), and she always knew when her brain was a little fuzzy. This wasn't like that at all.

This was like being awake. Fully, unconditionally awake. Even now, Herminia could feel every individual goosebump on her arms. She could feel the weight of the moisture that clung to her feet.

"It's always so frigging easy for you, isn't it?" Faustino said, and muttered a few curses under his breath. After several tries, he managed to get the Zippo to light. "Get your things. Let's go."

The flashlight lay on the ground, and Herminia retrieved it. To her amazement, it worked just fine. She played the light against the wall.

The painting no longer showed the Garden of Eden. It showed a human figure inside an animal. Before, when Herminia had copied this painting into her sketchpad, it had shown a man inside a crow. Now, the crow was no longer a crow. It was a sailfish. And the man was not a man. It was a woman.

Faustino didn't show any interest in the painting. He was trying to exit as fast as he could, but his wet clothes just wouldn't allow him beyond the choking point. The clothes clung equally to his body and the sandstone. He had to remove his shirt in order to pass.

Herminia winced at the abuse his nipples took sliding across the rock. Fortunately, she was a lot smaller. The squeeze didn't give her nearly as much trouble — and she kept her clothes on.

Wet, sticky and uncomfortable, they dripped from the cave and plopped before the fire. Faustino pulled his shirt back on. It was daylight. They had passed the night in the cave, if not several nights. Fatigue crawled up Herminia's forehead like a mental spider.

Don Esteban handed each of them a cup of coffee, steaming hot, in a black, metal cup. He had never shown them such courtesy before. He had never served them food or drink, period. Something had definitely changed in his demeanor.

"Now, apprentices," he said, sitting up taller. "I'm all ears."

Herminia let Faustino do most of the talking. She kept staring at El Brujo. He looked different. More hale. The improvement was more fundamental than a new haircut; if she didn't know better, Herminia would have sworn the witch's teeth had become partially repaired.

The story delighted Don Esteban, particularly the sailfish.

Herminia tried to remember all she had been taught about the Beyond. "Is it true that I made the raft?"

"No. Faustino created the raft out of fear. You were free to move about, because that was your place and your ally. You could have breathed underwater there, if you hadn't let yourself be affected by Faustino's fear."

Faustino pitched the dregs of his cup into the coals, causing them to sizzle. He made no move to get up, however.

"That was Physical, wasn't it?" Herminia said.

"Why do you pretend to be stupid?" Faustino said. "Of course it was Physical. Look at him."

The words hurt. Herminia tried to ignore them, for she had bonded with the sailfish ally on her first try, while Faustino had been trying for three years. The words had been driven by jealousy. Still, they hurt.

Don Esteban laughed in that mocking way, though Herminia wasn't sure if he mocked her, Faustino, or both. "Faustino understands, but you," El Brujo tapped his temple, "innocence is a stubborn child. Why else would a brujo spend years of his life trying to teach bumblers how to access the Beyond: out of the goodness of his heart? Of course not. I told you, compassion plays no part in the way of the brujo.

"The master shares in his apprentice's power. Just a trickle through the apprentice bond. If you had a Spiritual ally like mine, I would hardly notice the difference. But since you have a Physical ally, I now have some small access to Physical powers." Don Esteban held out his right hand. Nothing seemed to be any different — it was just his pudgy hand. The fingernails needed filing. And then a small mole on the back of the hand shifted into a smiley face.

It was both disgusting and funny.

"You said no brujo has ever had more than one ally," Herminia said.

"The natural state of all humans is to bond with three allies. We have been forced to live in pieces, forced to live in an unnatural state, thanks to Adam's sin."

"Adam was a witch?"

"He would be called so today. Adam and Eve lived eternally, no? No death. No disease. The painting of Adam and Eve — that is the key. If you could bond with two allies, you would be a witch without peer.

Your powers would multiply a dozen times. A hundred times. If you could bond with all three—"

"But that is impossible," Herminia said.

"It is the natural state of man. Adam's sin — no, God's reaction to Adam's sin — literally tore man and woman to pieces. We are now shells. Weak flesh, hardly alive, and hardly deserving to be alive. Only our pitiful self-awareness gives us dominion over the animals. Except for us, the brujos. One at a time the allies come to you. They accept you or they reject you. The sailfish accepted you on the first try. Perhaps you will be the one who bonds with two allies. Or more than two. Think of magnetic poles. They repel each other, but they belong together. The allies are like that: a trinity that belongs together but can never meet unless somehow the polar charge can be reversed."

"Or extinguished," Faustino said.

"Yes, extinguished. The brujo who extinguishes the charge that keeps the allies apart would save mankind."

Save mankind. What did Don Esteban mean by that? Such a proclamation! This, then, was the heart of the matter. Life without end, without disease. Herminia's fatigue faded, subsumed by the possibilities. Would she be the bruja who saved mankind?

Don Esteban leaned back onto one elbow and stared into the dark. She sensed that if she said the wrong thing, he would return to his usual, evasive self. She wanted to know more about this. What could she ask to keep him talking? A question about Original Sin? No. She could anticipate El Brujo's reply: That wasn't important. The sin happened. Live with the way things are, not the way they might have been.

A question about God's reaction to the sin, then, this sort of energy charge that kept the allies apart? If all this was impossible, why did El Brujo talk as if the charge could be eliminated? Why bring it up at all? Did he think he could defy God?

She was busy formulating a question when Faustino broke the silence. "If you steal our allies, Don Esteban, then you will have bonded with all three."

Herminia couldn't believe Faustino dared say such a thing. She wondered if she could stop whatever was to come. Although she had never seen El Brujo hurt another person, she had no doubt he would do so without a second thought. She wondered if she would have to intervene to save Faustino's life.

But instead of getting angry, El Brujo sank deeper into his own contemplation. It took several long seconds before he replied:

"Whatever it is you are planning, apprentice, rest assured you will fail."

ELEVEN

PRESENT DAY, PUNTA COLONET, BAJA CALIFORNIA NORTH

Abuelita didn't sit up tall as usual. She slumped in the kitchen chair, head wilted on a feeble neck, shoulders tilted forward. Her scalp was completely bald.

Mamá held Abuelita's head in both hands. She pinched the skin, pressed her fingertips into the purpleness, and muttered.

The splotch spread in eight directions at once, engulfing the Sharpie outline Lucinda had drawn. You could feel the heat pulsing off of it, as if the curse wanted to burn up grandmother Herminia's mind. Two legs advanced down Abuelita's forehead.

Lucinda wanted to cry and throw up at the same time. First, Abuelita had lost her memory. Now this horrid, disgusting illness. This blood curse.

"I'll call in sick," Mamá announced. "We will take mother to the clinic. The Flying Samaritans arrived today."

"What do you mean, *we*?" Lucinda asked.

"You, me, Abuelita. I am not going to leave you home alone."

"You leave me alone every day. All day."

That earned Lucinda a glare. And from the pointedness of that regard, Lucinda realized that if she pushed it, that might change radically. She could end up hauled off to the tomato cannery to work alongside her mother. Fifteen wasn't too early to quit school and start working in Punta Colonet. It happened every day.

Lucinda gulped and said nothing more. She had a lifetime to can tomatoes. For now there were more important things to do! If she and her friends were going to fix this curse and get Abuelita well, they had to work fast.

They had managed to witness two of Abuelita's memories. In the first, Abuelita drove into the mountains with three Americans. There, they encountered the shaman Don Esteban and his apprentice Faustino, who was sick and unconscious. The Americans took Faustino to get help; Herminia chose to stay and learn magic with Don Esteban.

When the memory ended, the friends found themselves back in the garden with the mirror pool. A second memory presented itself, a whirlwind hanging before them, expectant if not insistent, while the others danced away. Despite a wobbly feeling in their legs, Lucinda, Eva, and Mateo had reached out to witness the beginning of Abuelita's education as a witch, which seemed to consist of learning handcrafts and copying cave paintings. The memory ended with Abuelita visiting Faustino in the hospital — and the arrival of a note from the shaman.

How Lucinda managed to descend the hill from the cemetery into Punta Colonet proper, she would never know. The house felt a lifetime away. Watching.... No, living those memories drained energy like hoeing weeds in hard-packed clay under the midday sun. Without a hat. Lucinda had slept all afternoon and had skipped dinner, feigning illness. Or maybe not feigning.

It would take a lot to go through all those whirlwinds to discover who attacked Herminia, and Lucinda needed every spare bit of time and energy. Much as she wanted to accompany Abuelita to the Flying Samaritans, this was investigation time!

A headache greeted Lucinda from the corner of her eyeballs.

"Are you in pain?" Mamá asked Abuelita, oblivious to or at least uncaring of Lucinda's internal struggle. "Does it hurt? Anywhere? Does your head hurt?"

"Of course it does, with you pinching and prodding it," Abuelita responded.

Lucinda said, "You're sick, Abuelita. We need to take you to the doctor. The Flying Samaritans."

"I can't go to the doctor. I promised to make sopes when Don Pedro gets home from Gigante," Abuelita said. "He is bringing beans, goat cheese, cabbage, cream, and onions."

Lucinda would have been frightened if Don Pedro returned from the store with beans, onions, cheese, cream, and cabbage, because Don Pedro had died eleven years before when Lucinda was only four. Don Pedro was Lucinda's grandfather.

Lucinda patted Abuelita's hand.

"It's the stroke," Mamá said, bustling around to get ready to leave. "It makes you say crazy talk. Put some Fanta in your backpack, three bottles, and a book if you want it, or drawing paper. And my phone charger. We may be there a while."

Mamá made sure to hide Abuelita's condition under a floppy, straw hat. The clinic was on the opposite side of the Transpeninsular Highway, a small office next to a hairdresser. The sign on the door said *cerrado*, closed, but a man in blue jeans and a white lab coat bustled around inside.

Mamá knocked.

The man in the lab coat ignored them.

From the corner of the building, Lucinda peeked around to see El Jaguar's hacienda. Its forbidding, broken-glass topped walls gave her a chill. All of this began with El Jaguar and that fateful night at the Parade of Heroes.

Abuelita defending her. With magic.

By protecting Lucinda, she'd drawn a curse down on herself.

Mamá wanted to leave this to the doctors — and to God — and had said so the night before. Abuelita had lived a long, productive life, Mamá explained. If God decided it was Abuelita's time, then Lucinda must let her go.

Lucinda knew that God had nothing to do with the illness. Abuelita had defended her from a witch, and Lucinda owed it to grandmother to do everything possible to fight back.

"Hija, help with the door," Mamá said.

A little bell tinkled as Lucinda pulled the door wide enough for Abuelita and Mamá to enter.

It was a good thing they got there early. People began arriving with everything from a cleft lip to toothaches to warts as big as lollipops. The Flying Samaritans flew into Punta Colonet's little dirt airport once a month, medical providers combining their love of flying and Baja California with an unusual spirit of generosity. They always brought at least two doctors, a nurse, and a dentist. These Americans gave their time and resources, asking for nothing in return. (Although they flew home laden with tamales, mescal, and other hand-spun gifts such as the locals could afford.)

Wealthier families in Punta Colonet had donated enough for X-ray equipment and a real dentist's chair, which Lucinda hated.

The nurse had them fill out several forms, name, address, phone number, whether Abuelita smoked or drank and how much, and some embarrassing questions about Abuelita's sex life. Americans were famous for asking that kind of question — and not just at the clinic. The nurse offered to read the forms aloud, but thank goodness Mamá could read them fine. How embarrassing that would be!

Once completed, the nurse took them to the exam room. Abuelita sat on the medical bed while the nurse took her vitals. "So, what seems to be the trouble?" The nurse was a blond with a short, military-style haircut and a crisp voice to match. Lucinda had never seen her before.

When they pulled off Abuelita's hat, the nurse almost managed to control her surprise. Almost. Only a stiffening of the muscles around the eyes betrayed anything.

With her finger, the nurse traced the Sharpie marks Lucinda had made and mumbled to herself. She scribbled some notes.

"How long has this been here?" the nurse asked.

"A few days," Mamá said.

"She used to have hair," Lucinda added. "This made it all fall out."

The nurse muttered some more, scribbled some more, then fetched the doctor.

He bustled in, saw Abuelita's head, turned toward the filing cabinet and began reading her chart. All of that would have been normal, except the doctor's eyes weren't really reading. They simply stared, unfocused, as he decided what to say. Lucinda had seen that same look in the eyes of tourists pulled from their cars by the Federal Police.

With each passing second, Lucinda's hope dropped like a coin falling into an empty, dust-filled well.

After a time, the nurse broke the silence. "I think it might be a spider bite. Ms. García doesn't have a fever, but the discoloration feels warmer than the surrounding area. We don't have a surface thermometer, but I don't need one. I can feel it with my bare hands." When no reply was forthcoming, the nurse asked, "Should I call in Doctor Glass?"

The doctor finally turned to face them. The badge pinned to his lab coat read *Doctor Blake*. "No. No need. Ms. García's vitals seem to be normal, blood pressure is fine."

Mamá was nodding.

Couldn't Mamá see how scared the doctor was? "You've seen this before," Lucinda guessed. "The pharmacist? Remember him? He died of the same thing."

The doctor's Adam's apple bobbed when he swallowed. "I— I am not allowed to talk about other patients."

"Clearly, there is something wrong," Lucinda said. "People don't just lose their hair overnight. A few days ago, Abuelita was strong as a goat. Now it took us a full minute just to cross the road."

"Ms. García's muscle tone is fine. Yes. I suggest an aspirin and some rest. It looks like an allergic reaction of some kind. Nothing we can do."

The nurse's eyes bugged out.

"Nothing you can do?" Lucinda said. "What about the Hippocratic Oath?"

"Hija, let the doctor speak," Mamá said.

"You don't even know what the Hippocratic Oath means," Lucinda replied, winding up. "Clearly, Doctor Blake is afraid. Just like you are afraid. Just like everyone else in this one-peso town. El Jaguar is dead, get over it. Abuelita stood up to him for everyone's sake and now you are afraid of your own shadows."

A warm feeling began to creep up Lucinda's temples. The hair on the back of her neck actually stood on end — she could feel it do so, hair by hair. An excited rattling accompanied her outrage: a cabinet full of medicine seemed to tremble in sympathetic reaction ... though it must be in response to a heavy truck on the highway.

"That is about enough," Mamá said. "These people donate their time. They are doing the best they can. Be grateful, hija."

The sharp whistles of a red cardinal sounded from outside the window.

"This isn't even a real clinic," Lucinda said, wheeling on her mother. "We only come here because you are afraid to take Abuelita to the hospital in Ensenada."

She knew she had pushed too far — both Mamá and the doctor. She managed to seal her lips, barely.

The cupboard stopped rattling.

Doctor Blake began scribbling on a prescription form. His hands trembled; his penmanship was practically flat-lined. "This will take care of any reaction Ms. García might have had. There is a website there to check for any updates. If there is any swelling, particularly in the throat, she needs to get to the hospital right away. Check her pulse regularly for any sign of weakness." He tore off the form and handed it to Mamá, who looked visibly relieved to be getting out of there.

The nurse watched all this with a pale, astonished face.

A few more words were spoken, but Lucinda was too angry to even remember what was said. The nurse walked them to the door, probably to make sure Lucinda left without breaking any furniture. She suggested they return if Abuelita's condition deteriorated over the next two days, otherwise, the Flying Samaritans would return in a month's time. They could follow up then.

The nurse gave Lucinda a gentle squeeze to the arm and a sympathetic smile, and said, "If your grandmother feels warm, try wrapping a wet towel around her head."

The bell tinkled as they stepped outside, and Lucinda braced herself for Mamá's lecture on respect and remembering a daughter's place.

Mamá didn't disappoint.

Twelve

1967, MOUNTAINS OUTSIDE SANTA ROSALÍA,
BAJA CALIFORNIA SOUTH

Even though Herminia was living in the Sierra de la Giganta mountain range many miles from the ocean at an elevation of 2,500 feet, surrounded by high desert flora and fauna, water seemed to be her element. All of her sojourns into the Beyond had involved water of some kind, an ocean (usually), a lake (too big to swim to the shore), a river without end. Her ally's preferred shape was a swordfish, but if the body of water was shallow or freshwater, it might appear as any sort of fish.

That's what Herminia was counting on. With a great deal of meditation, concentration, and intent, Herminia had brought her ally through into the swimming hole near the cave. Her actual ally! The same way Don Esteban could bring his seagull through.

It was mid-November, and the nearby rivers had not started running yet; this twenty-foot-wide bowl was the largest body of water for miles.

A rainbow trout peeked up at her from the water, shy and a little angry. The rainbow coloration along its sides flung sunlight in all directions.

If the brujo Don Esteban was right, this wasn't really a separate entity at all, but more like a piece of Herminia that had been broken off when Adam bit from the Tree of Knowledge. That's why it was an ally, had some attraction to her, and constant knowledge of her location.

You're part of me, Herminia thought. *That explains your temper.*

Herminia grinned. "Come, little swordfish Ally. I do not want a trout, I want something that walks on land. Come to me. Come along." She gestured with her hand, wishing Faustino or Don Esteban were here to see this. It looked like it was going to work. It really did.

The trout thrust its expressionless face out of the water. It pushed with its tail, seeking to come to Herminia. Its gill flaps worked open and closed.

"No oxygen out of the water for you little trout, not in this shape. Try another." Herminia sounded like a mom trying to coax a smile from a baby — and she didn't care. She was having the time of her life.

Having the ally here made the whole place feel more alive. The wind from a dragonfly's wings tickled as it buzzed past. A clump of Brickell bush hidden somewhere under the chaparral provided lovely sweet aroma. Where a single blade of dried grass cast a shadow across her bare foot, a line of coolness crossed. And so much more.

The ally shifted into a toad shape and hopped closer.

"Ah, no," Herminia said, wagging her finger.

The toad blinked in confusion. Wasn't that what she wanted?

"Much too obvious. Try again."

The toad elongated, stretched. Fur replaced the spotted skin, became a shiny, black coat. Her ally grew a fluffy, gorgeous tail, and little claws, and sharp little teeth. (*A mink?* Herminia guessed, having never seen one in person.)

The mink-ally sprinted over and bit Herminia's big toe.

"Ow!" Herminia said, pulling her foot away and doing the one-legged dance.

The mink stood on its back feet, scolded her, and then faded from sight.

Despite the sting of her toe, Herminia pumped her fists in victory. She ran to tell the others.

. . .

Herminia followed the sound of shouting voices to El Brujo's pickup truck. She stayed out of sight until she heard the engine fire up and drive away. She debated leaving — Faustino would be in no mood to hear about her success with the ally — but Herminia's curiosity got the better of her.

"Don Esteban is letting the world fall apart around us while he bets on his horse races!" Faustino complained, slapping El Universal against his palm when Herminia revealed herself. Faustino read the political section of El Brujo's newspaper with the greed of an addict.

"More news about Vietnam?" Herminia asked, bored with all Faustino's talk of war.

With great drama, Faustino opened the paper and pointed to a headline from page 5: "*Mulegé Children Missing*." This was different.... Herminia took a closer look. The first paragraph said that as many as twenty children had disappeared in and around Mulegé and Santa Rosalía.

"*In the past year alone,*" read Faustino. "Poisoned by effluent from the copper mine, no doubt, their bodies discarded."

"In Mulegé? If it were pollutants, their bodies wouldn't simply disappear."

Herminia read the story with increasing horror. The missing children came from the most vulnerable groups — orphans and street children. In some cases, no one reported them missing for months after they disappeared. "It says here the police are investigating the mothers."

Faustino snatched the newspaper from her hands. "Sold into prostitution to the Americans, or kidnapped and then murdered. What I do know is this wasn't happening before the Americans reopened the mine. We were a community then; we looked after each other and each other's children. Now it is every man for himself. Greed. The gringos brought their greenbacks to destroy us."

"Or maybe it was happening and it wasn't reported because there were no local journalists before the mine reopened," Herminia replied, reasonably. "What is really wrong, Faustino?"

He began pacing, his tan shoes gradually erasing the pickup's tire tracks. The November nights could be cold, and Faustino still wore a sarape over his long sleeve shirt and blue jeans despite the late hour. He looked like a Western movie star with his scowl and sunburned face.

"You've been here all of six months, and I for three years. You are already a witch; I have nothing to show for it."

Herminia felt a small fear blossom in her breast. Was Faustino going to quit? Despite his moodiness, she knew she would miss Faustino if he did. And not just because she did not want to be left alone with El Brujo. (That was true also. Don Esteban made Herminia increasingly uncomfortable. He stared at her hungrily when they swam together, and she knew the brujo's ally spied on her even when he wasn't around.)

"What would you do in my position?" Faustino asked.

That was unexpected; Faustino never asked anyone else's opinion.

I would have quit long ago, Herminia admitted to herself. But she didn't want to discourage him. "You've been in the Beyond."

"With you."

"On your own. Your sketchbook proves it. The crow? The fox and the man, with the river in between?"

"You found those your first day!"

His pacing had brought him very close. She understood Faustino's frustration very well now, and she reached out and took his hand. "We will go in the cave together. Right now, while El Brujo is away."

"You promised El Brujo not to help me."

"I have helped you many times. And you me."

"Not like this."

"I wouldn't be helping you. I will just go to keep an eye on Lemon and Jefferson, in case they need me."

"I'm sorry I am so moody. My parents called me see-saw, and more saw than see."

"You had parents?" Herminia feigned surprise.

Faustino nodded. "I grew up in paradise, not far from here. The Americans—"

"I know, they ruined it. They are ruining everything."

"*Sí!* You are starting to understand."

He said this last with a grin.

They *were* beginning to understand each other, Herminia thought.

Herminia understood that Faustino was a fanatic of his own making. Faustino understood he couldn't con Herminia.

They also understood they liked each other — at least to a certain degree. It had grown on Herminia slowly. Much different than any crushes she'd had in the past. Those had been all passionate speculation. *Hormones*, her mother would have said. Faustino was a puzzle to be solved. And as the puzzle slowly pieced together, familiarity grew, caring blossomed. Paradoxically, curiosity also blossomed. What would he be like as a boyfriend?

Inexperienced was the word that popped to mind, making her smile.

She almost never entertained such thoughts in daylight, and she caught herself eying Faustino top to bottom. Yes, the man was handsome — when he didn't scowl.

They retrieved their mortars. Faustino's, shaped long before, had smooth sides. Herminia's sported three faces spaced evenly apart: a sailfish, an ocelot, and a sea turtle. As Don Esteban had predicted, Herminia's allies had come to her one at a time. Rather anti-climatic, really. The ocelot had appeared as Herminia explored a mountain path in the Beyond. No matter how fast she sprinted, the ocelot stayed out of reach. In sight, but out of reach, always rounding a corner just ahead of her. When she stopped seeking it, the ocelot padded away. Now and then Herminia caught sight of the feline when exploring the Beyond. Keeping touch.

The sea turtle had appeared in an endless, shore-less ocean. Herminia had hoped to lure it near by ignoring it. The technique seemed to be working; the sea turtle had drawn to within thirty yards. And then something unexpected happened. A gray-brown whirlpool grew from the seafloor. From nothing to a roiling storm. It swallowed the sea turtle and continued to grow.

Herminia didn't sense any menace from the storm. Nor did she feel any sense of power (other than a choppiness to the ocean). It was as if the storm were an absence rather than a presence.

She had the intelligence to swim in the other direction.

El Brujo told them the storm was called the Null Wind. One of the unpredictable features of the Beyond. One of the fatal features. The

Null Wind could appear at any time — though negative thoughts made its appearance more likely. Intent, as he said, ruled the Beyond.

A certainty: if the Null Wind overtook you, you would perish.

"What happens to the allies?" Herminia had asked, alarmed at the thought of her poor sea turtle.

El Brujo had shrugged. "I tell you this only because to learn it for yourself is impossible. I do not know. Your sea turtle will probably be just fine. But if you are overtaken, Herminia, the Null Wind will sever your ties with your allies. They will be gone, as surely as a wood splitter will sever a carelessly placed arm. On the unlikely event that you manage to return to this world from the Beyond without an ally, you will never again be a bruja." With startling tenderness, El Brujo had brushed some grit from Herminia's cheek with the back of his pudgy hand. "If the Null Wind takes you, Herminia, you will never again be truly human."

Faustino found Lemon and Jefferson without much trouble, then he and Herminia mixed up some masa paste with cornmeal, lard, salt, and a pinch of chili oil. On impulse, Herminia scraped some of her own paste onto her index finger and passed it to Faustino.

"For luck," she said, enjoying the feel of their skin touching.

His hazel eyes twinkled a pleasant moment.

Right away, Herminia noticed a difference in the pictograph cave. It was rougher. Wider. Machine-hewn. She placed a hand on the wall and felt a slight vibration, but when she sought her ally in order to enhance her senses, to expand her awareness of the physical world to confirm the impression, the sailfish would not answer.

Not entirely unexpected. The Beyond was a strange place — and surely this was the Beyond. Only those brujos with Spirit power fully controlled the Beyond. Almost fully. No one controlled the Null Wind. Herminia could only hope they didn't run into *that* in these tunnels — there would be nowhere to run.

She didn't mention that, of course. Since the Beyond was ruled by intent, Herminia didn't want Faustino thinking about the Null Wind — he might just bring it on them as part of his Saw moods, just when they needed a See mood!

"What are you snickering at?" Faustino asked.

"Just thinking," Herminia admitted. "You finally get to see it in person."

"See what?"

"Haven't you guessed where we are? El Boleo mine, tonto."

They passed a hydraulic shoring with CAT® painted on the side. Red LED lights overhead dropped eerie pools of light every thirty feet or so.

"You're right," Faustino admitted, patting the steel. "We are in the bowels of the enemy." He gave the beam a kick for good measure.

"Soon we'll get to see what your fear brings us," said Herminia.

"I'm not afraid." Withering under Herminia's stare, Faustino admitted. "Okay, a little."

"Remember the raft?" Herminia asked. That was the only time they had actually traveled into the Beyond together, and the memory was as vivid as if it had happened yesterday. "Your fear created the raft, and the surface, and even our need to breathe. Likewise, your fear created these tunnels." She touched Faustino's arm, felt it flinch. "Faustino, you are the most fearful man I have ever met. I don't mean to insult you, it is the simple truth. You think you are angry at the Americans for what they have done to the mine, to Santa Rosalía, to your mountains—"

"Don't forget the missing children."

"We don't know that. But fine, supposing it is the Americans, or some of them. Faustino, you think you are angry, but you are not angry. When I put my hand on your elbow.... I know you like me, I have seen the way your eyes linger on my face, the way they caress my body, and yet your arm flinches from my touch like it has been burned. Anger does not do this. Fear does this."

"Why all this talk about fear? Get to the point."

"These mine tunnels represent your fear, the very heart of it. If you don't master your fear, we will die here. And if we die in the Beyond, we die in truth. Do you understand?"

What Herminia did not say, could most certainly not say, is that she too was becoming afraid. If she could not access her ally, she could do nothing to protect them.

Faustino freed his arm and rubbed it defensively. "For your sake, I will try to control myself."

The tunnel branched and branched again. The lizards rode Faustino's shoulders stoically, offering no guidance. Without clues, Herminia and Faustino followed the vibrations as best they could, choosing tunnels with more vibrations rather than less, on the theory that silent, abandoned tunnels could go on virtually forever. In the working area, they would at least encounter something.

A rumble announced an approaching vehicle. Herminia and Faustino ducked into a wide place to avoid being run over by the strangest, most frightening machine Herminia had ever seen. It seemed to have metal teeth all over, front, sides, top, bottom, all at vicious angles and all on whirling disks. Clearly this contraption dug the tunnels, attacking the rock from every direction at once. If they got in the way, their bodies wouldn't even register to it as a bloody smear. The digger roared past in a screech of metal and power, an industrial-age Tyrannosaurus rex. The driver's head swiveled to stare at them, though it was no driver at all, but rather a three-dimensional shadow with dim glowing points for eyes.

"Follow it," Faustino said.

They did, at a brisk jog.

Dust assailed their lungs and stung their eyes. A metallic taste coated their tongues. Herminia tried clearing the air with intent, but her ally did not respond. She and Faustino began coughing every few steps.

The lizards became more agitated. Possibly a good sign.

The tunnel came to parallel a long conveyor belt on which ran a continual stream of blue-green ore. The pieces jostling along the belt had been shattered by the digging machine; their fresh cuts sparkled as beautifully as a beetle's carapace.

Both lizards gathered on Faustino's right shoulder, and Faustino cried out as their claws dug into his collar bone. He manhandled them on the ground.

"Hey, careful!" Herminia said. "They have been good to us."

"Something is coming," Faustino said, peering ahead.

At first, Herminia didn't see anything. There were no approaching headlights, just a tunnel continuing forward, forward at a slight downward slope, and red LEDs to illuminate the dusty haze. If there were turns, they were beyond sight.

"It is not really there," Faustino said. "It is, ah, an absence. Something in the dust."

Herminia saw nothing. The lizards turned circles, nipping at each other's tails. The conveyor rolled on, a continuous belt of—

"Um, Faustino, the conveyor belt," Herminia said.

Instead of shards of every imaginable shape, the conveyor belt hauled smoother shapes. Near ovals. One of them vibrated over, and the distinct bowl-like impression became obvious. The distant machine was hammering off copper ore in the shape of mortars. Herminia reached down and lifted one of the heavy bowls from the conveyor belt. Two of its sides were smooth, but the front had the beginnings of a face. Something pointed and hairy ... maybe an opossum?

A werewolf?

The face seemed to be straining against the stone, trying to manifest—

"Here they come," Faustino said.

They were a mockery of miners. Nothing more than shadows with outlines of safety helmets and overalls and work boots and pinpoints for eyes. Hundreds of them, filling the tunnel from one side to another. On and on they came, a shadow army.

The partly-formed mortar spilled from Herminia's hand to the ground.

Lemon and Jefferson bolted, and Herminia and Faustino followed. When the lizards turned right, they turned right, when the lizards turned left, they followed. No matter how their lungs burned in the dust-filled air and how their muscles cried out to stop, they kept running. Finally, the four of them, Herminia, Faustino, Lemon, and Jefferson emerged into a surreal landscape. To their right were the buildings of El Boleo mine: bunk house, water tank, rock crushers, vehicles, and outhouses. To their left yawned a giant, open pit, so wide they could not see the other side. The many layers of soil and rock were as colorful as the photos Herminia had seen of Copper Canyon, México's greatest natural wonder: gold, orange, yellow, pink, lilac, and lavender....

Herminia didn't have time to process whether the beauty of the exposed striations was the more breathtaking, or the scope of the hole (and resultant alteration of the mountain) the more shocking, for a murmur of voices began to fill her head. At first, she thought she was hearing the army at their heels, but this was more regular, more insistent than that. Voices without end. Not the annoyance of an argument outside your open window, nor the imposition of a phone call you were not a party to, but rather like when, as a child, you faced the nightly fear of turning out the light and sleeping between cold sheets, alone, and the reassuring sound of your parents talking came to you from the other room. A comforting, reassuring babble.

Indistinct yet familiar voices.

Coming from inside her own head.

Herminia's shoulders relaxed; she felt at once at ease.

The blind and deaf-mute lizards scurried over to a sedan and flushed a brown squirrel from beneath.

"Faustino," Herminia said, recognizing that the half-formed, pointy face on copper-ore mortars had been a squirrel. "Your ally. Your Mental ally."

From the mine at their backs poured the shadow-miners. Here in direct sunlight their forms could be clearly seen: boots, overalls, dusty jackets, and helmets. Their brown, dirty faces blurred when regarded too closely.

"I feel it," Faustino said, grinning. "I feel your thoughts. All of your thoughts. It is like—" He closed his eyes, put his fingertips on his temples.

The shadow miners stopped advancing. They became agitated.

Faustino's fingertips lifted and reset; his lip lifted into a triumphant snarl.

The shadow-miners started shoving each other. One of them clubbed another, knocking him to the ground.

"Faustino, what are you doing?"

"Pitting them against each other. I see it now. Yes, of course!"

The shadow miners began fighting, trading blows, stomping anyone who fell to the ground. Machinery fired up. An ore truck roared by and plowed through the shadows. Indistinct, male shouting filled the air.

Shouting and cursing....

Shouting and wailing.

Lemon and Jefferson took one last look at the melee and darted away. The squirrel ally climbed atop the roof of the sedan and stood in its hind legs, its little arms waving as if directing traffic.

Herminia didn't know what was happening, but she didn't like it at all. She had a terrible feeling that these shadow people were more than they seemed.

"Come on," Herminia said, tugging Faustino's arm. "You have your ally. Let's get out of here."

"I'm not leaving," Faustino said. "This is a place of my own creation. You said so yourself: a place of my own fear. I intend on facing it, here, now. Facing it — and destroying it!"

"These are not Americans. These are poor miners, Mexicans." Herminia tried to think of a language that Faustino would understand. The bunkhouse windows shattered; smoke billowed forth. "These are poor folk being exploited by greedy capitalists. They don't know any better. They are just trying to feed their families." Herminia let go of Faustino's arm and ran a few paces after the lizards. She paused and turned to catch Faustino's eyes. "The Americans did this. You need to go after the source, not these shadow people. That is why the lizard guides left. Come on, while we still have a chance to follow them. They went this way."

Reluctantly, Faustino followed.

The afternoon following the visit to the clinic, Lucinda met Eva and Mateo in El Jaguar's mausoleum. The three friends looked at the photos of Herminia's head. (Lucinda had convinced Mamá to take photos of it, and when Mamá went to the bathroom, Lucinda forwarded them to Eva.)

Mateo fingered his earlobe. "What did they tell you at the clinic?"

"The doctor said it might be an allergic reaction to a spider bite. The nurse suggested wrapping her head in a wet towel," Lucinda said, and scowled at the inane counsel.

"Anything else?" Mateo asked.

"No. They are going to look into it and post their recommendations online. They are afraid."

That wasn't exactly fair, Lucinda knew. The nurse had seemed kind, and only one doctor had seen Abuelita. Doctor Blake, the coward.

Mateo began tracing skulls in the dust on the sarcophagus. "El Jaguar liked to show me his work. Normally, he just liked to scare people. Along with selling dogs, that's how he made money. Mostly, it was just threats and big talk. People would pay him to leave them alone. But El Jaguar said if you didn't carry through with the hurt, the sheep wouldn't be scared. If they weren't scared, the sheep wouldn't pay."

Lucinda reached out and squeezed Mateo's free hand. She couldn't help it. He looked so vulnerable.

"The pharmacist was purple like this, as if a spider had woven a purple web all over his body. But the purple, the purple is on the inside. We are just seeing it through the skin. When he died, the inside of the pharmacist's mouth was full of webbing, as if his tongue were a trapdoor spider and it had spun its web between the teeth. El Jaguar pried open the mouth to show me. The pharmacist was lying on the floor of the shop, on his back...." Now Mateo wept openly. Snot crept out of one nostril. "The pharmacist's breath wheezed and made my hand wet and sticky. El Jaguar made me touch ... touch the webbing around the teeth." He mimicked his father's voice. "'*This is what happens when you resist me.*'" Mateo swept his hand across the surface of the sarcophagus, obliterating all the dust-drawn skulls. "Your grandmother is going to die."

"No, she won't." Lucinda said. "We are going to save her." She gave Mateo's hand a squeeze, then dropped it abruptly, crossing her arms. "Or are you giving up already?"

Mateo continued to weep.

To Lucinda's surprise, her best glare didn't seem to have any effect. Nor did insistent toe tapping.

Eva shrugged.

When it appeared Mateo's weeping would continue indefinitely, Lucinda reached out to his ear and gave it a sharp twist.

Mateo rose onto his toes and let out a yelp. His eyes widened in surprise. Which was, after all, the point.

He was so surprised, he stopped crying.

"I said, are you giving up already?" Lucinda asked.

"No," he peeped.

"I need you to focus. You are the only one here who has any experience with this."

Eva handed Mateo a handkerchief with an E embroidered on it. "Don't mind Lucy, she watches too much professional wrestling. We are going to buy her silver tights and a mask one of these days."

Mateo blew his nose in the handkerchief with a seal-like honk; Eva instructed him to wash it and bring it back.

When he'd recovered enough, from the shadowy recess behind El Jaguar's sarcophagus Mateo brought out a Gigante grocery bag. The bag contained Ziplock bags full of items — feathers, colorful kernels of maize, crystals. He also produced a small aquarium containing two lizards and set it over the engraved *Santiago Morales*. These were not the large Desert iguanas, but rather the little ones cats liked to pull the tails from. The lizards turned toward Eva when she tapped on the aquarium. On one, its mouth and ear holes were sewn shut; on the other, its eyes.

"Objects of Power," Mateo said, indicating the feathers, crystals, and maize. "El Jaguar was always muttering and casting these things in rituals. He never explained exactly what they could do, I picked it up by watching him and listening to his drunken rants. Except for these." Mateo opened the bag of maize and pulled out a single, purple kernel. No question, it was identical to the one Herminia had found in the sunflower. "These El Jaguar liked particularly. These were for cursing people. You could give them *la turista* — diarrhea. You could make them unable to have babies. You could give them headaches, smelly feet, or warts. Many warts, like a horned toad. They would have to remove them by surgery. When the skin doctor in Ensenada had bills to pay, he used to hire El Jaguar to curse rich people with warts."

"That's horrible!" Lucinda said.

"The worst was the Blood Curse, El Jaguar called it. He said it attacks somewhere that causes no pain, but affects the person here. He said it was a merciful death. I did not know what he was talking about, but I think I do now. Somewhere in that place we went, the Beyond, that's where the Blood Curse attacks. That is why you cannot heal it with doctors or medicine, but only a brujo can heal it. The sickness is rooted Beyond. Therefore, the healing must take place Beyond. Or so I think. El Jaguar used to threaten me with these things. Put maize next to my pillow at night, and I would spend days wondering what horrible disease I would contract. An itch on my nose, and I would be convinced I felt a wart growing there."

Lucinda felt a twitch on her nose, and resisted the urge to itch it.

"Your dad sounds horrible," Eva whispered, still trying to communicate with the lizards by tapping on the aquarium.

"He was not my dad. He was El Jaguar. I have no dad." Mateo shivered when he said this.

"And these?" Lucinda asked, indicating the feathers and crystals.

"For peace of mind, love spells, things people would pay for. He tried these on the dogs. They never worked the way he wanted."

"Do you think El Jaguar poisoned my Abuelita?"

"How could he? He was dead."

"Could he have done it at the Parade of Heroes, when they were struggling?"

"Maybe he was a ghost." Eva made a haunting sound that should have brought laughter but didn't. The walls of the tomb sucked in the sound and made it flat.

Mateo said, "Lucinda, you say that your grandmother fell down when the messenger brought the letter from the district attorney, that your grandmother lost her memories at that moment."

Remembering, Lucinda said, "A feather fell out when Papá opened the letter. Like this one." She pointed to a small, black and white feather in the Ziplock bag. "I didn't pay much attention at the time."

"She wasn't sick until that moment?" Mateo asked.

"No. Abuelita hadn't lost any memories until that moment. She was strong physically, tough as Patti, her goat. Normal. Her head didn't get splotched until—"

"Until after Mustache Man gave her the sunflower in church," Eva said, abandoning her project. The lizards seemed to be sleeping. "That's when Lucinda's grandmother found the kernel of maize. It dropped out of the sunflower."

"So, did two people attack her?" Lucinda asked, wondering aloud, "one with a feather and one with maize? That doesn't make any sense."

"Not a person," Mateo said, "a brujo. A witch."

A dad that is not a dad. A witch that is not a person. Lucinda was beginning to get irritated with Mateo's denials. "Fine. A brujo. That doesn't make him a non-person."

"Oh, yes it does," Mateo insisted. "It certainly does."

"He still has to act like a person. Eat and poop and all of that."

"Buy clothes," Eva said. "Get his hair done."

"Or her hair done," Mateo said. "There are brujas."

"With a mustache?" Eva asked. "This witch had a mustache."

"Don't assume anything," Mateo said. "Women from Argentina have mustaches."

"What?"

"Yes," Mateo said, "everyone says so."

"That's not true. They are the queens of waxing."

"That's Brazil."

Mateo and Eva got in a little argument about waxing and mustaches on women until Lucinda brought back the conversation to the here and now. "Maybe Abuelita resisted the curse the first time."

"Or maybe," Eva speculated, bouncing on her toes. "Maybe they decided just losing her memories wasn't bad enough. My dad is always giving me one punishment, and then my mom comes along and doubles it. So I get this, totally."

"That could be," Mateo said, "and here's why. There are three kinds of magic: Mental, Spiritual, and Physical. A witch can only perform one kind of magic. El Jaguar used Spiritual Magic. The crystals. He could give people emptiness. Hollowness. Despair. But cursing someone with Spiritual magic is long and slow, and he didn't have the patience for it. He preferred maize — Physical magic."

"If a witch could only perform one kind of magic, and El Jaguar could only do Spiritual magic," Lucinda asked, "then how did El Jaguar get the maize? How did he get the feathers?"

Mateo shrugged. "He was always searching for them. 'A brujo must always search.' But these are just maize and feathers and crystals until a brujo imbues them with power."

Lucinda put her hand in the bag of maize and let the kernels roll around her fingers. She estimated there were around fifty kernels in here. Fifty! So many curses.

Could the maize be used for anything good? she wondered. She pictured young Abuelita in her mind, a seventeen-year-old Herminia carrying the deer back to Don Esteban and laying it at his feet.

Don Esteban. The witch. El Brujo.

Abuelita wouldn't have studied witchcraft unless it could be used for good. Would she?

Lucinda scattered a handful of purple kernels across the slab of the sarcophagus. Many of them rolled into the engraving of the jaguar. Others stopped on their own, or fell with a tiny clatter to the floor. "If El Jaguar could only perform Spiritual magic, then how did he poison people with Physical magic? How did he turn simple maize into cursed objects?"

"Easy," Mateo said, "he paid another brujo to do it."

That stifled all conversation for a few seconds.

Eva broke the silence with, "You mean there are markets for witches?" She affected a market-monger voice, "Curse your neighbors, three hundred pesos, this week only!"

"He means," Lucinda said, struggling between laughter and irritation at Eva's irreverence, "he means that the witch who cursed the pharmacist is still alive. He might not even have anything to do with Abuelita. He might not even care who the curse affects. He simply sold his services to the highest bidder."

"Or she," Mateo added.

"If the brujo doesn't have any connection to Abuelita, it will make finding him — or her — much more difficult," Lucinda said, studying the random pattern of kernels across the yellow-veined slab.

"There is a connection," Mateo said, smacking his fist into his palm. "We have to believe that. And we will find out what that is — in the Beyond. The answer is in your grandmother's memories."

"So we have two crimes, potentially," Lucinda said. "One with Mental magic, and one with Physical. We think they are related, but we can't eliminate any possibility. And we have two places to investigate: Abuelita's memories in the Beyond, and Mustache Man here."

"Or the Argentinian woman," Eva added. She opened the aquarium and scooped up the lizards, cradling them in her arms.

Mateo put a few kernels of regular, non-powered maize into the mortar and pushed it over to Lucinda.

The pestle felt cool and comfortable in Lucinda's palm, more so than the previous day. She dropped it on the maize to shatter the hard shells so that it would grind and not simply push them around the stone bowl.

It was easier to believe this time. She had done it before.

Almost immediately a lifeline of power and sensory enhancement rippled through her veins — the red cardinal. Her ally? Yes, of course. Her Physical ally. She understood then they had bonded upon that first touch, when the cardinal's wing had clipped her, and she grinned.

A breeze ruffled Lucinda's hair, and the walls flipped away.

FOURTEEN

1967, Sierra de la Giganta mountains,
Baja California South

At a little rancho north of the mine, Herminia and Faustino rented a mule. The owner was an old man with more lines around his eyes than hairs on his head — and he was not bald. Faustino talked with the old man for some time, and though Herminia did not see any money exchange hands, the rancher became very helpful, providing a leather packsaddle, water skins, cheese, sausages, and tortillas for several days' journey, and even a sack of oats for the mule.

Estrella was the mule's name, for the white star on its nose. They hardly needed to hold the hand-braided lead rope, Estrella followed along so docilely. Faustino remarked that the farmer was an uncle of some kind by his mother's side, and that from then on most of the people they met would be relatives. The Arce family had raised cattle in these mountains for generations.

Faustino didn't talk much; he was distracted by the smoke that spread overhead in the shape of a mushroom cloud. The smoke had turned from black to white as the fire burned itself out, but since the wind had turned in their direction, it smelled worse than before.

They both knew all too well what had caused it.

Were the voices that accompanied Faustino's use of Mental magic tinged with disapproval?

That was probably Herminia's own bias.

Two nights before, upon Faustino and Herminia's return from the mine, Don Esteban had congratulated Faustino warmly, and showed his appreciation by causing the entire covey of quail to fly into their camp where he could twist their necks.

Through the apprentice bond, Don Esteban could access a portion of Herminia's and Faustino's powers, nothing to rival the magnitude of his own Spiritual power, but a sufficient quantity of Herminia's Physical power to make himself look younger and partially repair his broken teeth, and a sufficient quantity of Faustino's Mental power to make quail suicidal.

Herminia wondered just what El Brujo could do, what were the limits of his power, and how many apprentices he angled to enlist. She wasn't really comfortable with Don Esteban becoming more powerful … not with his lack of empathy for non-brujos.

She didn't think that becoming a witch was a mistake. It may have been possible to become one without apprenticing to Don Esteban, but how in the world would she have achieved it? Who would have trained her? The world was so alive when her ally was near. She had so much power! Power that could be used for good, she was sure. But there were…

…consequences. Yes, that was a good word. *Consequences.*

That evening, Don Esteban served roast quail to his now-confirmed apprentices. The smoke blowing over from El Boleo mine did nothing to sully his jovial mood. "Our work is done here," he said. "You are both brujos, and capable of making your own way. You are free to stay here with me to continue your training, or to find your own way wherever you choose — though I warn you that I have been putting off my own projects in favor of your training. My time will be limited. It is high time I looked after my own interests."

Considering that El Brujo had gained access to both Physical and Mental powers through his new apprentices, Herminia did not think he had neglected much at all. She said as much, and he practically choked on a quail-bone in mirth.

Later, *El Universal* confirmed Herminia's suspicion. A riot had broken out at El Boleo mine. The bunkhouse had burned. A number of miners were gravely injured — run over by a truck or beaten senseless by their fellows. The authorities were investigating what they called a "spontaneous outbreak of mass hysteria," possibly caused by LSD-laced food.

Faustino was very shaken up.

"I need to get out of here," Faustino said, whispering so El Brujo did not overhear. "The sooner the better. Come with me?"

Eying the quail carcasses littering the refuse pile, Herminia had agreed.

Sometime after midday and a meal of sausage and cheese, they came to another homestead. They had been walking since sunrise, and Herminia was grateful for the possibility of a respite.

This rancho resembled the place where they had rented the mule, and would have been exactly the same, Herminia thought, but for the confines of geography. Here, the canyons were steeper, the boulders larger, and the cacti more insistent, as if the forces of nature were purer here. From a distance, they saw the wooden structures of the compound, and a field perhaps two stone-throws in length across the canyon, leveled through obvious effort into the side of the mountain itself.

Herminia counted three buildings, including the common house with its wide porch, but more buildings were coming into sight as she, Faustino, and Estrella wound through the canyon.

A blue shirt worked the field across the canyon, and it rose and began an intercept course. It was the hottest part of the day, and they rounded the final bend into direct, oppressive sunlight. Estrella brayed, evidently happy to see a resting place ahead. Right on time with their arrival, the blue shirt arrived at the compound and resolved into a happy old man wielding a hoe. He gave them a grin with his three remaining teeth, one capped with gold, and doffed his wide-brimmed, straw hat.

"Don Ignacio," Faustino said.

"Welcome, Nephew!" The old man hugged Faustino. He turned cheerful, brown eyes to Herminia and gave a formal bow that would have done him proud at a royal ball. "Enchanted."

She held out a hand, and he kissed it gently. Whatever his status, despite having only three remaining teeth, he was as well-bred as any aristocrat.

Next, he kissed Estrella on the nose, and stabled her with the other mules. He insisted on doing the grooming himself. "I know Estrella, we are old friends," he said. "She would never forgive me if I let someone else brush her down."

Chatting all the while, he showed them his operation. First, the cistern, the ranch's heart. About a mile beyond the compound, hidden in the deepest part of the canyon, a natural spring had been improved with a wall of rock, making a permanent source of water that could be pumped along rock-lined ditches for gravity irrigation. Everywhere could be seen the love the Arce family had for this rugged land, manifest in generations of hand-work.

Faustino enthused about everything, and remarked on improvements since the last time he had visited. More rock lining to the southern ditch. A wider porch on the common house. A new outhouse. Herminia had never seen Faustino so animated. His cheeks practically glowed.

"Pardon me for making you walk after your long day," Don Ignacio said, leading them at last to the great porch. "I am trying to delay you. My family will return shortly and I want them to meet Faustino's new paramour. So, before my wife returns and makes me behave properly, who is this who makes your eyes sparkle so?"

Though this was often the way of the older generation, Herminia was slightly miffed that the old man had spoken as though she wasn't there. "I am Herminia Carrillo," she said, emphasizing the *I*. "And Faustino's eyes sparkle at all the women, so don't let that put ideas into your handsome head."

"Well said," Don Ignacio laughed, "and you see, I knew I was running out of time."

"Out of time for what?" came a woman's gravelly voice.

Herminia started. Even with her enhanced physical senses, she hadn't heard anyone approaching, let alone a woman and the dozen goats that had just sauntered into the yard. These were angora goats, with sagging udders and shaggy coats of the softest wool.

Don Ignacio bowed to his wife. "Nephew has brought a guest —
Herminia Carrillo. Time to put the beans on the fire, *mi amor*." He
scurried off.

"No doubt flirting like a rooster in a hen house," the old woman
said, coming over to embrace Herminia and kiss her on both cheeks.
"Or that other kind of house he's more accustomed to."

"Auntie!" Faustino said.

"You think I don't know what he does when he brings our wool to
Santa Rosalía? First the church, then the market, then, with his pockets
full of plata, the pink zone. Well, if he complains about what he eats
here or the lumps in his mattress, he can look no further than his own
empty pockets the next time he leaves town."

From the doorway sounded a long, happy violin note.

"You see, Herminia?" Auntie said. "He hopes to woo you with
music."

Somehow Don Ignacio managed to prepare a luxurious taco
dinner without ever seeming to abandon his violin. "Non-tradi-
tional," he admitted when Auntie was out of earshot, "but Auntie
could burn a cup of water. Better for a man to learn to cook than
to suffer or starve." Two more couples joined them after dark,
and they danced deep into the night and their bellies were full
and their faces hurt from smiling so hard. Auntie showed
Herminia and Faustino to a small room with two beds of straw,
and Herminia and Faustino lay down with their heads nearly
touching.

"Tomorrow, freshly laid eggs," Auntie said, kissing Herminia gently
on the head. "I can cook those without burning them, no matter what
Don Ignacio says."

When they were alone, Herminia rolled over to look at Faustino. In
the dark room he was but a shape, a familiar smell, and the sound of his
chest moving against the hand-woven blanket.

"How could you have ever left this?" Herminia asked.

The silence dragged on long enough that Herminia thought he may
have fallen asleep. Finally, she heard a substantial inhale, as if Faustino
planned to say much.

"In due time," was all he said.

. . .

The following day, after traveling an hour along the same mule trail as before, Faustino turned abruptly along what looked to be an impassable cliff. Indeed, their shoes slipped so on the sand-sprinkled granite that Herminia removed her sandals, relying instead on the steady grip of her bare feet. They meandered over solid rock, behind a stand of manzanita, and onto a secret path. That the path was meant to be invisible was obvious, for the path took great pains to slink behind rocks and dodge into the shadows. Even from the air, it would seem at most an animal track, appearing and disappearing with no deliberate direction, yet the weedless bottom showed it was much used by foot and mule traffic.

After a time, Herminia could not restrain her curiosity. "Why the secrecy?" she whispered.

"We will be killed if found along this trail."

She wanted to ask, "So why on earth are we taking it?" but refrained. This must be part of the explanation he promised her. So instead, she asked, "Killed by whom?"

"By Don Ignacio and his family."

"No mames!"

Don't suck tit! seemed appropriate. The cheerful old man and his family, kill them?

Faustino smiled. "We all have a dark side. All of us, Herminia. You, me, Don Esteban, my aunt and uncle. It's time for you to get in touch with yours, if you are to survive."

"Everything is so dramatic with you, Faustino. Just tell me already."

"You'll see soon enough."

Herminia didn't want to wait. She let her mind wander enough into the Beyond that the sailfish — her ally — became aware of her. Suddenly Herminia could hear a black bumblebee hovering by the yucca flowers, hear that its wings beat differently than the wings of the two wasps drinking nectar from the fireweed nearby. Besides the dim smell of smoke and charcoal — perhaps from the mine — Herminia didn't smell anything unusual, and so she dipped a tad deeper in the Beyond, until she could distinguish the very sweetness of the yucca nectar. The trail seemed to shimmer, and she thought with a little push she could go directly into the Beyond without the help of mortar or cave. Perhaps she could transport directly to their destination—

Herminia's foot dislodged a loose rock and she nearly rolled her ankle. To pay more attention to the trail, she reluctantly drew back into this world, where the colors, smells, sounds had become paler.

"Have you been practicing?" she asked.

"A little." Faustino's breath was heavy. "I do not want Don Esteban to see me practice."

"Do you feel embarrassed?"

"Something like that."

"You found your ally! It does not matter if you make mistakes, or if you don't know exactly what to do. El Brujo will show you. He can be hard, cruel even, but he is a good teacher. He has led us so far. Where else will you get knowledge like this?"

"You are right, of course."

"Yes. Except for El Brujo's dark side. Which is—?"

"He left me to die."

"Pish-posh," Herminia said. "That's not why you hold a grudge. El Brujo wants to elevate people, lead them to their ally, their full potential. Where is the dark side in that?"

"The trouble with El Brujo's Utopia," Faustino replied after a bit, "is that it is an exclusive address. Only a few are allowed in; the masses are excluded — unlike communism, which is made specifically for the masses. Now, be careful to walk on the stones so we don't have as much sweeping to do. We can't leave footprints or we will be hunted."

There was a twenty-foot band of fine dust across the trail devoid of prints. This obviously had been left there in order to see if anyone came or went.

The palm tree grove was larger than it seemed, and water ran in the bottom. There were fallen trees and boulders, and many places to hide. A number of palm trunks had been washed down and jammed together into a chaotic mess. Water marks ran halfway up the standing trees and along the sides of the canyon, where the floodwaters sometimes rose in the sudden thunderstorms of the mountain. The dampness carried the aroma of worms and decay — but also of fresh, green leaves. The creek babbled happily as it dropped from shelf to shelf.

"It disappears in the sand below," Faustino said. "It is a fickle river. But here it always flows, even in the driest year."

"So why isn't your uncle farming here?"

"He is, in a manner of speaking," Faustino said. "Come on."

The mule brayed behind them. They could see nothing wrong, but they hadn't been as careful as they'd thought. Occasional tracks betrayed their passage. Faustino began gathering palm fronds to sweep them clean.

Herminia drew on the power of her ally. She blew wind across the pathway, obliterating the marks in a matter of seconds. Faustino blinked at the fronds in his hand and the now-smooth sand, and let the fronds drop.

Up on the other bank, above the flood zone, they found the still.

"Let me guess," Herminia said, "they sell mezcal to the Americans."

Faustino shaped his hand like a gun and shot his index finger. "The secret of the mountain folk. To get hard currency, most resort to mezcal production. I do not begrudge them this, nor the fact that they pay no taxes. The mountains are a hard place with their own rules. Which, my beautiful Herminia, we are breaking by staying here. I am doubly breaking the rules by bringing an outsider. We rest a few minutes, then be off swiftly."

The still consisted of two copper vessels. The first, explained Faustino, comprised a pot, a hat, and a serpent coil. The pot was as round and tall as a black bear sitting on its haunches. A sizable hunk of copper. Nearby was a charcoal-fired clay oven through which ran a complicated irrigation system.

Cold to the touch.

Faustino indicated that they steam-cooked the agave plants in the oven for 24 hours. Once finished, they put these agave plants into the copper pot and add water. A fire under the pot would evaporate the water through the serpent coil, and little by little, drop by drop, concentrated mezcal would fill up the second copper vessel.

"How did you know no one would be here?"

"Because, my beautiful Herminia, today is November 20, a very important day for the Arce family." Herminia raised one eyebrow in question. "El Día de la Revolución, when we finally overthrew that dictator Porfirio Díaz."

"*Aye yi, yi*," Herminia said, shaking her head. "*Mi pobre Faustino*. I have a far more important reason to celebrate."

"Well?"

"Tomorrow is my birthday."

Faustino looked to see if she was joking.

She wasn't.

"Eighteen," she added. "Born November 21, 1949."

"Then you will see my home on your eighteenth birthday. What do you think of that?"

"We'll see." She smiled. At that moment, the prospect of spending more time in these lovely mountains was pleasant indeed. So, too, the thought of getting to know Faustino more intimately. As a man rather than as a rival apprentice.

They filled their water skins, rested, and after crossing the line of soft sand on the return journey, blew their tracks away again. It was a long walk back to the authorized trail, and if anyone came, anyone at all, they would be in a prickly situation. Fortunately, their luck held, and they made many miles before nightfall.

They slept exhausted on the naked sand without even lighting a fire, and Herminia wished Faustino would come closer. She dreamed that he was hovering over her, floating as if on a cloud, watching and admiring her body as she slept. Faustino wasn't the perfect man, that was for sure. He wasn't handsome like that actor or his friend, Curtis or Brennan. And he wasn't as fit or as agile as Herminia herself....

And he could be moody. *That* was the more important consideration. Could she live with someone moody?

On the other hand, he had the conviction of belief. The same sort of conviction as El Brujo. Faustino and Don Esteban shared that character trait, while Herminia drifted along the surface, adventuring, exploring, learning, observing.

Should she have conviction? About what?

She rolled to the other side, trying to ignore the lumpy ground.

Yes, conviction was attractive. Faustino was attractive. And convincing ... convicting. Whatever that word was.

She dreamed that they soared together on the surface of the ocean, surfing on the soles of their feet. They talked much and laughed more. Faustino tried to convince her of something, and Herminia wouldn't take it seriously. "What if you're wrong?" she asked, just to tweak him.

She awoke. The moon was cold, a sliver. Faustino lay about ten feet away. She called out his name to see if he was awake. They made eye contact, more a feeling than a seeing. Barely visible in the dark, a scorpion meandered between them. Herminia realized she was about to tip into a point of no return, and she welcomed it.

"*Venga*," she said. "Come."

Padding over in bare feet, Faustino skirted the scorpion. "Check your boots in the morning," he cautioned.

He lay down beside Herminia. Platonic, but not overly so with his body against hers, keeping her warm. Herminia was able to find the dream again, and she slept with a smile.

FIFTEEN
PRESENT DAY, PUNTA COLONET, BAJA CALIFORNIA NORTH

The three friends stood around Grandfather Pedro's slab in the Punta Colonet cemetery. Mateo unrolled a map over the cement slab and placed stones in the four corners to hold it in place. Lucinda rather thought Grandfather Pedro would approve. He had always been a practical man ... and it was a lot more pleasant to be outdoors in the cemetery than inside the Morales mausoleum. At least early in the morning when it was still cool.

The map was a confusing grid of pathways and rectangles, and it took Lucinda a minute to realize they were looking at a map of where they were standing: the Punta Colonet cemetery.

After circling, Mateo's finger landed on a rectangle. "This is where we are now, García — Eco family. Right next to it is where we found the flowers. Two of the plots are unmarked for a reason — they haven't been sold. But the third, the one that abuts your family plot, Lucinda, is owned by Carlos Serra, born August 1, 1947. Which makes him seventy one, almost seventy two. Best of all, he lives in Punta Colonet."

The names and some sort of number were scribbled in the "purchased" rectangles in an almost-indecipherable handwriting.

"You mean he's not dead?" Eva asked. "But who is buried there?"

"No one, I think." Mateo passed over a poor photocopy of some sort of ledger. About halfway down was a receipt for Herminia García for the purchase of her family grave site, February 26, 2011. Abuelita must have purchased the plot when Grandfather, Don Pedro, died. Just below that, entered one week later, was a receipt for Carlos Serra for the adjacent plot.

"The grave diggers helped me find this — an entry from the log book from 2011."

"Okay, that is just weird," said Eva.

"Or a coincidence," said Lucinda.

Mateo studied the map again. "Yes, I am sure of it. Your family plot is here, and Carlos Serra's family plot is right next to it. And the sunflowers were right between them. We could stake out his house, see if this Carlos Serra really is Mustache Man. If he is, I could threaten him with El Jaguar's Objects of Power. He'll know what they are."

"I've got something also," Eva said. She unfolded a full size piece of paper from her red purse. On it, Eva had drawn a charcoal sketch of Mustache Man. The clothes were well detailed, the sarape just as Lucinda remembered, but his face was very rough. "Didn't want to make his face too perfect as I didn't notice everything," Eva said, noticing their confusion. "False details could give us the wrong impression. But that's about it. Besides, I'm more of a fashion person."

Eva's rough sketch was better than Lucinda could have drawn in a million years. If they saw this man, they would recognize him against the drawing. Eva had even made photocopies.

It was all falling into place.

"This seems too easy," Lucinda said.

"What is easy about this?" Mateo said. "I happened to have grave diggers as friends. The grave diggers have the keys to the church. They were able to go in, find the log book, and copy the information. For anyone else in our class, this would have been impossible."

Eva eyed him incredulously.

"Bueno, not *impossible*, just very difficult. Give me some credit. Am I part of the team or not?" There was a hint of desperation in Mateo's voice.

Eva let him worry just long enough before conceding, "Probation. Pending administrative review."

"I still say it sounds too easy. The big boss must be concealed behind levels of lies and deceit."

"Unless he's not afraid of being found out. If he's powerful enough...." Mateo shrugged as if to say, '*El Jaguar* certainly hadn't been hiding.'

Lucinda had to admit, the idea of threatening Mustache Man with the Objects of Power was a plan, if not a good one. Other than that, she had no idea what to do if they found Mustache Man besides reason with him.

Since that second visit into the Beyond, when Lucinda realized she had bonded with her Physical ally, the three friends had gone to the Beyond twice more. They had gathered in El Jaguar's tomb in the late mornings (midnight would have been better for magic, Lucinda thought, but they had to go when their families were occupied), and Lucinda used the mortar and pestle. They had experimented, swapping the mint candy and maize for chilies (third visit) and sesame seeds (fourth). This had a small effect — the herb garden where they landed grew respectively a patch of serrano chilies, and small shrubs with long, thin leaves that must have been sesame plants.

Honestly, Lucinda preferred the mint.

Each time, Young Abuelita had been waiting for them in the herb garden. She wanted to know all about the memories they had watched, soaking up their descriptions with the eagerness of a child. She asked many questions, especially about Faustino, what he looked like, how he talked, what he said. She urged them to visit as many memories as they could, and to come back soon and tell her all about it.

Lucinda felt sorry for her. Young Abuelita didn't even have the run of the hotel — only that tiny herb garden. Lucinda would have died of boredom — if such a thing were possible in the Beyond. She began to speculate that this whole construct was a manifestation of the curse. The hotel may represent Abuelita's mind: the woman was locked in a tiny herb garden while her memories were trapped in the Mirror Garden. Maybe the hotel represented Abuelita's body, or her autonomic processes.

Whatever.

The important thing was that, thanks to the magic of the mortar (or to Lucinda's ally, or both), Abuelita's memories were accessible. She and her friends were unlocking the mystery, little by little. They had witnessed Herminia meeting Faustino and Don Esteban in a restaurant, and they had seen Herminia and Faustino find the blind and deaf lizards. In the final visit, they had seen the stunning water-world where Herminia bonded with her sailfish.

When they returned from that memory, Lucinda had confessed to her friends that she, too, had bonded with her ally — the red cardinal. Lucinda was officially a bruja. A Physical witch.

They were envious, of course, especially Mateo, who shut down upon hearing the news, hunched his shoulders and refused to talk the rest of the morning.

That just made Lucinda mad. Why did Mateo have to be so sensitive? It wasn't as if Lucinda had tried to bond with her ally — it had just happened. Not her fault! Her friends would have plenty of time to bond with their allies once this mystery was solved and Abuelita healed.

It felt as if they were on the crux of something big. There were answers in the Beyond, whirling in those dust devils. Lucinda was sure of it. She only hoped they wouldn't be too late. And she wasn't going to let Mateo's hurt feelings slow them down.

Other dust devils had led to unimportant memories — Lucinda lost count of how many. All of this took energy. A lot of it. One memory made you tired. Two was like staying up all night. Three, well, just thinking about that many memories made Lucinda's eyelids heavy. And they took time; watching a single memory required several hours of real time.

There was just no way to speed up the process.

Every day, Abuelita became sicker. Neither Mateo nor Eva witnessed it firsthand, but Lucinda lived it day by day.

They had to stay focused. They *had* to.

If Mateo's feelings got hurt, if he got jealous, so be it.

Mateo's blind and deaf lizards also had an effect on the magic (larger than grinding corn instead of mint). Their presence made Lucinda feel more in control. It didn't matter that Eva held them; their nearness was enough. Lucinda's intent became more focused. Figurative scales fell from her eyes. What was previously concealed became plain:

A passage from the Mirror Garden, another arched tunnel that led deeper into the labyrinthine hotel. And a doorway. Although closed, Lucinda was sure that doorway led outside, to the greater Beyond.

Two new places to explore — after they had viewed all the memories in the Mirror Garden. Not now. They *had* to stay focused on Abuelita.

That's why they had gathered in the cemetery with Mateo's map and Eva's sketch, to continue the investigation of Mustache Man in this world. Two worlds, two investigations.

Mateo said, "We were lucky this log was one of the old records. The new ones are all on computers and we'd have to figure out how to hack into that. Or get Father Ramón to look for us. That would cost us."

He was implying that Father Ramón might take bribes. Lucinda didn't like that assertion, even unspoken. She preferred to think of clergy as honest — unless Mateo knew something concrete.

"What sort of disguise should we use?" Eva said.

"No disguise. He won't be expecting us," Lucinda said.

"Are you sure this is a good idea? Mustache Man might be a brujo." Eva loved disguises. Once she dressed up as a clown and convinced random people she had gotten separated from the circus. 'Have you seen a big top around anywhere?' she'd ask. 'Bright color canvas? Flags snapping on top? Elephants?' It was truly amazing how long she could keep people going.

"Three kids hanging out together, that's our disguise," Lucinda said, wanting to nip the disguise idea in the bud before it blossomed. They didn't have an extra afternoon to create fake wigs and beards. "Find out where this is and we'll go there. Now."

Thank God Punta Colonet finally got a cell tower a few years prior. Before that, the town had been completely isolated. Eva typed the address in Google Earth and zoomed in on a small, nondescript rooftop on the far side of the famous bridge (at least famous in Punta Colonet), which crossed the arroyo on the northern part of town. This part of Punta Colonet wound around the beginnings of a canyon. The further north you went, the steeper things became. The buildings faced the riverbed, dry most of the year. It had two landmarks everyone knew: El Pajaro restaurant, which Lucinda's family had never been able to afford, and Las Conches Hermosas, a shell emporium. Kids could earn a few pesos selling shells to the owners, if they found a pretty one on the beach. Las Conches was about the only reason for *norteamericano* tourists to stop in Punta Colonet. That and a Pemex gas station whose public restrooms had never been open in Lucinda's lifetime.

A short bus ride dropped them at the shell emporium. They walked from there.

The houses on Carlos Serra's street were nicer than Lucinda had imagined from Google Earth. They had windows with shutters in bright, primary colors, and wooden doors instead of metal security ones, and the doors had fancy bronze handles instead of knobs with black paint. They weren't haciendas like Mateo's house, but they were comfortable. Carlos Serra's house was painted sky blue with white trim.

Lucinda noticed all this because they walked back and forth in front of the house about a dozen times, singularly and in pairs, in an effort to stake it out. Staking out was about the most boring thing a person could do, Lucinda decided. She would never, ever become a policewoman if staking out were part of it. Eating churros with black coffee she could handle. Shooting hoodlums and saving cats stuck in trees — fine.

Staking out:

No way!

Mateo seemed right at home drawing skulls in the dust with his finger. Eva wanted to play word games, which were okay, but then they forgot to watch the house.

Many times they had passed the sketch back and forth, trying to decide if Mustache Man from the sketch and Faustino from Herminia's memories were the same person. Both were skinny. They had similar cheeks and a similar bump in the nose. But so much time had passed — fifty years from the time of Herminia's memories until now. They just couldn't be sure.

Wait, was that— Did the curtain actually move when they walked by?

Lucinda stopped in the middle of the road and stared, and Eva had to drag her away by the arm. "He'll notice you."

"Who?"

"Mustache Man. That's who we are supposed to find, remember?

"He's seventy one. He's probably bedridden and calling for

someone to change his diapers," Lucinda muttered in frustration. She lost count of how many flies she had smashed. They kept landing on her sweaty arms — probably to get a drink, there was so much sweat. Soon, they'd be taking a bath. She could open up a fly spa in the crook of her elbow. "Forget it. I'm done."

She walked directly up to the house and knocked.

This time there was no mistaking it. The curtain got pulled aside.

Lucinda scrambled, very conscious of eyeballs staring at her back as she sprinted away with her friends.

"I saw him. He had a mustache," Eva said, ducking behind a parked car.

"You sure?"

"I think so."

Mateo just shrugged.

"Well," Lucinda said, "he saw me. That's for sure."

The sun crept past noon, and afternoon. The earth slowed its rotation. Hourglasses everywhere clogged. This was worse than sitting through a class with a substitute teacher who hadn't received the lesson plan. The most fascinating thing they learned was that Eva could wind her hair exactly eleven times around her index finger. Lucinda seven times. And Mateo one and a half.

Everyone in the neighborhood knew about the three teenagers watching the sky-blue house. A nice lady even brought them tamarindo juice in plastic bags tied around straws, which they sipped gratefully.

Toward evening, the door of the little house rattled. A rotund man wearing slacks and a straw fedora hobbled out. He used a cane in one hand. In the other he held the leash of a black dog. A Rottweiler.

Taking the dog for a walk.

The fat man's face was smooth and kind. It was most definitely not Mustache Man from church, who was skinny and tall. Lucinda felt a sense of both relief — the staking out was over! — and disappointment — their great idea had failed.

Mateo tugged on the hem of Lucinda's shirt. "One of our dogs. I don't know its name, but it's definitely one of ours."

So the man had money, and felt some need for protection, since all El Jaguar's dogs were guard dogs. This dog had a slow, arthritic walk that matched the old man's, and wouldn't offer much protection anymore.

"We need to talk with him," Lucinda said.

Her friends hung back a little, letting Lucinda lead the way to the man's stoop. There they waited.

After a few short minutes, the Fat Man returned. In his cane hand, he held a plastic bag holding a large lump that bounced against his cane with every step. He didn't seem the least surprised to see them. He placed the poop-filled bag in the dirt by his stoop, filled a bowl with water from an outside faucet, and sat on the top step facing them.

"Hello," he said in a friendly voice. Again, Lucinda was reminded of a substitute teacher: the Fat Man's voice projected, but without the confidence of a regular teacher. "Her name is Waffles. She likes to be petted."

Taking a deep breath to steady her nerves, Lucinda knelt and petted Waffles, noting its knobby joints. It didn't look mean. Or excitable. It lapped the water noisily. Its tail thumped against her leg.

Eva approached and took a photo of Lucinda and the dog, angling the camera to capture the Fat Man as well. "I'm María Hernández," Eva said, making up a name as easily as breathing.

Lucinda nearly panicked. She could never invent a name in a heartbeat!

"I'm Carlos Serra," the man replied. "*Mucho gusto.*" He shook Eva's hand without standing up.

Lucinda was thinking furiously of a name to give him. *María? Eva had already used it! What about Adriana? Yes, she liked that name. But what about a last name?*

"It is not nice to spy on an old man," Carlos Serra said. "What are you doing here?"

Lucinda felt her ears blush. She refused to move her gaze from Waffles, though she was acutely aware of Mateo and Eva trying to catch her eyes. Why didn't Eva say anything? Eva was the one who was good at stories.

Finally, after what seemed an eternity, Lucinda accepted that responsibility fell to her. She mumbled, "I'm waiting for my grandmother."

Waaaaay too close to the truth — but it was all she could come up with. She blushed some more.

Carlos Serra smiled, but Lucinda didn't believe its warm innocence anymore. Why would he need a guard dog if he were warm and innocent?

"I haven't seen you three around here before. What is your grandmother's name?"

"It's um.... Nice to meet you," Lucinda said. She stood, and the three friends backed away from the stoop, the man, the dog.

Mister Serra removed a cell phone from his pocket. He seemed to be aiming it at them to take a photo, and the three friends sprinted away, around the corner, down the lane, leaving a trail of dust in the air.

Later, waiting for the bus to take them across the bridge to their side of town and home, they went over what they had learned. Apart from the fact that Lucinda never, ever wanted to be on a boring old stakeout again.

Eva noted that Mister Serra's iPhone was the latest model. She also recognized his shoes as Rockports. "Expensive," she said. "And you can only get them in Ensenada or online."

Mateo added that the Rottweiler was expensive, too, and no one would get one just for companionship. So Mister Serra, if that was his actual name, had money, and some reason to think people would try to rob him. He must be corrupt in some way, since that was the only way to get rich in México.

"But," Mateo said, "that does not mean the man is a brujo. He didn't seem like a brujo to me."

"Abuelita didn't seem like a bruja to me, either," Lucinda said. "Did you expect him to fly in on his broomstick?"

"He would have," Eva said, "except it's too hard to balance Waffles on the shaft."

"How can you keep laughing when you're so sweaty?" Lucinda asked, but she grinned as well. She felt they were missing something, something obvious, and said as much. But after much discussion, none of them could figure out what it was.

They examined Eva's sketch again, smudging its corners with sweaty, dirty fingerprints. But no matter how they held it or squinted at it, there was no way to make the rotund Carlos Serra match the drawing. The Fat Man and Mustache Man were definitely two different people.

The bus came. They had to wait for an orange and white chicken to get out of the way before plopping on a bench seat next to an open window. An elderly woman on all fours chased the hen down the aisle. The bus was all squawking and rattling, diesel fumes and dust.

"All we are doing is collecting memories that don't seem to be doing any good. And chasing fat men and lazy dogs," Lucinda said. "We need a different approach."

She looked at Eva, who nodded understanding.

"My turn on the pestle?" Eva asked, her voice lacking its usual bubbliness.

"Your turn," Lucinda agreed.

Mateo pursed his lips. Although he didn't say anything, Lucinda could tell from his lips and the tightness around his eyes that Mateo was jealous that he hadn't been chosen for a turn. The mortar and pestle was his, after all. Or more precisely, El Jaguar's.

Which made Lucinda a little nervous. All those skulls Mateo drew in the dust; the way he had spied on her house with binoculars when Abuelita had been cursed; the fact that El Jaguar was his father; the gravediggers his friends. There was a sort of nihilism to Mateo that she couldn't put her finger on ... a darkness to his character ... and she'd rather not dig too deeply into it. Better to remain surface friends. Keep him close, but not too close. She'd heard that expression somewhere about enemies, and it seemed to fit Mateo just as well.

Close, but not too close.

From the aisle, the elderly woman shouted in dismay. The hen fluttered past and through the open window, clucking victory at its newfound freedom.

Sixteen

1967, Sierra de la Giganta Mountains,
Baja California South

"A thunderstorm is brewing," Faustino said. "Do you feel it?"

Herminia squinted up at the sky, crisp and blue, and seeming to shimmer from barely contained force. She was annoyed with herself for sleeping past sunrise. *The best part of the day, wasted. Some fisherman's daughter you are.*

Herminia rolled over, groaning. The soft sand of her bed had somehow turned to cement overnight. Usually she was first up, but this journey into the mountains had made Faustino a new man. Remembering the scorpion from the night before, she sat up quickly and examined her clothes and the dark hollows her body had made with the ground. It was well known the creatures liked darkness and warm bodies.

Nothing. And nothing in her sandals either. What had Faustino said the night before? Check your boots? Herminia had never owned a pair of proper boots and didn't want to. Too constraining. Too hard to shuck off if you fall into the ocean. Too likely to develop a fungus in the swamp of a boot's toe.

"Here, beautiful," Faustino said, handing her a small jar. "Homemade toothpaste. Coconut oil, baking soda, vanilla. You could do other flavors, but I like vanilla."

Not having a toothbrush, Herminia dipped her finger in the paste. "Yum, vanilla," she said, and used her finger to rub it all over her teeth, the gums, and across her tongue. Then she spat beneath a bush. "This doesn't mean you are going to get a kiss," she said, meaning it as a joke, but surprised at how easily her mind had dallied into the thought of kissing Faustino. Obviously, part of her was more than a little curious how such a kiss would feel. And the way Faustino had begun calling her *beautiful*. Unlike the sort of compliment machos used to try to make a conquest, this rolled off Faustino's tongue naturally, as if he had been thinking it for some time, and only on this trip had given himself permission to articulate it.

He smiled as she wiped the back of her hand across her mouth. "The morning will be more pleasant if I do get a kiss."

"You know, you are almost charming when you aren't so sullen."

"Don't forget bitter. And angry."

"See-Saw, I do believe you are developing a sense of humor."

After breaking their fast, they took a moment to appreciate the view. They were in the bottom of a gully, with steep sides leading to rocky ridges. Flower-covered yucca plants ornamented the walls like beautiful sentinels. Thunderheads piled up over the western horizon. From the bottom of the gully, it was impossible to tell how far away the clouds were.

"We get out of this canyon, we will be able to see Cerro de la Giganta, the highest mountain in the Sierra de la Giganta range," Faustino said.

"And why did you wake me up?"

Faustino pointed to a rounded form traversing the terrain. "He's slow, but—" he shrugged.

Herminia gave a delighted squeal. "A turtle!" For a second she thought it was her Mental ally, the sea turtle come to visit her on land. But no, this was a normal animal.

"Tortoise. Desert tortoise. Rare."

"Its wrinkles look like crumpled paper," Herminia said, and ran over to stand in front of it. The tortoise altered its path slightly to avoid her, but didn't appear alarmed.

"Enter its mind," Herminia suggested.

"Slow down ... I just met my ally. I'm not sure I can do that. This is an alien creature."

"Go on, try it." Reaching out to clasp Faustino's hands, Herminia said, "It will be easier to call your ally if we are already in the Beyond."

She hoped this were true; she'd never tried such a thing.

Opening herself to the Beyond, Herminia arrived in the middle of a shoreless sea and crafted from memory the log raft from their first visit. The sea was flat in every direction. In the deep water, a circling white form was all that could be seen of the sailfish ally.

Faustino materialized. His weight rocked the raft so that water lapped at their feet.

"I am not as ... bonded ... with my squirrel as you and your sailfish," Faustino said, a hitch of fear in his voice.

"Wait," Herminia replied, "let me try something."

She willed herself to feel the humid, mountain air of the Sierra de la Giganta Mountains, the trail and the stone, the altitude and the tortoise ... and also the wobbly raft and the briny ocean, to be in the Beyond and in this world simultaneously. On Earth, Herminia felt Faustino's hands in hers. In the Beyond they stood side by side on the raft, Herminia's sea legs keeping it from unbalancing. It was very odd.

"The squirrel isn't even here. You know I don't like the ocean—"

"Shush!"

Slowly, little by little, working one sense at a time — touch, gravity, smell, taste, and finally sight, Herminia changed their surroundings. The Beyond morphed into a mirror of this world ... though not a perfect mirror. Instead of standing on a raft in the ocean, they were in a gully, a dry creek nearby. But the sky was pink, the brewing thunderhead purple and green, a cotton candy nightmare that flashed black lightning over the sand and scrub brush.

"Call your ally," Herminia said.

A pleasing murmur of voices sounded in Herminia's head. Not loud. You could miss it if you weren't paying attention. But it was there: the sound of Faustino connecting with his ally.

With a Physical ally, one felt the hairs on the nape of the neck rise. Faustino must be feeling this, with Herminia and the sailfish ally so close by. (Herminia hardly noticed this response anymore.)

With a Spiritual ally, such as Don Esteban used, nearby brujos — and others sensitive to such things — smelled cinnamon.

With a Mental ally, one's head was filled with pleasing voices.

Faustino's rock squirrel ally scrambled onto the tortoise's back.

"What do you see in the tortoise's mind?" Herminia asked.

"Not what I see," Faustino said, slowly. "What I know. What I remember."

"Speak," Herminia urged.

In a sort of mesmerized voice, Faustino began. A minute or more passed between each sentence, as if it took Faustino a long time to sift through the tortoise's thoughts, or as if the tortoise thought as slowly as it walked.

"Many blades of grass, many cold seasons, and many trails. Tortoises, friends I remember by smell." Faustino shook his head in slow motion; his eyes drooped closed. "Shell patterns. I— I don't have the words. Beautiful, distinctive patterns. Familiar smells." He looked wobbly, and Herminia helped him to sit cross legged. "Sun. Dryness. Alkali — bad water, belly sickness. Desire. Males I loved, and males I accepted because..." he grinned suddenly, a grin that actually belonged to the tortoise, "...stronger than the others. Males I ran from as fast as my legs would go — I wished to be a deer."

Herminia couldn't help giggling. Faustino had obviously entered the mind of a female tortoise. *If all men had to do this,* she thought, *maybe they would have more sympathy for pregnancy and childbirth — and so much more.*

All this was taking forever. The sky had turned dark. She counted only four seconds between the flash of lightning and the thunder's boom. If they were on the panga, they would have anchored and hunkered below deck to wait the storm out.

But she didn't have the heart to call an end to the experiment.

Faustino's face now wore the content, feminine look of a mother remembering her children. "The feel of laying eggs. The feel of rain-drops on my shell. A welcome feeling. Happy. Abundant drink. Remembered rain from many times before, floods, pools, and easy travel, green shoots. Eat. Eat while you can. Alarming memory: rain and water, too much too fast, water that washed away the sand covering my eggs, then my eggs, a flood that caught me fleeing and flung me down a great canyon to an unknown place." His eyes twitched behind the closed eyelids, a sort of waking Rapid Eye Movement. "Ache all over. Climb — dryer places. Starting over. Puddles, springs dried. Many, many cold evenings. Alone. Moons changed. Days grew, shrank, grew. Loneliness again before I saw another of my kind."

All of this took over an hour. During that time, the downpour became real. With a force of will, Herminia left the vibrant Beyond and came back to the pallid beauty of this world. "Faustino, we have to go."

"Maybe eat a leaf," he droned in a sedate baritone. "A delicious blade of grass...."

"We have to go," Herminia repeated. "Pull yourself free."

Little by little, the voices that accompanied the Mental ally grew quiet. Faustino's eyes became his own. Herminia and Faustino still held hands. The tortoise was about thirty feet away.

Marble-sized drops of rain pelted them, so large as to be almost painful on their scalps. The gully was fast filling with water. It was a good eight feet wide and several inches deep. Lightning vaulted from cloud to cloud.

"We need to get out of here," Faustino said, blinking away his lethargy.

Good idea, swift. "Up or down trail?" Herminia said, slightly breathless. "Or do we climb the walls directly?" While the danger from lightening was real — and it didn't need a direct hit to fry you, not if you were soaking wet — in the bottom of this canyon a flood was the higher likelihood. In the oasis where the still had been cached, they'd seen the damage of a recent flood — debris deposited twenty feet or higher above the creek bed. A wall of water, mud, and rock could come upon them in no time if the rains had been falling in higher elevations.

"Up," Faustino said, still blinking away the daze. "In a few hours we will be at my home. I don't want to wait any longer. I have been away too long. Come on, this trail leaves the bottom in a mile or so. We can make it." He began stuffing their belongings into the pack, and Herminia hurriedly fed Estrella a bag of damp oats and brushed its coat to keep it calm.

Herminia walked beside Estrella with her arm across its neck. Each time the thunder boomed, its muscles twitched. "Faustino, can you calm it?" That would be a good use of his Mental power, she thought.

"I will try if the storm gets too close," Faustino said, a blur in the trail ahead.

Up, up they toiled. Breathing was difficult; the warm, humid air labored against their lungs. The clouds gave the earth a gray appearance, reminding Herminia of the way everything felt when she wasn't connected with her ally. Gray. Less vibrant, less colorful than the Beyond. But more ... tangible, Herminia thought. That was it. More tangible. Solid. She knew that dying in the Beyond was the same as dying here. But on this earth, the dance of life and death were all around: in the bugs, the branches of the trees, the desiccating cacti that rattled like maracas in the storm, the empty wasp nest made of mud, sloughing away from its perch drop by pounding drop.

A happy noise from Faustino caught Herminia's attention. A square rooftop had become visible, tiny in the distance.

"Your home?"

"Sí."

Herminia tugged and clucked at Estrella until it broke into a trot. The trail was too narrow to pass, and so Herminia simply shoved Faustino playfully. He stumbled, tripped and fell, as lightning flashed and the clouds laughed in great sheets of rain.

"What are you sitting around for?" she called over her shoulder, passing him by, laughing with the clouds.

His reply was muffled in the boom of thunder. Faster they ran. Estrella's tongue lolled to the side, spraying Herminia with saliva almost as fast as the rain could wash it away. It had a warm, grassy smell.

She looked back. Faustino labored to catch up. Fatigue showed in his broken posture. Whatever spirit coming home had given him wasn't enough to turn Faustino into an athlete.

The trail zigzagged out of the flash flood zone. Estrella's breath changed. Perhaps the mule was digesting food in a separate stomach, for its breath smelled spoiled, almost fish-like in decay. It was slowing. Herminia didn't want to win without Estrella, didn't want to leave the faithful pack animal behind — though she sympathized. This path seemed to go on forever, winding, winding up and up. The sand became slipperier. The rain, bother the rain. How she hated it!

All was labor and breath. Chore. Why struggle? Her legs were sponge-filled bags, holding water. Wind dipped into the canyon and blew against her, whipping her hair away, down the canyon. Her calf muscles burned with the effort of finding purchase on the slippery trail.

Faustino jogged past, grinning like a mischievous monkey. If Faustino had just kept his head down she might have relented, might have given up. But he just had to rub it in.

He's using his ally, she thought. *He's in my mind.*

Estrella wasn't slowing anything down. Herminia herself had been leaning against the lead rope while berating the mule to move faster. Poor Estrella! No wonder the mule looked confused.

Herminia cursed at Faustino good-naturedly, considering the use of Mental magic fair play for the shove. It wasn't cool that he had entered her mind without permission … but she dismissed this niggling unease. After all, she'd practically encouraged it with all the talk of entering the tortoise's mind and trying out his powers. It was good for Faustino to experiment, wasn't it? Later they would discuss entering a lady's mind without permission.

Never okay. Not now, not ever.

But here, under the deluge, Herminia had a race to win.

Besides, this was more evidence of Faustino's playful side. Brilliant! Playful, fun-loving, brooding brujo. As long as he didn't mind losing. For Faustino was going to lose.

The dwellings were in sight. Not one square roof, but several. She recognized the large public house right away. The others must be bedrooms, a loo, storage. Through the rain and darkness, they were geometric impressions. Faustino was already halfway there.

Herminia had come to a complete stop without realizing it. A thunderclap burst overhead.

He's still in my mind; still affecting me....

It was hard to come around, hard to break from the grip Faustino held over her thoughts. The way he impeded and slowed them. The way this storm makes walking so very difficult....

My ally is the Physical ally, not yours. I will win a contest of speed, not you.

Herminia reached into the Beyond and joined her sailfish ally. Strength filled her; her respiration expanded. Pain vanished; the storm became a caress. She wished to shed her clothes to feel the rain all over, to savor each and every touch. The headwind hadn't been real — that had been Faustino. His power pressed against her mind, but Herminia shunted it to the side, began to run as she had never run before. Her thigh muscles were sinew and strength; her calf muscles pressed her feet into the sand, digging in, tearing forward the way a badger tore open a hole in the ground. Sensing Herminia's newfound resolve, Estrella galloped also, glad to have firm, steady direction.

A good effort, but too late. Faustino had too much of a lead. It had taken too long to realize his trick.

Herminia pulled more power from her ally and unleashed a deluge on Faustino: blinding, driving sheets of rain just for his benefit.

Still not enough. He had nearly reached the compound. A few steps only.

Herminia released the lead rope and shifted form. Hardly a conscious thought (if she had tried to puzzle it out she never would have succeeded), her clothes slipped off like the film on a kettle of burned milk; she dropped onto all fours and bounded ahead at fifty miles an hour.

A puma.

The pressure on Herminia's mind disappeared in the instant of victory. In the wide open space between buildings, she regained human form, naked. The hair on Herminia's nape stood on end, quivering like a wire brush — a characteristic of intense Physical magic. Herminia's body, still in touch with the sailfish ally, felt every drop of water that pounded onto her flesh, the rivulet that gathered between her collar bones, poured from her navel over her belly, and caressed her thighs.

A barrel stood at the corner of the stable to collect the roof runoff, and by stepping behind it she could conceal her bottom half. Sort of. She did so, then crossed her arms across her chest, suddenly self-conscious.

Thank goodness the clouds made it dark.

Faustino arrived, heaving with the effort to breathe, holding Estrella's lead rope. He praised Herminia's victory, and burst out laughing.

"Well?" she said, joining in the laughter.

"Hmm?"

"My clothes, tonto."

"Oh, right."

He gathered them and, eyes averted, handed them to Herminia.

She dressed quickly. Teasing Faustino no longer brought a sense of power; now it made her feel self-conscious, vulnerable.

Did he find her attractive? Would he like her? Was he the right man for her?

The pulse in her fingertips thumped with awakened questions.

The stable had not been used in some time, but it was dry and full of old straw. They stabled Estrella and put on its nosebag. Then she and Faustino faced each other. Uncharacteristically bold, Faustino leaned down and kissed Herminia on the lips. His mouth tasted of homemade vanilla toothpaste. The stubble on his face itched pleasantly against her cheek.

Everything was so electrifying when holding the Physical ally, Herminia was afraid her body would betray her. She wanted her decisions to be completely hers, not the result of overstimulated, ally-enhanced senses. Reluctantly, she released the sailfish.

Faustino sensed the change. He stepped back, brushed a strand of hair from her face. "I want to show you my home."

"Now? In the rain?" she said, noting how lovely Faustino was with the fire of home in his eyes.

"No better time."

Today I am eighteen, Herminia thought, *and it is very good to be alive and a bruja. I think I am falling in love.*

She reached out and took Faustino's hand.

SEVENTEEN
PRESENT DAY, BEYOND

Dusk, the sun setting over the rough countryside, turning the mining relics orange and black. The smell of cilantro, chili, and tomatoes in the air. Eva had wanted to go all out for her turn at the mortar, and had brought to El Jaguar's tomb myriad baggies filled with ingredients for salsa.

It certainly had made a difference: different time of day, the aged look to the hotel's plaster, the fact that they had arrived outside the hotel rather than in the herb garden, the lack of dust devils, the absence of Young Abuelita.

There was also a different feel to the place.

Emptiness. That was how Lucinda thought of it. Emptiness. Possibly because no one was here to greet them, though Lucinda doubted that. The feeling was too fundamental.

Eva dipped a tortilla chip in the mortar and crunched it. Her blond eyebrows shot up appreciatively. "You guys have to try this."

Lucinda smiled at her friend's irreverence to the place's solemnity, and noted that the mortar and pestle had come into the Beyond with them. Maybe she could do that too, Lucinda thought, if she had food worth bringing. She would have to try next time. It made sense — lots of other things had come with them also. Their clothes, for example. Thank God.

If the hotel was a real place in the real world, Lucinda was pretty sure this wasn't its real setting. They were at El Boleo copper mine. No one would put a fancy hotel in the parking lot of a mine, would they? No, this was the Beyond playing tricks — or reading their intent. They had seen the mine in Herminia's memories, maybe the Beyond drew the hotel and the mine together for the experience.

Lucinda and her friends stood before a tall, plastered wall and wooden door, closed. An ornate, cement frame surrounded the door. It must have been something in its day. They could see the tile rooftop of the two-story hotel behind it, and also the palm trees in the Mirror Garden.

Turning away from the hotel, the mine's buildings lay all around them — bunk house, water tower, elevator, and ore-crushing machinery. On the far side of this yawned the colorful striations of the open-pit mine.

"Do you have the lizards?" Lucinda asked suddenly.

"Right here," Eva said. The little critters had climbed inside her shirt.

A flight of bats startled them. The girls ducked. Mateo shooed the bats with his hands as they flitted around his head before flying off towards the setting sun.

"I think you have found your ally," Lucinda remarked to Eva, straightening.

"Bats?" replied Eva, "That should be Mateo's ally."

Lucinda pointed to a large knot-hole halfway up the wood frame of the water tower from which a bird watched them with curious eyes. "A Gila woodpecker. Don't ask me how I know that."

They walked closer, feet crunching on dried weeds and pebbles. Zebra-like stripes marked the woodpecker's wings; its body was tawny; and a red, thumbprint-like mark crowned its head.

Mateo offered his arm for the woodpecker to perch on, but it remained in the hole, head cocked to the side. Disappointed, Mateo said, "Tell it to fly to your arm, Eva."

Eva put her two index fingers next to her temples like little antennas.

Her voice took on the quality of a horror film actor. "Fly to me, my little chickadee. Fly, peck, sing at my command!" Nothing happened. "All right, on the count of three, then. *Uno, dos, tres!*"

"Little communication problem," Lucinda said. "I think it pooped."

"Ah ha," Eva boomed, stretching out her arms to embrace the universe, "that is what I was telling it to do with my mind."

"Really?" Mateo asked.

"Okay," Lucinda laughed, "so maybe it's not your ally."

Eva hit Mateo's shoulder to emphasize that she had been joking, which was really a nice gesture. Ordinarily, she would have kept the gag going as long as the mark followed along. Mateo must be growing on her.

The laughter died, and the strangeness of the Beyond returned stronger than before. Eventually, Eva said, "I do think I feel something from the woodpecker. Some connection. Gila Woodpecker, you said? I don't know why I should be surprised. And yet—"

"And yet it feels different," Mateo said. "Odd. Very odd. Though the herb garden was odd as well."

"So where is Young Abuelita?" Lucinda asked, looking around. "This place looks abandoned. Weeds everywhere. Rusty equipment. Cracked plaster. No whirlwinds." She thought maybe Young Abuelita was not here because Eva did not have a special connection to her, and that made Lucinda feel warm inside.

Mateo pointed across the open pit mine. "What is that?"

What Lucinda had taken as the coming night was something else, a brown smudge on the horizon, more tangible than the absence of light. Smoke from a wildfire? She didn't like the looks of it. It almost appeared to be watching them, though that couldn't be possible ... could it?

"Let's um, keep an eye on that," Lucinda said.

"Yeah, good idea," Eva agreed.

Tearing his eyes from the brown smudge, Mateo asked. "So ... the mine or the hotel?"

"The hotel, definitely," Lucinda replied. The mine frightened her. The hotel was familiar; and that was where they had found the memories before.

They turned to the plaster-covered wall and the door. Some of the nails in the door frame had worked partway out. With a lot of trepidation, they wrapped their knuckles on it. No one answered the knock, nor Lucinda's call. After a suitable period of waiting, they tried the handle. It lifted easily, and the door opened. They stepped over a line of ants to get inside.

There was a long, empty courtyard, with doors to both right and left that appeared to belong to guest rooms. Straight ahead was a sweeping staircase and a grand entryway. They mounted the stairs, stopping before another closed door of knotted oak with iron bindings. In one window, the curtains were open and they noted a single electric lamp on an end table. Bathed in the yellow glow, Young Abuelita sipped from a sweating glass.

So, she is here. Lucinda wasn't sure how she felt about that. A part of her felt relief; there was always something comforting about having Abuelita around, even if it was a younger version. Another part of Lucinda felt a tad jealous to know that through the mortar, Eva could connect with Abuelita as well. She wondered if even Mateo could make that connection. That would be ... strange. He wasn't an enemy, but he was El Jaguar's son.

She sighed. They would find out soon enough; Mateo would certainly want to try his hand at the mortar.

This version of the hotel sure looked dilapidated. And that brown smudge: What could it be? Lucinda looked over her shoulder. It loomed higher than before. She didn't like the idea that it might be getting closer, nor did she like the way it seemed to frown back at her.

Mateo was already pulling open the door.

Young Abuelita started to her feet, recognized them, and sank back onto the flower-print armchair. "Ah, you came here also? There are no memories here. I have been all over."

"No whirlwinds?" Lucinda asked.

Young Abuelita invited them to look around with a gesture.

They explored. The main floor held the reception area where they had encountered Young Abuelita, a kitchen with old copper vessels still hanging to the walls, a large empty room that may have been for banquets (the room was empty; Lucinda's eyes were drawn to the beautiful wooden beams holding up the ceiling), and a chapel. The chapel's entire back wall was plugged by a dark, wooden altar with Jesus in the center, Mary to the left, and a saint or an angel to the right whose identity was hard to discern with the cracking age of the wood. The friends said a short prayer (Father, please keep us safe; we pray we aren't doing anything wrong by being here; help us cure Abuelita. Amen). Down a few stairs from the kitchen was a cellar where one broken, twenty-pound sack spilled flour to the floor. Otherwise, like most of the building, it was empty.

They mounted the main staircase. On the upper floor, rather than heavy wooden beams, the ceilings were smooth and painted white, stained in places where rain had leaked through. The hotel's bones creaked as they traversed the hallways.

It must have been built in stages, Lucinda thought, *no one would have designed such a strange floor plan otherwise. Just like a mind, built haphazardly, in stages, with elevations, cellars, captured moments, spirituality, and cooking — and more than a few broken windows.*

They saw the Mirror Garden and reflecting pool (black with scum) through second-story windows, but could find no way down to them. Nor were there any memory-dust devils in this version of the Beyond.

In its glory, with people bustling and the smell of food, the place would have been grand. With only Young Abuelita hanging out downstairs, it felt like a horror movie set. The beds were made, but very musty. The floors were swept. The cupboards were bare; when a knob pulled off yet another empty chest drawer, they stopped pulling on them. Their exploration passed in a frustrating blur.

Back downstairs, Young Abuelita was gone.

"Why is this place falling apart?" Lucinda asked.

"Think about it," Mateo said. "We are in your grandmother's mind. The curse is aging it."

"But why is it empty? Why are there no memories here?"

Eva touched Lucinda's arm. "More importantly, why is it not *completely* empty? Why is your grandmother's younger self here? Remember, Young Herminia said she was trapped in the herb garden ... and yet she seemed perfectly at home in the main room of the hotel, and even said that she had explored the hotel and that it was empty. So she is not actually trapped at all."

Lucinda berated herself for not noticing this before. "Or is this one aspect of Abuelita's mind, and another is trapped in the herb garden…?" Lucinda rubbed her temples in frustration. "Oh, I don't know. The longer we stay, the more questions we have."

"Do you think this is even your grandmother?" Mateo asked. "It could be some bruja impersonating her."

The three friends looked at each other, considering whether or not to be more afraid than they already were.

"Mateo's right," Eva said, "we can't be too careful. Is there some question you can ask that only your Abuelita could answer?"

"How can I do that — being as she doesn't remember anything?"

"Reverse psychology," Mateo suggested, "ask her something that she should not remember. If she answers correctly, we will know she is an impostor."

"You guys will make me distrust my own shadow. Let's get out of here; there might still be time to go back to El Jaguar's tomb and try the mortar again," Lucinda said, moving toward the door. "If I use the mortar, we can cross-examine Young Abuelita to see if she remembers seeing us." Not that that would prove anything.

Outside on the grand staircase, Young Abuelita stared into the distance. She did not turn upon their approach.

"Did you discover anything?"

"No, Abuelita," Lucinda said. "How about you? Are you getting better?"

"I think so, in that sense." Young Abuelita gestured to the brown smudge on the horizon. "I remember that. It is called the Null Wind. Within its boundaries, all power ceases. Your ally abandons you. You forget yourself. You are stripped bare. Very, very dangerous."

Suddenly the Null Wind towered above them. One instant it was a distant smudge, the next it dominated the sky. It resembled a sandstorm of enormous proportion, the kind of thing one might find devouring the Sahara Desert.

"Who did that?" Young Abuelita said, alarmed. "One of you three. Who did it?"

Tan, primordial dust comprised the storm, a tempest that moved without wind, a tsunami ready to break over their heads, a sandstorm trapped in amber.

"You need to get out of here. Go!" Young Abuelita flicked her fingers at them and the Beyond flipped away.

They arrived back in El Jaguar's mausoleum disoriented. The three friends shared a bottle of Señorial, having discovered that the tart, fruity soda helped combat the fatigue that came with memory surfing.

"This is good news," Eva enthused. "Don't you see? Your grandmother has begun to control her powers again. She sent us home! The memories we are recovering are beginning to have an effect."

"If it really was her grandmother," Mateo grumbled.

"But the hotel is falling apart; we're running out of time," Lucinda said, mentally comparing how dilapidated the hotel looked with how frail Abuelita had become. "Mateo? Did you notice anything that could help with the curse?" Lucinda had come to respect Mateo's powers of observation and analysis. He also had more experience with witchcraft than anyone else in Punta Colonet, except perhaps his mother ... and Abuelita.

"Why have the memories come to us as they have?" Mateo replied. "Why do we come every time to the hotel, when for all we know the Beyond is infinitely big? Faustino and Herminia even arrived underwater!"

"Go on, don't play Hector Belascoaran Shayne," Eva said, naming a famous Mexican detective.

"I think I know," Lucinda said. "We are looking for Abuelita's memories, so we arrive right where they are hiding, and see the ones we need to see."

"We see the ones—? We don't know what we need to see. Whose intent is working?" Eva asked, guzzling the last of the Señorial as if drowning confusion with real, wine-based sangria.

Lucinda shrugged. "Our intent, maybe. Or Abuelita's."

"The Beyond may have its own intent," Mateo said. "El Jaguar believed it was alive. He saw the Beyond as a dark thing, evil, but I think he carried his own pollution that tainted everything around him. The Beyond seems to me to be, what is that word, between good and evil?"

"Ambivalent?" offered Eva.

"Weird," supplied Lucinda.

"Yes and yes. Ambivalent and weird. Willing to mold itself around our intent."

"So why did the Null Wind nearly sweep us away?" Eva asked. "Whose intent was that?"

"I think the woodpecker was your ally," Mateo said to Eva, in one of his awkward conversation shifts. "Congratulations. Next is my turn. I wonder what I will get."

Lucinda frowned. She still wasn't comfortable with letting the moody Mateo run the show. "Mateo, we have to stay focused on why we are doing this. To save my grandmother! We can go back to get your ally any time. I promise, once we save Abuelita, that will be our first priority."

Eva nodded in agreement.

Mateo ran his finger over the rounded head of the pestle and didn't respond.

EIGHTEEN

1967, SIERRA DE LA GIGANTA MOUNTAINS, BAJA CALIFORNIA SOUTH

Faustino and Herminia wandered around the camp, getting soaked until it was almost more of a burden to get under shelter, knowing they would get wet again. Water poured down everywhere. It poured from the corners of rooftops and dripped from their eyelashes. It splattered into open barrels and pushed sand away to make new channels in the yard. It flattened the dead grass and, with the noise it made, turned the leaves of the yewleaf trees into chattering cicadas.

Faustino pointed out various buildings, along with a memory for each one. The mule stable. The hay barn. The well. The tanning vats and drying racks. *This is where Mamá would spend the day cooking and weaving. This is the woodshed where Dad would beat me if I slept in. This is where I would sit and carve toys from soft wood with an obsidian knife. Not that anyone would buy them, with plastic American soldiers available for centavos.*

They visited each of these rooms but the wood shed — that one was off limits. Too many painful memories, Faustino explained. In the children's bedroom (a separate building), they found where Faustino hid his carvings beneath a loose floorboard so his father would not take them to town to sell. Three were still there, a horned lizard, a coyote, and a turtle, and he gave the turtle to Herminia. Two he hid again as souvenirs to come back to the next time they visited.

Herminia turned the turtle over and over in her hand. It was a very touching gift — a very piece of Faustino's childhood. Was it a coincidence that, as a child, he had carved Herminia's Mental ally? Or was there some sort of cosmic connection between Herminia and Faustino? Almost surely the former; children loved turtles, and the rounded shells were probably easier to carve than mammals. Still, she liked contemplating that their meeting may have been preordained.

Back outside, a roar was building in the canyon — a flash flood.

"Stills will be lost this day," Faustino said.

"Are you happy about this?"

He shrugged, still keeping his face averted. "I don't begrudge the bootlegging of mescal. It is an old tradition here. But the gringos pay more, driving up the price and creating dependency on their currency. Of the two, I would take dependency on mescal over dependency on American dollars a thousand times over. Their money changes attitudes, outlooks. And when they leave — and they will leave when the copper runs out — things will be much worse. Better they had never come."

Herminia decided not to confront Faustino's hatred of the Americans with logic — easier to paddle a panga against a strong current ... with a banana leaf.

"Where is everyone, Faustino? Why did your family leave its home?"

"My family serves the Americans now." He said it flatly, without emotion, and she wondered if some of his family had been hurt in the riot that Faustino had engendered, and how he would feel about that.

Not much, she guessed. Certainly not regret. Anyone who sided with Americans was lost to Faustino.

They stood side by side, he looking out over the canyon, she taking in the abandoned camp. How many generations had lived here? How many hours, backaches, days without sufficient food to carve this homestead from the unforgiving mountain? Water pooled on the matted strands of Herminia's hair and drizzled down her chest beneath the shirt. She shivered and wondered at the hour. It was dark as night, but surely night hadn't fallen. Had it?

"Poor México, so far from God, so close to the United States," Faustino said.

"You quote dictators?" Herminia said.

"You know it? Most people have forgotten the source."

"Porfirio Díaz, El Presidente," Herminia said, referring to the man who had been México's president a total of seven times. Her parents were fishermen, and they didn't have much formal education — but they were also readers, and for years their debates competed with the lapping of water on the panga's hull to put Herminia to sleep. "I have often wondered, would México be richer if its neighbor were, say, Ethiopia? Russia?"

"At least we would not be their slaves!"

"Do they really steal our resources," Herminia countered, "or do we prostitute them to our corrupt politicians?" She said this partly to be a contrarian, and partly because she had seen the mordidas — the bites of corruption — more times than she could count. Fishing licenses, docking fees, health inspections — the seas were rife with opportunities for petty extortion. It disgusted her — and it had nothing to do with México's neighbors to the north or to the south. Corruption was México's problem, no matter which way the fingers pointed.

Faustino began walking back towards the great house. A few steps later, he said in a conciliatory tone, "It is a good question for philosophers, Herminia. I'm sorry for being angry. This is, for me, personal." His sweeping gesture encompassed the abandoned compound. "Not philosophy but blood."

Gloom once again furrowed his brow, and she regretted the way the conversation had turned.

They built a fire in the chimney of the great house using wood already gathered, very old wood, crumbling like the native Sierra de la Giganta culture. Hips touching, they sat in the fire's embrace and talked a long time, the conversation drifting to the safe topics of the Beyond, allies and magic, and El Brujo, whom Faustino feared.

Herminia let herself relax against Faustino's shoulder. On the ride up the mine road with Sybil Kersey, the conversation had drifted to men and Herminia had pretended to be experienced, while secretly envying the hippie's devil-may-care attitude. It seemed so liberating, like the wind in her hair and the thundering of the Jeep in her thighs.

Now, in the moment of choice, Herminia remembered her mother explaining how precious innocence was; Herminia should guard it like a treasure, her mother had said, making doe-eyes at father. Father responded by telling Herminia men would say anything, give her flowers and gifts, pledge eternal devotion, lie, whatever it took, to trick her into loving them ... as long as there was no commitment involved. On this one subject, there was no debate between her parents; they had agreed completely.

A relationship without the commitment of marriage was as useful — and as everlasting — as a sopping wet piece of paper.

In the ruddy, flickering light, Faustino's cheekbones looked strong. His teeth flashed white when he spoke, when he smiled. Smiled. *Faustino can smile.* Herminia leaned over and kissed Faustino on the lips. The stubble on his cheeks felt virile and masculine. Herminia savored the way his lips softened and molded to hers....

A colorful tear ripped cross-ways through the wooden roof, splitting the building in half, and pulling Faustino's left eye from his right. Everything pulled apart, revealing bright green grass, roses and palm trees. Herminia didn't react; she was enjoying the feeling of Faustino's warmth...

...and then the memory dissolved. Lucinda and friends sprawled on the grass in the Mirror Garden with a feeling like waking up in the backseat of a moving car at night, dizzy and unsure where exactly you are....

The memory wobbled next to them, a near-stationary cloud, various wisps and strands drifting apart. It looked like it was on the verge of breaking up. And then some internal energy started the spinning again, the dust devil regained cohesion, and the strands were sucked back inside. The whirlwind looked less concrete than before; Lucinda could see bits of green grass through the striations.

"Yuck, yuck," Mateo said, wiping his mouth and spitting into a white rose bush. "He was kissing me!"

"What happened?" Eva asked, rubbing her temples in confusion.

"Faustino was kissing me, and I got out of there!"

"You— What? You pulled us out of the memory?" Lucinda asked.

"That was disgusting!"

Lucinda managed to rise to her elbows, wanting badly to vomit, but not wanting to do so in front of her friends. She swallowed sour bile and tried to think neutral belly thoughts.

Rice. Corn tortillas. Rice again.

When her belly had regained some semblance of normalcy, she said, "I didn't know we could leave a memory halfway through. Useful. That could save us time if a memory is not getting anywhere."

Lucinda wasn't about to admit how disappointed she was. Reliving Herminia's memory was like staring in the world's most titillating romance. No matter that Lucinda thought Faustino was a disgusting creep who cursed Abuelita — Young Herminia didn't think so: she was floating somewhere on cloud eight on the way up to nine, and the memory ran through the experience from Herminia's mind. Recalling it with such vivid detail, Lucinda could practically feel Faustino's lips against her own.

"Maybe Faustino wasn't so bad back then," Eva mumbled, her beautiful cheeks as flush as plums. "Something changed — obviously."

Lucinda trembled, unsure her knees could hold her weight.

The girls caught each other's eyes.

"I don't think it's over," Eva said, glancing at the whirlwind next to them and winking at Lucinda.

"I don't think so, either."

"I'm not going back in there," Mateo said. "Disgusting!"

"We can't take any chances," Lucinda said. "What if this is the most important clue? We have to find out if Faustino cursed Abuelita. And why."

"I'm not—"

"Okay, Mateo, we got it. Just stay here and don't do anything. We'll be back as soon as it's over. Right, Lucy?"

"Right."

"Why don't you go talk with Young Herminia in the herb garden?" Eva suggested. "See if she remembers anything about our visit to the hotel, when she warned us about the Null Wind."

Mateo wiped his nose vigorously with the back of his arm, as if the memory was a booger he could wipe away. "Yeah, okay. I'll be in the herb garden."

The girls held hands and crawled into the dust devil.

The drumming of the rain had become irregular. Herminia was uncertain whether it was still coming from the clouds, or if the sounds were simply the soaked roof and yewleaf trees dropping their burden of water.

Listening to the drumming rain was a lot safer than acknowledging her panting, the quiver of desire, or the way Faustino's hot breath matched her own. Faustino's homemade vanilla toothpaste breath smelled delicious, and behind it drifted the sweet smell of strawberries — her favorite fruit. Herminia's mouth began to salivate. They relaxed back on the floor, and Faustino threw one leg over Herminia's. It didn't feel heavy or awkward — it felt right.

She grabbed a playful fistful of hair and squeezed.

"I've never wanted anything the way I want you," Faustino said.

"Did you see that in a telenovela?" Herminia asked, stealing another kiss so that he wouldn't ruin the moment with cheesy lines — they reminded her too much of her father's warning. *Men would say anything....* "Just keep kissing me."

The patter of rain became a languid murmur. The coals crackled and sparked, as if even they serenaded her.

"I want this to be perfect," Faustino said. "You are the only person who has ever understood me, Herminia. Can I say your name again? Herminia." He drew out the vowels as a caress. "Beautiful Herminia."

It was as if they drifted on a raft, as if the entire room caressed them. Faustino's kisses fit her mood — contemplative, exploratory, not demanding, while his fingers sent tingles that ran around and over her skin. It was almost too good to be true....

She blinked.

The smell of strawberries; the murmur of the rain; the serenade of the coals? Just like hypnotic voices in her head.

"Faustino?"

He nibbled her neck. "Close your eyes and enjoy it."

The nerve tingles increased in intensity. Strawberry smell flooded the room — too strong — spilled leche con fresas. "You're in my head. Stop it." She shoved him languidly, muscles reluctant to respond. The floor grew cold and hard. Had Faustino been so deep in her mind that he had made the wood floor comfortable? The thought soured her belly. "I am not some tortoise for you to read."

"I just wanted to make it—"

"Get off of me. I told you what I thought of Mental magic." She had meant to say "of compulsion" but "Mental magic" was what came out and she wasn't going to take it back.

"Come on, beautiful. Everything had been so nice. Don't spoil it."

The words fired her nerves like scratching on a chalkboard — with a nail. *Spoil it?* Her anger grew so sharply that if the carved turtle had been to hand she would have snapped it in two. The sailfish responded, and she drew on its power. Just in case. Faustino still hadn't removed his leg.

Faustino's eyes narrowed. "So it's okay for you to use Physical magic, but not for me to use Mental."

"That's different. I can't get in your head."

"That's what I do. That's what I am. My ally — it's part of me now."

He rose to his knees. She sat up as well and folded her arms across her chest.

"I brought you to my home," Faustino pleaded. "I opened myself up to you completely — every secret, every thought. I even showed you my uncle's still, and the carvings I made when I felt completely alone."

Herminia's scowl should have been enough to shut him up, but listening wasn't Faustino's strong suit. The murmuring voices revealed the Mental brujo hadn't completely let go of his ally.

"Do you know why I apprenticed with Don Esteban? While I love these mountains more than anything, more than anything in the world, I was not suited for them. I was a weak child — tuberculosis sapped my strength. I nearly died. And while my family would have cared for me even though I could not pull my weight, I could not tolerate being a burden to them. I wandered away, looking for ... I don't know what. I thought of suicide. I thought of prostituting myself to the mine. Don Esteban offered another possibility, another way to fight."

Crossing arms, Herminia said, "Do you want me to feel sorry for you, is that it?" She hated that nothing could be trusted anymore — not the warmth of the fire, not the smell of the air, not the thoughts in her own head.

Faustino took a deep breath. "You helped me. Without you, I would have not bonded with my ally. My *Mental* ally." He emphasized the word *Mental* as if the nature of his ally were somehow Herminia's fault.

"This is not about your family history," Herminia said, poking a finger in his little chest. "This is about borders and limits — and you crossed way over the line when you got in my head. I swear, if you ever do that again—"

Faustino reached out tentatively and Herminia slapped the hand away. She had to restrain herself not to fling Faustino's away as well — her sailfish was eager to fight. A puma-like growl escaped from somewhere in Herminia's throat. A tightness in her cuticles indicated that her fingernails thickened, grew claw-like of their own volition. One mental intrusion and she would transform. Yes, a puma. Black, shiny coat, sleek muscles, sharp fangs. How would this weakling deal with her then!

Faustino crawled backwards once, twice. "I see. Your ally is pure. Mine is dirty. Well, I'm telling you, this is me." He pounded his chest. The thump sounded weak, barely reverberating in his tuberculosis-thin frame. "I am my Mental ally. If you can't accept that, you can't accept me."

The desire to strike, to claw, to bite was so strong, Herminia barely managed two words. "Leave me."

The words sounded final, as final as the banging of the door at Faustino's back.

It took some time for Herminia to come down off the adrenaline and Physical power surge. She threw more sticks on the fire, even going outside to get some rain-soaked deadwood that would take longer to burn. All night, if she was lucky. She didn't want to have to use Physical power in order to stay warm.

She replayed the previous hours in her mind, trying to pinpoint exactly where it had gone wrong. Not seeing anything, she recalled the journey into the mountains. Was it the tortoise, when she had encouraged Faustino to enter its mind? Was it the race, when they had that contest of allies in the rain, and she had allowed Faustino to slow her down, delighted in it even, delighted in pitting her sailfish against his mole lizard? If she had said something then, when they had first arrived at the homestead, could the night have been salvaged? Could their relationship have been salvaged?

Did she even want it to be salvaged?

The only thing she knew for sure: They had gone too far, too fast. With Faustino's newfound powers, with their relationship. With everything.

She shivered in her damp clothes, wondering what the morning would bring. Wondering if she should even stick around until morning.

NINETEEN
Present Day, Ensenada, Baja California North

Lucinda's mother searched the house. ("Have you been sniffing glue?" Mamá asked. "Don't lie to me, I know you're hiding something.") Herminia was now bedridden, and Mamá actually shoved the old woman aside to feel all over the bed, seeking some hidden cache or seam, looking for a chemical explanation to Lucinda's fatigue. When that didn't pan out, she insisted Lucinda disrobe and undergo an inspection for malady, needle marks, anything.

It was humiliating, to say the least. Lucinda, of course, knew the real explanation would dismay Mamá even more than drugs. Lucinda and her friends had been using magic, traveling in the Beyond, and seeking some clue to Abuelita's malady.

Even worse, Lucinda herself was now a bruja. Albeit an inexperienced, bone-tired one.

"I should keep a better eye on you," Mamá muttered, mostly to herself, as she turned Lucinda's arms over looking for tracks, scars, or some sign of substance abuse.

Lucinda drew the line at her underwear. "Whatever you read on the Internet, I am not shooting drugs in my butt."

"Okay, okay. Maybe you have mono, the kissing disease."

"Maybe I do!" Lucinda retorted.

It wasn't Lucinda's fault surfing memories took so much energy. It felt as if she had run a hundred miles and then an elephant had sat on her head. Her temples throbbed that much.

Mamá had peered into her eyes, pulled the eyelids back to look at the whites, and grounded her for three days.

Lucinda groaned, crawled into bed next to Abuelita, and slept like never before. It was catching up with her, all this memory surfing. They'd followed Herminia's training — Abuelita's training — step by step until Herminia became a bruja, and Faustino a brujo, and the two had run off into the mountains together. So romantic. And ultimately, so tragic.

Mateo had exited the final memory in mid-stream (*That might come in handy some time,* Lucinda thought), and Eva and Lucinda continued right through the fight and Abuelita telling Faustino, "Leave me."

Lucinda was dying to know what happened next. When they returned to the Mirror Pond Garden, another memory was awaiting, beckoning with its closeness and its human-like, hourglass form. But neither girl could muster the strength to reach out and enter it. Without speaking, Lucinda and Eva agreed it was time to go home. They had to lean on each other to trudge from the garden, through the covered hall, into the herb garden. Without each other's support, Lucinda wasn't sure they would have made it. To lie down and sleep was nearly irresistible.

(*What if one dreamed in the Mirror Garden? What a weird idea. Would the dream go spinning away to join the other whirlwinds...?*)

Arriving in the herb garden, Mateo's back was to them. He was speaking with Young Abuelita — she with a hand on his shoulder, leaning in as if confiding some secret, the young woman's hair spilled around Mateo's face. He must have liked that. Despite being just some fragment of an old woman's mind, Young Abuelita's seventeen-year-old form was stunning in the white, knee-length dress.

Young Abuelita looked up at the two girls with a wide grin. "Well, did you have any luck figuring out what ails me?"

It almost felt like they were interrupting something, which was weird. Slowly, Lucinda shook her head. "We didn't find anything in the memories. Not yet. Though we did see where Abuelita and Faustino got into a big fight."

"Yes—?"

"It's sort of embarrassing."

"More than a little embarrassing," Eva said. "More like the Montezuma of embarrassment. Mateo practically heaved onto his shoes from having to watch it — and he pulled out halfway through."

Young Abuelita laughed, a tinkle of delightful wind chimes. "You can tell me anything. I'm older than I look. Right, Mateo?"

At this, Mateo spun rather reluctantly on his heels, and Lucinda got a first look at his face. If anything, it was paler than before. Scratch that. *Greener* than before. His eyes roved incessantly, as if he had been caught making out with someone else's girlfriend.

"Start at the ending; Mateo told me what happened up until he pulled out from the memory," Young Abuelita prompted.

"Faustino used magic on you," Lucinda said, "while you were kissing."

A pause, considering. "He forced me with Mental magic?"

Lucinda ran tongue around teeth, trying to recall exactly. No matter what she thought of that pig Faustino, she didn't want to exaggerate. "He brought you into— Well, I don't know. I think he brought you to the Beyond, but maybe not. I don't really know how Mental magic works. He made the smell of strawberries appear. He made the floor comfortable, and the fire and rain seem like a musical serenade." It didn't sound so bad out loud. But it was terrible. She knew it was, like El Jaguar and how, without Lucinda's permission, he had dragged her to a mockery of the Parade of Heroes. She knew now that he had been showing her the Beyond. A place where, as a Spiritual bruja, El Jaguar would have had complete control over the surroundings ... and of her.

Gross.

Worse than gross.

Revolting.

How to explain this to Young Abuelita without exaggeration? Lucinda took a deep breath. "The point is, Faustino entered your mind without your permission. He invaded you, made you experience things that did not exist for real. So yes, he violated you. He violated the integrity of your mind."

"Ah." Young Abuelita's grin melted away; her eyes glistened. Was that some remembered pain? Were they finally getting through, drawing memories into the old woman's subconscious?

It appeared so.

"Then you learned much. Do not be discouraged, Lucinda. I have confidence in you."

"I wish I could do more, Abuelita. I wish I had your strength."

"You have great strength, granddaughter. Great strength."

Lucinda wished Young Abuelita would call her Little Chicken. It would just feel nice. But of course, Abuelita invented that term for Lucinda many decades after quitting Southern Baja California for good.

In Punta Colonet, between waking and dream, Lucinda snuggled deeper under the single blanket and took Abuelita's hand. The gnarled fingers were cold, and Lucinda pressed them to her belly.

"I will be strong for you, Abuelita. I promise."

On day two of being grounded, unbelievably, Mamá forgot her cell phone. Lucinda could hardly believe her luck. She didn't believe it. She circled the phone, still plugged into the charger, like one might circle a wounded badger. Was this a trick of some kind? Mamá *never* forgot her cell phone. Had the phone been turned into a listening device? Did Mamá plan on checking the history when she returned?

Lucinda imagined some Jason Bourne-type software running on it, Mamá with an ear piece, listening and recording, John Williams music playing in the background.

A snatch and grab and the phone was to hand.

Lucinda returned to the bedroom, lay back against a pillow, and set her free hand gently on Abuelita's shoulder. Every now and then a tremor snaked through the old woman.

First, Lucinda texted the tomato cannery. "Hola, Lucinda Eco here. I'm writing to let you know my mom — Magdalena Eco — forgot her cell phone at home. Can you let her know? Gracias." The most grammatically correct text Lucinda had ever written.

Next, Lucinda visited the Flying Samaritans website, entered the ID and password. It was all in English, of course, but Lucinda could read that well enough to understand that the result was *nada*. The doctors had discovered nothing apart from the fact that Abuelita was dying.

That taken care of, she FaceTimed Mateo. He picked up, groggy. A pimple fiesta had broken out on his cheeks.

"I'm grounded," Lucinda announced.

"Mande?" Mateo's nose sounded stuffy, his voice thick.

"Grounded. I can't leave the house. We need to comb your list of customers. Can you get it?"

"What customers?"

"Your dog customers. One of them may have cursed Abuelita."

Mateo coughed up some mucus. "I thought we agreed this wasn't my family."

"We don't know yet. I'm looking for clues, okay? We don't eliminate anything until we have the answer. Until Abuelita is healed. Here." Lucinda turned the camera on grandmother Herminia, who, by this time, had opened her bloodshot eyes.

"Oh! It's crawling down her neck."

"It's lower than that. Want to see?"

"All right, all right. One list of dog customers coming up. I'll send it to Eva too."

"Good. Use your own eyes. You know these people. Pick the most likely ones to start with."

"Likely ones?"

"Ones that might be brujos or brujas."

Lucinda didn't think she had the energy to travel to the Beyond, and judging from Mateo's voice, he didn't either. Nor would he until his cold ran its course. The investigation would have to focus on this world for the moment.

When the list came through, it was photos taken of a handwritten ledger with columns for dog name, age, weight, litter, pedigree, and price — this last typically crossed out with a slash and another, lower number penciled in. On the far right, a column marked Customer. Lucinda sat a little straighter and pulled the blanket over her bare legs.

R. Hagrid
    Moliere, J.B.
    Zapatistas R Us
    F.T.B.
    Morgan Chase. Co.
    Liza Imports
    ...

The ledger went on and on. Initials, nonsensical names, company names. Temple throbbing, eye hammering gibberish. Maybe Mateo had an idea what they meant ... Lucinda certainly didn't.

No. Don't give up. Abuelita needs me.

Lucinda opened the sketch of Mustache Man. Maybe some holistic neurological connection would happen if she looked from the image to the list. What name did this sketch evoke? A movie character? Fake initials?

Looking from the sketch to the list, back again, Lucinda wondered if in the Beyond she could find this person simply through *intent*.

One thing was sure, Eva was a fine artist. If acting didn't pan out, Eva could pursue art. She'd captured the proportions perfectly. The string tie with horse-head fastener. And the clothes, just as Lucinda remembered them.

The clothes.

There were millions of sarapes around, all of them the same. Well, not exactly the same, but only a few variations of bright colors and horizontal stripes. All but this one. Lucinda had never seen one quite like it. This had subdued tones, crosses woven into the fabric, lines running diagonally rather than horizontally. High-end work. Even Lucinda could tell it was quality. Probably handmade, not mass produced.

Lucinda FaceTimed her friend.

"Eva, I've got an idea. How do you find an item of clothing on a celebrity? Like if you see an actress wearing something and you want to buy that same thing. Mustache Man's sarape is unlike anything I've ever seen. You look awesome, by the way."

Eva was wearing a black, one-shoulder romper. "Why, thank you. I had to use cold spoons to get rid of my eye bags. A lot of times the magazines will have it listed."

"And if they don't."

"Hmm. There are apps for that — Inspo can match just about anything using visual recognition. It's really geared for international stores, fashions in catalogs. There are millions of sarapes out there."

"Not like this one. Not the way you drew it. Is this exactly right, or did you take some creative liberty?"

"You know me, girlfriend, I always take liberties."

"Well—?"

Eva paused, clicked her tongue loud enough to register on the Samsung micro, and said "How do you remember it?"

"Eva! I'm no good at this sort of thing."

"Anything. Less stripes? Wider stripes? Use your ally. Go on. Try."

"Wait a minute." Lucinda carried the phone into the kitchen, retrieved the family mortar and pestle and some sesame seeds, and returned to bed. It wasn't like being in a mausoleum, but maybe it would work.

The walls didn't flip away.

She concentrated on the memory, ground the sesame seeds, tried to connect with the cardinal in the Beyond. *Yes!* The sleep-shirt hem between her bottom and the mattress became intolerable — she had to shift to be comfortable. The tag began tickling the back of her neck where the hairs started to lift.

Ignore those. Give me the memory of the sarape, she thought to the red cardinal. *Mustache man's sarape, what's different about it?*

The cardinal responded.

"It's not wool," Lucinda said, the words coming in a slur, fatigue-heat rising like a tidal wave of sleep. She'd pushed too hard, too hard... "It's goat, like Patti. I can smell the difference. And, oh, is it soft. I'll have to get ... one ... like ... that."

"Right, Mohair," Eva said, her voice distant. "Soft goes without saying. That should help."

Lucinda mumbled a reply, and the phone slipped away. *Yes ...* she thought *... I did something with intent ... I ... am ... a ... bru—* A red cardinal's trills sent Lucinda into a dreamless sleep.

Until midday. A message from Eva sent her scrambling.

Eva had found the store: Mercado Californio in Ensenada. They could take the bus there and be back by seven in the evening. The text continued, "Get this, Mercado Californio only carries crafts made by indigenous people of southern Baja."

This was it, then. If they took the sketch to the store, they were bound to find Faustino. Because Mustache Man and Fausino were one and the same — Lucinda was sure of it.

Ensenada pulsed with foreigners and Mexicans, booze and neon, hope and despair. Eva disallowed any speculation on the success — or lack thereof — of their prospects. Mustache Man had purchased his sarape in this store, recently, she insisted, and a clerk would remember him.

That decided, Eva distracted Lucinda by pointing out the well-known thespian establishments of Ensenada: University Theater and La Covacha Foro. The former was a modern, boxy structure that, at first glance, made Lucinda think more of bureaucrats and pointless waiting than a theater. But the longer they stared at it, the more interesting its architecture became. The roof didn't look quite square, and there was a giant crest or shield of some kind above the name. The interior, she was sure, was every bit as magnificent as Eva described.

The other theater was less impressive. All they could see from the road was a narrow alley and a sign: La Covacha Foro: Concert Hall and Art Gallery. From Eva's description (she had performed there — twice) "dive" was a word that came to mind, "cozy" was another. Lucinda thought the place would suit her more than the University Theater.

Mercado Californio was only two blocks away from La Covacha Foro, near enough to the touristy part of Ensenada to attract American dollars but far enough to discourage drunks. Sepia prints of *gente de razón* — early Baja Californios of mostly European descent — frowned over the merchandise. Gente de razón: people like the Arces, Faustino's family.

(Eva might be descended from a gente de razón, Lucinda thought; that blond hair must have come from somewhere.)

Many styles from these sepia photograph prints were echoed in the fashions for sale in the store. For the women: loose shirts with colorful neckline hems, pleated skirts with three distinct layers (great for twirling, a clerk explained to a couple of tourists — and demonstrated), sashes, practical shoes with low heels. For the men, flat-brimmed, straw hats of various shapes, stockings and durable trousers, tall boots with sheepskin uppers and leather bottoms. All of it modernized just enough to be attractive and unusual.

Soon enough, a sharp-looking young man bustled over to them. Eva showed him the sketch, now rendered in color, of Mustache Man wearing the unique sarape.

Lucinda let Eva handle the clerk. Eva could be demure, flirty, forceful, and vulnerable all at once. The employee kept searching Eva's face with his eyes, perhaps seeking her true age. Or wondering if she had a boyfriend.

"Yes, yes. We have several like that," he said, showing them a number of choices. "These are very similar. Mohair, you can't get softer."

"Hmm." Eva thrust out the sketch again. "They are all very nice. But I wanted one just like this. 'Similar' won't do. We know it came from here; a friend of ours bought it."

"Mercado Californio changes its inventory all the time," the clerk explained, pulling open another drawer. "These are all handmade — the highest quality. No two are exactly alike."

"What I'd really like is to ask my friend about it. This one here," Eva said, and pointed to the sketch of Mustache Man. "But I lost his contact info when someone stole my phone. What a bother! I hate that. Have you seen him? Does he come in often?"

The young man stared intently at the drawing, then raised a hand to signal. "*Clara, un minuto?*" He leaned forward and confided, "I haven't been here that long."

A neutral smile in place, a middle-aged, no-nonsense woman came over. Her smile disappeared immediately upon seeing the sketch.

"They are asking—"

"Yes, are they buying? Do they even have any money?" The woman had a hawk-like face to match her attitude. She pulled the sketch from the clerk's hand and creased it neatly in fours. "José, please go help those women over there. My English isn't good enough."

When he had gone, she said to Eva and Lucinda, "We don't release information on our customers." In a quieter voice she added, "José has already taken note of you, you can be sure of that. Please leave before he decides, well, just leave. It isn't safe." Hawk-nose returned the squared up piece of paper, with a whispered "Burn it."

In the few seconds of this exchange, fear had already made its acrid imprint on the woman's armpits. Lucinda could smell it.

Then Lucinda and Eva were back on the streets of Ensenada, losing themselves in the crowd.

"Don't you see, this is a clue, a real clue," Lucinda said, practically skipping down the sidewalk toward the bus station. "She knew who the customer was."

Lucinda was trying to figure out how they could stake out Mercado Californio — though she hated staking out and had decided at the Fat Man's house would to never do it again. She would for Herminia. Bother it all, she would.

"José had us rolled," Eva muttered. "I was sure he didn't know anything. And the whole time he knew."

"If what Hawk-nose said was true."

"Oh, it was true. She was no actress. But José, he could be on Broadway. Let's hope he didn't take note of us. That woman, the way she got so frightened upon seeing the sketch." Eva shook her head. "Lucy, do we really know what we are getting into?"

"You aren't giving up on me, are you?" Lucinda asked, semi-playfully.

"No! Of course not. It's just that ... witches, curses, attack dogs, weirdos, communists, and who-knows-what. It's getting a bit overwhelming."

Lucinda took her friend's arm. "You brought us here; I never would have found it on my own. Together, we are unstoppable."

Jangling and rattling in a diesel-fume haze, the girls dozed most of the ride back to Punta Colonet, and Eva nearly missed her stop. Later, as Lucinda trudged up the hill homeward, after having risked life and limb crossing the Transpeninsular, her mind replayed the events of the day. Her brief buoyancy had faded during the bus ride. What had they accomplished? They found out Mustache Man shopped in a particular store in Ensenada. Big deal. So did everyone for fifty miles around. They found out he wore sarapes from southern Baja. Which meant that he could be Faustino — something Lucinda had suspected for some time. Or even El Brujo. She'd have to pencil out the years and the ages and figure out if that worked.

When was Abuelita born? November 21. The year she couldn't remember for sure. Like, a few years after World War II, which was way hard to believe. Faustino was about the same age, so he'd have a similar number of wrinkles ... but El Brujo wasn't that much older than Herminia.

I mean Abuelita.

I'm getting too sleepy for this, Lucinda thought, *calling Abuelita Herminia in my own head.*

If only they had a photo of Mustache Man.

Oh, one more thing. The employees of Mercado Californio — Hawk-woman feared him; José reported to him. Mustache Man had power.

A brujo in Ensenada, maybe?

A brujo shouldn't be too hard to find, not if he made money pedaling curses.

Trudging uphill, mind duly occupied, Lucinda didn't notice the cars parked on the street in front of her house until practically walking into a bumper. Sunset was a couple of hours away, but clouds had gathered over the Pacific, and the light, although diffuse, splashed gold across the hoods of Papá's pickup and two newish cars, Aunt María's Mercedes and a deep blue BMW sedan.

Lucinda pulled up sharply.

Abuelita has died, Lucinda thought. *That's why Papá is here. That's why all these strangers have gathered. She doesn't belong to them. They don't know Abuelita the way I do.* Tears fought their way from Lucinda's squinting eyes. *Abuelita ... Herminia, I love you. I'm sorry I wasn't here. Dios, please protect my grandmother.*

She steeled herself before approaching the door.

Mamá opened it before she got there. "Where have you been?"

Really? Lucinda thought. *Abuelita is dead and that's all you can say?* She burst into tears.

Aunt María exited behind Mamá next, followed by Papá, and then The Fat Man.

The Fat Man?

Twenty

1967, Sierra de la Giganta mountains and Santa Rosalía, Baja California South

Without offering to help, a lump growing in her throat until she could hardly breathe, Herminia watched Faustino bundle up their gear and load it onto Estrella.

If the mule had kicked her in the gut, it wouldn't have hurt half as bad.

"We can be at the stables tomorrow evening if we push hard," Faustino said.

Now Herminia wondered what had kept her from leaving the night before. With the skills she had learned working with her parents on the panga, she could have easily navigated off the Sierra de la Giganta. And her Physical magic would have made the physical strain easy to bear.

Faustino had slept in, as usual, expecting the world to slow down and wait for him. Rather than apologize, or argue, or do anything to make matters better, upon awakening, Faustino had started packing. Now the gear was stowed, the lines of conflict drawn, and nothing could make it better.

Herminia lay an arm over Estrella's back, and her head atop her arm, partly to feel the mule's comforting warmth, and partly to allay mental fatigue. "Faustino, are we going to talk?"

"What for?"

The mule pawed the ground and whimpered.

Faustino's eyes, devoid of anything but anger, searched hers. "I have nothing to say that you would understand. That became abundantly clear last night." He placed a shoe against Estrella's side and, using the added leverage, pulled the pack girth strap one final time and secured it. "Let's get going before it is too hot."

As if to mock their distress, a spectacularly beautiful bloom greeted them on the trail, a sudden flowering engendered by the surprise rain: red ocotillo flowers on spine-covered, kelp-like branches; boojum trees like upside-down carrots sporting hanging clusters of yellow flowers; golden butterscotch poppy; royal purple lupine; and glorious desert sunflowers; not to mention stately vanilla yucca spires. Happy bees came out in force to serenade the flowers.

Herminia wanted to rip the blossoms off and tear them to pieces. Passing a desert sunflower, she reached down to do just that, changed her mind, and made Faustino stop the mule. Ignoring Faustino's exasperated look, she dug into the saddle-pack until she found her sketchbook, and where she pressed the flower between its pages. "There," she said, "something beautiful will remain of this day."

They traveled in almost total silence. Tension built rather than diminished.

We can't even be friends now, Herminia thought. *It would have been so much better if we hadn't come to these mountains.*

It was over. Their friendship. Their courtship. Even Herminia's training. No way could Herminia return to Don Esteban now — not even if Faustino wasn't there. Too many memories. She would learn on her own or she would give up magic. She could give it up. She *could*. She didn't have an ally before — she could learn to live without.

Everything had changed.

Everything was ruined.

They returned Estrella. The nice old man wasn't there, and there was nothing to say to the boy who took the mule.

Shouldering their respective packs, they stared up the trail, seeing the caves in their minds' eyes, considering.

"Are you going back?" Faustino asked.

Herminia shook her head against the stiffness of her neck. "Did you get what you wanted, Faustino?"

"Ha! What I wanted — I never came closer to what I wanted than when I made El Boleo mine burn."

"I was talking about us." Herminia hated the desperation in her voice.

Faustino simply stared across the mountains, pursing his thin lips.

"I can't help it if you can't control your impulses. I can't help it if you don't know what you want," Herminia added in a whisper, "but leave me out of it."

No wonder hippies are so casual about physical intimacy, Herminia thought, remembering Sybil Kersey. *They become numb to protect themselves. No emotional entanglements to complicate things. It is, I suppose, freedom of sorts. Though I am glad that with Faustino we didn't do more than kiss.... This is difficult enough.*

Faustino led the way back to the split in the trail, a T that could take them left to Don Esteban or right to the coast, and turned toward the left. "Once apprenticed with Don Esteban," Faustino said, "we will never really leave him. It is impossible. I have much to learn. Will I see you there? I will stay until the spring and then decide." Faustino was talking to himself as much as to Herminia.

Tears threatened to well up. Even though technically nothing had happened, Herminia decided to go to church and confess to cleanse herself.... But no, that avenue was closed to brujas. What clergy would forgive her? Only divine grace would do, not human forgiveness.

"No, my brujo friend," she said, adjusting the straps on her pack, feeling its lightness, realizing how few belongings she actually had. "Our paths diverge."

They kissed each other on the cheek and Faustino gave her a brief hug. Herminia hated how much she wanted to continue the embrace.

Numb, dazed, Herminia arrived at Santa Rosalía, hardly noticing when the meandering path spilled onto a bumpy, well-traveled road. The bakery beckoned, Panadería El Boleo, named after the copper mine. Its distinct, corrugated metal roof lifted in four peaks like a cubist's vision of ocean waves. She joined the line waiting to get in, mixed Americans and Mexicans jabbering in English and Spanish. Every time the door opened, the aroma of fresh, buttery croissants caressed the senses.

Hermina pulled her hair forward and tilted her face downward, afraid of being recognized by family (her mother had a weakness for the European pastries) or friends. With one glance, they would read the story on Herminia's face: love and betrayal and deep secrets. Herminia shivered, could almost hear Mother badgering her to go confess, calling her name, quietly, questioningly, not knowing that Herminia was a bruja and beyond earthly forgiveness.

"Herminia? Herminia Carrillo, pictograph guide?"

A question posed in Spanish in a feminine voice with a thick, American accent.

Herminia blinked. "Umm?"

"I thought I recognized you."

She'd been imagining Mother, but the voice came from Sybil Kersey, the woman in the back of the Jeepster who had shared the trip to the cave so long ago, the trip that had divided life in two. Sybil offered to buy Herminia a croissant here and a coffee at the restaurant nearby, which was what Americans did: American men offered to buy you a beer (if they thought you were cute), and the women coffee.

After they were seated outdoors at the cafe, Sybil switched to English and asked, "So, have you returned to work at the Loma Linda hotel?"

It had been some time since Herminia had had to speak English, and while embarrassingly out of practice, she was grateful for the extra privacy it offered. "No, I am, how do you say, loose ends."

"Loose ends are good," Sybil said, winking, "as long as they are not too loose, if you know what I mean."

"No, I don't. Is that an expression?"

"Just my silly double entendre: loose women? Never mind. I'm glad to find you available. In fact, I'm thrilled with it." Sybil laughed in a friendly way. "I am in need of a friendly ear."

Herminia nodded. "Good to see you too. I wasn't here in too long."

"So, are you going back to Loma Linda to apply for your old job? I'm sure they would take you back in a second with that smile of yours."

"No sé, mi amiga. No sé...."

The table outside offered a good view of the Iglesia de Santa Bárbara, a prefabricated metal church shipped directly from France, and designed by Gustave Eiffel himself. It was tall and slender and white, as churches in America were supposed to be. As with the entire town of Santa Rosalía, the church looked incongruous to Baja California, as if the town had been pulled out of time and place and set down here. In a way it had, by the first owners of the El Boleo mine, the Rothschilds, who imported most of the town piece by prefabricated piece in 1885.

"Your thoughts are far away," Sybil said.

"I occupy them with the history of the town."

"Easier that way?" Sybil cocked her head, like a bird who knew the worm had taken refuge in the acorn. "I am a woman, too."

Herminia cleared her throat — which must certainly have confirmed to Sybil whatever she had been thinking — and said, "I thought you returned to Hollywood long ago."

"I found something here more important than Hollywood," Sybil said, and waved a hand to indicate something here in town. "But this is neither the time nor the place, Herminia, trust me. These croissants, they are to die for! Too bad Mexicans don't know how to brew coffee.... I honestly didn't know you could burn it."

Herminia chuckled and let Sybil change the subject. Why not? They both had secrets. It felt good to be with someone who had no idea that Herminia was a witch. Someone to relax with.

As they made small talk, the American sought out Herminia's eyes a little too often. She asked questions, not out of interest ... or rather, yes, out of intense interest — the interest of a salesman or a seducer looking for some point in common to exploit.

It didn't take much intuition to guess that Sybil was recruiting.

Later, when the other patrons had vacated and the waiter went inside, Herminia tried again. "We are alone; what is this thing that is so important?"

Sybil's shoulders dipped a tad. "I can't tell you."

The hairs on Herminia's nape crept up. Her ally was close. "Are you in some trouble?"

"In the daylight no one will bother me. After sundown—" Sybil moved to sip her coffee, then looked at her cup in surprise. The cup was empty.

Instantly, Herminia's own troubles seemed further away. She embraced the sailfish, thinking *Physical power may come in useful outside of my training, after all.* "Let's walk," Herminia said, linked arms with the American and steered her toward the coast road. With heightened awareness, Herminia felt a slight tremor through Sybil's arm, whether from fear or too much caffeine was impossible to say. When the American indicated they should turn away from town and led them to a sedan, Herminia piled into the passenger seat without even asking the destination. With nowhere to go, no destination in mind, and plenty to avoid, she wasn't sure who had been leading whom.

One of the Chevrolet's valves closed slightly late, something a non-bruja would have never noticed. To Herminia, charged with Physical power, the engine rattled like a hundred drunken woodpeckers. With the smell of gasoline and the dirt road passing under the tires, Herminia put Faustino and Don Esteban out of mind.

Another trip into the unknown with Sybil Kersey, she thought. This one couldn't possibly be as eventful as the last ... could it? Still, something mysterious was going on here in Santa Rosalía, something that made Sybil afraid to be out after dark.

It hung there, between the two of them, the American still unwilling to discuss it:

What had Sybil found?

TWENTY-ONE
PRESENT DAY, PUNTA COLONET, BAJA CALIFORNIA NORTH

Lucinda's brain spun circles. Why was The Fat Man here? Did he know her mother? Her grandmother?

Of course! The Fat Man must be a brujo like Abuelita.

"I should have been here," Lucinda gurgled.

"Yes, you should—" Mamá began, and then stopped, sympathy softening her eyes. "Your grandmother is not dead, hija."

"What?"

They gathered around, this posse: Mamá, Papá, Aunt María, The Fat Man. All looking stern. Little by little, the adults moved in such a way as to give The Fat Man the place of power. He took Lucinda in under bushy, black eyebrows.

"You remember me, no? Señor Serra?" he asked, the dead smell of cigarettes puffing with each word.

"Sí."

Mamá patted Lucinda's back twice, gently. "We are going for a ride, hija."

The Fat Man opened the back door to the BMW; Mamá and Lucinda climbed in; and he shut the door. The Fat Man doffed his hat and drove off determinedly. Aunt María followed in the Mercedes with Papá. They paused long enough to get safely across the Transpeninsular

Highway, and paused again in front of El Jaguar's hacienda to pick up the Morales' car. Mateo rode in the back, his mother driving, he looking zoned out and lost, she looking stern.

The three-car caravan bumped down the dirt road that led, after two miles or so, to the peninsula with its cliff-edge view of the coast. Mamá stared at the progressively dirtier windows, hands folded in her lap. The Fat Man drove with both hands on the wheel.

Lucinda had never understood why the Transpeninsular Highway didn't border the ocean — what a spectacular view that would have had! Here was scrub and sand and steep cliffs, and the will-o'-wisp promise of a deep water port that would never come. If things had turned out differently: if the road fronted the ocean, if the government had kept its promises, Punta Colonet could have been a beautiful seaport instead of a dusty way-point for cars short on gas and bellies short on food.

Rounding a corner, three hulking, metal derelicts like beetle carapaces came into view. No one could remember how the ships ran aground or when exactly it happened. They lay sideways in the sand, defying the ocean to the last rusty girder. With her older brothers and sister Tina, Lucinda played in the wrecks as a child, played until the high tide sent spray and water-song through the rusted hulls.

Perched on one of the iron hulls, a red cardinal twitched its wings. Lucinda craned to keep it in sight as long as possible; the sight of the bird helped calm her stomach.

The caravan turned aside from the cliffs and took side roads that Lucinda had never explored. It was a long walk to the peninsula; she had never bothered to take detours. After a time, the road swung toward to a burned-out foundation and two chimney husks. From one chimney grew a substantial beavertail cactus.

Lucinda wondered if her body would be found here someday, buried in the ruins of this house, along with her family. What had the investigation got them into?

Wait. She had power. Abuelita's mode of power.

If Lucinda embraced the red cardinal she could shapeshift, could turn into a snake and slither into a hole, or a bird and fly away. Or a mountain lion and protect her family from The Fat Man.

Palms becoming slick with nervous sweat, breath coming in short spurts, Lucinda's mind had trouble staying focused. She didn't even have a mortar to help connect with the Beyond; any access to Physical power would have to be without props.

Wait, watch, be ready, she thought, biting her cheek in the hope that a little pain would help her stay centered. Whatever was happening, it was nothing good. Mamá and Papá didn't know — or didn't understand — the forces allayed against them. The Fat Man would wait to make a move until they were off their guard, but he would move quickly. Not physically quickly; she doubted the big man was capable of that, but a trigger could be pulled quickly even by someone old and out-of-shape.

A curse could be woven even quicker.

Lucinda tried to bring the cardinal closer by thinking about it, but that didn't seem to work. She couldn't sense its presence, nor could she see it, and those red feathers should stand out against the tans and olive greens of the chaparral.

Not a good portent. Not good at all.

So, they were right about The Fat Man, and about the shop in Ensenada as well. She, Eva, and Mateo were digging close to the truth, and the murderer had decided to stop them. Well, he wouldn't. Not with all the pesos in México. She didn't think The Fat Man was the ringleader, probably just a stupid henchman. A stupid, dangerous henchman.

One by one, the caravan cars parked next to the house foundation, the doors opened, the riders exited. Of them all, Lucinda was most surprised to see Aunt María.

Lucinda caught Auntie's eye. "Who is Carlos Serra to you," she asked, suspicion blossoming like a wildfire, "and why are you both here at the same time?"

"Hija, your tone," Mamá warned.

"This can only mean one thing: she betrayed us! Didn't you, Auntie? I can see you look guilty."

Aunt María lit a cigarette and sucked greedily. "We have ... I have a story to tell you," Aunt María said, blowing plumes of foul-smelling smoke from her nostrils. "Many years ago when I was a little girl, a brujo lived in this house. He was well known in Punta Colonet. The brujo lived extravagantly, with women and drugs, all the pleasures, all the money. The police knew and did nothing. We in the town knew. He would cure our ailments, cast our spells. Our mother's spells. We knew, and did nothing."

Lucinda looked sharply at Mamá, who shook her head. "I was not born yet. That is why Aunt María is telling you. She saw what happened."

"As did I," said The Fat Man. "I am older than I look. Much older. Listen to your aunt, hija."

Lucinda reminded herself that Aunt María was actually her great-aunt, her grandfather's sister — this story must have taken place a LONG time ago.

Mateo was scuffling a rock with his shoe. His mother was nodding. Lucinda felt like she had started a fight in school and everyone had come against her: the principal, teacher, hall monitor, the other girl's parents, and her own mother.

Lucinda wondered if Mateo, too, could be turned against her. He manifested no sign of courage, and didn't seem inclined to resist or even question what was happening.

"The brujo was cruel," Aunt María said.

"They all become cruel," Mateo's mother, Doña Yolanda Morales, said. "It carries with the magic."

The Fat Man nodded vigorously at this. "Francisco López could be — was — a cruel man. I heard about the cruelties."

"We do not say his name," Doña Morales spat, "no more than I will utter the name of my husband."

"Sí, you are right. El Diablo," The Fat Man corrected.

How strange that neither Mateo nor his mother would use El Jaguar's given name, as if they wanted to erase him as a person. Either that, or they considered that he was no longer kin to humanity and didn't deserve a name. Or some combination.

Aunt María continued, "We tolerated El Diablo's cruelties and did nothing because he cast our spells, and because we were afraid. El Diablo made our crops bloom without rain. He healed our hands from the dryness of the cannery. As a little girl, I counted the days until I would be old enough to call on El Diablo myself — I had favors to ask. I dreamed that he would grant my boons; and I had nightmares that he would choose me as one of his brides." She ran her tongue around her red mouth.

The Fat Man reached out and put a hand on Aunt María's shoulder in a familiar way.

Mamá took an old, rolled up paper from her purse, unfurled it like the deed to a valuable property, and handed it to Lucinda. On the dry, yellowing poster paper, the photo of a beautiful young girl, beneath which were printed in block letters:

Marisol Sisson, muerta June 6, 1961

Aunt María said, "El Diablo chose my friend Marisol to be a bride. She would never have gone voluntarily; she was better than all of us. The best. We were twelve years old at the time, in eighth grade, and she refused El Diablo's advances. El Diablo killed her there on the street of Punta Colonet, in front of Avila's restaurant where Marisol had been busing tables on the weekends."

Lucinda let her gaze wander over the foundation, the two chimneys. Teardrops of oat grass seed hung from golden stalks, the grass sprouting between cracks in the stone walls. A whisper would have broken the fragile connection that held seed to stalk, dropped them to the barren soil.

"The people rose up. They came here in mass and burned the house — and El Diablo in it. He had women here, putas, who trapped him somehow, so he could not turn into smoke and leave. They were slaves; we do not blame them, and they waited for their moment."

"Heroes," The Fat Man said.

"When the smoke cleared, and the walls fell, all that was left of El Diablo was a puddle of grease."

They stepped across the foundation wall and into the remains, and to Lucinda's astonishment much of the floor had turned into glass where sand had been melted by the heat of the blaze. On top of that was a gooey, human-sized blob.

Mateo bent and touched the glass, and then to the hiss of discomfort of his mother, put a finger to the grease and sniffed it.

"I don't know what games you are playing, Lucinda, Mateo," Mamá said. "But brujos always end up like this."

"Consumed," Doña Morales said, bitterly.

"Burned like a puddle of grease," The Fat Man added.

Mamá hugged Lucinda tight to her soft bosom, an embrace both comforting and suffocating. "I beg you, stop whatever you are doing. Herminia, I love her. She is my mother. But there is nothing we can do. Herminia brought this on herself. Let her go, hija. Let your grandmother go, and stop pursuing this path to El Diablo."

Twenty-Two

1967, Santa Rosalía, Baja California South

Sybil's car climbed inland for a mile, turned up a steep drive, and stopped in a large, irregular shaped parking lot. Dirt, of course. Nothing was paved in Santa Rosalía. Before them was a wall and a locked — or at least closed — gate. Playful voices lifted on the other side. Women's voices.

Herminia remembered playing here as a girl. It had been a labyrinth of abandoned hallways, staircases, gardens overgrown with weeds, and cobweb-invaded rooms. Some hotel that had been added onto year after year, becoming grander and grander, stranger and stranger in its form, until it finally went bankrupt with the opening of modern hotels with airstrips such as the Loma Linda.

She was surprised to see gleaming whitewash on the walls, healthy pruned trees within the compound, a shiny brass knocker on the gate. No signpost indicated the name of the place.

Sybil wrapped the knocker and a wide orderly in a white uniform opened the door. Herminia stared as they filed past — he looked like a barroom bouncer.

Inside, women played soccer, three different games with nothing resembling a goal in sight. They looked to be teenagers for the most part, a few in their early twenties. Long buildings with red tile roofs flanked either side of the corridor, with doors to either side that may have led to bedrooms. The destination lay ahead: a two-story building with a grand entrance.

Memories drifted into Herminia's consciousness: Many archways and porticoes. A cute, enclosed courtyard where the ground always remained damp and wild mint poked up between the weeds. A larger, enclosed garden with a dry mirror pond; Herminia's cousin stealing her first (very chaste) kiss in that garden. They giggled about it later.

"Didn't this used to be a hotel?" Herminia asked.

"Yes, the Agua Escondida. Our guests stay longer now — though we hope their stays are not permanent." Sybil smiled without humor.

The kids began cheering — someone had made an imaginary goal. Everyone seemed to be celebrating, as if they all had scored.

Herminia and Sybil mounted the sweeping staircase. A plaque by the door read "Women's Clinic." Another bouncer-type orderly opened the door for them.

"Should I be nervous?" Herminia asked.

Passing indoors, they arrived in the registration. Apparently, it was still used for the same purpose. A receptionist looked up expectantly, but Sybil ignored her. The receptionist's television droned with half talk, half static.

"We work with abused women," Sybil said, signing a form. "I'm sorry for all the secrecy. The women's identities must remain anonymous beyond these walls. I know you are from Santa Rosalía, and, well, if you recognize anyone...." She let the sentence die.

"Don't worry. I understand having a secret identity." And to Sybil's raised eyebrow Herminia added, "We all do — to one extent or another."

Sybil busied herself with the form, but it was apparent that she was stalling more than anything. Herminia reached out, touched her arm gently, and nodded for Sybil to go on.

"Yes, Herminia, even a lost reputation in a small town—"

"That isn't the real issue," Herminia guessed.

"No. No, it isn't. I shouldn't tell you this; you won't come in. We desperately need help, and you are so good with people. You have caring eyes." Sybil ran a fatigued hand across her forehead. "Our patients have disappeared in the middle of the night. Or … or been taken. Husbands, pimps, the gangsters that run the brothels. We don't really know who is responsible. And the police are incapable of doing anything."

"Incapable? Or being paid off?"

"Who knows. One can buy anything with a mordida around here."

"Cómo es differente en Los Estados Unidos?" the receptionist said, eyes narrowed in disapproval. "I've seen your movies. I know what it's like. *Gangster Story*, eh? Tell me it isn't certain."

Placing her hands over mouth, ears and eyes, Herminia made the signs of the no-seeing, no-hearing, no-speaking monkey. All of this sounded exciting. Important. More than that, it sounded like a place a bruja's powers might make a difference.

"We have had to expand our mandate, take in abandoned children," Sybil said. "We just can't turn them away! Their moms come in with them, then the moms return to work in the brothels. Sometimes the pimps bring them. We place the kids in foster families as fast as we can. They are good kids, not mentally retarded or anything. Not dangerous. Just lost, abandoned."

"I've read about children gone missing in and around Santa Rosalía," Herminia said. "Is this where they went? Are you hiding them here?"

"Oh, no, no. We have two missing children ourselves. Officially, the mothers returned for them — easier on the paperwork. Bad business, that. Vanished into thin air. We had all the orderlies watched in case it was an inside job, but I'm convinced whoever did it came over the walls. Some sort of serial killer or something working Baja. But it seems to have stopped. As usual, the newspapers are two bus tickets behind the ride, reporting on a problem after it's gone away."

The receptionist tried to hand Sybil a clipboard, but the American waved it away. "Not now. I am recruiting my friend, Herminia Carrillo. She is a registered nurse." Sybil winked at Herminia.

"Thank the Virgen. Don't let her run away," the receptionist said. "We have another guest," she added, as if this were an afterthought. "Room 2-F."

Sybil snatched the clipboard. "Why 2-F?"

"The first floor is full." There was an undercurrent of animosity, or perhaps rebellion, in the way the receptionist responded.

"What about the wings?"

"When you can get the cleaning staff to work faster, you let me know." The receptionist turned back to her black and white television set and adjusted the rabbit ears to little effect.

Herminia decided she liked her.

Clipboard in hand, Sybil led the way upstairs, grumbling, "I thought Mexicans were supposed to respect El Patrón."

"You are not a doctor. And you are a woman."

"Yeah, well, the feminists will come here, one day. You'll see."

Paint was beginning to peel off the walls in pastel scabs. It looked like a recent job, done on the cheap without primer or sanding. Boat captains would never have stood for such a shoddy job. Everything smacked of razor thin budgets and overworked staff. At least it didn't smell of disinfectant like so many clinics. Herminia remarked on this, and Sybil replied that they didn't have trauma wounds there, not unless they were self-inflicted.

They passed to a balcony corridor. The waist-high walls and ornamental pillars had been carved of real stone. The balcony overlooked a renovated herb garden, complete with sweet-smelling herbs and colorful chilis.

Sybil approached 2-F, but her eyes kept falling on the door marked 2-G. Her steps were uneven against the weight of it: Sybil feared something there.

A madwoman?

Herminia embraced her ally. With enhanced senses, she detected breathing from behind that door, a single person, but could discern no more than that.

Inside room 2-F, a bed, a chair, a desk, and a lamp. Gossip magazines spread out on the bed like blades of a fan. But no girl.

"Another runaway," Sybil said, sorrowfully jotting something on the clipboard chart, then cursed. "That little — she knew I'd forget!"

Sybil rushed back downstairs, and Herminia followed. As they passed reception, the receptionist called, "Conference room B."

Though unsure Sybil deserved it, Hermina smiled at the little revenge of the little people. Faustino would have approved.

They burst into a nondescript conference room. In a circle facing inward sat at least 15 women on folding chairs. Most were around Herminia's age, but carrying the scars of several lifetimes. Herminia noted a few things right away. Tears had flowed here recently from most of the eyes, though all were dry presently. There was one man wearing a white doctor's smock and a bored expression. He looked American. Apart from the man, who seemed to be pulling his mind back to the present now that Sybil and Herminia had arrived, the women's attention was on a pregnant woman — little more than a girl, close to term, with bruises on her face.

Sybil made her way to the pregnant woman and bent down so that their faces nearly touched.

"You're late," the doctor said in English.

Ignoring the doctor, Sybil offered her hand to the woman, who took it hesitantly. In Spanish she said, "Sybil Smith. Pleased to meet you. This is our new nurse, Herminia Carrillo.

The doctor's scowl softened somewhat. "New nurse? About time. Yes, well, you will excuse me." The doctor departed, and the room relaxed.

After a moment of silence, a woman said, "It's like confessing to a priest."

"A priest who doesn't believe in God," another added.

There were cynical chuckles all around.

"So are you a sex worker, too?" the first woman asked Herminia. "You'd fetch a peso or two."

Herminia's jaw dropped as fast as the blush came to her cheeks.

"This is Gabi," Sybil said. "One of our 'lifers.' I don't know what we'd do without her. She recruits the new girls. She's fearless."

"I'm only here for the fish Fridays."

They all laughed again, implying the fish wasn't good. The laughter came easily, a way to release tension more than actual mirth.

The pregnant woman hadn't participated in any of the conversation thus far, nor in any of the laughter. She was younger than Herminia, possibly as young as twelve, and Herminia found herself staring, thinking they weren't so different. If Herminia's family had perished in a storm, for example, could she have ended up as a sex worker instead of a bruja?

"And your name is—?" Herminia asked.

"We don't use real names here," Sybil interjected.

The pregnant woman wrung her fingers in her lap.

"We've been calling her Christina," Gabi said. "She wants to leave."

Sybil leaned over and put her hand on Christina's wrist. "Where would you go? Back to your boyfriend?"

"He doesn't want you," one of the women offered. "No one would pay for a pregnant woman. No decent man."

"Decent men!" another scoffed.

Some of the others nodded.

"There is a place for you here, a fresh start," Sybil said.

"If you return to your boyfriend, he will kill the baby," Gabi said.

"What baby? What are you talking about?" Christina sprang to her feet and the chair flew back from her straightening legs with surprising force. "You are all insane. Don't you understand? That is why you are in this insane asylum. I'm getting out of here. Alfonso loves me. He *will* marry me."

Herminia hadn't let go of her ally since trying to read what Sybil feared in room 2-G. Thus she knew Christina was bracing to run away. If Christina's bitter adrenaline wasn't enough of a clue, the minuscule, outward turn of her right foot was as obvious to Herminia as a shot off the block in track.

The patient was going to rabbit.

Herminia dropped into the Beyond and pulled Christina there. They were swimming, fully clothed. Christina's legs kicked in a parody of a sprint — still responding as if they were on hard ground.

She handled it pretty well, in Herminia's opinion. Most people would have gone hysterical, screamed and kicked, or shut their eyes tight, refusing to believe. When her legs did no more than churn the room-temperature water, Christina simply went limp. A bubble escaped her gaping mouth.

Herminia and Christina were both lean and strong, petite and brown. They could have been sisters. Overhead a storm lashed the surface, and Herminia knew the storm was caused by Christina's confusion.

A talented girl. Bonded to her ally, Christina would make a powerful bruja.

This clinic would be the perfect place for Faustino, Herminia thought sadly. She had wondered if Mental magic could be used for good, or if compulsion was its only benefit. Here in this Women's Clinic was true need, true good that could be accomplished through Mental magic ... just when Herminia's friendship with Faustino was ruptured forever.

Possessing only Physical magic, Herminia could see no way of healing Christina.

The sailfish, sad in its inadequacy, languished nearby.

"Where are we?" Christina asked. "Have I gone insane? Is that why I am at the Women's Clinic?"

Herminia took Christina's hand. "Swim with me. Not a word. Just swim."

They swam in the clear waters through schools of silver corbina and green jack fish. They breathed underwater. Their muscles fatigued and they kicked off their shoes and their troubles.

All this happened in the blink of an eye, because Herminia willed it so.

"I want to stay here forever," Christina said, turning circles with little movements of her hands.

Herminia felt another presence with them: the child in Christina's belly. Herminia amplified the sound of the fetus's heartbeat so that Christina could hear. "This is your child," Herminia said. "The other women at the clinic are not lying. You are pregnant. You are going to be a mother."

Christina's eyes relaxed, as if entranced by the rhythm. She let herself drift. Content with the water, and with the knowledge that she was with child.

"This is only a dream," Herminia said. "Or rather, a small gift. I am sorry I cannot offer more." She cradled Christina's face between her fingers and, instinctively, not really knowing what she was doing, projected physical power into the girl. The girl's bruises faded. The swelling went down. Something about Christina's need made learning come easier. The friction between Herminia and her sailfish diminished; they grew closer to being one than ever before.

Herminia held Christina for a time, reveling in the joy of helping another human being as much as in the feeling of wholeness. And then she returned them to the present time. A few seconds had clicked by on the wall clock. Everyone looked a little confused, but not overly so. Herminia was kneeling before Christina, fingertips pressed to the girl's face.

Christina pushed Herminia's hands away and stood. "I'm going to my room now. The baby and I need to rest."

When the girl had left, Sybil said, "Thank you, Herminia."

"Thank you—?"

"Christina has never acknowledged her pregnancy before. I don't know what you did, but thank you."

The other women murmured their appreciation.

After the meeting, Sybil came to Herminia. "We need you here. We can't pay very much."

Herminia nodded in acceptance. "Nor can I do much. Not as much as—" She almost slipped and said, 'not as much as Faustino.'

"—not as much as I would like."

Faustino could accomplish so much in a place like this, she thought. With his Mental ally, he could assuage the women's pain, restore their dignity, heal their trauma, their mental scars. Faustino wouldn't be interested in any of that, of course. Only hurting the Americans interested him. That, and making his girlfriend's experience *just perfect*.

Hiding her conflicting emotions as best she could, Herminia shook hands with Sybil in that peculiar American fashion, when they should have hugged. Or perhaps not, since Sybil had just become her *patrona*.

Now that she had the run of the place, Herminia returned upstairs. She knocked on room 2-F and entered. Christina was sitting on the bed, a confused but serene look on her face.

"Do you need help packing?" Herminia asked.

The masonry walls carried sound. Footsteps on the stairs. Voices from downstairs. Springs of an old bed next door in 2-G. Creaking, creaking. Over and over. Manic repetitiveness.

Christina didn't seem to notice. She flipped a magazine closed. "Packing? I'm not going anywhere. Tomorrow I will talk at the next circle meeting. Today, rest. Thank you."

"For what?"

"I— I don't know."

With a few words of reassurance, Herminia departed.

Gabi, the 'lifer,' was wandering the hall, but that didn't matter. Sybil had hired Herminia with the official title of *Nurse Practitioner;* she outranked just about everyone in the clinic. So Herminia strode the few feet to room 2-G.

She knocked and tried the door, but it was locked. A simple matter for a Physical bruja to manipulate the lock and let herself in.

There was a boy shackled to the bed by the arms and legs.

This she hadn't expected. A boy, in a women's clinic, bound like a dangerous criminal.

He was around seven years old. Red welts covered his wrists and ankles where he had struggled against the bonds. His chest under the white shirt heaved as his breath normalized. His rounded back faced Herminia, but there was no question that he was aware of her.

Gabi joined Herminia in the doorway. "He can't speak," Gabi said, making the sign of the cross, "nor can he hear. Though he senses when we open the door; maybe he can feel the air moving. If you ask me, he senses all kinds of unnatural things. His mother.... Well, anyway, a woman the right age left him here and disappeared. No one has come for him. We tried bringing him to an orphanage, but no one will take him."

Herminia and Gabi were frozen in the door, afraid to set foot in the room. Herminia acknowledged and accepted the fear, and still could not bring herself to move forward.

"Things happen around him. This door was locked earlier."

Herminia only nodded.

"Water turns to blood. Food spoils. No one will stay near him. Except the rats."

There was one in the corner, staring at the two women as if they had interrupted a conversation. A gray rat so dark it could pass for black. It chattered and squeaked, and then disappeared under the bed. Herminia wondered if it had a hole down there, or if it bunked in the stuffing of the mattress.

"Hello, child," Herminia said, embarrassed at the weakness of her own voice. She hadn't been this frightened since that first trip to the Beyond. "What is your name?"

The boy's only response was a slight stiffening of the neck; a slight tug against the restraints on his wrists. It was uncanny; he certainly knew that Herminia had spoken to him.

How could he know that with his back turned?

After a few seconds, Gabi whispered, "They call him El Jaguar."

Twenty-Three
Present Day, Punta Colonet, Baja California North

Papá returned to the United States. He hadn't said much this whole time, but Lucinda felt terrible that he had come all this way because of her. The greenhouse in Fallbrook never slept, and the bags under Papá's eyes showed the strain the commute from and to the United States exacted.

Aunt María was assigned the job of chaperon, which consisted of taking Lucinda to Ensenada to the movies every afternoon and buying lime paletas for the ride home. She talked about how Abuelita had had a long, eventful life, and it was okay to let her go. Everyone had to go some time; it was the Lord's will. Abuelita would be going to a better place, would be watching over Lucinda from above. Auntie also taped the poster of *Marisol Sisson, muerta June 6, 1961* on the inside of the front door so that poor Marisol's wide eyes could guilt Lucinda from anywhere in the living room.

At home, the old woman noises of Abuelita had been replaced by the old woman noises of Aunt María. They were not the same noises. Abuelita had rattled pots with conviction. She dragged the rug outside and beat it with the broom. She whipped together warm milk and leftovers for Patti the goat, and called for help in unabashed bellows.

Aunt María ironed their clothes — everyone's clothes. (Abuelita *never* ironed.) She flipped pages of gossip magazines and gasped quietly at the celebrities latest peccadilloes. She watched television so loud it made the window panes vibrate in their frames. The whisper of hot metal on cotton, the snick of turning pages, and the exhortations of game show hosts — these were not bad sounds. They might have been comforting to Aunt María's grandchildren, if she'd had any. The problem was they were different sounds. Replacement sounds.

They were driving Lucinda mad.

At eleven o'clock precisely (which seemed to take *forever* to get here)...

...there it was: *100 Mexicanos Dijieron*, the game show.

Lucinda cracked the door. Auntie was sitting up on Papá's recliner, her red-rimmed spectacles firmly in place, a certain gleam in her eye for Marco Antonio Regil, the presenter.

"Care to join me, Lucinda?"

"Um, no, thanks. I want to do some chores. Outside."

"You will have your whole life to do chores," Auntie said, leaning forward to catch a contestants' name. "Don't live like a housewife until you have to." Her eyes never left the screen.

"I just need to take a walk. I can't stand being cooped up like this." Watching Abuelita die.

"We're going to the market. Didn't I tell you? Just as soon as *In Family* ends. You'll get plenty of fresh air."

Lucinda had to count to ten to answer civilly. "Yes, Auntie." With great restraint she managed to close the door softly. And not kick it.

Okay, she *would* have kicked it except she had bare feet.

If she threw herself down on the bed, she'd roll and thrash and bother Abuelita, who was sleeping the sleep of the ill.

Maybe she *should* watch *100 Mexicanos Dijieron*, Lucinda thought, get trained up to be a spinster—

A tap on the window startled her, and a familiar blond head made her smile. Lucinda leaned over the skeletal form of Herminia to throw open the green-framed window.

"Eva!"

"Girlfriend!"

"...and Mateo."

He gave a half-smile.

Lucinda wasn't sure how she felt about a boy coming to her bedroom window, but supposed that as long as he came with Eva it was all right. More than that, it was a relief! Finally, they were together again. Finally, they could do something.

"I'm coming with you," Lucinda announced, and with Eva's help, climbed through the sill. They used the opportunity for one of their signature hugs.

"Come to the back," Lucinda said, leading them behind the house where no one would see them. The bedrooms had windows only on the side of the house, and the little bathroom window, the only one to the rear, was glazed.

They could hear faint applause coming from the television — more than enough noise to cover their conversation.

For the first time in several days, Lucinda smiled. Certainly, her friends wouldn't have come without some news. "What have you got?"

Eva's emerald eyes sparkled. "What do you think unites Mustache Man, The Fat Man, and Mercado Californio?"

"Um, the fact that you're keeping it from me."

"Well, yes. Ownership is what I was looking for. Ownership. Who owns the grave?"

"The Fat Man," Lucinda replied. "Carlos Serra." Mateo's map of the cemetery indicated that much.

"Right. But Carlos Serra doesn't own his own house. I checked on Zillow. He sold it to Nuevo Ibero LLC the same year he bought the grave site. The money just moved from the LLC to the purchase of the grave site."

"You have to purchase a gravesite?" Lucinda asked. That just didn't seem right.

"Duh! Nothing is free in this world."

"Maybe Carlos Serra owns the LLC." Lucinda wasn't ready to let The Fat Man go, not after he'd led the posse to El Diablo's house.

"That doesn't make sense," Eva replied. "The LLC wanted the grave, but didn't want its ownership traceable. The Fat Man wasn't trying to hide — the LLC was."

"Hmm?" Lucinda was starting to get frustrated trying to follow the convoluted logic.

Mateo, now squatting in the dirt, appeared to be tuning out the entire conversation.

"Here's the best part. The LLC also owns the shop in Ensenada. Zillo shows it selling in 2009. There haven't been any sales since. Zillo, that's a real estate app, shows Carlos Serra's house selling in 1983. Also to Nuevo Ibero LLC. They are the same owner."

"Okay," said Lucinda, "if that's right—"

"It's right," Eva said, confidently.

"If that's right," Lucinda repeated, louder, "What is an LLC?" She'd been wondering this for some time, but Eva was so sure of her vocabulary that Lucinda didn't want to admit she didn't know.

"I don't know," Eva admitted. "I googled it. It says, and I quote, *blah, blah, blah, blah.*"

"That's helpful."

"Some kind of company, I think," Eva said. "You'd have to be a Spanish teacher to understand it. Or a lawyer. It means the owners have limited responsibility, like if you slip and break your back in Mercado Californio you can sue the LLC, but you can't sue the owners of the LLC. It's a shelter for their assets. I checked out what I could. I couldn't find who the owner of the LLC was, but I found an on-line article about Mercado Californio. The store donated a hundred thousand pesos to City of Angels orphanage right here in Punta Colonet. The lady who kicked us out of the Mercado was shaking hands with the orphanage person, along with the mayor and some other wealthy types."

"Okay, I'm officially lost," Lucinda said. "Maybe we'd better call 1-800-go-figure so they can explain it to me."

Eva laughed. "Stop interrupting, silly. I'm getting to the best part. The man standing behind the clothing store woman was identified in the photo. Faustino Arce. Don't you get it?"

"Faustino? Are you sure?"

Eva awakened her phone and loaded one of those setup shots with people shaking hands and an oversized check. The check was from Mercado Californio made out to City of Angels orphanage. Standing in the background, with a silver bolo tie and cowboy hat, was Mustache Man, a.k.a. Faustino Arce.

No question: Faustino Arce was the man who had handed Abuelita the flower in church. The man who had poisoned Abuelita with the blood curse.

Lucinda could hardly contain her excitement. Mystery solved. They had the guilty party. "Good work, girlfriend. Did you find out where Faustino lives?"

"That's the best part— just kidding. Do you think I'm Jason Bourne? I did pretty good with Zillow and Google, but I'm no hacker."

Lucinda stroked her chin a few times, then looked at Mateo. "Did you check this against your list of dog customers?"

"Huh? No. I didn't think of it."

"Well, don't you think that would be a good idea?"

He shrugged.

Before Lucinda could get angry, Eva stepped between them. "Breathe, girlfriend. We're all doing our best."

Realizing her fists were balled at her sides, Lucinda relaxed the fingers with difficulty, one at a time. Relaxing her shoulders was too much to ask.

Eva raised a thin, beautiful eyebrow.

"Right. I've got it in my room. I'll just nip back and get it," Lucinda said.

With a boost from Eva, she climbed through the window, over Abuelita, and retrieved the list. On the return trip, Abuelita shifted, partly because of too much bouncing on the mattress, and partly because Lucinda bonked her head on the window frame with a loud "Ow!"

"Everything all right?" called Aunt María from the living room.

"Yes, Auntie."

Drat, a commercial!

"Leaving for the market in three commercial breaks. Remind me to get queso panela for tonight."

"Okay. No problem. Will do."

Auntie wanted cow cheese. Another reminder of the changes — no Patti and no goat cheese.

With a sorrowful glance at Grandmother Herminia's wasted form, Lucinda climbed back outside.

Together, Lucinda and Eva checked the list of dog customers: New Spain, Co. was listed in El Jaguar's childlike hand.

Eva flicked the name, saying, "A poor pseudonym for Faustino's company, though El Jaguar probably thought it clever."

Lucinda nodded. Even with limited English she understood the translation.

New Spain Company

=

Nuevo Ibero LLC

"Faustino owns Mercado Californio. He hired the Fat Man to purchase a cemetery plot right next to Abuelita's plot. He must still be in love with her or something in a sick way," Lucinda said, thinking aloud and then wishing she hadn't spoken. She gulped and went on, "He even bought dogs from El Jaguar — and El Jaguar, king of blood curses, gave Faustino the poison maize to kill her. We have our—" What did you call him? Attempted murderer? Future murderer? Curse giver? Lucinda settled on, "—our assailant."

Squatting on the ground, Mateo was refining the eye-holes of a particularly large skull.

Eva tapped her foot on the ground in that pretty way. Finally she said, "One thing that's bothering me, if this was all Faustino, why did he do this on two different occasions? Why did he steal the memories on the day the district attorney cleared your grandmother, and use the blood curse," counting on her fingers, "nine days later at church?"

That had been bothering Lucinda for a while.

She didn't want it to bother her. They had an answer, why complicate things?

She wanted the doubts to just go away so she could fight someone, heal Abuelita, and get on with life.

"I think there are some things we will never understand," Lucinda said, trying to convince herself as much as anything. "Do the police wait to understand every last little clue before making an arrest? No. The suspect will reveal some information, confess here and deny there, and some things will never be resolved. Once the police know who is guilty—"

"Once they get a bribe," Mateo muttered.

Came Aunt María's voice from right behind them, sober and sharp. "Who is guilty, Lucinda? Pray tell. And who are you planning to bribe?"

Auntie stalked up, grabbed Lucinda's ear and twisted, then unleashed a string of words Lucinda had never heard issue from an older woman's mouth.

Or younger, for that matter.

Not even from the fish market mongers.

No matter how much her ear hurt, Lucinda refused to rise to tiptoes. She grit her teeth so as to not cry out — and so as to not say something she'd regret later.

After all, this was Auntie. And Autie had caught them red-handed.

Lucinda sort of deserved it.

Auntie concluded with, "After everything your mother and father have done for you, sneaking around like robbers! You'll bring down curses upon us all. Do you think El Jaguar is the only brujo around? And you, Mateo, you of all people should know better. Your mother will be hearing from me." Auntie turned to scowl down at Mateo, for he was hunched over, working something with his hands. "What are you doing down there, boy. Don't you know it's not polite—"

Looking up, Mateo whispered, "Your TV show is back on," and a feather drifted from between his fingers. "The commercial break is over. You'd better hurry back so you don't miss anything."

Auntie released Lucinda's ear and blinked a few times.

"And don't worry about us," Mateo added. "We are just cleaning windows. We didn't do anything wrong."

"The windows. Yes, right, they are filthy. Use lots of soap! Thank you!" Aunt María rushed around the corner of the house to catch her show. Then poked her head back. "Close them first, eh?" And then she was gone.

Eva looked from Mateo to Lucinda and back again, hands clasped, face frozen in a laugh she wasn't sure it was safe to release.

Lucinda didn't know what to think. Outrage battled with relief. Mateo had just saved their collective bacon, and possibly salvaged the entire investigation — maybe even saved Herminia's life. On the other hand, he just used Mental magic on Auntie. He'd just spun her mind like the dials on a cheap bicycle lock — and snapped it open.

Mateo had attacked Auntie's mind the way Faustino had attacked grandmother Herminia.

Outrage won.

"How dare you mess with Auntie's mind! What the hell are you doing, using magic on my family? You slimy little—." She wished she had written down some of Auntie's phrases. The ones she knew seemed so inadequate. "I forbid you to ever, ever cast a spell on a member of my family again, do you understand me?"

Mateo nodded and scuffed his shoe.

Softly, Eva said, "Um, Lucy, he probably just saved us like a year's detention."

"He could have seriously screwed Auntie up. He could have made Auntie like Abuelita, destroyed her mind. Who knows what damage he might have done—" Tears jumped from her eyes of their own accord, and Lucinda let them come. She cried, and eventually Eva hugged her and they cried together, blond and brunette, green eyes and brown. Eva's hair smelled like almonds. Best friends. When it was over, Eva's shoulder was soaked and Mateo had drawn six new skulls in the dirt.

Typical.

Lucinda decided she was definitely going to buy almond oil shampoo.

The girls took a deep breath, then wheeled on Mateo.

"So you have been traveling to the Beyond without us?" Lucinda said. "You've actually bonded?"

"No, never!" he said, looking more ashamed than usual ... if that were possible. "I used a feather. You saw me." He retrieved the little down feather and shoved it in his pocket. (Lucinda wondered if the feather would disintegrate and dirty Mateo's pocket the way the blood curse maize kernel had disintegrated after use.) "And yes. You wouldn't let me. So I went to the Beyond by myself. They were my mortars anyway! If you'd seen the things I've seen..."

"Seen where?" Lucinda asked. "In the Beyond? Why did you want to see more if it were so awful? What did you see there?"

Eva said, "I think he means 'awful' as in at home. With El Jaguar."

"Well?" Lucinda said, ignoring her friend.

In the silence that followed, when it became clear Mateo would say no more, Lucinda finally allowed her ire to smolder on the back burner, and put more important things to the front. There was a lot left unsaid. She knew that, but to talk to Mateo right now would be about as rewarding as talking to an open manhole ... and less edifying. To Eva she asked, "Well then, Nuevo Ibero, LLC, is that the news?"

"No, silly," Eva replied. "That was just me talking. Mateo found something far more important. In the Beyond."

"You knew he went traveling?"

"He told me just today. You need to get a grip, Lucy, like right now. This is going to knock your socks off." Eva went and put a hand on Mateo, though whether to reassure him or to keep him from running away, Lucinda couldn't be sure.

"She told me not to use magic," Mateo pouted.

"Lucy told you not to use mind tricks on anyone in her family, and that includes me as her near sister. Me or my family or anyone I know." Mateo started to protest but Eva shushed him. She squatted down and filled the mortar with sesame seeds. "I know you didn't mean it, but using *compulsion* is like a mind rape. Do you understand? I think I'd rather face a year of detention than have you do that to someone — even an enemy." She turned toward Lucinda and mouthed 'Not.'

Mateo nodded morosely.

"This is different. Going to the Beyond to look at memories is just sight-seeing."

He nodded again.

"The clinic, Mateo," Eva said, placing Mateo's hand back on the pestle. "Don't tell Lucy. Show her."

"Yes, Mateo," Lucinda echoed, anticipation churning her belly, "show me."

In Mateo's hands, the pestle turned with the whisper of murmuring stone, stone versus unyielding stone, crushing the sesame seeds to paste. "You are going to hate me," Mateo warned.

Twenty-Four
1967-1970, Santa Rosalía, Baja California South

At Herminia's request, two orderlies stood to either side of El Jaguar, one holding each arm. Sybil was there, also, punctuating the momentous occasion with worry.

"El Jaguar," Herminia said, sitting on the bed next to the boy, "the orderlies will release your bonds now." She made sure the boy could see her face, for while he was as deaf as he were dumb, he could read lips quite efficiently.

The bonds had never been off in front of Herminia. Too dangerous. The orderlies took his wrists in their meaty hands, exchanging padded bonds for human connection, and undid the buckles strapping his wrists to the bed. The bonds were for El Jaguar's protection as much as anything — he often scratched his own face or tore out his hair.

Herminia sat on the bed next to El Jaguar. His legs remained attached; flailing legs were every bit as dangerous as scratching nails.

Herminia called her sailfish.

El Jaguar's head cocked a bit. Yes, he was sensitive. Of all the people in the room, only El Jaguar had reacted to Herminia embracing her ally. She wondered how far the boy had come as a brujo, if anyone had trained him.

Herminia placed a gentle hand on his shoulder, felt the deltoid jump in response. The orderlies tightened their grip. "I have asked to work with you. The doctors said this was okay." (More than that — they were thrilled someone would take him on.) "But I want to be sure you agree. I will read to you this wonderful book by Jules Verne, *Twenty Thousand Leagues Under the Sea*. We will visit such places together — the bottom of the ocean. We will find out who your allies are."

She trusted that the other people in the room would not know the significance of the word *ally*. El Jaguar seemed to — more tightening of the face.

She intended to open a pathway to her world, which is why *Twenty Thousand Leagues* was such a good choice. One brief visit to the under-water Beyond had helped Christina immeasurably, and Herminia had run out of other ideas for El Jaguar.

Herminia flipped open the book and read the first few pages. The room relaxed. Sybil actually smiled.

El Jaguar's neck relaxed; he seemed to enjoy the story, watching her mouth with open-mouthed anticipation.

"Are you ready?" Herminia asked, pausing in the recitation, watching the boy's face carefully.

His eyebrows lifted.

And she pulled them into the Beyond.

Her intent became confused with El Jaguar's almost immediately. Rather than arriving underwater, they arrived on the side of a moun-tain, a level terrace lumpy with grass covered mounds. The orderlies, Sybil, the Women's Clinic had been left behind.

El Jaguar was free of his bonds, as she had intended. They were alone.

The terrain didn't make much of an impression on Herminia, for her eyes were consumed with El Jaguar's true form. A boy, yes. A six-and-a-half year old boy, gangly, with his mouth and ears sewn shut — a human lizard guide. Someone had sewn his ears and mouth shut!

As quickly as her mind tried to seize up upon seeing this, El Jaguar raked his nails across her face. She shouted in pain and surprise, pain made worse because of her connection to her ally, surprise made worse by the sudden understanding of why El Jaguar was dumb and deaf in this world.

She dropped them back into room 2-G. El Jaguar had slipped the orderlies' hands. His fingers sought Herminia's eyes; hissing escaped his mouth.

Before the orderlies could react, Herminia slipped behind him and pinned him to the mattress with the strength of the Physical ally. Keeping her face down, averted from Sybil and the orderlies, Herminia willed the scars on her face closed, all but one that crossed her eye. That one she left deliberately red.

The orderlies regained control of El Jaguar's limbs, bound them back into place. Sybil shouted at the orderlies for being incompetent. Using Sybil's lecture as cover, controlling her voice with difficulty, Herminia said, "Like the scratches on my face, we will heal together, you and I. I promise."

Herminia and El Jaguar alone in his room, both standing.

"Are you ready?" Herminia asked.

He stopped rubbing the circulation back into his wrists. As much of an affirmation as he could manage.

She pulled them into the Beyond, no longer surprised that they arrived on the terrace at the side of the mountain. With El Jaguar, there was no other place. Of an unnaturally deep green, with a sheer drop-off on one side, mesas in the distance, and to their backs a cliff disappearing into a cloud bank, the terrace must have meant something of such significance to El Jaguar that it focused his intent the way the magnetic pole focused a compass's iron needle. Herminia shuddered to think what may have happened here, what trauma would so stain the mind as to leave open no other destination. One tree, a sprawling thing with white bark and oval leaves, roots half exposed on the eroded cliff face, marred the green of the valley.

"Here we can have some privacy," Herminia said.

The cloud bank stirred, turned a pale brown. The Null Wind. It often appeared around El Jaguar. So far, it had never gotten closer than the edge of the cliff, a latent nihilism.

El Jaguar kicked Herminia's shin.

Herminia smiled grimly. "You know that won't work. I tried cutting the threads last time, and the time before." And countless times before that. It was a ritual that El Jaguar insisted upon. She had come to believe that the threads were not made of Physical bonds — those she could have severed. Nor did she think Mental brujos could make this kind of bond. No, these must be of Spirit magic. Don Esteban had told her that the Beyond was the domain of Spirit brujos — they could control it like no others, the Beyond bent itself to their will.

She did not know if Don Esteban could have done anything to help El Jaguar or not; El Brujo had vanished. Consumed by personal projects, no doubt. She did not know how to contact him, though she had tried, for El Jaguar's sake. The pictograph cave was deserted. Seeking El Brujo in the Beyond, using her intent and her ally as a guide, had also proved fruitless.

Other thoughts, guilty as thieves, crept into her mind when it was distracted, in the dead of night, at the tail end of a shower. At these times, with her subconscious working through the puzzle, suspicion gurgled that Don Esteban himself had sewn the boy's mouth and ears shut. She felt guilty suspecting her former teacher, but intuition told her it was possible. She knew no other Spirit brujos than Don Esteban. (She knew of no others of any persuasion outside El Brujo and Faustino — true brujos must be few and far between.) How callously El Brujo had left Faustino when the latter's lizard guide had become trapped! Seemingly uncaring whether his apprentice lived or died. And Don Esteban was working on some sort of project to try to reunite all of humanity with its allies. Would he care if a few children were hurt, if the possible outcome were so beneficial?

No, of course not. El Brujo had the odd distinction of loving humanity and detesting humans. To her knowledge, El Brujo had never hurt any individual deliberately, but he didn't care if they got hurt, either.

El Jaguar kicked her shin again. She knew from experience he would do this until the shin was so bruised she would have to use Physical magic to heal herself — or spend several days limping. A kick was one form of communication that the Spirit bonds didn't object to.

"Well, if I cut through your bonds," Herminia said, "then do you promise to do what I ask?"

He could not answer, of course, but his shoe scuffed the ground instead of Herminia's shin.

She lifted her full-length skirt, revealing powerful calves — she had taken to swimming again — and the old ankle knife. It slid smoothly from the sheath, an unadorned skinning knife half the length of her forearm, her prized possession, nicked from years of use. She channeled Physical power into the knife, honing its edge better than any whetstone, hardening it better than any blacksmith's hammer. One by one, thread by spiderweb-white thread, she sliced across El Jaguar's mouth. It seemed to be working. Herminia's hand trembled with excitement, the handle grew slick in her palm—

—but the threads reformed immediately after the blade passed.

The emptiness of failure was worse than not trying. Herminia had thought herself immune to disappointment after so many tries. She wiped the moisture from the sides of her nose. "I'm sorry."

El Jaguar's shoe scuffed the ground, gently.

"Now tell me, where is the other child, the one with his eyes sewn shut?"

El Jaguar's eyes widened a tad.

She dropped to her knees so as to be at his level, and smiled grimly. "I have been thinking about this. If a witch did this to you, so that you could act as some sort of lizard guide, then there is another, blinded child. How else could the witch hope to communicate with you?" She laid a hand on El Jaguar's bony shoulder; the boy never seemed to be able to put on weight no matter how much he scarfed down. "If we can locate the other boy, we will be able to talk, you and I, in a manner of speaking."

She could discover the identity of this evil brujo who mutilated children and reverse the magic, heal both children, and make sure the brujo never, ever harmed another child again.

She didn't know what she expected to happen, but it certainly wasn't for El Jaguar to walk a few feet and begin to dig with bare hands into one of the grassy mounds. The mounds that rumpled this entire terrace, which had appeared to her a natural phenomena, took on a sinister significance. Her heartbreaking assumption was confirmed when a hand was exposed, then an arm in a white, knitted sleeve, a little girl's cloak. The body should have decomposed, but here on the terrace, it did not, for the body was retrieved intact by El Jaguar's intent, the little girl as he remembered.

The grassy mounds, all those little mounds. Herminia had found the missing children, but there was no way to report them, no way to inform the parents or the police. A brujo had killed them; only a brujo could find them. Herminia did not know where the bodies were located on earth, or even if they could be found on earth at all.

El Jaguar continued digging.

Maybe eight years old, a scarecrow thin body, a long nose, tight lips, the girl was rangy and wild and beautiful in a tomboy sort of way.

Herminia combed the dirt from the girl's hair with her fingers. That it was done by hand was important — she had to overcome aversion and establish a connection, both with the deceased child and with El Jaguar. Then she used Physical magic to clean the body the rest of the way, buffeting away the dirt and grime with tiny whirlwinds. The girl was perfectly preserved; a taxidermist couldn't have done a more perfect job. Herminia shuddered at the thought.

El Jaguar sat beside the body and took the girl's hand in his own.

Already knowing the answer, Herminia asked, "Your sister?"

Herminia emerged from Panadería El Boleo with an armload of pastries for the Good Friday celebration. As always, a line of customers curved out the door. From these anonymous people hissed a familiar voice.

"Lots of bread for such a svelte figure. How do you manage?"

Startled, Herminia fumbled with the brown bags full of pastries, nearly dropping them. "I have been looking for you," she blurted, too surprised to remember pleasantries.

Don Esteban tapped his head with a finger. "The power of intent, eh?" Since they were in the world and not the Beyond, this must have been a joke. He took a croissant from an open bag without asking and began munching. "Shall we walk together?"

Herminia wondered how much to say. She didn't really want El

Brujo to know where she worked, and she didn't want him to know about El Jaguar — not until she was sure he was innocent of sewing the boy's mouth and ears shut. On the other hand, she had no way of determining El Brujo's guilt without talking to him. Faustino could read minds, but Herminia most certainly could not.

This was a dilemma she had been considering for some time and still hadn't come up with a satisfactory plan.

Well, planning wasn't really her strong suit. Improvisation usually worked out; she'd go with that.

They walked along a quiet street next to prosperous houses, brine tickling their noses from the breeze. Tree shade and sun alternated every few steps. It was a pleasant morning and a pleasant place to spend it, especially with a butter croissant to hand. Don Esteban seemed content to walk at Herminia's side without speaking; he had always been content in silence. A knee-high retaining wall fronted a hotel, with people sitting here and there along the top. Behind the wall was a small cactus garden with a meandering foot-path for the hotel guests.

"Let us sit here," Herminia said, choosing a spot on the wall away from any listening ears.

"It is not like you to hesitate to say what is on your mind," Don Esteban said, making himself comfortable. "What troubles such a powerful bruja?"

Herminia connected with her ally — she wanted to test the air for any cinnamon to be sure El Brujo didn't use Spirit magic. With senses at maximum, she explained El Jaguar's condition, and her suspicion that the bonds on his ears and mouth were made of Spiritual magic.

She focused all her senses on El Brujo. He seemed genuinely surprised. Not dismayed — that would have been out of character — but surprised. And curious. To him, El Jaguar was a mystery to be solved. She didn't detect any use of magic, any smell of cinnamon, a too-intelligent seagull, or anything out of the ordinary.

"Bring this boy to my house," Don Esteban ordered when the story was told. "I will see what I can do." Chuckling at Herminia's raised eyebrows, he added, "You do not think I camp all the time, do you? I appreciate plumbing as much as the next person, not to mention a roof over my head. Here, my address."

Rather than giving Herminia a business card or jotting an address on a piece of paper, El Brujo opened up a kind of window in the Beyond through which Herminia could see a little house with a blue tin roof. A flood of cinnamon smell accompanied the vision. "In Mulegé," he said, "across from the Misión Santa Rosalía de Mulegé."

Herminia was picking a little bone from between her teeth. The fish Friday's were every bit as bad as the women had said, but after three years in the Women's Clinic, Herminia had grown used to it. She ate in the little staff dining area so that for twenty minutes at least she would not be bothered by any patients. One other staff member sat on the opposite side of the windowless room, both needing quiet as much as food.

How could it be possible to have such *fishy* fillets with the Gulf of California a stone's throw away? Herminia wondered if any of these gulf corvina had been caught by her parents. If so, they would die of shame knowing how long the fish had been held before serving, and how incompetently prepared.

Herminia had suggested using the patients to prepare the food — they could do a better job than the staff, and it would give them purpose. The cooking staff could be put to better use ... well ... anywhere but in the kitchen.

That idea was as popular as a shaved cat — it seemed even here in Santa Rosalía there were labor laws and protected employees. She couldn't even convince the staff to soak the fillets in milk before preparation to ameliorate the smell a little bit. Not her department. Mind your own business, *registered nurse*.

Sybil joined Herminia at the table. Herminia blinked away her musings and mumbled a welcoming platitude.

"Promise me," Sybil said, placing both hands on the table, "promise me you won't make up your mind to do anything for at least a full minute. Okay?"

Herminia pushed her plate to the side, grateful for an excuse to abandon it, but concerned also. Sybil wasn't one for unnecessary drama.

"El Jaguar ran away this morning."

Herminia's wrists got that hollow feeling, like all the blood had drained from them. Could he have gone to the Beyond without her? Could he have gotten stuck there?

She didn't think so. Although she was sure the boy had connected to his ally at some point, he didn't seem to have one now. His intent was wild. Not untamed but driven so by the terrible experience. Perhaps he could make it into the Beyond with a mortar and pestle and proper training, but not without the training.

If he had run away, it was to somewhere in the world.

"We have to go looking for him," Herminia said, beginning to rise.

"That wasn't a full minute."

"Why didn't you tell me before?"

Sybil looked down at her hands, then back at Herminia.

"You didn't just find out. You've known for hours," Herminia guessed. "You were hoping he wouldn't come back."

"That's not true."

"Then why—?"

"What would you have done? Plenty of people run away from here. We don't have the staff to bring them back. We let the police know. A few are found; mostly they disappear forever. Listen, Herminia, El Jaguar is a special case. He has no family. Nowhere to go. If he had a family or something, even a pimp or drug dealer father, my concerns would be different. But in this case, El Jaguar is not going anywhere." Sybil's repetition of the fear-name the women had given him reminded Herminia the boy was still a nameless John Doe on the paperwork. Herminia had tried many times to think of a name to fit the boy, but nothing seemed right. He would need a unique name, something special.

"What do you mean, a 'Special Case'?"

Sybil gestured back at the seat, and with reluctance Herminia dropped from a half-crouch back into the chair.

At the nearby table, the other staff member was listening attentively.

"He is testing you. You specifically. If we go after him—" Sybil bit her lip, unwilling to say more.

Herminia tapped her fingers on the table, considering. She understood what Sybil was trying to say. If they went after El Jaguar it would cement their connection, he would become Herminia's burden forever. Did she really want to shackle herself to a psychotic, deaf-and-mute near-brujo for the rest of her life? She was young, twenty years old.

Sybil retained something of a hippie in her yet, and wanted to remind Herminia that this much burden, this much permanence, was a grave decision indeed. What about freedom? What about youth, falling in love, following a movie star to an exotic land just because you felt like it? Signing up to work at a women's clinic to find meaning in your life ... and leaving the door open to abandon it just as fast.

If you felt like it.

All those things Herminia wanted to experience:

Wild, frivolous fancies.

Bold adventure.

Freedom.

Romance.

A man's love.

And yet she had chosen to train as a bruja, and El Jaguar had been wounded by a brujo or bruja. If God had a plan for her, a plan to use these powers that had been granted to Herminia, that most people had been denied from Adam's sin, well, this must be it. She could see no other reason to have landed here. Besides, she had developed more affection for El Jaguar than she cared to admit. He had grown on her like a pair of shapeless, wool slippers, until she could hardly imagine walking without them anymore.

On the other hand, Sybil was right. This was more likely a test than an escape. Unless...

...unless whoever had mutilated the boy had showed up again. That thought brought with it a cold swell of fear. Did Herminia have the power to fight such a brujo?

"We need to try to find him, bring him home," Herminia said. "I can go on my own."

"We don't need to try. The police have already found him. Someone must sign for him. A guardian. If not, they will take him to the orphanage. We have taken in children in the past, but the government is getting more persnickety about legalities. The orphanage in Cabo San Lucas has expanded; they have beds to fill, and an empty bed means fewer government pesos." Sybil touched Herminia's forearm. "That may be the best place for him."

They had made such progress! El Jaguar didn't need to sleep with restraints anymore. He hadn't hurt anyone in months. He went to the bathroom by himself, and could be trusted with wooden spoons. He still couldn't communicate, but he was so much better.

Had all of that been a ruse to make them relax their guard? Had El Jaguar been planning an escape for these months, winning their trust only to betray it?

More likely it was as Sybil surmised, a test for Herminia alone, a test to see how much she really cared.

It certainly would be better for the Women's Clinic if El Jaguar ended up in the orphanage. Less fear in the halls. Less resources devoted to what everyone but Herminia considered a lost cause. But who would have Herminia's patience or powers to help him? No one.

Not for the first time, Herminia thought how much Faustino's Mental power could help. It wouldn't be able to remove the bonds of Spirit, but it could certainly help heal El Jaguar's mind. At the very least, Faustino could seal away the terrible memories the boy must be replaying over and over and over. The mutilation. The abandonment. God only knew what else.

Over the years, Herminia had sought Faustino, willing to put aside pride and dignity to ask for help. Beg for it, if necessary. But Faustino had left the area — and Herminia — without a forwarding address.

"Only one question," Herminia told her friend. "Do I walk to the police station or do you drive me?"

Sybil sighed, slumping in the chair. "I told the police to bring him here. They are at reception."

The boy, El Jaguar, was docile enough to be holding the female police officer's hand. The officer obviously didn't know his reputation or she wouldn't have such nonchalance. She even held him on her gun-side, the firearm within El Jaguar's easy reach!

Standing at the receptionist counter, Herminia gave El Jaguar a disapproving look and pulled the paperwork over.

"Do not run away a second time. Okay? The police have better things to do than babysit." Herminia made sure El Jaguar was watching as she used Physical magic to heal the scar the boy had made across her cheek and eye. She meant it to convey many things. *You disappointed me — I will no longer carry your mark. You cannot hurt me, even by running away. My powers are greater than you can imagine; you have much to learn.* And especially: *We will heal together.*

She signed her name as guardian, *Herminia Carrillo, April 9, 1970.*

TWENTY-FIVE
PRESENT DAY, PUNTA COLONET, BAJA CALIFORNIA NORTH

The three friends sat side by side, Lucinda in the middle, their backs against the cool wall of the Eco house, the first rays of dawn beginning to peer over the distant hills and creep down the roof-line. All night they had passed in the Beyond. Herminia had stayed in the Women's Clinic for *years*, producing far more memories than they could possibly witness. Being very selective, picking and choosing and jumping out of the memories the moment they seemed to veer off course, the three friends had only been able to see a smattering of the whirlwinds that came to their intent; and while interesting, Lucinda failed to see how any of them related to Abuelita's current condition.

Yes, they showed a tight relationship between Herminia and El Jaguar, one Lucinda had never suspected existed. But how did that shed light on Mustache Man's poisoning — Faustino's poisoning — of Herminia years later?

They were wasting time!

Eva cleared her throat. "So, you are like Mateo's cousin or something?"

Mateo leaned his head against the wall and groaned softly. After each viewing, when they reemerged in the Mirror Garden of the Loma

Linda, Mateo had sunk further into himself. And no wonder he was distraught; seeing his father like that. Who wouldn't be?

Eva added, in a tone that certainly was intended to be kind, "At least we understand your father now, how he came to be the way he was. We need to find out who put that curse on El Jaguar, and how he was healed."

"We need to forget all this," Mateo responded.

"Don't you want to know—?" Eva began.

"No!"

Silence.

Lucinda scrounged around for pebbles, picking them from the hard-packed clay, and tossed them toward the neighboring house, around 30 feet away and slightly uphill. No way would she actually hit it from here. The sun crept another few inches down their wall.

Eva said, "Whoever healed El Jaguar can heal Lucy's grandmother."

Lucinda's hand froze in the act of digging up a particularly stubborn pebble as aloud she realized, "No, they can't. A Spiritual brujo can only heal a Spiritual curse." In her mind, she replayed the scenes of Herminia trying to cut the Spirit bonds that covered young El Jaguar's mouth and ears, and Herminia's thoughts that Lucinda, Eva, and Mateo somehow shared through the magic of the Beyond.

Herminia had come to believe that the threads were not made of Physical bonds — those she could have severed. Nor did she think Mental brujos could make this kind of bond. No, these must be of Spirit magic. Don Esteban had told her that the Beyond was the domain of Spirit brujos — they could control it like no others, the Beyond bent itself to their will....

"The bonds on El Jaguar's mouth and ears were made of Spirit magic," Lucinda said. "Abuelita believed that the threads were not made of Physical bonds — those she could have severed. Those she could have severed! This Blood magic is a Physical curse, so a Physical bruja should be able to reverse it."

Mateo retrieved the mortar from where it had fallen on its side. "We have enough sesame seeds for one more try," he offered, and Lucinda took the stone bowl.

Eva said, "Lucy, you're fatigued from the viewings. Maybe you should wait until you feel better."

"No, Abuelita has suffered enough. Help me through the window. I'm doing this. Now."

While clamoring over the windowsill (ouch, the knees!), and then Grandmother, Lucinda wondered what had happened to Aunt María. Was she doomed to watch *100 Mexicanos Dijieron* for all eternity due to Mateo's *compulsion*?

She'd check on Auntie in a minute. First, heal Abuelita.

Their bedroom felt cold. Poor Abuelita had had to sleep with the window thrown wide all night. (The dry desert air cooled considerably at night even in the middle of August.)

Seven sharp whistles — the red cardinal had responded to her need, sat even now on the windowsill, a red splash next to Eva and Mateo's earnest faces.

Lucinda hadn't trained for this; didn't know what she was doing.

She could do this!

She was exhausted beyond measure.

Her need would inspire her!

To do what? How?

Maybe she should sleep....

Lucinda vacillated between confidence, grogginess, and trepidation.

Why hadn't she thought of this before? She'd had the key in her hands this whole time. No matter. Things had worked out. Her cardinal was there; her friends were there; even Abuelita, skeletal as a shrouded mummy, yes, even Abuelita would help.

Round and round the pestle mashed. Churro smell filled the room. Lucinda's fatigue bled from her the way water disappears into the ground from summer puddles.

Once her ally's strength flowed into her, not knowing what to do, Lucinda brought her hands toward Abuelita's infected head. Before she even touched flesh to flesh she felt the taint, the blood curse, a reverse pole to any Physical healing. A disgusting, viscous poison. Lucinda wanted to gag, to run to the sink and wash the filth from between her fingers. Instead, pushing against invisible resistance, she touched her fingertips to the feverish dry skin.

It was as creepy as plunging your hands into the sea and accidentally pressing them into the body of a sea cucumber. An alien touch, punctuated with a quiver that shouldn't be possible over the bone-and-skin cranium. Dry, infectious heat.

"Heal. Heal," Lucinda breathed.

Abuelita began to moan piteously. Then, horrors, her eyes flew open, the pupils dilated to the edge of the iris. Practically no color left, bloodshot white and then black, empty, memoryless holes.

"Ohhhh," Abuelita moaned, a raspy, bottlebrush kind of moan.

Eva shrieked.

Mateo's face had gone ashen.

"Heal. Heal!"

It wasn't enough. Lucinda didn't know enough, hadn't trained enough, was too fatigued … why hadn't she listened to Eva. In her weakness she would ruin it all!

"Enough, enough!" Eva shrieked, now pointing to Lucinda's face.

What is it? Lucinda thought. *What is wrong with my face?*

And, *Just a little more. Just a little more.*

Her ankles grew cold, then her legs, and her forehead could have iced a paleta out of fresh juice. But it seemed to be working. The spider's legs crawled from Abuelita's shoulders, shimmied up the wrinkles of her neck, began tiptoeing along the strong line of her jaw. Healthy brown skin showed through the splotches of disease.

"Heal! Heal!"

That is when Mateo, gulping in fear, lunged through the open window and shoved Lucinda back. The connection broke. Lucinda's heightened senses heard the flutter of the cardinal's wings … then all went dark.

She came around seconds later, lying on the floor, both friends peering down at her.

"You all right?" Eva asked.

"I could have saved her," Lucinda groaned, voice trembling.

"You could have died," Eva said. "I was just about to push you but Mateo reacted first. Lucy, your forehead had turned blue. Like Blue Man Group blue."

Feeling pain from her fingertips, Lucinda held them up. Several fingernails had cracked; blood pooled around the cuticles.

"Help me into bed," she croaked.

Eva wrapped Lucinda's fingers in tissues and pulled the covers up to her neck. Arranged next to Abuelita, Lucinda mumbled, "Can't give up now."

The mattress compressed as Eva and Mateo climbed over the two bodies and through the open window.

According to Mateo's timeline, Abuelita had eight days to live. Lucinda had given one hundred percent last night, had put all of her Physical power and knowhow into trying to heal her grandmother, and failed miserably. According to her friends, she'd nearly died.

Blue Man Group blue. Sheesh.

Certainly, her throbbing headache — and Lucinda wasn't prone to headaches — argued that she'd done some damage to her system.

Reflecting on her failure gave Lucinda the courage to do what she needed to do.

Lucinda first checked on Abuelita (asleep next to her, breathing shallowly, splotches the same as before); then on her own fingernails and toenails (several of them cracked, none bleeding); and finally on Aunt María. The old woman appeared just fine. Chopping cabbage in the kitchen and humming, she gave Lucinda a healthy grin.

Lucinda smiled back, crossed the main room, scooted around the ironing board and stack of freshly pressed clothes to the kitchen, and began searching.

She needed help, and she knew of only one person who had both a connection to Faustino and the power to combat him. Don Esteban, El Brujo.

She had to make contact.

The mortar and pestle wasn't where it normally should be, in the top, left cupboard. Lucinda frowned and moved the various pots aside — the ones she could reach. Still no sign of it. She climbed on the counter and removed everything, and felt around in the back where the shadows were deepest and a few abandoned cobwebs had lost their sticky.

No mortar. No pestle.

Lucinda sucked on her cheeks. Mamá was taking no precautions:

first, she brought great Aunt María to live with them, ostensibly to help take care of Abuelita (really to spy on Lucinda), then she had hidden the mortar and pestle. Or gotten rid of it. Knowing what was in the marriage trunk, Mamá must have guessed that Lucinda would become desperate enough to try to use this mortar and pestle — any mortar and pestle — to cast a spell.

Eight days to live.

"Looking for something, dear?"

"No, Auntie."

"Why are you climbing on the stove, then?"

Lucinda returned the pots to their place and descended from the white stove-top, her mind racing too much to feel chagrined. "Just thinking. Never mind."

"Why don't you help me by chopping cilantro?"

Lucinda almost agreed; after all she owed Auntie that much ... but time was wasting. Every second counted. So instead she pointed at her head and said, quite truthfully, "I've got a killer migraine. I'll just go lie down." With Auntie's drinking habit, the old woman probably sympathized.

Against the sound of Lucinda's bare feet swishing on the tile, Auntie remarked, "What a strange girl."

Just as Lucinda shut the door behind her, a skeleton shifted on the bed. Abuelita had lost so much weight the thin covers dimpled against each individual rib. "*Hija?*"

"Yes, Abuelita."

"Why is my bed wet? Someone spilled on my bed."

Lucinda couldn't stop herself; tears dripped from her chin before she even realized they had overflowed her eyes. She swallowed back a hiccup.

The wrinkled face rolled toward her. "What's wrong, *hija*? Why are you crying?"

"Everything's okay. I'm here. Aunt María is in the next room. Do you remember great Aunt María, grandfather's sister? She ironed my jeans. Can you imagine that — ironing blue jeans? Don't worry, Abuelita, there is nothing wrong, just something in my eyes." As she murmured comforting nothings, as she began to pull the covers from the twin bed, Lucinda's voice trembled from fatigue, from the throbbing in her temples, from emotion. It wasn't easy changing a bed with a person lying on it. It wasn't easy facing the purple curse of failure growing on Abuelita's head.

Whistles came from the window. Standing in the sill, the red cardinal pecked once on the glass.

Lucinda embraced the Physical power and was able to move her grandmother with no trouble, change the sheets, replace everything flatter and cleaner than it had been before.

The headache retreated.

Lucinda opened the door. "Accident," she called.

Aunt María glanced up from the stove. "I will help in a minute."

"No need. I've already done it."

"Hija, don't do that, you'll hurt your back trying to move Herminia all on your own. You're no good to anyone with a strained back."

Lucinda dropped the soiled sheets on the floor where indicated. "Auntie?"

"Yes?"

"Thank you."

The door safely closed, Lucinda shed her clothes, threw open the window, and climbed outside starkers. A road passed the house leading uphill to more houses, and a brown sedan wheeled by all squeaky springs and chugging exhaust, and Lucinda's heart nearly stopped. What excuse could she have possibly made for being naked outside....?

She eyed the laundry, ready to make a grab for whatever was there.

Thank goodness it wasn't necessary. The car chugged on by, the driver intent on the road.

The strongest flier Lucinda had ever seen was the golden eagle, and to this she decided to transform.

Slipping out of human form was spectacularly easy, like becoming a viscous Lucinda, a wax figure slightly melted from the sun. Settling on *golden eagle* was tricky. Her mind kept slipping. Lucinda's face puffed out like a puffer fish; her vertebrae drew together like a shepherd's crook, her feathers billowed into Eva's beautiful, blond hair. The more mistakes made, the more her mind bounced from one form to another. Her skin felt taut, loose, cactus-spiky and lizard-scaly.

Wait, that was close. Scales, quills, feathers. Okay, concentrate on feathers.

The red cardinal chided her with a series of chirps and bird whistles, laughed a bird-laugh, and flew away.

Lucinda tried to say, "Golden Eagle," but without a proper face, it sounded more like "Glud Diggle."

What was she trying to do?

Fly to Don Esteban's house. *Fly.*

She blinked slowly.

She was trying too hard.

A deep breath, a relaxing of the trapezius muscles, and change suddenly overtook her. She simply transformed, flapped her wings, and lifted from the ground.

Ponderously lifted.

This golden eagle form wasn't the agile flier Lucinda had supposed; keeping this body aloft took work. Her pectorals worked overtime, got her to about twice the height of her roof-line, when a surprise updraft lifted her twenty feet, and Lucinda chirped in surprise and delight. She floated up until the rooftops of Punta Colonet became a patchwork quilt and wheeled south.

TWENTY-SIX
PRESENT DAY, PUNTA COLONET TO MULEGÉ, BAJA CALIFORNIA SOUTH

Lucinda kept both the Transpeninsular Highway and the coast in sight for as long as possible, for the Pacific foam that sharpened the knife-edge cliffs had a mesmerizing beauty, and Lucinda wanted to enjoy the uniquely beautiful perspective of her first flight as much as possible, but finally the two landmarks separated, the coast continued due south, blacktop veered inland, and Lucinda followed the blacktop towards Mulegé and a surprise meeting with El Brujo.

The 500-mile flight should take around fifteen hours — but that was for a real bird. At this rate, Lucinda figured, flapping furiously to escape a downdraft, she had to add two or three hours to the margin. Minimum. No matter how she cut it, she was going to be in BIG trouble. She was officially a runaway. She had every intention of returning home as soon as possible — but Mamá didn't know that. Nor did Auntie. Nor Papá.

For all they knew, Lucinda had been kidnapped.

Calling in frustration (frightening a couple of voles, who abandoned their piñón nuts and scurried back to their hole), she veered inland where updrafts were more frequent. Little by little, hour by hour, Lucinda figured out the flying thing, used her keen sight and sensitive feathers to seek out the appropriate thermals and let air currents do most of the work, glided south at nearly forty miles an hour with almost no beating of wings.

The flight gave Lucinda time to think over their entire investigation, all the memories they had reviewed, and her times tables through thirteen times thirteen, which she had never mastered at school. It was hard since she couldn't count on her feathers, but she was pretty sure that beginning at one hundred thirty (ten times thirteen — easy!) she could just add thirteen three times and get the right number.

Let's see. That would be thirteen plus, um, twenty-six (thirteen times two). Plus the ten times thirteen, um, one hundred-thirty plus, that's, well, one sixty-nine?

She came to the same number three times before deciding that yes, thirteen times thirteen was one hundred sixty-nine.

She counted giant cardon cacti (some of them six stories tall) until she reached one hundred.

She counted stream beds, and Pemex stations, and cars with one headlight out, for the flight lasted into the night.

Mamá would kill her when she got home, that was for sure. She just hoped it was worth it. She also hoped that Aunt María wouldn't get in trouble on her account. It wasn't Auntie's fault that Lucinda was impulsive.

Impulsive! Hah. Fifteen plus hours of flight could hardly be called impulsive. What choice did she have? (*Letting Abuelita go*, as Mamá put it, was a coward's choice.)

Despite all the work Eva had put into investigating ownership and LLCs and whatnot — that girlfriend was awesome — they had reached a dead end. Great. Big. Nada. They had no address for Faustino Arce and no way to get one before Abuelita passed away.

Nor did Lucinda have the power, nor the training, to cure Abuelita on her own. She'd proved that in spades this morning. Or was that last morning? She couldn't keep track.

The only road that remained was to ask the help of a real brujo. Don Esteban. If he couldn't remove Abuelita's curse himself, he probably knew one or more Physical brujos who could help. Hadn't he talked about Brujo councils or something? She had a vague memory of that ...

or maybe Eva had said that. Whatever. Don Esteban could find Faustino if anyone could, and that was where all of this eventually led.

All roads lead to the mental brujo, Lucinda decided, the one who stole away Herminia's memories.

For what? What secret had Herminia uncovered that cost her her memories?

Her life?

Lucinda only hoped Don Esteban was still alive.

Oh, is that crushed possum? Ah, delicious pungency. Her stomach growled.

That would be the carrion feeder in her, and Lucinda welcomed it, for the bizarre feelings made the flight pass quicker.

The moon was nearly full when her keen eyesight spotted three volcanoes to the north — Las Tres Vírgenes. An hour later and the Gulf of California slipped into view, black and reflective as gasoline in the moonlight. Santa Rosalía was a galaxy of lights, and those over there by that white mountain scar were probably El Boleo copper mine. Still in operation, despite Faustino's best efforts. Lucinda tried to smile, but her beak wouldn't cooperate.

Finally, the sun already ablaze over the Gulf of California, Lucinda spotted the palm-filled river bottom and oasis town of Mulegé. Not much larger than Punta Colonet, it looked neater, more prosperous, more cars, more likely to have delicious roadkill.

Just in time. Any longer and she was sure to eat something regrettable.

Lucinda followed the tree-lined canyon upriver, wheeled around the Misión Santa Rosalía de Mulegé a number of times, and finally spotted Don Esteban's blue tin roof. The little house had a walled-in garden — different from in Herminia's memory, but then again, it would have changed after this many years. An elderly woman in an orange, Hare Krishna-like robe was raking between rows of bean plants, face shielded by a wide sombrero. Lucinda landed on the wall. The elderly woman paused in the raking, her face pinching in curiosity, her knuckles whitening on the rake handle.

Lucinda transformed into a human again, fell backwards off the wall, landed in a bush. Her chest felt as if she had done a thousand push-ups. She shook all over. She was upside down; it wasn't clear where the hair ended and the bush began. Worst of all, she was buck-naked.

She began to cry.

A blue, metal gate opened, and the gardener's brown face peeked out. There was amusement on the corners of the eyes, though the lips remained neutral. "He's inside," said the woman.

Lucinda was sobbing too hard to reply.

The woman's face disappeared, and Lucinda heard the sound of a rake begin again from behind the wall. A car went by at the end of the alley.

Eventually Lucinda managed to right herself, untangle her hair but for a few broken twigs, and wipe her tears onto her forearm.

Well, she thought, *not too bad for having flown about a million miles. I hope Don Esteban offers me something to eat ... something besides roadkill. And some clothes. A sheet or something, at least. Or a Hare Krishna robe.*

She didn't figure he'd have teenage girl clothes just lying around.

Lucinda knocked on the garden gate and pulled; the metal door was not latched. The garden was neatly laid out, beds of red and white roses offering their aroma, slate paving stones, little birds in a birdbath.

The home's back door had a curtained window at head height, and at a nod from the gardener, Lucinda opened the door and stepped inside. Due to lingering Physical power from the Beyond, she smelled immediately the scents of age. There was a brown couch (dust bunnies, crumbs between the cushions), a little table with two wooden chairs (dry rot setting in on one leg). Old tomato paste was spoiling within the refrigerator in the next room.

On the couch was a fuzzy blanket, and Lucinda wrapped it around herself. Better the blanket than one of those cultist robes.

Just in time. An elderly, orange robe-clad manservant pushed Don Esteban into the room and pressed a lever so the wheelchair would not roll. El Brujo hadn't aged well. His neck was so frail his head looked like a marshmallow on a stick. His shoulders held up the corners of his shirt like tent poles. A few gray hairs clung to the sides of his blotched head, roots dangling from an eroded wash.

Don Esteban smiled, and Lucinda recognized a single, broken front tooth. The others must have fallen out over the years.

Lucinda was shocked. In Herminia's memories, El Brujo had been young and vivacious. He'd seemed only a few years older than her grandmother, and Herminia had guessed as much. Now, he looked about a thousand years old. Rough living ... disease ... or some combination of both had taken its toll.

"Diego, agua de limón for our guest." El Brujo's broken tooth made him lisp the "st" in guest. Lucinda would have recognized that voice anywhere. "Alone?"

"Yes, sir. I came alone."

He stared at her until Lucinda felt uncomfortable. Finally, he said, "Probably you have heard that you are beautiful. That is a lie. Young women are not beautiful in that sense. They have potential — or they do not have potential." Don Esteban's red tongue made its way around cracked, old-man lips. "You will be every bit as lovely as your grandmother."

Lucinda took the proffered lemonade and tried not to let her creeped-out shiver show. "Thank you, sir. I am here for her, for Abuelita. She is dying."

"You cannot reverse time. Not even the greatest brujos have been able to do that, and Herminia was not one of the greatest. Nor was I, I am afraid. A good brujo, a powerful brujo, but not one of the greatest." He looked about to say more, but then lowered the hand that had been gesturing at the sky or the sun, gesturing as if the ceiling were no barrier. It fell to rest on the brown trousers of his lap. "Tell me."

"She has been cursed."

"Ah." He made a slight wave, and Diego, the manservant, bowed and went outside. When Diego had left, Don Esteban made a steeple with his fingers under his nose. He blinked and stared, as if trying to see into Lucinda's head. Although watery, his brown eyes were alert.

The story came out, beginning to end, from Herminia's falling on the day they got the letter from the district attorney's office to the puddle of grease on the burned-out foundation. Only El Diablo's story elicited any reaction from the old man, and it was the last reaction Lucinda would have expected. A tear and a smile, both at once. He told

Lucinda he would explain later. And so Lucinda told of their suspicions about Faustino, the taming of El Jaguar, Lucinda's flight to Mulegé.

When she had finished, El Brujo said, "The puddle of grease was named Francisco López. And I, I was the apprentice who escaped. No, don't be sorry. I can be sorry, for I knew the good and the bad in Don Francisco, but to Punta Colonet there was no good at all. El Diablo used his power to enslave women. He didn't understand that the Beyond holds the power to liberate, not to enslave. I escaped that day, the day Punta Colonet burned my master alive, and I have turned these many years toward the opposite vision of Don Francisco, toward liberation of the human race. Such years as remain to me, I will continue the struggle. So now you know something of me. And we come to the crux of the thing: Why do you put yourself into my hands? Why do you fly here as a golden eagle, alone, into the house of a dangerous brujo?"

Lucinda discovered that her body could not budge. The movement of her lungs, in and out, was barely allowed against the still frame of her rib cage.

"The mark of my training is all over you. Your grandmother, I suppose? Dear, dear Herminia. So lovely. I thought she had given up magic for good. And now I find her training her granddaughter without a single word to me, her true master. Drink, please. Not too much."

Lucinda took a sip of lemonade. But it was not Lucinda's will to drink; her muscles moved on Don Esteban's word, lifted the glass, pursed the lips, swished the drink around her mouth more than normal even though the lemonade was too cold and hurt her teeth. She swallowed faster than she would normally swallow, as Don Esteban himself must swallow.

Lucinda heard a door open and two sets of footsteps take up station behind her.

"Speak," Don Esteban commanded.

Lucinda found she could talk. "I need help ... help finding Faustino Arce. He has cursed Abuelita."

At this the old man laughed, which faded into a wheeze. "Faustino loved your grandmother. He would not curse her."

"*Sí*, he did."

They sparred, the watery brown, old man eyes and the young, dry, determined eyes.

"Will you help me? Or do you want to play games?"

"Forgive me for showing off," said El Brujo. "I have little skill in compulsion; only such skill as a master gets through the apprentice bond. Only a trickle of Faustino's power that I can channel to force silly girls to drink lemonade."

At that, Lucinda's muscles became her own. She slumped onto the seat back.

"You have much to learn, Lucinda. A master takes power from his apprentices. He gets stronger. If the apprentice is of a different power, he gains a certain amount of control over that power. For example, because Faustino was and remains my apprentice, I have a certain amount of Mental magic. Because your grandmother is my apprentice, I have a small amount of Physical magic. I see from your face that you have been taught some of this, no?

"Despite the sundering of the trinity at the Garden of Eden, through apprentice bonds the master can wield a certain amount of control over all three powers."

Finally starting to recover, Lucinda said, "I'm fifteen. I'm not a 'silly girl.' I'm a woman. A bruja. I have my ally!" From outside, the cardinal responded to Lucinda's defiant tone and vitality flooded into Lucinda's limbs. If necessary, she knew she retained enough magic to transform and make a break for the door. A bear would be good — she could scatter these servants like bowling pins and break through the door if it were locked.

"I have been working my life long to bring the three allies together," Don Esteban said. "Once, I was close; I had a key. Your grandmother was the Physical part of that trinity, and she abandoned me — and the world itself. The world may be condemned to its divisions, its poverty and its weakness, what we call 'humans' condemned to live as little more than animals, thanks to your grandmother. Why should I help one who betrayed me so thoroughly?"

Lucinda had not expected Don Esteban's complete, utter conviction. He *believed*, with every fiber of his being, with a power that projected from his eyes like an electric current, that Abuelita had foiled his chances of bonding with the three allies and remaking the world into....

What?

Paradise?

A Garden of Eden?

She hadn't seen Herminia's betrayal in the memories. Maybe Abuelita was hiding that one, the way people hid secrets even from themselves.

It made Lucinda want to rush back to the Beyond and view all she could, as fast as she could. Did the alleged betrayal have something to do with that meeting between El Brujo and Abuelita in Santa Rosalía? Had Abuelita taken El Jaguar to this very house to be cured? If so, what had transpired?

Given unlimited time and energy, Lucinda would have explored the memories further, would have tried to see if El Brujo's accusation held any truth.

Time and energy. Both were finite.

Both drained from Lucinda like grains in an hourglass.

Perhaps that was why Faustino had poisoned Abuelita, so there wasn't enough time to comb through the memories and discover what really happened between Herminia, Don Esteban, and El Jaguar.

Perhaps Lucinda's investigation had actually forced Faustino to poison Abuelita....

Seven days left.

Lucinda swallowed, trying to come up with an argument to convince Don Esteban to help her. "You should help," Lucinda said, sorting through all the possibilities, "because I am asking you."

Twin chuckles came from behind her shoulders, as if El Brujo's helpers found this particularly amusing.

Don Esteban frowned. "Is that the best you can do?"

"Yes. Yes! I could tell you that if Herminia dies, then there is no chance of uniting the three allies. I could tell you that I will be able to convince Abuelita to help unite the three allies, to start using magic again at least, but these would be lies.

"I don't know what happened between you two. So unless you care to tell me, I cannot promise anything. Abuelita is as stubborn as a goat.

If she feels wronged, she'd just as soon butt a brick wall as make amends. The best I can give you is that I am asking for your help. Please. Help."

El Brujo braced both hands on the metal rims of his wheels and, despite a spasm in one arm, rolled his chair closer. The metal rim brushed Lucinda's knee as it slid past.

The gardener put out a sandal-clad foot to stop the chair's forward momentum.

"And what," Don Esteban asked, a mouth-hole on the end of a wobbly neck, "what will you give me in return?"

The saliva in Lucinda's mouth fled, leaving her tongue dry and thick. She couldn't swallow. The fuzzy blanket seemed a meager covering indeed to her naked, fifteen-year-old body.

Only one thing came to mind.

One, awful, terrible thing.

The same sacrifice her grandmother had made so long ago.

"I will become your apprentice," Lucinda offered, a cactus blossoming in her stomach.

The broken tooth appeared. A smile. "You are making a correct choice. The strength from your Physical ally will comfort an old man in his final days."

Impulsive? Yes, this time the word fit. Lucinda had blurted out *apprentice* with the naïveté of a tourist just off the cruise ship in Ensenada trying to find a bargain — and paying triple the normal price! Every fiber in Lucinda's being was shouting *Fool*.

She didn't want any lasting connection to this ... this brujo. The way Don Esteban had taken control of Lucinda's muscles and made her drink lemonade just for laughs. What kind of man would do that? Someone who thought himself above the rules of man. Don Esteban considered himself a brujo, a complete human, as opposed to the near animals that walked on two legs and called themselves *men*.

Lucinda knew this was a dangerous, evil belief.

Once you put yourself above others, once you considered other men to be less than human, then what happened to those people mattered not at all. Just like slaughtering cows for carne asada didn't matter, or scything wheat for grain.

No matter what happened, no matter what awesome Physical feats

Lucinda could accomplish with her ally, she would never let herself believe that.

No, Lucinda did not want to apprentice to El Brujo. She did not trust him.

She feared him more than a little. As did Faustino. As did Herminia.

But what choice did she have?

What else could she possibly offer this powerful Spirit brujo than the apprentice bond?

She channeled a bit of Physical power and tried to sense Don Esteban's helpers. Yes, they had allies, she was sure of it. So, El Brujo had at least four apprentices to draw from: the two helpers here plus Faustino and Herminia. He would have five apprentices if Lucinda bonded.

Just how powerful would he become?

The gardener brought a cutting board and sliced open Don Esteban's thumb. Lucinda rubbed her hands against the fuzzy blanket, trying to build courage.

The knife had sliced the old man's skin like it was nothing; it was REALLY sharp. It wouldn't hurt much. Nor could Don Esteban make Lucinda do anything she didn't want to do. They would make this exchange, this one bargain, and never see each other again. She would leave him just as Faustino and Herminia had left him.

El Brujo was so old. What harm could he do with a trickle of Physical power?

Besides, he wasn't evil. Faustino was the villain here. Faustino had cursed and poisoned Abuelita, hadn't he?

Hadn't he?

Lucinda's thoughts bounced from place to place, but kept resolving to the same truism: What choice did she have?

She seized the knife, closed her eyes, and cut deeper than intended. The blood dribbled onto the cutting board. Lucinda and El Brujo pressed their thumbs into the growing pool, side by side. A membranous, magical wave descended from the tip of Lucinda's head to her toes.

As the bond took, Don Esteban's neck gained musculature. His head sat purposefully, less ready to fall at the slightest pressure, more willfully maintained. Some of the blur left his eyes.

He inhaled deeply, with apparent satisfaction at the expansion of his ribs. "So, now, my apprentice, what help do you request?"

"First, we need to heal Abuelita. She has been cursed by a blood curse. She doesn't have much time."

El Brujo reached out, took hold of Lucinda's thumb, and channeled a bit of Physical magic. The cut sealed to a thin, white line.

"No."

The old brujo continued smiling, content as could be. The gardener and manservant snickered.

Lucinda's momentary optimism melted away. The scar on her thumb throbbed for several heartbeats before she had the courage to speak again.

"But I thought—"

El Brujo dismissed this with a wave of his hand. "Perhaps the blood curse I could reverse, thanks to the Physical power I gained from you and some other … skills I have learned over the years. But I will not. Faustino has attacked Herminia's memories. Even now, they weaken to the point of instability. If they are not released soon — the next day or two — they will disintegrate. I will not heal Herminia's body without her mind. That serves me no purpose, and would be cruel to your grandmother. But I can do one thing for you. I can help you find Faustino."

"Can you travel with me?" Lucinda asked.

"As you can see, I cannot travel at all. Even in my youth, I could never have harnessed enough Physical power through our bond to transform and fly as you do. The power I siphon is—" he wiggled his fingers, "a trifle, really. No, dear Lucinda, I'm afraid you will have to do this on your own."

"How? I am only fifteen years old. I just got my ally a few days ago."

"A moment ago you were a woman and a bruja!" Her scowl made him chuckle. "So, you come for aid and you gain wisdom. A worthy trade. One more morsel of wisdom I will impart: Appeal to Faustino as Herminia's granddaughter. He loved your grandmother; he will love you. Do not try to overpower him or he will crush you — and Herminia's memories will be lost. Appeal to him in love.

"Now, come. Let us enter the Beyond together. Open yourself to it, as Herminia has taught you."

With that, the walls rolled back exactly like the peel of a banana, changing into terrain with vaguely the shape of Mulegé, except with bas-relief paintings instead of houses, and video-game renderings instead of vegetation.

"It is getting late, your mother will be worried about her little Golden Eagle."

Don Esteban flicked his hand, exactly the same way Young Herminia had flicked her hand to get Lucinda, Eva, and Mateo away from the Null Wind, and Lucinda found herself flung across the Beyond, high into the sky above Punta Colonet. Plummeting. Toward the ground. Falling. Toward real vegetation, real Punta Colonet.

"Do not panic, Golden Eagle," came Don Esteban's voice inside her head. "Fly."

"Wait!" Lucinda called, beginning a wind-whipped tumble. "How am I supposed to find him? How am I supposed to find Faustino Arce?!"

No answer.

Lucinda pierced a cloud, white blindness, and came out the bottom, cold attacking her bare arms. The fuzzy blanket whipped from her body and fell beside her. She grabbed for it with the vague notion of using the blanket as a parachute, but it had spread wide and dropped more slowly than she did, just out of reach.

Wait, she didn't need a parachute. She could fly.

Lucinda willed herself into golden eagle form again, felt her bones hollowing out, her chest growing, and sore, overused muscles attach between her gigantic sternum and her super-long fingers, fingers that became wings that eased the dive into a glide. (Wait, the wings came from *fingers*? Weird!) The rooftops all looked the same at first, but patterns emerged, the ribbon of the Transpeninsular Highway, and the hairdresser — clinic, and Javier rolling his orange juice away. It must be past noon.

If she went home, Lucinda would be grounded for all eternity — she had spent the entire night away without a word to Mamá or Aunt María. She needed a place to hole up and plan.

At most, Herminia had seven days to live. And her memories would disappear in a day or two! There was no time to be grounded and make peace with Mamá and Aunt María.

She had no idea how to find Faustino Arce, and no idea how to force him to help. *Appeal to him in love.* What nonsense!

She should have known better than to trust a brujo.

Lucinda needed help. And fast.

The golden eagle landed next to the laundry rack outside of her home and transformed back into Lucinda. Naked, exhausted, wobbly Lucinda. The driver of a passing car gave a wolf whistle. Thank goodness Auntie had left the laundry outside. Lucinda pulled on a pair of undies, jeans, and a faded blue scoop neck tee. She stuffed a pair of socks into her pocket in case Mateo had any spare shoes, jogged across the Transpeninsular Highway, and wrapped her knuckles against the green gate of the Morales compound.

TWENTY-SEVEN
PRESENT DAY, PUNTA COLONET, BAJA CALIFORNIA NORTH

A cacophony of barks answered Lucinda's knock, and Lucinda took an involuntary step back. No matter how much time passed, she didn't think she would ever forget that Rottweiler goring her at the Parade of Heroes. Not the pain — overwhelmed, her pain receptors had shut down almost immediately — but the fear, fear taken to the point of helplessness, to the certainty that there was nothing she could do to stop the dog from devouring her. Deer must feel something like that when faced with a mountain lion's overwhelming force.

When no one opened the gate for several minutes, Lucinda mustered the courage and knocked a second time.

A deep voice admonished the dogs, and with an oil-requesting squeak, a bolt was thrown back. A burly man opened the door, perhaps one of the thugs Lucinda had seen at the church, she wasn't sure. He looked very uncertain about letting her past, but she scooted under his arm and he bolted the door behind her.

The barking came from Lucinda's right: six separate chain-link cages, each holding two or more adult Rottweiler's. No puppies or cuddly cuteness, just muscles and jaws and violence.

Once certain that none of the cages had been left open, Lucinda eyes were drawn to the yard, an area large enough to park five or six cars. There, a thug held a snarling Rottweiler by the collar to keep it from attacking Mateo. The thug's eyes were nearly as wild as the dog's, the man's with worry, the dog's with fury, the man's forearms bulging and blood-engorged, the dog's body quivering and straining toward Mateo.

Mateo was covered head to toe in a thick, padded suit. Only his head was exposed. A piece of foam had been torn from the suit's arm and hung like a flap of living flesh.

"Again," Mateo said, between panted breaths. He didn't even spare a glance for Lucinda.

"Patron," said the thug, "the dog needs a rest." The Rottweiler didn't look like it needed a rest; it looked like it was ready to tear Mateo to pieces.

"You have let the dogs go soft," Mateo responded. "Who will buy them if they cannot even pull down a miserable boy?"

"Patron—"

"One time more, release the dog," Mateo ordered, his voice low, his glower black, a glower that reminded Lucinda so much of El Jaguar she shivered.

The thug released the collar with a shout of "Fahs." The dog rushed forward, a bullet train of bone and fur. It didn't leap as Lucinda had anticipated; it came in low for the groin, but Mateo dodged with surprising agility and flung his club-like, padded arm in the way. The Rottweiler seized the appendage and dragged it down and back, pulling Mateo off-balance. He tottered and fell face-first. The Rottweiler released the arm and attacked the back of Mateo's neck. The two thugs rushed forward, pulling the dog off before it could root into bare flesh. They seemed to be yelling "Fuss!"

"Patron, you have to stop. Your suit is damaged; the dog—"

Mateo staggered to his feet. This time he regarded Lucinda, perhaps noticing her for the first time. His eyes widened just a bit, then narrowed. Whatever passed in his mind, it wasn't good. Lucinda would have said it took courage to wear that training suit, to let a dog tear at you with all its might, but she didn't see courage in Mateo's eyes, she saw flat, emotionless, brown paint. A desire to die.

"Desire" was the wrong word. Desire wouldn't make irises that flat.

Mateo's irises bespoke nothing.

Lucinda wanted to stop this somehow, but didn't have any idea how to go about it. It was like seeing a friend pick a fight he couldn't win, taunting the school bully, saying things in the heat of the moment that could never be taken back and must be paid for.

"The dog couldn't take a priest," Mateo said, heaving so much he could hardly articulate. Sweat dripped from his forehead. "You haven't been working them since El Jaguar died."

The thugs knew better than to protest. They returned to their positions.

Again the command "Fahs," again the dog attacked. This time Mateo kept his feet, which seemed to infuriate him more. He loosed a series of insults at both dog and trainers. The Rottweiler hung onto Mateo's arm with jaws powerful enough to break bone. A feeling, a connection came to Lucinda's attention — the red cardinal, and a memory flash of Abuelita turning into a puma, shaking the dog, tossing it aside. The Parade of Heroes again; El Jaguar's compound brought those memories back to the fore.

That was one way to stop this. She could do it, Lucinda knew, summon enough Physical force to manhandle the Rottweiler like a puppy — and Mateo to boot.

She chose not to. The Rottweiler was doing no harm, just training, just following orders. And Mateo needed to work this out himself. Or so she reasoned, though Lucinda allowed that her decision may have been simple conflict avoidance. Not really in her nature, but not impossible.

Beyond the yard was El Jaguar's home, a blocky structure without character.

During the next pause, she told Mateo, "I'll be inside when you're done," and marched to the front door. This should hurry things up, she figured, force the issue and protect Mateo from himself at the same time.

She was prepared to use Physical power to open the door if necessary — better to cheat than to turn the big statement into an epic fail — but the door wasn't locked.

After an entryway lined with racks of high-priced shoes (Mateo's and his mom's), the home opened to a family room where a large, flat-screen TV showed Real Madrid versus Manchester United to no one. Paintings adorned the walls. Little Mesoamerican statues stared from every nook. Real leather sofas flanked the TV; fancy white armchairs with carved feet faced each other. Wealth everywhere, though not drug-lord quantities of wealth. Down a hall, Lucinda passed a powder room. Two open doors led to bedroom suites, each large enough to hold her entire house. The bedroom suites looked sterile, the corners of the bedspreads crisp as envelopes, the decor as blah as a cheap motel: unused guest rooms, no doubt. Who would visit El Jaguar who didn't have to?

With no destination in mind, only a vague notion of waiting in Mateo's room — or at least seeing what it looked like — Lucinda allowed curiosity to guide her. Despite their adventures, she didn't know much about Mateo, his likes and dislikes, his hobbies (besides drawing skulls and hanging out in cemeteries), his favorite color and food.

Here was a closed door, the only one she had seen. She paused to examine it. The hinges were ornate, black metal; the knob irregular cut glass. The door looked to be made of one piece of wood, the tree-rings evident and countable if you had an hour to spare.

Lucinda felt a tingle in her wrists, and a deep desire to connect with her ally. She faced the door, and the growling and the television noises faded. She hesitated a moment. Whatever had happened beyond this door, it had a connection with the Beyond that hadn't entirely faded. Her ally was aware of it; Lucinda was aware of it. This must have been El Jaguar's office. His lair.

Lucinda knocked and entered, leaving the door open.

The room was lit by red glass lamps. Sunlight filtered through red curtains across a fancy mahogany desk. Something wet slithered along Lucinda's palm and she jerked her hand away, gasping.

Satélite had come from behind and licked her hand.

Relieved, she scratched the dog's ears.

There were bookshelves and sparkling knickknacks everywhere, a bewildering array of crystals, feathers, carved Mesoamerican figurines, and leather-bound volumes. The office of a psychic hoarder. A mattress and sleeping bag cut across the floor, the mattress with Batman sheets pulled to tight corners.

Mateo must be sleeping in El Jaguar's office in the sleeping bag, Lucinda mused. Which was nonsensical, since he wanted to forget El Jaguar's abuse. This room was clearly the confused, ill heart of El Jaguar's hacienda — why would Mateo spend more time here than necessary?

Lucinda plopped down on the only comfortable-looking chair in the room, a wooden rocker with black and white, zebra-print upholstery. That flight to El Brujo's took a lot out of her. Despite the bizarre surroundings, despite the growling and barking from outside, her eyes slipped closed.

Much later, she awoke. Disoriented.

Red lamps?

A rocking chair?

Feathers and crystals ... oh yeah.

She stretched, rubbed her eyes, and blinked a few times.

Mateo was propped on his elbows on the mattress, scowling at her. He'd taken time to change into baggy, charcoal trousers and black, button-down shirt. His face was ruddy, though no longer sweaty. He greeted her with, "You shouldn't be here."

Lucinda wiped her mouth with the back of her arm in case she had drooled. She had fallen asleep in El Jaguar's office — Eva would never believe it! She wasn't sure she believed it herself.

"You shouldn't be here," Mateo repeated. "We will get in a lot of trouble for this."

Lucinda stifled a gigantic yawn. "Don't you want to help me figure out who poisoned my grandmother?"

Mateo turned to examine a semi-precious stone chessboard with a half-finished game on the floor next to his mattress. After a couple of awkward minutes, he moved a white marble knight.

Lucinda scratched Satélite's ears and resumed the inspection of the office. The room was chock full of witch-y objects: mortars and pestles (including a green-veined marble one), bags full of crystals, a pen-holder filled with feathers, several bat skulls, one set of reed pipes, a jar full of ornamental corn kernels of every hue. With her red cardinal ally nearby, Lucinda could detect power radiating from some of the objects like lingering heat from an extinguished stove burner.

Several moves later, Mateo removed the onyx king from the chessboard. "How long I have hated you," he told the chess piece. "And now you are gone, but not really gone. You're here, aren't you? In my head. In here, in this room, in these objects of power. This maize, these crystals, this mortar. Everywhere I look, you are staring back at me."

Lucinda wondered if Mateo were seeing El Jaguar in the polished black ... or merely his own reflection.

Eva would have a witty remark about Hamlet and soliloquies, but Lucinda didn't dare, afraid she'd use the wrong word and blow the moment. Instead, she said, "If you see El Jaguar in these objects of power, I'll just take them." She gave a little smile and pocketed a six-sided quartz crystal and a feather.

Mateo opened and closed his mouth as if to say something, thought better of it, and reset the chessboard.

Since he didn't make any objection, Lucinda went ahead and pocketed several more charged objects. *One just like this might have been used to attack my Abuelita,* she thought, pocketing a couple of kernels of purple maize, *but they might have the power to help as well.*

She noticed something else in the room, an aquarium holding two lizards: the cuties that had been accompanying them into the Beyond. Both lizards turned toward Lucinda when she tapped on the glass. The glass was warm from a heat lamp inside the artificial log.

Eva's hello sounded from down the hall.

Lucinda raised her eyebrows.

"I called her while you slept," Mateo explained. "We might as well all get in trouble together."

"In here," Lucinda shouted, more than a little relieved. She gave her friend a hug.

"Whew, cree-ee-py," Eva announced, looking about. "I mean your hair, Mateo. Don't you own a hairbrush? This room is awesome! I brought tortas." She pulled pork shank sandwiches out of brown paper bags and handed them around, then proceeded to sit on the desk.

Lucinda couldn't imagine anyone having ever sat on the desk before.

For a moment, objects of power and curses, lizards, and chessboards were forgotten. Much of the gloom fled the room.

"So, Lucy," Eva said, between giant, footballer-sized bites, "your mom called my mom and said you went missing — and I find you hanging out in Mateo's room with bags under your eyes. I assume the worst. Do we need to order a wedding dress?"

Lucinda choked on her torta.

"She slept in the zebra chair," Mateo supplied.

Eva sat up straighter. "The suspense is killing me. Start at the top, and give me all the details." While she said it nonchalantly, there was a slight hitch in her voice. Almost as if Eva were jealous. But that couldn't be. Eva, the most beautiful, talented girl in Punta Colonet, jealous of Lucinda and Mateo?

Nah.

After Lucinda finished her story, Eva burst out, "So you're El Brujo's apprentice?" Her voice managed to convey excitement, surprise, relief, and dismay. "Lucy, did you ever consider that Faustino and Don Esteban might be working together? That would explain everything, including the fact that your grandmother was cursed twice, once for losing her memory and once with the Blood Curse. One curse from each brujo."

A chill passed through Lucinda's belly. No, she had never seriously considered that possibility. In her mind, it had always been one or the other. Either Don Esteban or Faustino had cursed her grandmother. She shook her head, all the while thinking, *Yes, it is possible. It would fit perfectly. Faustino never actually left El Brujo after all, not in the memories we witnessed. Abuelita left, but Faustino said he would return for more training.*

"Now that you are his apprentice, El Brujo feeds on your power," Mateo said, moving a pawn into a kill zone. "You are like a blood-bank for a vampire, one of those victims who offers themselves voluntarily. You gained nothing, and we are no closer than before to finding the memory thief. He didn't even give you Faustino's address or a place to start looking."

"We know for sure that Faustino stole Abuelita's memories. That's something," Lucinda said.

"We've known that for a long time," Mateo said, adding, "if you believe El Brujo."

"We know that Faustino loves Herminia," Lucinda added. She didn't want to admit the heroic flight south had been for nothing.

"We've known that also."

"Yes, well, we know that it is still true," Lucinda said, "and El Brujo told me it is important somehow. If we can use it."

"From Herminia's memories, we know that El Brujo speaks in riddles," Eva said. "Why would he change now? He probably told you exactly what to do; we just have to figure out the riddle."

They sat for a long time with nothing to break the silence but chewing, swallowing, and chess pieces being moved around. Lucinda was so distraught she couldn't look ahead at what she needed to do. Instead, she kept peering into the past, kept trying to think what she had gained from becoming El Brujo's apprentice. She had wanted him to reverse Abuelita's curse. She had wanted him to kill Faustino if necessary.

(*Kill him?* Yes, if necessary. Though she didn't relish the idea of anyone dying on her account. Imagine that, extinguishing a human being...)

Mateo interrupted her thoughts. "Have you ever wished your grandmother were dead?"

"What? No!"

"All right, your mother, then? Have you ever been so angry at her that you thought, 'I wish she would die.' Just for that one second."

"Oh, sure," Eva said. "Come on, Lucy, fess up."

Lucinda thought hard. Normally she put bad thoughts from her mind as fast as she could: Why dwell on what hurts? She ran her tongue around her teeth. "Maybe, like when Mamá took all my money from my quinceañera, said we needed it to pay taxes and I had to start contributing sometime. That was so unfair!"

"She did that?" Eva asked in disbelief.

"But I only thought about that for a second!" Lucinda protested, her face getting hot. "Mostly I thought about giving her a good hard slap, and then packing my suitcase—"

"And what if," Mateo interrupted, "in that exact second, someone burst through the door and pointed a gun at your mother. What if it was the Joker, and he said, 'I'll do it right now!' What would you do?"

"Protect her."

"How big is the gun?" said Eva, simultaneously. "Is it loaded? Do I know kung fu?"

"I think I see," Lucinda said, nodding. "You are trying to say that because Faustino loves Herminia—"

"He would protect her," Mateo said. "He poisoned her for some reason. Maybe he was angry, or jealous, or doesn't want her to get old and wrinkled. Doesn't matter. But if someone else threatened Herminia, Faustino would protect her out of love. Maybe, I don't know, maybe that's what El Brujo was trying to say with his riddles."

"I got it," Eva cried. "Maybe he has to make her death last. Otherwise, why didn't he just shoot her? Maybe Faustino is using the remaining time to steal Herminia's memories. He needs time to gather all those memories, break down her defenses, so he cursed her with a blood curse. Your grandmother Herminia will die, but Faustino gains the time he needs to get the memories first."

"That's good," Mateo said, "and if he needs time and someone else threatens to kill Herminia quick, he will have to stop them."

"But it doesn't fit with what El Brujo said about Faustino being in love," Eva said, tapping her pretty chin with a finger. "I think we need to stick with that."

Lucinda looked from one friend to the other in shock. "Where did you come up with all this?"

"Haven't you seen Othello? People who love each other kill each other all the time," Eva said.

Mateo shrugged. "I've been thinking a lot. Also, I talked to your grandmother. When I pulled out of that gross memory when Faustino was kissing me — I mean, kissing Herminia." He wiped his lips and spat into a gold embroidery adorned waste basket. "She said something about it taking time to remove a memory. It can't happen instantly when the memories are protected by whirlwinds. Something like that. You know Young Herminia, she remembers some things but not others. Most of it I came up with on my own."

An odd feeling crawled up Lucinda's neck from knowing that Mateo had spoken to Young Herminia in the herb garden, though she couldn't quite put her finger on what was odd about it.

Had he gone to practice magic ... or to talk with Young Herminia?

Odd.

"So we need to threaten Lucy's grandmother?" Eva asked, legs swinging in excitement. She wore electric blue, low vamp heels. Which looked fabulous, of course.

"Yes. It has to be real, a real threat. Something that spurs Faustino to action."

"Hey, I'm right here. That's my Abuelita you're talking about."

"Lucy, listen a second. Mateo is just twisted enough to think this through."

Mateo started pacing. Satélite's tail began thumping. It lifted out of the way just as Mateo passed as if this were a dance the two had perfected. "We have to make sure Faustino is watching. We have to make sure he believes it."

"Yeah," Eva breathed.

Inside, Lucinda steamed. Mateo was too smart for his own good. Bast it, this made sense. They didn't have many options. Sit back and watch Abuelita die ... or try something radical, do or die.

What would Abuelita do?

Emergency surgery: that's what Abuelita would have tried, every time.

"There can't be any real danger," Lucinda said. "This is a bluff. Right?"

Mateo took the chess king in both hands and tried to snap it in two, tried until his face turned red and a grunt escaped his gritted teeth. Distressed, he tossed it into the fancy waste basket.

"I'm sorry, Lucinda," Mateo said, pushing the trash can under the desk with his toe. "Faustino will read our minds and see through a bluff in a second. There can be no turning back, no escape for your grandmother. Faustino rescues her, or she dies. This has to be real."

"Wow," Eva breathed, and gobbled the last of her torta.

Twenty-Eight

They took everything, sensing that one way or another, this was the final act. The blind and deaf-mute lizards poked their heads from Eva's stylish purse. Mateo walked Satélite on a leash, and carried a backpack weighed down with the mortar and pestle. He had also lent Lucinda an over-sized pair of sneakers that she intended to change as soon as they got to her house.

Lucinda had the objects of power in three baggies in separate pockets in her jeans: feathers, crystals, and maize kernels. And some peanuts, in case they got hungry. The crystals — six-sided, rose and plain quartz, rubbed against her leg like a pocketful of nails as they walked. Too bad cargo pockets weren't part of women's fashion.

She could have let Mateo carry the objects of power, of course, but after witnessing his dark combat with the dog (really with himself, she thought), she didn't trust him to carry what amounted to live grenades.

Despite the nap in El Jaguar's office, Lucinda's mind was still fatigue-fuzzy. Which made it hard to poke holes in the plan. They were going to take Abuelita into the Beyond, summon the Null Wind, and wait. It sounded simple enough. Too simple, even. Mateo seemed to think the Null Wind would come when he asked it to, and Lucinda had no doubt that it would. What better accessory to his flat, blank irises than a wind that negates everything?

The Null Wind, a storm of nothingness, was the threat to Herminia.

So far so good.

If Faustino was somehow keeping tabs on Abuelita, they reasoned, he would come to the rescue. His love for Herminia would force him into the open. The three friends would get the jump on him. Negotiate if possible, use force if necessary.

A risky plan, but they'd already established the necessity of taking risks. Lucinda was down with that. What really worried her was this: What if Faustino didn't come?

Or this: What if he didn't care?

Or this: What if he and Don Esteban really were working together?

Sigh.

They agreed to stay until the last minute, but if the Null Wind got too close, they would leave Abuelita there. Abandon her to the Null Wind.

Pondering that caused Lucinda to stumble in the middle of the Transpeninsular Highway.

"Chica!" Eva cried, taking her arm. "Be careful."

The draft from a speeding semi pulled them sideways. Cars and trucks were always speeding on the Trans.

"Thanks," Lucinda mumbled.

Mateo and Eva were sure the plan would work — and just as sure that Faustino wouldn't show unless they were one hundred percent committed to abandoning Abuelita. Being a mind reader, skilled in Mental magic, Faustino would discover any sort of feint. The threat — the intent — had to be real.

Fine and good for them, Herminia wasn't *their* grandmother.

Lucinda shook her head. If only she could rest a few hours, clear the fatigue from her brain, maybe she could come up with something better.

If the Null Wind came, it would strip Abuelita of her allies. That seemed to be the only certainty. Abuelita would feel empty, sensory-deprived. Suffering from curse-induced dementia, she would wonder why Lucinda had abandoned her....

Would the end come quickly? Would Abuelita die of thirst or would the blood curse run its course?

Step by step, the road passed beneath her down-turned eyes. Lucinda was surprised when they arrived at her home. Mamá's car was gone; Aunt María's black Mercedes sat in the drive. A huge collection of cigarette butts decorated the cracked cement. The TV blared.

Mateo suggested using a mind spell on Aunt María.

Lucinda hesitated at the front door, not at all comfortable with using compulsion on Aunt María ... or whatever "mind spell" Mateo had in mind. She had firsthand experience with compulsion, and even being forced to do something as innocent as drink lemonade had left a scar.

"Where are we going to get Mental magic?" she sort of growled. "Did you just promise never to use this on anyone in our entourage ever again?"

Mateo pointed to Lucinda's right, front pocket, where she had put the charged feathers. "You have them, not me. I didn't say anything about *me* casting a spell."

Lucinda frowned. It wasn't the worst idea. Maybe tell Auntie to forget they were there, or to let them do what they wanted for an hour. Something benign and simple. And Lucinda was a LOT more comfortable doing it herself than giving Mateo another crack at Auntie.

On the other hand, they had few objects of power (unless Mateo had squirreled some away he wasn't talking about). Not knowing how to procure or produce more, they should use them judiciously.

"Let's just play this by ear," Lucinda said, and knocked.

Aunt María opened the door shortly, Tecate in one hand, doorknob in the other, her hair suffering from a wrestling match with the couch. "Can I help you?" Auntie fumbled for the glasses dangling between her breasts.

As Auntie pushed the glasses up her nose, Lucinda linked with the red cardinal, reached out with Physical power, aligned with the crystals of the lenses, their neat, orderly layers, and bent them a tiny bit. Lucinda's strength diminished that much more.

Auntie staggered back a couple of steps, took off her glasses and rubbed them against her flower-pattern blouse. "Are you deformed?" she slurred and wiggled her eyebrows, trying to focus. "What's the matter— Oh, Lucinda must have stepped on my glasses without telling me. Now I'll have to get a new prescription. I'm sure you're all perfectly normal and, uh, beautiful." She didn't look too convinced.

Seeing Auntie's semi-inebriation, a giant grin formed on Eva's face. "Do you know where you are going when you die?" Eva slipped into the house. "I mean, do you really know which layer of heaven you will wind up in?"

"Layer? I don't remember— What book is that in? Are you Mormons?" Auntie's head swiveled from the group on the stoop to Eva inside. Finally, she shrugged and followed Eva. "I'm sure you are nice people," Auntie said, dropping the spectacles to the kitchen table, "but I really have no time for this. My niece is missing."

Satélite charged between Auntie's legs, nearly knocking her down. Eva patted a spot on Papá's armchair, coaxing Aunt María to sit next to her. After a bit of hesitation, Auntie sat and scratched Satélite's ears absently. Although the chair was designed for one, Eva's hips were narrow enough that they both fit.

"Genesis III contains the entire angelology and layers of heaven — where you'll end up and what you might expect to do there," Eva continued. (Lucinda was pretty sure Genesis III didn't exist.) "You don't really want to end up in the harp-playing layer do you? Do you even like harp music? I didn't think so. Imagine having to play it all day for eternity!"

"Aren't you a little young to be canvassing the neighborhood?" Auntie asked, stifling a yawn. "The priest will be angry if he catches you. They get territorial, you know. Father Owens used to put screws in the tires of the Methodists."

"I promise you, if you just give us a little of your time, and," Eva was thinking furiously, "and meditate with your eyes closed, enlightenment will be much closer."

Lucinda slumped to the floor next to the armchair. Her strength ... needed to replenish her strength. Her eyelids felt so heavy.

"Well, okay," Auntie said, "let's get this over with. I know you have quotas to fill. You don't do mass weddings or anything, now, do you? I'd have to open another one of these," she joked, guzzling the last of her Tecate.

Mateo sat on the floor across from Lucinda. Everyone crossed their arms as Eva instructed and held hands with their neighbor as best they could. Auntie closed her eyes.

Nothing happened at all.

A few minutes later Eva said, "You can open your eyes now. Did you feel it?"

Aunt María made a mouth raspberry. "Didn't Jesus make wine as his first miracle? I was hoping for sherry, at least." She blew another raspberry.

Everyone burst out laughing, Auntie loudest of all. "Oh, I needed this," she said. Her eyes moistened. "My little Lucinda is missing. You don't know how worried I've been. Maybe God did send you. Thank you for the laughter."

Rising from the couch, Eva said, "Now you have something to pray for — think 'free wine' really hard the next time you set foot in church."

Auntie nodded and dabbed her eyes with a handkerchief, and Lucinda felt a little sorry for her. "Okay, then, say, have you seen my niece? She's about your age. I have a picture right here on my phone."

"No," Eva replied, not giving Auntie time enough to pull up a photo. That might be risky with Lucinda right in front of her. "We haven't seen anyone our age about, but we'll be sure to induct her if we find her. Bye, then."

They waved, but instead of leaving the house they filed into Lucinda's room and closed the door behind them.

"Hey, excuse me! Cultists? That's not the door out," came Aunt María's voice.

From the bed, Abuelita rolled over and opened one eye. Lickety split, Mateo dropped his backpack to the floor and unzipped it. Eva began rummaging around her little red purse.

Lucinda flopped down beside Abuelita. Seeing the comfortable, beautiful bed, all she could think about was closing her eyes ... and not thinking. "You're on," Lucinda mumbled to her friends. "I don't have the strength for this."

If she were a steam engine, she'd be out of wood and water both.

Auntie rapped on the door. "Cultists! That's not the way out."

"Lucy? Lucy!" Eva hissed, "Your aunt — she's going to come in here. What do we say now?"

A series of whistles came from the window — the red cardinal trying to get Lucinda's attention.

The mortar's third leg had snagged on the side of Mateo's backpack. He jerked it ineffectually, grunting like a frustrated Chihuahua.

Eva sorted out a package of breath mints and held them in excited fingers, whispering, "Come on, come on, come on...."

Mateo gave up on the mortar, straightened up, closed his eyes, and scrunched up his face in concentration. A murmur of voices slithered fore.

The doorknob turned. The door opened, and kept opening wider and wider. Auntie's surprised face blew up like an expanding balloon until it became so thin it vanished entirely, and the doorway enveloped them and took them to the top of a solitary mountain, beneath which agricultural fields ran to the horizon in every direction, neat squares of wheat or barley or something like it, with a network of shining canals to feed them.

The Beyond.

Lucinda and Herminia were lying on straw grass. Not as comfortable as her mattress, but not hard either.

Straining with effort, mouth slack with wonder, Herminia managed to sit up and wrap her arms around her knees.

Eva nearly died of laughter. "Aunt María is going to need a six pack when she finds your empty room! A missing Lucy and a missing Herminia. 'Really officer, these cultists just disappeared. It was that dog; I know it was!'"

Even Mateo chuckled.

Lucinda just stared at her friend. Mateo had been acting strange all day. Well, that wasn't so unusual, though his strangeness was stranger than usual. Which could be a tongue twister if she tried to say it really fast. What was strange ... she blinked ... was that she knew why he was acting strange this time. She rose to one elbow.

Mateo's brief laugh faded to self-conscious shoe scuffing.

"Mateo, when did you bond with your ally?" Lucinda's tone caught Eva's attention immediately. Mateo cocked his head so that one eye was looking at her, the other off center. "It seemed awfully easy, awfully natural the way you took us here without the benefit of the mortar."

The Null Wind began to gather. Tan dust obscured the distant fields and rolled up the slopes on all sides. It happened faster than ever before, hardly giving Lucinda enough time to stand. Lucinda's red cardinal landed at their feet, flicking its tail feathers nervously.

The Gila woodpecker flew overhead. Lucinda had no doubt it was Eva's ally. If they kept coming to the Beyond, it wouldn't be long before those two bonded. At their feet, a clump of dirt lifted and rolled away. A pink, diamond-shaped head emerged, a curious blend of lizard and worm. It was so strange that it could only be one thing: Mateo's ally.

"The feather…" Mateo offered.

"I'm holding all the objects of power, so I know you didn't use one of those," Lucinda said. "And I heard the murmur of voices this time. That didn't happen when you used the feather before." Nor did it happen with the maize kernel in church, she realized.

"I didn't do anything wrong," Mateo insisted. "It was my mortar and pestle, my tomb. You have my objects of power in your pocket. Mine."

"Mateo," Eva said, "these are not yours; they belong to El Jaguar."

They sort of *were* his, now that El Jaguar was dead, but Lucinda had never heard Mateo take ownership of them before.

"What's wrong with you?" Eva asked. "Why are you acting this way?"

"Who are you to ask about acting?" Mateo retorted. "That's all you do."

"You're not making any sense," Eva said. "I trusted you."

"So what?" Mateo replied, raising his chin in defiance. "Who cares what you trusted?"

Her friends seemed to have changed the subject in a really weird direction, and Lucinda didn't like where it was going. Not at all. Mateo seemed overly defensive, the sort of defensive people took when they had something to hide.

Eva had become unusually aggressive. The sort of aggressive you used to cover your own feelings — fear, guilt, embarrassment...

No, she didn't like this direction at all.

"Never mind that," Lucinda said. "You two can work it out later. The Wind is coming."

Scowling at Mateo, Eva removed the deaf-mute lizard from her purse, put it on Abuelita's shoulder, and draped a shawl over it. Satélite lay beside Abuelita, burying its nose under its paws, ears flat and back. It didn't like the gathering Wind, not at all.

Mateo didn't move until Lucinda punched him in the arm, at which time he bent down and put a hand on Abuelita's back. "We push Herminia into the Wind when it comes," said Mateo, then considered the old woman's frail form, skin vein-blue and bruise-yellow from the poison, isolated strands of hair blowing in the gathering storm, gnarled fingers wrapped around bony knees, shivering. "Okay, no pushing. We leave her and let the Null Wind bring oblivion." Lucinda moved to the other side and put her hand on Abuelita's back as well. Eva joined them.

"Are you sure it will work?" Lucinda asked.

This was their prearranged dialog. Eva had made them rehearse it over and over again.

"Yes, of course," Mateo replied. "The curse is made of magic — the Null Wind will eliminate the curse."

After a couple of breaths, Lucinda prompted, "Eva?"

"Oh, yes." Then, in her theatrical voice, "Let the Null Wind come! Come, Null Wind, come cure Lucinda's grandmother!" It wasn't Pablo Neruda, but Eva's voice was steady and she managed to make the dialog sound spontaneous.

It really started blowing now, brown, dust tentacles seeking them from the valley floor. Straw grass picked up from the hillside bit at their eyes. Lucinda began to feel a leavening of her ally, like the feeling of lightness when an elevator changes direction, only a lightening to her power.

"From the sea, from the mountains, from every which way, bring the dust of nothingness! Remove this evil blood curse with your sacred power!" Eva spread her arms to embrace the gusts snatching at her voice. She'd gone off-script, caught up in the power of the moment. "We offer you Herminia Carrillo, take away the magic that poisons her. Remove..."

The Wind snatched the rest from Eva's lips. Lucinda wished she'd worn a stretch tee; hers flapped and caught at the blasts, a sail in a squall, a rudder in whitewater, a drag that threatened to make her stumble into the storm proper.

Which, in any case, would overtake them momentarily.

Abuelita wrapped her bony arms over her head. She may have moaned; she probably had, but the sound blended with the groan of the tempest. She looked so old, so infirm, so completely isolated and helpless ... so lovely. It was as if this Wind were in the process of consuming the last, best part of her.

'For dust thou art, and into dust thou shalt return.'

Lucinda bent and kissed Abuelita on top of the head. But for a strand of hair that tickled Lucinda's lips, the head was smooth, warm, soft fragile skin stretched taut over bone. She stayed there, could have stayed there forever kissing Abuelita, squinting against the blown debris...

She couldn't imagine a way she'd rather die. She didn't want to die, but if she had to—

"Guys, time to leave," said Eva.

The Null Wind whirled.

Abuelita would not want me to die so young. She would not want to go on living like this ... but she would want me to live.

"Guys, come on."

Mateo and Eva both tugged on Lucinda's sleeves. Two friends, two more reasons to keep on.

Reluctantly, she stood. The three friends backed away.

The Wind reached for Abuelita.

"Guys?" Eva repeated, frightened. "We have to go."

The Gila woodpecker and red cardinal flew in tight circles overhead, dodging strands of Null Wind. The weird mole lizard crawled back underground.

"Abuelita, I love you," Lucinda said, sure they have made a mistake, but unwilling to turn back now. The three friends had made a bargain with one another. They were out of choices. It was this ... or nothing.

She would not want to keep on living like this. I think.

I think.

…

Who am I to make that choice?!

Who. Am. I?

She swallowed hard. "I'm … I'm sorry."

And then a male figure appeared in the maelstrom, lifted Herminia in his arms, and disappeared.

The roar of the Null Wind made it hard to talk.

"Do you have it?" Lucinda asked Eva.

He came.

Faustino came!

Eva lifted the deaf-mute lizard to one shoulder, listened. The blind lizard allowed the bruja to see clearly through the chaotic and malleable Beyond, and the deaf-mute kept the bruja's other senses from becoming overwhelmed. And they always knew where to find their sister lizard.

The three friends were counting on it.

"Got it," Eva said, grinning.

Twenty-Nine

Present Day, between Punta Colonet and Ensenada, Baja California North

They arrived in dry, ankle-high grass next to a well-groomed, dirt airstrip. A small, twin-engine plane was just taking off, banking into the wind, rising over the nearby mountains. Lucinda could almost feel the rush of air under her wings, as the plane recalled the vivid memory of flying as a golden eagle.

It looked like they weren't too far from Punta Colonet, judging by the scrub brush, the familiar mountain skyline, and the heat. Satélite whined, and they turned to see a portly man in jeans and blue flannel shirt pointing a machine gun at them.

Mateo raised his hands. "You don't see us."

The portly man blinked and, thankfully, didn't pull the trigger. Wearing a puzzled expression, he walked forward. The three friends shuffled aside. The man toed the grass where they had been standing with his thick boots. Then, using a walkie-talkie, he reported finding footprints.

"How many of those feathers do we have?" Mateo whispered. "They should be able to do the same thing."

Lucinda checked their inventory. Four feathers, five maize kernels, and five quartz crystals.

"You all right?" Eva asked.

"Feeling a little woozy," Mateo replied. "I've been visiting memories."

Of course he had. Lucinda removed the feathers from her pocket and handed them over. Thinking a little more, she gave the bag of crystals to Eva (grateful not to have them chafing her thigh), who seemed to be leaning toward Spiritual magic. She kept the Physical maize kernels for herself.

The portly security guard barked into the walkie-talkie, asking if whoever was on the other end was talking to him. Then he fiddled with the controls, stuck his finger in his ear, and rubbed vigorously.

"He can hear us," Eva whispered.

They took off running, trying as best they could not to flatten the grass and leave a trail. Thank goodness that guard wasn't trigger-happy or he might have begun shooting in random directions!

Near the airstrip crouched a ranch-style adobe house roofed with orange tiles. Shaped like a giant horseshoe, the house wrapped around an idyllic swimming pool and patio, chaise lounges, and parasols.

"This way," Eva said, listening to the deaf-mute lizard on her shoulder, and they took off running.

The lizards didn't really talk per se, but they had a way of making you understand directions, like at the dead of night when none of the normal landmarks look the same but your subconscious still knows exactly how many steps to take and which way to turn. That's what it felt like to let a lizard guide you.

A sliding door by the pool let them in, and they charged through the great room, the kitchen, past a maid, a gun-toting thug, two gentlemen smoking cigars, the laundry, an exercise room, to the bedrooms. Mateo spent three feathers, and Lucinda wondered how long these people *wouldn't see* them. Forever? What if she used that on Mamá? She almost thought somebody *had* used that on her mom until that incident with El Diablo's house. That was when she realized Mamá really did care — the worst possible way to find out, with Mamá trying to block the investigation's progress!

They arrived outside a clear-wood door at the end of a tiled hallway, a beautiful, Chinese rug underfoot. The deaf-mute lizard did a few push-ups on Eva's shoulder and stuck its tongue at the door.

Lucinda knocked.

"Faustino? It's Lucinda. Herminia's granddaughter. We want to talk with you."

Appeal to Faustino as Herminia's granddaughter, El Brujo had advised. *He loved your grandmother; he will love you.*

She couldn't hear anything until she opened herself to her ally. Behind the door, her enhanced senses heard clothes rustling slightly against the hiss of a gas fireplace, someone trying to be quiet. It sounded like a cozy room, no windows, or maybe a curtained one, little air circulation but for the chimney puffing warm air up and out.

Lucinda embraced the lock tumblers and began to line them up, smoothly, the way they liked to sit.

"Mister Arce?" Eva said. "My feet hurt like crazy in these heels, and Lucinda's grandmother is dying. You don't want that, do you?"

Mateo had been moving his hand closer and closer to the door handle. When Lucinda was sure the tumblers were aligned, she nodded.

There was a crack that rang Lucinda's ears. A fistful of plaster beside her head blew apart. Mateo twisted the door handle and threw it open. Lucinda dropped to hands and knees; more bullet holes smashed through the wall, one, two, three, clouding the air with white dust and shattered drywall. A black streak bolted into the room. A shout turned into a high-pitched shriek. Lucinda poked her head around the door frame: Satélite had locked its jaws over Faustino's gun hand and was dragging the man to his knees in a crackle of hand-bones and torn skin. The pistol clattered to the floor.

Lucinda crawled inside as fast as her knees would carry her, followed by her friends. It was a small bedroom, lavishly appointed, with a mural embracing all four walls. Half the room was taken up with a four-poster bed in which lay Abuelita, covered to the neck by a white comforter despite the heat of the fireplace.

Lucinda stood so as to look down on her enemy.

The pathetic man was whimpering. His hair was thick, full, salt and pepper — the only thing remotely handsome about Faustino. His face pinched to a point on which perched his waxed mustache. No question: Faustino was the same Mustache Man who had cursed Abuelita in Camino Hacia Dios.

"Faustino Arce, I am Lucinda Eco. You cursed my grandmother. You are going to restore her mind, and then we will talk. I think I will let Abuelita decide what to do with you at that point. If you are fortunate, she still holds some affection for you."

At a sign from Mateo, Satélite released the hand and Faustino squeezed it under his other armpit. Dressed nicely in new jeans and a white, collared shirt with the sleeves rolled up, Faustino sat on his boot-heels, nursing his hand.

Eva picked up the gun between index and thumb, and slipped it in her spandex waistband like they do in the movies. This really stretched her Lululemon's. She frowned and tugged it out, holding it awkwardly, barrel pointed at the floor.

Mateo said, "You're about to shoot off your toe."

Eva straightened her index finger away from the trigger guard, held the gun away from her like a scorpion.

Faustino's whimpers turned to broken, near-hysterical laughter. "An actress, the son of a lunatic, a bruja's granddaughter? A motley group of executioners. This is where I offer you a mordida to spare my life, no? Would you accept an iPod? Justin Timberlake tickets?"

"Who cares about those things?" Eva said, horrified.

A muscle in Lucinda's neck began to twinge. "You will heal my grandmother, or we will kill you. If you don't think I will do it, Mateo will. He is the son of El Jaguar, I think you know that. He is loco."

Eva handed Mateo the pistol, and he palmed it much more expertly.

Faustino's head tilted. His cheeks had become ruddy like raspberry filling through a thin pastry. "Herminia will die with the turning of the moon, and I am glad for it."

At this, Lucinda lashed out with her foot, connecting with Faustino's back like a mallet banging a drum. She could tell it hurt — but not as much as it would when she kicked the back of his head next time.

"Lucy!" Eva said, alarmed.

Lucinda tried to remain expressionless, as though kicking people in the back were no big deal. Faustino was evil, and he would show no mercy if he captured them, that was for sure. Abuelita's life was at stake! Life, memories, everything. She could end up like those Alzheimer's people who repeated the same things a million times and forgot their own grandchildren! She could end up dead, ashes and dust. "Abuelita trusted you. Lies, that's all you offered. You took everything for lies. We've been watching; Abuelita showed us her memories in the Beyond."

Eva stared as if Lucinda had sprouted a second head.

"Spying on the past, have you? Dangerous business," Faustino said. "How exactly did Herminia show you anything?"

"You don't need to know."

"All you need to know," Eva said, "is that I have never seen Lucinda this angry. And I've seen her really, really angry. Like smash her own cell phone angry. And like I said, my feet are killing me in these heels. You know what I'm capable of when my feet are killing me?"

In reply, Faustino's nervous eyes invited them to look more closely at the mural, portraits of the great Mexican bandidos Pancho Villa and Emiliano Zapata over and over, one after another, very stylized with flowers and the Mexican flag surrounding them. It matched the red, yellow, and green linens of the bed perfectly.

"You know all of this, no, the history of my country? Emiliano Zapata, a murderer of Indians. Pancho Villa, a thief of the highest order. México's greatest heroes, Emiliano and Pancho taught me about acquiring power. Hatred, that I learned on my own."

Mateo turned the gun sideways like a gang-banger. It looked as awkward as it was dangerous, like if he pulled the trigger the recoil might break his own hand. "I know these are assassins like El Jaguar."

"You would know all about that, wouldn't you, Mateo Morales? For the pain El Jaguar gave you, I am sorry; without purpose, cruelty is wasteful. That is why I gave the blood curse to Herminia; to keep her alive in this state would be cruelty. Nevertheless, I did not do it on my own. Someone asked me to do it. I refused, many times, but she insisted. With tears, with her beautiful, brunette eyes pleading, she made me promise."

Lucinda knew what Faustino was about to say, knew who he was going to blame, and she didn't want to ... couldn't ... hear it. Faustino's power was Mental; he might be as good at manipulating people in this world as he was in the Beyond. She heard no murmur of Mental voices, but would she if Faustino targeted them with Mental power? He'd been practicing for decades.

"Fine, if you won't heal Herminia's body, restore her mind. Give Abuelita her memories back. Let her remember my name, who I am. Remember her own dignity." Lucinda knew she shouldn't start bargaining this early. Faustino had offered nothing! Eva should do the talking. (That girlfriend knew how to bargain!) But Lucinda wanted this so badly, she couldn't help herself. If only Faustino restored Herminia's memories, Don Esteban could heal her body.

Don't give him a clue. Don't let Faustino see hopefulness; he might guess that she had a backup plan.

A faded photograph in an ornate silver frame seemed to speak to her. Lucinda remembered taking the self-timed photo as Herminia: Don Esteban seated on the tailgate of his truck, Young Herminia and Faustino to either side, arms held wide as if presenting Don Esteban as a triumphant athlete — he *was* then, wasn't he, their idol? — the red eye of the camera blinking slower and slower, until ... click.

Lucinda worked her jaw a few times; in her fatigue, she was beginning to confuse Herminia's memories with her own.

Faustino followed Lucinda's gaze to the silver-framed photograph. "My love for Herminia, my love for your Abuelita, is the only true thing in my life. The only thing of beauty."

The murals bubbled and streaked. The ruined faces of Pancho Villa and Emiliano Zapata elongated, smeared. Paint vapors tickled the friends' eyeballs, wrapped fingers around their brains, and squeezed. Dizziness pulled from their heads to their stomachs, drawing them together like saltwater taffy.

The gun dissolved into sand that slid through Mateo's fingers; Eva pulled a crystal from her pocket and tried casting its power; the clear, six-sided crystal grew smoky and opaque, sparks twinkled up and down the edges and burned themselves out, and finally the stone cracked. Eva let fall the jagged shards to the floor.

They were in the Beyond; neither Abuelita nor Satélite had come with them.

They were on the grand entry of the Women's Clinic, though the structure had decayed considerably since their last visit. One of the windows was shattered, two pieces of glass remained in the bottom like fangs; the paint had grayed; now devoid of furniture, the reception room inside (viewed through the window-hole) was dimpled with mounds of termite dust.

Lucinda tried to shift to cougar form and found herself incapable; she had used too much energy on the flight to Mulegé, and she hadn't rested sufficiently. The effort brought blackness to her eyes. She would have fallen had not a post been nearby to lean on.

Faustino remained on his knees, one hand under his arm where a dark stain spread around his armpit, the other hand on his lap as if in church. In the distance, over the Gulf of California, the Null Wind began to blow.

"If you would know the truth, Lucinda, there is a memory you must see. Sí, I owe your grandmother this much, at least. But know this: nothing, nothing you can say, nothing you can do, will bring me to restore Herminia's mind or body."

"I don't trust you," Lucinda said. "Whatever you have to show us will be lies."

"*We* don't trust you," Eva added.

The double doors opened and a breath of wood-rot enveloped them. "We won't be going on a tour of my past," Faustino said. "We will visit Herminia Carrillo's past — your grandmother's past, before she took the name of another. You are familiar with some of this, no? We will skip right to the climax. The most important memories are still here, buried deep. You will find them upstairs. I myself don't know everything, but Mateo's lizard friends will be with us. We will learn together."

Eva bent down and retrieved the blind lizard so that she carried both.

Lucinda released the wooden post that had been keeping her upright. Her legs wobbled, but she was determined to go on. As long as Faustino kept talking, as long as he was showing them something, they had time. Faustino was bound to make a mistake.

"We came here before when Eva used the mortar and pestle," Lucinda said. "There was nothing here; it was empty."

Faustino's white hair began to lift and flutter. "One of you is drawing the Null Wind. Come inside with me, or stay out and learn what true emptiness is. You are free to choose."

Clothes billowing, all three followed Faustino inside the Women's Clinic. They must have looked a sight — the wounded old man, blood-soaked hand clutched under his armpit; Lucinda, staggering from one step to the next in weariness; Mateo and Eva trailing, one angry, tired and sullen, one wide-eyed and beautiful, all of them scared.

The double doors shut behind them. The building groaned against the lashing of the Wind.

THIRTY
1972, BEYOND

Faustino hustled Lucinda, Eva, and Mateo upstairs. "We haven't much time," he said. "The Null Wind will break this place apart."

Lucinda could see no alternative but to follow his lead for the time being. She was acutely aware that they had left Herminia and Satélite behind. Their only hope lay in outwitting Faustino. He may have been a bumbler in Abuelita's memories, but he had had forty or more years to perfect his magic. Lucinda had been practicing all of a couple of weeks ... and without a mentor to guide her.

The baggie of maize kernels was a reassuring weight in Lucinda's pocket. She hoped Eva and Mateo were standing ready to use magic also, if necessary.

The memory awaited in room 2-G. In the corner of the otherwise barren room was a metal frame bed. Restraints dangled from the head and foot. Dismal. Without hesitation, Lucinda, Eva, and Mateo stepped inside the room. Never mind the strangeness of a whirlwind spinning inside a wood-paneled room, they reached for it. The whirlwind dropped them in a valley on the shoulder of a mountain, a valley of an unnaturally deep green, with a sheer drop-off on one side, mesas in the distance, and to their backs, a cliff disappearing into a cloud bank. Wounds of fresh dirt defiled the grass. Apart from freshly-turned earth, only one tree, a sprawling thing with white bark and oval leaves, roots half exposed on the eroding cliff face, marred the smooth green of the valley.

"Where are we?" Eva asked.

"A graveyard," Mateo said, calm, at home. His kind of place. He wandered over to kick dirt clods across one of the closer mounds. He managed to do this without any disrespect.

Faustino had not come, or he was invisible, though no doubt he was watching. What did he want them to do here? The sky was a uniform purple. Uniform, that is, but for a split through which they could see the water-stained ceiling of room 2-G. So, this was a broken memory. Not intact.

Lucinda had expected to drop into Herminia's point of view and watch the memory as if she *were* Herminia. Apparently, Faustino's way of viewing the memories was different, for Lucinda, Eva and Mateo were standing there in person.

Two figures appeared near the cliff, holding hands. El Jaguar looked calmer, older. A son taking a stroll with his mother. Herminia had become a beautiful woman in her twenties. Her hair was long and braided down her back.

"You know this place creeps me out," Herminia said.

A shovel appeared next to one of the graves, and Herminia took it. With a shrug she said, "It's your birthday."

Herminia dug. Time warped, and in seconds Herminia dug out the body of a young girl, completely intact, without any signs of decay, the girl's dress as blue as the day it was purchased. A young girl, maybe thirteen, with her eyes sewn shut.

"They don't know we are here," Eva said, doing the floss just to be sure.

Lucinda punched her shoulder.

The girl that Herminia dug up was more of a fairy tale princess than a corpse — porcelain-smooth skin, curly eyelashes, dimples — she might have been sleeping if it weren't for her complete stillness. Lucinda guessed that the girl's perfection was a measure of El Jaguar's intent rather than an actual viewing of the girl. After all, El Jaguar certainly wasn't handsome.

Herminia carried the body over to the tree, lay it back against the trunk, and proceeded to clean it. Wiping a film of dirt from the girl's lips, she said, "She's aged with you. The last we came she was a year smaller. You don't want to be older than your sister, eh, Santiago? Do you think you could reverse the aging process in me, keep me from getting wrinkles?" She grinned sideways at El Jaguar. "No? I didn't think so. You're the one who gives me wrinkles."

So, thought Lucinda, *Abuelita has already named him...*

The purple sky chose that moment to close, Lucinda lost sight of her friends, lost sight of her own body, lost awareness of anything but the memory.

"Well, I brought something for you," said Herminia, aware that Santiago was pleased. She had long since gotten used to touching this girl who must have been Santiago's sister, though Santiago had no way of communicating that. He could write as well as he could talk, which was to say not at all. Not after all these years. Something beyond the threads on his mouth kept him mute, some magical hooks that ran to his very core. She patted a spot next to the girl, and they sat together, the three of them. From the pocket she had sewn onto her store-bought skirt, Herminia pulled a sheaf of colorful cardboard decorated with cartoon images of happy strawberries, ludicrous bananas, and assorted anthropomorphic fruit. "I know you can't eat here, so I didn't bake a cake. But look, strawberry, your favorite. You scratch it, see?"

Santiago clapped his hands, awkwardly, a gesture a much younger boy would make — and he and Herminia scratched and sniffed the bright drawings. It was the happiest Santiago had been in months. What a bizarre family they made, thought Herminia. Mamá witch, mute son, and the corpse. Why couldn't El Jaguar have an imaginary friend like a normal kid?

Herminia knew Santiago loved her without restraint; and she loved him back, cautiously. The way a mother must love someone who pulls the heads off insects. You love them, and you know, somewhere, that they are going to wind up in prison. You pray they don't hurt someone else's child before they get locked up. Not too much. Please.

Let my love temper his anger.

Herminia managed to keep all this off of her face, her carefree face, the one she used to keep Santiago on an even keel. "We make wishes on birthdays, no, when we blow out candles? Let us make a wish and blow this out." Drawing power from her ally — which fluttered in hummingbird form through the branches of the tree — Herminia made a flame appear on the end of a blade of grass, a round flame, as if you dipped the head of a dandelion in gasoline and lit it. "Have you wished? I think I know your wish. My wish is to find whoever did this to you, wrap them with a thousand little threads, and pull the ends until their head pops off, like this." Together, they blew, and the flaming dandelion head sailed over the cliff.

Santiago pointed to his mouth, and then to his sister's eyes, and Herminia replied, "If only you would let Don Esteban—" El Jaguar shook his head frantically. "I have tried everything I know. I cannot. I cannot cut your threads; I cannot cut those on your sister. God knows why you want me to do that, but I can't. This was made with Spiritual magic. Nothing I have tried does any good, and I just don't know anyone else who has bonded with their Spiritual ally. If you just let Don—"

El Jaguar broke down in sobs, and it took time to calm him. Herminia didn't understand his fear of Don Esteban. El Brujo had never shown Santiago anything but patience.

As always, Herminia acquiesced. "I understand you. I do. We will get revenge on the brujo who did this, I promise."

Again, Santiago pointed to his mouth, and to the girl's eyes, and Herminia sighed. "I will try again."

Despite her pessimism, Herminia still spent many hours concocting new ways to try to rid Santiago of the binding threads, and one idea had come to her in the middle of the night. Maybe it was an answer to her prayers. God sometimes worked that way, through one's dreams. Holding her ankle knife reverently in both hands, she chanted: A grainy sheen flowed over the blade, liquid stone, raw Physical power. She'd never tried liquid stone before, not like this. One by one, thread by spiderweb-white thread, she sliced across El Jaguar's sister's right eye. It seemed to be working. Tight as guitar strings, the threads sprang apart against the liquid stone ... and stayed open. As the stitches disappeared from his sister's eyelid a crescent-moon of brown iris appeared. Herminia's hand trembled with excitement; the handle grew slick in her palm. She moved the knife over the girl's nose to the left eye...

...but the second the knife lifted the threads drew back together from the corner of the first eye, reweaving, reforming, and piercing Herminia's heart.

Santiago made a strangled sound, misery and disappointment choking him.

Herminia released her breath. "Santiago, your sister is dead. Someday we will find a brujo with Spiritual power — not Don Esteban — who will help us open her eyes, and more importantly, open your voice. Your wonderful, live voice." Santiago placed his hands on the knife handle and tugged. For a second, Herminia panicked, thinking he wanted to commit suicide, but El Jaguar rotated the blade away from him, and she allowed this to happen, curious, wide-eyed, as the boy guided the tip of the skinning knife to his sister's abdomen. Santiago leaned against the handle, pushed the knife tip through his sister's brilliant blue dress, through the skin.

Through the handle, with the sickening reminder of raw meat, Herminia felt fabric and skin spread. Deeper now, the muscle wall suddenly gave and the knife plunged with a sound like a rotten tomato hitting the floor.

Herminia began slicing the belly open. She was in a sort of nervous trance, unable to stop, unaware of just what she was doing or why. The knife tangled in the dress. She released the handle, used her bloody hands to rip the fabric open. It was all there now, tan belly, gaping watermelon wound, gore emerging like curious beasts from hell. Once again, Herminia seized the knife handle and cut further, deeper, wider, like a butcher possessed. When the incision crossed the whole belly. Herminia slithered her hands through the opening, pushing aside the gore, the intestines, the spleen, until she encountered something hard. It throbbed.

Herminia withdrew a spiny, bloody mess.

Santiago clapped, and together they wiped the thing clean on the grass until they were surrounded by stain, as if a battle had taken place around them. It looked like a dragon fruit. One end was bulbous, smooth and red, the rear had scales that tapered to a point, with green accents on the tips of the leaf-like scales. The fruit warmed her like nothing Herminia had ever felt: nascent, life-giving, as if her hand was on the bellies of all the pregnant mothers in the world.

Herminia concentrated some Physical power on it, seeking to pry apart its secrets, and the power multiplied, knocking her backwards to the ground. Blinking the flare from her eyes, she picked up the fruit again. *This could only be one thing.*

"You were hiding it there? You were hiding this inside your sister all this time? You found it, didn't you? Fruit from the Tree of Knowledge. With this, Don Esteban could unite the two worlds, the Beyond and the mundane. We *all* could be brujos."

Herminia contemplated what that might mean. She turned the fruit over again and again in her hands, savoring its pulse. "With this, I could cure you."

The Null Wind blew up from the valley, sending a chill across Herminia's shoulders. She turned to look. Two creatures stirred within the Wind, a sea-turtle, and an ocelot, seeming to swim in the air. She understood these were respectively her Mental and Spiritual allies. Around them, just outside the brown tendrils of Wind, fluttered the hummingbird, her Physical ally.

With just the proximity of this fruit, the three allies no longer repelled each other — this fruit of the Tree of Knowledge. In that moment, Herminia knew she could bond with all three allies. What had sounded so wonderful in her youth, when Don Esteban had explained it, when she had first tasted Physical power, now frightened her. This fruit could change everything, everything in this world and the next. "We should put this back. I need to think about this. I need to talk with someone."

Santiago put his thumbs over his sister's eyes, the ones sewn shut with Spirit thread, and caressed them gently.

"Ah, well. I did make a promise, didn't I?"

Still, she hesitated. Was it her place to change the balance of the world? She used her forearm to wipe the sweat from her brow. The scientists on the Manhattan Project must have felt something like this, she thought. They could let millions die fighting Japan ... or they could usher in the nuclear age. There was no going back from something like that...

...there would be no going back now.

How much was her promise to Santiago?

How much was the allure of power?

How much simple curiosity?

Something pushed her over the edge, some impulse that welled up from within or without, and Herminia drew a stone from the cliff and shaped it into a mortar and pestle with pure Physical power. Her knife carved a neat hole into the side of the fruit — a shame to mar something so beautiful, but she knew the flesh hid something more important.

The seeds.

The flesh was the brilliant white of fresh snow, the three seeds blue, silver, cinnamon. The silver seed looked different, plain, and Herminia knew instinctively that was because she had already bonded with the Physical ally. It had no role to play. So, blue for Mental, silver for the Physical, cinnamon for Spiritual.

Herminia withdrew this latter seed and crushed it in the mortar. She ground the seed to a bronze paste.

The ocelot exited the Null Wind. A whiff of cinnamon came from its fur.

Santiago's eyes widened.

Herminia wiped her index finger through the paste, ready to eat it and finish the ritual. But she didn't. It didn't feel right. Maybe it was the mother instinct in her. Maybe it was pity. Maybe it was something else that made her crawl forward, embrace Santiago's head against her chest, and allow El Jaguar to suck the paste from her fingertip. The tentative bond with the Spiritual ally, with the ocelot, moved from Herminia to Santiago.

Santiago gasped, bound now with Herminia's Spiritual ally. A full range of emotions warred over him: pleasure, surprise, nostalgia, fear, terror, his posture, his face reacting to each and all. They wept together, adopted-mother with almost-son, happy tears. Unbelievable, happy tears.

A Spiritual fog rolled in and obscured the purple sky. The Null wind seemed to retreat.

"Stop! Stop! We won't be able to see each other if you keep going." Herminia was half-laughing, too happy to be worried. "We'll have to teach you to control that, Santiago. Now, something that's too advanced for you, but I will guide you. It cannot wait any longer."

Herminia took El Jaguar's hands and put them on her knife. With Herminia's guidance and a couple of false starts, he managed to surround the blade with Spiritual magic — a mercury coating rather than the liquid granite of Physical power. That this would work, Herminia had no doubts. Nevertheless, best to practice on a corpse. Using the blade of Spirit power, they cut the bonds on the poor girl's eyes. The instant the last thread parted, the body disappeared.

Then, with an easy stroke, they released Santiago's mouth.

El Jaguar made a few sounds, vowels, mostly. He tried various configurations, mouth wide, mouth narrow, tongue rounded, tongue against the roof of his mouth. A caveman choir. Once the sounds began to sound like words, Herminia put her hands on Santiago's knees.

"Santiago, *mi hijo*, what was your name?" She had never called the boy her son before, but now that he was bonded to her Spiritual ally, no other label applied. "*Mi hijo*, do you remember your name?"

"Santiago."

"That is the name I gave you. What was it before? Do you remember?"

He nodded slowly, then said, "I am Santiago. Santiago Carrillo."

Herminia bit her lower lip. "Do you remember your mother? Your father?"

"Don Esteban," he said.

"We have to tell Don Esteban," she said. "Yes. There are two seeds left, and he already has Spiritual power — he can bond—"

"Your wish with candles." The enunciation sounded alien, but she could understand.

"Yes. With all three allies, Don Esteban will finally achieve what he always dreamed: uniting the Beyond with this world. Don Esteban already has a Spiritual ally, so it does not matter that we used this seed.

With the other two, he will have full power. Unless you want to tell me where the Tree of Knowledge is so we can harvest more fruit."

"Don Esteban-did-this-to-me."

Herminia shivered, a deep primordial fear. "That can't be true."

"It strange, you understood better before I talk."

But Herminia did believe. She recalled vividly her first encounter with El Brujo, when he had left Faustino to die, when he had known full well how to free the lizard and save Faustino's life.

"Tell me, Santiago, what did Don Esteban do?"

"He tried many ways to find Tree. He knew it hid in Null Wind, and lizard guides no find it. He needed different guides. Human guides. Children, easy to bond, easy to manage. We didn't matter, only the Tree."

"I don't believe it. Don Esteban tried to heal you. I was there—"

She had brought El Jaguar to Don Esteban several times to attempt to heal the boy. Each time had been a terrible struggle. Herminia had had to use all her Physical skills to restrain the terrified boy without hurting him; each time El Brujo had made a great show of using magic to attempt a healing ... to no avail. Had that all been a sham?

"My sister, we caught in Null Wind. Our allies deserted us, but ... we walked the maze. My sister died. I didn't, and then the Wind passed by. The fruit, I hid it so Don Esteban could not find it."

"Maze, what maze? You are not making any sense. Are you talking about maize — a kernel of corn, an object of power? Don Esteban couldn't have done this to you." Seventeen graves. She had counted them on every one of El Jaguar's birthdays. Seventeen children murdered in Don Esteban's quest for the Tree of Knowledge.

Herminia couldn't, wouldn't believe it. She shook El Jaguar until the ocelot hissed at her. "Are you sure? It could have been a mind spell."

"I would not lie ... to you."

"No, no you wouldn't." She could take Santiago to Faustino — he could dig through Santiago's mind for the truth. No, no, she couldn't expose Santiago to that.

Faustino, why did his name come to her just then?

Footfalls in the spring grass caused them to turn. El Jaguar scrambled behind Herminia; the ocelot ran to the tree and climbed out of sight.

Don Esteban approached between them and the cliff, the Null wind at his back. "Whisper a name over a grave," he said, a broken-toothed grin spreading across his face. "Better make sure the person is buried inside before you do." With a gesture, a net of Spirit wrapped up the ocelot. Unable to balance, the cat fell to the grass. The Spiritual net looked like a spider-cocoon around a struggling moth.

"Santiago found it, didn't he? I wondered why he didn't die like the others."

Herminia hid the fruit behind her back. Had Don Esteban seen it already? She couldn't be sure. She dug her fingers into the pulp as fast as she could, concealing her actions by her body and her ire. "Children! They were children!"

El Brujo would pay for this, Herminia thought. His head would pop like the dandelion flame they had blown earlier. Just exactly like that.

Still holding the fruit behind her back with one hand, Herminia bent down and retrieved the knife. Before Don Esteban, a mirror-like barrier appeared, something Herminia had never seen before. But she didn't doubt its effectiveness. El Brujo was powerful, secretive. He'd been perfecting his defenses. And the Beyond was a Spiritual domain after all; he ruled here.

Herminia took her time, lifted the knife to her shoulder, coated the blade with Physical power, drew as much energy from her ally as she could, and threw. Don Esteban's barrier flicked wider, almost wide enough to block the knife ... but Herminia wasn't aiming at Don Esteban. Instead, she threw at the base of the Spiritual net, where the various strands gathered around the ocelot. Guided with Physical power, the knife sailed true, sliced more effectively than any normal knife, and freed the ocelot.

Herminia didn't notice a strand of Don Esteban's barrier elongate and reach behind her back, not until it snatched the fruit from her other hand.

"No!" Herminia yelled.

Don Esteban saluted her. "You will thank me before this is over, my apprentice. We will be gods." He disappeared.

Santiago tugged Herminia's shirt sleeve. "Into the Null Wind. Safe."

"First, we destroy these," Herminia said. Concealed in her waistband were the two remaining seeds. She had extracted them while the fruit was behind her back. She put the two seeds in the mortar and stabbed them with the knife, breaking them into pieces, mingling them. She mixed that with grave dirt and spit, hardened it with Physical power, and threw the resulting ball into the Null Wind as hard as she could.

"You're right," she said, eying the Null Wind dubiously, "Don Esteban would never follow us there. He couldn't bear to live without his ally."

Santiago tugged her hand, tried to get her to enter. Herminia's hummingbird fluttered and chirped, awaiting her decision.

The answer came at once, fully formed, irrevocable. She could never go back to being less than she was, less than a bruja. She would rather die.

"You'll understand, once you learn what you have here," she said, indicating the ocelot, pulling Santiago away from the Wind, "once you learn how to swim in the air, to fly underwater, to bathe in the trees and the stone. Or whatever it is you Spiritual brujos do. Come, we take our chances."

A flick of power, and the skinning knife returned to her hand. Herminia and El Jaguar exited the Beyond, and the dream ended.

Thirty-One
Present Day, Beyond

The Women's Clinic complained, a whole litany of complaints from a death-bed patient: the stairwells moaned, the beams popped, the joists creaked, the shutters banged.

"We're almost there," Faustino said, reassuringly, as if he believed they were on his side now that they had seen the memory. "One more I want to show you for your grandmother's sake."

Did Lucinda trust Faustino? She couldn't flip her feelings like heads-to-tails on a coin. She needed time. She needed to work all this out by running, walking, swimming. Get it all out and start over. Even a shower would help. A good, lukewarm, summer shower, with no need of stove-heated water.

Don Esteban — a mad brujo scientist.

Lucinda — his apprentice.

Don Esteban would know exactly where and how to find her; Lucinda had used magic inside Faustino's house. El Brujo would have tracked her there through the apprentice bond.

Nowhere was safe anymore.

Before Lucinda could decide what to do, whether to warn Faustino or not, Faustino led them to another open door, another room with another whirlwind. He tried to shoo them inside but Mateo wedged himself in the door frame.

"I'm not budging until I get some answers," Mateo said, uncharacteristically defiant. "We were inside the last memory. Why?"

"What do you mean, 'inside'?" Faustino asked.

"We could see what was happening from the inside, as if we stood next to Herminia. There was a tear in the sky, too, and the room behind it — I could see it."

"The memories are dissolving," Faustino said, rubbing his mustache in thought. "The Null Wind is speeding the dissolution of Herminia's memories."

"If it falls apart when we are in there?" Mateo insisted. "If the crack widens or something and we step through, will our minds erase, too?"

"You expect life without risk?" Faustino asked. "Life doesn't work that way."

"That's not what I asked. I want to know—" Mateo was pleading, "will we forget?"

"You should have learned by now — a brujo never answers directly. *Andale*, inside."

An alleyway in a smog-filled city. The sun setting. Herminia knocked on an iron gate. A bolt slid on the far side, and the gate opened inward.

Good. Otherwise it would have banged against Herminia's sage-green Chevy Impala, and she liked the fenders as they were.

The courtyard hummed with activity, young men and women in black pants and camouflage pants with black shirts, some wearing neckerchiefs across their faces, restless youth who moved importantly between three Jeeps, a bus (spray-painted black, though Herminia was sure it was a stolen school bus), a wooden table carrying pro Fidel Castro placards, and a home. They made room for the Impala — grudgingly — and Herminia parked near the home. She braced her hands on the steering wheel, relieved to not have to be driving. She needed sleep. Food. A warm bed and a break from running. A break from Santiago, too.

"Mamá?"

"Sí, *mi hijo*. We are here. Uncle Faustino will help us."

Herminia prayed that it were so. She couldn't keep running much longer. El Brujo had found her again and again and again. Each time they had barely escaped with their lives. On her own, it wouldn't have been so difficult, but Herminia had to protect both of them. Don Esteban could wring the information he needed from Santiago as easily as from Herminia.

At least El Brujo needed them alive, needed to learn how to find the Tree of Knowledge to achieve his Utopian vision. He could have killed them half a dozen times.

Herminia gave a final squeeze to the steering wheel and exited the car, holding her head proudly. "Eh, Faustino Arce?" The first two people she spoke with ignored her. The third replied by pointing at the house. She felt like punching the snooty youth in the mouth — he had no physique beneath his black shirt, probably an UNAM student. Probably had never worked a day in his life.

So these were Faustino's revolutionaries, eager to break some windows and shout their support to El Comandante. As if Castro could hear all the way in Cuba across the Gulf of México. America would take El Comandante out with a sniper's bullet, and that would be that, Herminia thought, and Faustino's dreams of communist revolution would disappear.

Thank God for that. She knew enough about communism to know it would only bring misery to México, as if they didn't already have enough. And these so-called revolutionaries would go back to mamá and papá for another tuition check.

Herminia couldn't see the gap, the ceiling where the sky should have been, the split in the wall that showed the bedroom in the Women's Clinic, but Lucinda, Eva, and Mateo did. They shared Herminia's consciousness and their own in the crumbling memory. Mateo stepped in and out through a gap, now-you-see-me, now-you-don't.

Lucinda pushed her consciousness in as deep as she could — she wanted to share Herminia's thoughts.

Inside the house now, an office with shades pulled down. Wearing a traditional sarape, a bolo tie, his hair greased back, Faustino looked at Santiago sideways.

"He is not mine," Herminia was saying, "I have — I have adopted him."

Santiago had fallen into the habit of silence again, though he *could* talk if he so desired. The boy flinched as Faustino rested a hand on his mop of hair.

Faustino said, "He holds your power, and yet he is not yours. I sense Spiritual magic. An ocelot. *Your* ocelot ally, Herminia. How is this possible?"

"Santiago found the Tree of Knowledge. I was able to— He lost his own allies in the Null Wind, and so I helped Santiago bind with my Spiritual ally.

"Faustino, he has done terrible things. If he ever found the Tree—"

"Who?"

"Don Esteban. El Brujo. He has been using children as blind and mute guides, substitute lizards. He has murdered at least seventeen of them in this way. I've seen their graves. It's horrible."

A knock at the door.

"Later," commanded Faustino.

"Time to leave," a woman said through the door.

"You know the plan. Stick to it."

"You are not coming?"

"*Que te importa* if I come or not! Do not knock on my door again."

Outside, trucks powered up, the gate opened, the courtyard emptied.

"*Comunistas*," Lucinda whispered.

"Of course they are, it was the '70s," Eva replied. "Everyone who was anyone was a communist."

Herminia said, "I cannot use magic or El Brujo can find me. We have been running. Running like scared cockroaches." The fatigue caught up with her, and Herminia sagged into a chair.

The memory shifted.

Nighttime had fallen, Herminia and Faustino were performing a ritual. Splits rippled all along the memory showing Lucinda, Mateo, and Eva flashes of the Women's Clinic and Faustino in the present day, though of course Herminia took no notice.

"You know that I love you, Santiago?" Herminia asked El Jaguar.

The boy nodded. Swallowed.

"I have adopted you. You are my son." Herminia thumped her breast. "Here and forever."

Faustino rubbed his thumb in a paste from Herminia's mortar and pressed it to El Jaguar's forehead. The boy wobbled and passed out. Faustino then pulled a ski mask over El Jaguar's head — backwards — so that the boy could not see. He taped it on with duct tape.

Herminia's heart nearly broke — they were binding the boy just as Don Esteban had done with threads of Spirit. How frantic he would be upon waking! She choked back a sob...

...but she had to trust Faustino completely — or not at all.

She wondered where Faustino had learned all this, but now was not the time for stories or long-winded explanations.

"Are you sure he will remember nothing?"

"I have taken Santiago's mind back before you met him, before he ever found the Tree of Knowledge. He will remember nothing. Even if El Brujo captures him, El Jaguar no longer has any knowledge to reveal. He is as safe as he can be."

"But he will have my ally?"

"Nothing I can do about that. Santiago will be a brujo now and forever. A Spiritual brujo. With your ally." Faustino's voice held bitterness. "He will wake up with the mind of a child. I don't know what all it will do to him. The emotional scars may heal over time — he will have forgotten whatever Don Esteban did to him. But it won't be pretty."

"And the silence?"

"Your knife slit the Spirit threads that made Santiago mute." Faustino shrugged. "No barriers to Faustino talking now."

"Now you must erase my mind," Herminia said, "so that I do not remember what Santiago told me about the Tree of Knowledge. With even the slightest clue, El Brujo might be able to find it."

Faustino shook his head. "We cannot take that risk. Don Esteban would feel me tampering with your mind through the apprentice bond. He would come here, and even together, you and I could not defeat him. You have no idea how powerful El Brujo actually is, even with only a single ally."

"The risk is that he strips my mind and finds the Tree of Knowledge!"

Faustino said, "Herminia, you are still El Brujo's apprentice. You must never, never use magic again."

"I would rather die." The truth just came out. She would rather die than let Don Esteban find the Tree of Knowledge, and she would rather die than live without magic.

Faustino stroked his mustache. "Oh, too good to be one of the people? Do you consider them animals now?"

"No, of course not," Herminia said.

"Remember our conversation in the cafe when we ate lobster, Don Esteban laid it all out in plain sight; only you refused to listen. He considers all non-brujos expendable. They are no more than animals to him. He would like all humanity to become brujos, yes, that is his dream. But those who do not pass the test, those who fall to the floor of the cave and cannot immediately find their ally, those are chaff for the wind." Faustino moved to where he could drape an arm across Herminia's shoulders. "My love, my one and only, do not think that way. Before you ever entered the pictograph cave, you were God's marvelous woman."

Herminia cradled Santiago and wept for everything she had lost. Some time later, perhaps a minute, perhaps an hour, she lifted her head. Faustino still held her, and she still held Santiago. "What now? Do I keep running forever?"

"We have saved the boy," Faustino said, "now we will set a trap for your memories. If El Brujo ever comes calling, your memories will be whisked away into the Beyond where he won't be able to get them."

"Are you sure?"

"Oh, yes."

"They will disappear?"

"Memories do not just disappear in the Beyond. They have resonance there even after the physical brain forgets. But yes, the memories will fade long before El Brujo accesses them. He will not find the Tree of Knowledge on my account. I want revolution, not Armageddon."

"Why can't we do that now?"

"It's like my Agent Orange spell," Faustino said, grimly. "It does the job, but leaves behind nothing but scars. You will have to learn everything again. You will forget me, Santiago, your parents, the pictograph cave.... I am not sure you will remember how to eat without help."

Herminia found a black neckerchief and used it to wipe the tears from her cheeks. She made a point of blowing her nose on it. "Well, I should put several hundred miles behind me before daylight. And you have a revolution to lead."

"You are the bravest woman I have ever met."

"Braver than your revolutionaries?"

"Hah. Intellectuals. Paper revolutionaries and window-breakers."

"You are fighting on the wrong side, Faustino," Herminia said. "You should be fighting for freedom — not totalitarianism."

"I will not let you go with an argument," Faustino said, taking Herminia's hand and pulling her to face him. He was close enough to kiss, and she wanted to. Dearly. She had been so mistaken for so long. "If you want to pursue that thought," Faustino said, "spend the night here. With me. There are better ways to resolve our differences."

"One question."

"Yes."

"Why did you use Mental powers on me that night?"

Faustino pulled away as if burned.

"Why didn't you let it happen, let love happen as God intended?"

"You still believe that Mental magic is a form of rape." Stiffly, Faustino walked to the far side of his desk and sat down.

"Faustino, why do you insist on misunderstanding?"

Herminia knelt and lifted El Jaguar over her shoulder in a fireman carry. She paused in the doorway. Outside, the moon shone smoky topaz through the smog. A crow cawed. Somewhere, men and women in black shouted their support to El Comandante.

Her back to Faustino, Herminia said, "We will disappear, Santiago and I. Some no-name, no-nothing town, I think."

Bitter as a dry leaf, Faustino muttered, "You still despise me, don't you?"

Herminia let the door slam behind her. She muttered, "We will never know."

The memory ended. For a second, Lucinda, Eva, and Faustino stood in the creaking, protesting Women's Clinic, then Faustino returned them from the Beyond to his hacienda. Strangely, Mateo's tongue hung out of his mouth as if he were in a stupor.

"What's with him?" Faustino asked.

"He's weird," Eva affirmed.

A murmur of voices caused Lucinda to look around ... and then she realized that this was an indication that Mental magic was being used. Since she hadn't heard the voices before when Faustino had used magic (he must be skilled enough to be able to mask that), perhaps Mateo was setting up some escape. She eased her hand toward the pocket that held the maize kernels and asked, "What happened then?"

"I followed her, of course. Your grandmother dropped El Jaguar off in an orphanage in Punta Colonet, and stayed nearby to keep an eye on him. It tore her apart to be near him and unable to do anything to help. She blamed herself for his corruption. We ... I had to take the boy's mind back to before her healing touch, her love, had made El Jaguar almost whole. I did what I could to keep El Jaguar's violence in check. Twice, I intervened directly before he could hurt anyone, but I had to be careful about using magic. I am still Don Esteban's apprentice, and I know he checks on me from time to time. I hired Carlos Serra, whom you call the Fat Man, to keep an eye on things.

"El Jaguar always felt an attraction to Herminia even though he didn't remember. He saw your mother — and later you, Lucinda — as taking his rightful place, though he didn't really understand *why* he felt that way. He would have violated you at the Parade of Heroes, violated you and killed you and Herminia both. The corruption inside him — the experiments of Don Esteban, or something that had always been broken within his psyche — were more than El Jaguar's brain could process. Herminia had no choice but to use magic to defend you — do not feel bad for what happened.

"Through the apprentice bond, Don Esteban felt it when Herminia changed into a puma to defend you. I had hoped he had died, I had not seen him in several years. El Brujo is very old, very weak, but he has managed to cling to life. And now he is a greater threat than ever."

Lucinda said, "He has two other apprentices, at least two, a woman and a man, one Physical and one Mental." She chose not to confess her own apprenticeship to El Brujo. What good would that do?

"Well, I suspected as much. El Brujo felt Herminia transform into a puma, and he found her. When he tried to bore into Herminia's memories, the old trap whisked them away. The Agent Orange spell I had woven so long ago. Herminia's memories disappear now; in a few days this all will be over. The Women's Clinic will crumble. And nothing Don Esteban can do will change that."

"You killed my grandmother," Lucinda accused.

"Several weeks after Herminia left me, I received a letter in the mail from your grandmother. Inside was a burgundy kernel of maize with the instructions that, should my Agent Orange spell take away all her memories, I use the blood curse to end her life. Herminia did not want to re-learn everything as if she were a child again. Imagine it! Herminia is old, too old to recreate her beautiful mind. She would rather die in peace and dignity. Trust me, it tore me apart to have to use that object of power on my beloved."

"Mamá will kill me," Lucinda said, very confused about all of this.

"I would like to care for Herminia, if you agree, until the end," Faustino said.

"How can we explain to Mamá that Abuelita just disappeared?"

"I can help with that. I do have a certain facility with persuasion." Faustino took a jar from a shelf and pressed his thumb inside. It came out coated in indigo powder.

Eva sat on the four-poster bed next to Herminia and crossed her legs.

Mateo sat beside her.

Mateo panted.

Lucinda's defiance was slowly draining away. "We figured it all out — and we've accomplished nothing. Abuelita is still going to die in a few days. With your Agent Orange spell, Don Esteban wouldn't have caused Armageddon anyway—"

"One last issue," Faustino said. "You three have seen Herminia's memories. Don Esteban will try to wrest the location of the Tree of Knowledge from you. We must prevent that." Faustino presented his thumb. "Let me press this to your foreheads."

That thumb grew closer, bigger, bluer. So big Lucinda couldn't see anything else.

Eva hugged Mateo, hard.

"We won't be vegetables, will we?" Lucinda asked.

"It will all be over in a second," Faustino said.

Mateo started to lick Eva's ear.

"Yuck! Mateo!" Eva cried out.

"Relax," Faustino said. He hesitated, turning his head between Lucinda and Mateo and back again. He apparently decided Mateo needed the treatment first; he reversed direction and put his thumb to Mateo's forehead ... and Mateo dissolved into Satélite, who barked.

"What?" Faustino said. "Mind powers! Son of a dog!"

The bottom dropped from Lucinda's stomach. "How did you not see that?"

"I wasn't expecting— Where would Mateo have gone? What does he want?"

"Oblivion," Lucinda answered. "He has gone to see Don Esteban, to forget. The garden."

Summoning her red cardinal ally, Lucinda spun them to the Beyond, to the Women's Clinic, the herb garden.

The fake Herminia was there waiting.

Not alone. Oh God, not alone.

Mateo was on his knees. Fake Herminia had her thumb pressed to his forehead. She gave a little finger wave at them and disappeared.

Mateo fell flat on his face.

"What the hell?" Eva said.

"That was never Herminia," Lucinda replied. "That was Don Esteban."

Thirty-Two

Present Day, Punta Colonet and Beyond

There was a time of pledges: Pledges to help one another. Pledges to warn one another if anything untold happened. Pledges to keep studying magic, to arm themselves for the coming war. Pledges to heal Mateo if they could.

Pledges to resist until the end.

There was a time of waiting — the longest weeks in Lucinda's life. She was punished, grounded, reprimanded, and consoled.

"What happened to my Mateo?" That was Doña Morales, blaming Lucinda.

"How dare you accuse mi hija!" Mamá, defending Lucinda ... until Doña Morales left, then spinning on a peso: "What did you do to Mateo?!"

How could Lucinda explain? How could she say anything?

None of this would matter. Not the yelling. Not the grounding in her room. Not Mateo acting like a one-year-old baby, relearning how to eat with utensils. Not the complete phone privation. (That hurt!)

There was a time of rejoicing. Not having a secret to keep, Faustino showed Lucinda how to heal Abuelita (it required all of Lucinda's power ... and two maize kernels from El Jaguar's dwindling stores), and he performed the complicated magic to restore Abuelita's memories. They didn't return as they had left, with the alacrity of a thunderclap, but rather with the gradual clearing of the eyes, as of a disease finally responding to antibiotics, and the sharpening of the wit, as of a critic reluctantly admitting to his favorite actresses' terrible performance.

It truly is easier to harm than to heal, Lucinda thought, unsure where she had seen that meme before.

September came and went. The last week in October, Lucinda and Mamá made sugar skeletons to place on Grandfather's grave for the Day of the Dead, and dyed them various colors. Lucinda didn't try to slip out the door, and her friends didn't communicate.

Until the world ended.

Fabric snapped outside the bedroom window, unexpectedly, as this had been a calm, dry, October afternoon. The kind of afternoon where an autumn leaf falls so straight you can look up and guess which twig it came from. Lucinda pressed her nose against the windowpane and saw a flock of granny panties tear loose from the clothes drying rack and ripple over the rooftop.

Herminia was in the corner of the room doing knee push-ups in her nightgown. ("*If you tell anyone I have to do these from my knees, I'll spank your bottom until it's so red your mom thinks it's a canning tomato*," Herminia had muttered after a shaky number three.)

"What is it?" Herminia asked.

"The Null Wind."

With a pop of old knees, Herminia brought her legs to her hands, stood, crossed to the window, frowned. "We are still in this world, Little Chicken. The Null Wind only exists in the Beyond."

"Don Esteban has brought it here. We should have guessed. He's brought everything here. He is merging this world and the Beyond. He had chosen the Day of the Dead for its symbolism — of course. The death of the human 'animals,' the rebirth of the witches."

"Little Chicken—"

Lucinda shouted, "There was no wind, and now there is wind. It's the Null Wind, get it?"

Abuelita's eyes widened; her lips drew tight against her teeth. Never had Lucinda talked to Abuelita in this way. To *any* adult in this way.

The old woman seemed to waiver between slapping Lucinda and believing her. With menacing quiet, she said, "Call your friends."

"I'm grounded."

"Nobody is grounded when Apocalypse comes, tonta. Call your friends. Call Faustino. Call everyone you know." Abuelita squares her shoulders. "I'll deal with your mother. Where is Pedro Armendáriz Junior when you need him?"

"Who?"

"Mario Almada? Clint Eastwood?"

Lucinda didn't recognize any of those names. "Are you feeling okay?"

Abuelita shooed her with hand gestures. "Go, Little Chicken, go."

Lucinda pocketed three bags: feathers, crystals, and maize, the charged objects of power they had scored from El Jaguar's.

Out of the bedroom they went, Abuelita and Lucinda. Mamá, too, was staring out the window. She had a baseball bat in her hand. "So soon?"

"*Sí, mi hija.*"

"I had hoped to spare Lucinda all this," Mamá said.

"You did your best. We all did."

The three exited the house and stood looking over Punta Colonet, the Transpeninsular Highway, the Flying Samaritan clinic and hair salon, El Jaguar's hacienda, the dusty road to the Pacific. Wind whipped their hair and clothes. Here, it was a clear, normal wind. Over the Pacific Ocean a brown, world-ending storm brewed.

"He made the breach at El Diablo's house," Lucinda guessed.

"Revolutionaries and corny symbolism," Abuelita lamented, shaking her head. "A diet of saccharin, Hollywood, and Karl Marx."

A semi-truck driving south on the Trans Highway sounded its air horn, the back wheels slid forward, sideways, the cab and trailer jack-knifing nearly in two, the whole tipping, wheels sagging on the axles as if seeking some purchase. A car slammed into the side of the truck, pushing it over the balance point.

A two-hump camel vaulted over the wreckage. A California condor sailed overhead.

"The allies," Abuelita said, "he's brought them from the Beyond."

"*Díos mío*, how many?" asked Mamá.

"Enough for the whole world, hija mía. First the Null Wind, then the allies. Next, chaos. Lucinda, you need to go straight—"

"No! First, we pray," Mamá said fiercely. "God's will, not our own."

They huddled together as the Wind mingled their hair and prayed with closed eyes to Christ for guidance.

Allies streamed past at a faster and faster pace, filling the world. They were cute, frightening, funny, mammals and reptiles and fish and impossible things. Punta Colonet was beginning to warp, as if titans had grabbed hold of either end and had begun twisting. The effect was subtle but Lucinda knew she wasn't mistaken.

Herminia growled — very animal sounding. "Whatever you do, control your intent. If your mind wanders, no telling."

"Like what?" Mamá asked. She had no experience with the Beyond; it was a legitimate question.

"Like Punta Colonet becomes Whoville, and you a Whatsit."

A car rumbled up from a side road, a blue BMW — the Fat Man. Faustino was in the back. Riding shotgun was Eva, who opened the door before the car was fully stopped and rushed over to Lucinda. (We're wearing the same thing! Lucinda noted, both with stonewashed jeans, though Lucinda had a blue tee and Eva a black one.)

"What's the plan?" Eva asked, over the Wind and the hooting, roaring, cawing of the allies.

Lucinda responded, "We are going to the Tree of Knowledge, take another bite, return things to the way things were."

Lucinda and Herminia had discussed this many times. It was the only way.

"You know that's ironic, right?"

"If we recommit the original sin, then God will split humanity from its allies ... again." At least Lucinda hoped that were so. As far as sinning in this way, well, death was already a thing ... and she didn't think God would object. Much.

"You're leaving me?" Mamá asked.

"They will be safer in the Beyond than here," Abuelita said. "Trust me. Faustino and I are going to war."

Mamá nodded.

Lucinda closed her eyes to call her ally. Closing the eyes wasn't necessary … but it helped eliminate the distractions. Like the pink narwhal that just swam over the house.

"Wait, Mateo," Eva said.

"He's a vegetable," replied Lucinda, offering her shoulder as a perch to the red cardinal. "Not to mention that he betrayed us."

They would never know everything, but she and Eva figured they'd puzzled out the gist of Mateo's scheme. He been living a double life. Without telling his friends, he had traveled into the Beyond many times, long enough to bond with his ally — among other things. At some point, either he figured out that 'Herminia' in the herb garden was really El Brujo, or when Mateo went to the herb garden on his own, El Brujo had revealed himself.

Either way, El Brujo made a proposition:

"Mateo, how painful it must have been to have El Jaguar as a father. How much did he hurt you? How did he *shame* you?" All the while, El Brujo himself had caused the warp in El Jaguar's mind. The witch must have considered that a great joke. "I could make you forget, Mateo. You've seen Lucinda's grandmother, no? You see how she no longer suffers from memories of the past. They have been snatched away to a safe place.

"This I can offer you – no more nightmares. No more shame. Peace, I offer you. Peace, and forgetting. All you have to do is tell me how to find the Tree of Knowledge."

Mateo accepted the offer. He agreed to betray the world, betray Lucinda and Eva, his best and only friends, in return for oblivion. Maybe Mateo actually believed that it wouldn't hurt to tell El Brujo how to find the Tree of Knowledge. Maybe he believed we all could really be 'completely human.'

In a sadistic way, El Brujo kept his end of the bargain. With his thumb to Mateo's forehead, he erased every memory. Mateo became like a child, like a dementia sufferer.

Lucinda almost pitied him.

Almost.

Eva tilted her hip to such an angle that half the boys in school would have fainted to have seen it. The other half would have fainted to see the way her pretty, right eyebrow rose, giving her twinkling green gaze the intensity of a bald eagle discovering a trout pond. "Remember Gandalf — 'My heart tells me that he has some part to play yet.'" Lucinda's confusion must have been apparent. "Gandalf? Gollum? You really need to read, chica."

"I don't like it," Lucinda said, meaning both reading and retrieving Mateo. But she didn't want to waste time on pointless discussion. Eva was right, Mateo had been with them from the beginning. Unless 'betrayal' was his only role, they had to take Mateo with them.

They sprinted.

Lucinda had never felt so magical here in the mundane world. Powers were surging; it was becoming like the Beyond here in Punta Colonet. She had to resist the urge to become a golden eagle and fly. A steady stream of ally animals flowed past, as if all the zoos in the world opened their doors to this one spot. Accidents up and down the Transpeninsular Highway had stopped traffic completely. Around Javier's fresh juice stand, a grove of orange trees sprouted head-high with glowing, orange fruit. Javier danced around, collecting oranges into his already bulging shirt.

"The world really is ending," Eva said.

Lucinda couldn't have agreed more.

Thirty-Three

Lucinda, Mateo, and Eva walked into the force of the Null Wind, had always been walking ... sore ankles, tired feet, so tired they could hardly lift their toes to avoid dragging the point of their shoes on the ground. Their lips were impossibly dry, wind-cracked; their eyes hardly functioned; tears had been shed until twin roads dried down their cheeks. The three of them held hands: Lucinda, Eva, Mateo.

They toiled to the top of a ridge, peered between gusts of dust.

"We're never going to make it," Lucinda said. "These ridges and valleys go on forever."

"You thought this would be easy?" Eva asked.

Lucinda didn't bother getting angry, nor did she bother to reply. Both actions took energy she didn't have.

Almost immediately upon arriving in the Beyond, the Null Wind had enveloped them, responding to their combined intent. Three stimuli embraced them along with the Wind — a sonorous chorus of talking voices, a sort of tickle to the back of the neck, the smell of cinnamon. The three friends had looked at each other in wonder. A long pink lizard missing rear legs dug its way out of the ground and climbed atop Mateo's left shoe. A Gila woodpecker landed in Eva's hair — or possibly the Wind had blown the hair around it, and bird and hair had become entangled. (Thank goodness the woodpecker hadn't started pecking!) Lucinda's red cardinal flew so close to her head she had to duck. It scolded her with a series of rising and falling whistles.

And then the Null Wind cleaved Lucinda and her ally.

She could best describe it as stepping off a curb. What once supported her had become insubstantial. The earth had given way. An instinctual reaction caused Lucinda to reach out to catch the red cardinal, retain it for her own. It was, after all, as much a part of a bruja as her arm.

The cardinal, her ally, had dodged the clumsy hands easily, whistle-scolded her again for being so careless as to get caught in the Null Wind, and disappeared into the storm.

Hollow, that was it. Lucinda felt hollow as an empty urn.

Eva and Mateo's allies had likewise deserted them.

Eva and Mateo clung to each other, mouths agape, hardly able to stand. Lucinda had to pull them forward until the shuffling forward became habit.

Habit.

Moving forward.

Moving ... somewhere.

In the endless storm, it was impossible to know exactly how much time had passed. Lucinda tried to will time to move faster here in the Beyond and slower in the real world so that they could accomplish their mission before Don Esteban caused too much harm, but she had no idea if that had any effect. Particularly now that the red cardinal had deserted her.

Since she was no longer a bruja, nothing she did would make any difference. It all seemed so impossible. So hopeless....

"What did you say a minute ago, Eva," Lucinda asked, "about being easy?"

"I said, 'You thought this would be easy?' I meant it as a question."

"'This would be easy,'" Lucinda repeated. "That's it. Our expectation. We have to change it."

"Lucy, no one has ever found the Tree of Knowledge since Adam got us booted out of Paradise with his stupid fruit! Why did he eat the fruit anyway? Why didn't he eat a taco?"

"El Brujo found the Tree. El Jaguar found it. What did they do differently?"

"You are asking the wrong girlfriend," Eva said. "My powers of deduction went out with the conditioner on my hair — about an eternity ago. If this genius wasn't stuck with the brain of a two-year-old, maybe he could guess."

"What rules the Beyond?" Lucinda asked.

Eva sighed. "Intent."

"Let's try it."

Eva bumped her hip into Mateo. "You, too."

"What?"

"Think about something different. Change your expectation."

"I not think about nothing. I don't like this place."

Okay, Mateo's mind is better than a two-year-old's, Lucinda thought. Maybe four. Minus a toddler's cuteness.

In this Wind, it was hard to think about anything other than discomfort. And hopelessness. Lucinda supposed it must be like that for sailors when the wind whistled in their ears day and night, the sun beat their skin, scurvy started to make their teeth loose and their skin yellow, no land in sight.

Wait, no, sailors *liked* the wind. The wind drove the ship. There was a word for what sailors feared. What was it? Lucinda racked her brain, finally coming up with:

Doldrums.

A period without wind, without a way forward — much as Lucinda and her friends were now. No horizon and no way to navigate. Endless swells.

"Lucy, something's happening," Eva said, "and I don't like it much. My feet are sinking."

The ground felt spongy. Was it going to turn into water? Lucinda wobbled to her knees, pulling Eva and Mateo down.

"This is not working," Lucinda complained.

A snarl cut through the dust. A deep, guttural snarl. Lucinda thought immediately of a Jaguar.

"Mateo, cut that out!" she said.

"But—"

"Stop thinking."

"I'm tired," Mateo complained. "Did you bring snacks?"

"Do not — and I mean this," Lucinda said, "do *not* think about food."

If Lucinda's guess were correct, their combined intent was affecting their surroundings. Lucinda had been thinking about ships and doldrums ... and appeared earthen waves and sinking feet. Mateo had probably been thinking about his father.

Another snarl. Coming closer.

"Let's get out of here," Eva suggested, then remembered to whisper, "quietly."

"But I'm hungry," Mateo said.

"It's a game. We're playing hide-and-go-seek," Lucinda said. "We really, really don't want to be found. We need to win this game. It'll be fun. Come on."

They dropped below the ridge on the opposite side from the snarling monster and, quietly as they could, jogged in the bottom gullies, shifting from one to another at the intersections until they ran out of breath. (*Definitely waves*, thought Lucinda.) An outcropping of sandstone provided some shelter from the wind, and a decent place to hide from whatever was out there. It's rim sure looked like the crest of a roller about to break over them.

"Well, that was helpful," Eva breathed, as they crammed into the small space. "I thought about Aladdin's cave and voilà! Maybe there's a genie in here somewhere."

But it was just a small, empty shelter.

"I'm tired," Mateo complained.

Lucinda glared at him — the one chiefly responsible for their predicament. After all, Mateo gave El Brujo Abuelita's memories. After everything they had gone through, and all the trouble Faustino and Herminia had taken to hide the memories, Mateo went and gave away everything. For what? To become a child again.

The traitor.

Once they had caught their breath, Eva said, "There is something else El Jaguar had that we don't have."

"What?"

"A guide. El Jaguar's sister was blinded by Spirit thread. El Jaguar had a Spirit-bound mouth and ears. They were like their own lizard guides."

"No, no we're not going to do that. I know what you're thinking, and it's not going to happen. Anyway," Lucinda added, "it's too late for that. With my ally gone I don't have enough magic to warm a plate of refried beans."

"Thread is Spiritual," Eva said. "Let me try."

She wiggled her fingers in a sort of yarn-pulling motion. Nothing happened except a pretty crease on the bridge of Eva's nose.

Retrieving a shard of sandstone, Lucinda tried to fashion it into a needle with her non-existent Physical powers.

Nada.

Lucinda threw the rock shard into the Wind, heard it clattering downhill. "We have lost our allies. Even if we managed to exit the Wind — and I'm sure we are lost — we would be helpless as babes. We didn't even think to bring lizard guides. Some heroes we are! I wish I were back with Abuelita and Mamá and the Fat Man. We could be fighting Don Esteban right now with my red cardinal and your Gila woodpecker and that — whatever that disgusting pink lizard is that bonded with Mateo."

"That is gross, isn't it?" Eva said. She hesitated a bit, then with a shy smile admitted, "It's called a Mexican mole lizard. I looked it up online. It likes to dig in freshly turned earth and hang out in graveyards — so perfect for him! Did you notice it doesn't even have back legs?"

The two girls vented some stress by talking about how disgusting that ally was, and how perfect for Mateo. The reptile probably ate false teeth and rotten eyeballs and slept in hollowed-out skulls.

Ignoring their chatter, Mateo rested his cheek against the shelter wall, his eyes unfocused. Lucinda found it hard to remain angry at him. She had no doubt that Mateo had suffered terribly at the hands of El Jaguar, and that if Mateo had thought he could find peace in any way other than betraying his friends, he would have chosen the better path.

Still, Lucinda wouldn't have betrayed her friends for inner peace ... or for anything.

Would she?

Would she?

"Pretty feather," Mateo commented.

"Hmm?" The girls followed his gaze. One of the objects of power, their last remaining feather, had almost worked its way out of Lucinda's pocket. She started to stuff it back into the plastic baggie with the others.

Eva stopped her. "Spirit magic. We don't need allies; we have the objects of power."

"We can't. I — I can't bear to do that to you. To either of you."

"Lucy, we're lost. A jaguar is hunting us out there in the Wind, and who knows what other monsters this one will conjure up," she said, indicating Mateo. "It's time for drastic action."

"But that—?"

"Yes, that. We know how to cure it. Faustino and Herminia both know. If it doesn't work and El Brujo wins, well, there will be plenty of Spirit witches around to cut the threads."

"Girlfriend, we don't even know that this will work!"

Eva held out her hand. "Give me the feather."

Given Eva's determined nose crinkle, there was no arguing this.

"Feathers are for Mental magic," Lucinda corrected, digging in her pocket. "Maize kernels are for Physical. And crystals are for Spirit."

Reverently, Eva received the last four rose quartz crystals in her palm. "We'll need needles. And a spell for baby-brain so he doesn't try to run away or scream and attract that monster."

"What are we going to do?" Lucinda asked.

"You are going to find the Tree of Knowledge, Lucy. It's your grandmother we are trying to save."

"It's the whole world!"

"Too big. We will save the whole world," Eva said, and smiled, "one crinkled old butt at a time. Starting with your awesome Abuelita. Now, sew my eyes shut. Not my mouth, I couldn't bear to live without talking. Do you think I can be a famous actress if I'm blind?"

Lucinda blew across a Mental feather. "Mateo, let me sew your mouth and ears shut, okay? And then guide me to the Tree of Knowledge."

"Whatever. When are we going to eat?"

The feather began to dissolve and Lucinda dropped it.

The maize worked just as effectively to fashion stone into a needle. So, the Null Wind separated brujos from their allies, but did not harm objects of power. If ever they returned here, Lucinda would definitely be bringing cargo pockets full of objects of power!

"This won't hurt a bit," Lucinda said, praying for it to be true.

Burning through two crystals to fashion thread, she sewed Eva eyes and Mateo's mouth and ears closed.

Holding hands, not missing a step despite Eva's blindness, Eva and Mateo walked confidently into the Wind. Lucinda kept one of the two remaining maize kernels ready lest they encounter that snarling beast. She surveyed any overhangs and dark recesses in particular.

Sometime later, reflecting in what had happened thus far, Lucinda said, "Eva, I want you to take the crystals."

"Oh, why?"

"In case something happens to me. Like I get dragged off by the jaguar. Or ... well, just about anything. If we get separated, I'd rather you have some magic. I'll keep the maize kernels. It makes sense."

Eva took the crystals and nodded reverently. "We are getting out of here, girlfriend. Mateo and I know the way, you know? Just stick with us."

They hugged.

When the human guides veered toward a blank wall, Lucinda sprinted forward and caught Eva's hand. Just in time. A cave entrance appeared that Lucinda couldn't see without direct contact with Eva. The opening led to a twisty grotto of stalactites, stalagmites, cave bacon, and other formations she knew no names for. Holding Eva's hand, Lucinda could see fine. She experimented by releasing it for a split second, and everything became pitch dark.

"Are you seeing the cave?" Lucinda asked.

"It's like V.R.," Eva said. "I'm not seeing anything; I'm experiencing it like a dream. It's hard to explain."

Mateo followed along docilely. Lucinda didn't ask what he saw or didn't see; she didn't want to trigger a change of intent and some weird monster attack.

The cave emerged on the rim of a valley. Lucinda blinked against the brightness. On this side of the cave, the brown of the Null Wind thinned to a slow-moving haze. From time to time, slivers of purple sky came into view as if they were in the eye of the storm. The valley, or rather the garden in the valley, reminded Lucinda of something. Every square inch was filled with a hedge maze. From here, it was impossible to tell exactly how tall the hedges were, though Lucinda was certain they were not of a uniform height. Some might have been waist high, others probably towered several stories. Either that, or the floor of the valley was monstrously uneven. From this angle, a familiar, spiral pattern could be discerned. With binoculars and enough time, they might have been able to draw it and avoid many of the wrong turns and dead ends.

Lucinda thought for a moment, and then looked at her own thumb. "The maze is a thumbprint. I'll bet anything. Just like you need a bloody thumbprint to complete the apprenticeship ritual." She shivered, thinking about how she had bound herself to El Brujo.

"Do you suppose that is God's thumbprint? Like, if God went to the notary he would have to put that in ink and roll it on the signature paper?"

"You are so lame!" Lucinda said.

"I'm serious," Eva said, laughing. "Or maybe ... maybe it's the thumbprint of the very first brujo. Like Adam or something."

"Can you see it, even with your eyes sewn shut?" Lucinda asked.

"Like I told you, it feels like V.R."

"I see nothing but shrubs," Mateo said. "And I'm hungry."

"If he says that again, I'm giving him the blood curse maize to munch on," Lucinda threatened.

The path meandered into the valley at a gentle slope. Now in the lead, Mateo pulled them forward eagerly, as if he knew that Lucky Charms were hidden within the maze or something. The path led to a split between two ten-foot-high hedges and they entered. Nothing grew on the level pathway, as if someone raked it and sprayed it with herbicide regularly. Not to mention trimmed the hedges to crisp corners.

Lucinda had always loved mazes. She loved the feeling of getting lost without really being lost. She loved deducing the direction by process of elimination. She'd been in a pebble maze in La Bufadora — the place where the waves crashed through a cave and exploded into the air over the gawking tourists. Better yet, she'd mastered a corn maze north of Ensenada that took over two hours to exit. Mazes in Lucinda's book were the perfect combination of mystery and physical activity.

This one circled around and around as you might expect from a thumbprint design. It was far harder to keep track of their direction than if it had had perpendicular rows. Lucinda wondered if, in fact, this maze were a fabrication of her subconscious expectation, wondered if Eva and Mateo had come here alone they would have found something else entirely.

"I can't believe I'm El Brujo's apprentice," she murmured half to herself, considering thumbprints, mazes, and bonds.

"It means nothing."

"He feeds off my strength."

"Well, he doesn't anymore. You don't have an ally, remember?"

"I walked right into his house and gave myself to him. I'm no better than Mateo."

"You should give yourself a break," Eva said, the pitch of her voice rising, "and give one to Mateo while you're at it. You can't imagine what he went through."

"Why are you getting so quarrelsome?" Lucinda glanced down; Eva had worn Vans sneakers rather than heels so it wasn't sore feet. Maybe it was this place.

They made turn after turn, always careful not to let go of each other's hands. No telling what would happen if they did. The whole thing might disappear. The true path might become overgrown. No, Lucinda did not want to experiment here in the maze of Paradise.

The Garden of Eden. Were they truly here?

She didn't believe it was a maze when Adam and Eve lived here. The Bible would have mentioned that, right? All the book of Genesis said, as she recalled, was that the Tree of Knowledge stood at the center of the

Garden of Eden, and that Adam and Eve were not to eat of it. It might have been in a maze. More likely this grew up afterward to make sure no one found it.

"You don't have a crush on Mateo, do you?" she asked Eva.

"Me? No. Sheesh."

No more was said for a minute.

"Lucy, it's hard to explain, but I liked some things about him. He was nice, for one thing. And he is the only person I know who doesn't give a fig that I'm, well, beautiful, and an actress, and all of that."

"Um hum. I don't give a fig."

"That's different! You're a girl. You're beautiful, too, you know." Eva sighed. "Okay, I liked him a little. But, to quote my BFF, 'It's too late for that.'"

"Eva and Mateo. Mateo and Eva. It has a nice ring to it," Lucinda said.

"Cut it out."

"Think of the fun you'll have teaching your boyfriend his ABCs."

Mateo pulled up short and Eva and Lucinda practically bowled him over. He pointed at a corpse lying in their path. It was El Brujo's gardener, still clothed in her orange Hare Krishna style robe. Just beyond the body, to the side of the path, was a golden statue on a pedestal, about six feet tall. The statue depicted a winged creature with four faces: that of a man, a lion, an ox, and an eagle. Lucinda seemed to remember from Bible study that the statue was called a cherub.

"Do you smell that?" Eva said, breathing in through her nose. "Cinnamon. Yum."

"It's a dead body," Lucinda said. "It's not supposed to smell good. It's supposed to smell like an egg that rolled behind the stove for a couple of weeks and just cracked open. You're smelling magic — Spirit magic."

Eva stepped beyond the statue. Eyes lingering on the dead woman, Lucinda followed, hardly noticing that the three friends no longer held hands. The gardener's corpse wore a fierce grin. Lucinda had once seen a blow-up photo of a ladybug face and it had worn the same grin.

She felt like an aphid about to be chomped.

"Lucy, Lucy, come on. It's Paradise."

Another step, and Lucinda saw nothing. It wasn't until she touched Eva's arm that entered her mind a vision of paradise, technology, prosperity beyond her wildest imagination. It was like a millisecond trailer for the latest Star Wars movie ... after the Empire had been defeated. Lucinda jerked her hand away, and all she saw was the hedge maze and the grinning corpse.

"This is the future!" Eva said. "Can you feel it? This is what Paradise will be like when we defeat El Brujo."

"This is a trap," Lucinda warned. "I don't see anything like that. Mateo?"

He shook his head.

"Reality is right here. Eva, come back here to the statue; come and look at this body."

Reluctantly, her friend returned. "She looks so happy." Eva giggled. "Who wouldn't want to die in just this moment?!"

"Okay, BFF, you have gone a turn too far," Lucinda said, moving between Eva and the statue the way a basketball player would move to screen someone from the hoop. "I don't want you ending up like the cultist, here." She wanted to tie Eva in place, but it didn't work like in the movies. First, where was she going to find something to tie her friend with? She didn't have any rope, nor any clothes to spare, and removing them from the corpse was just too icky. Besides, even if Lucinda got the orange toga-thingy off, how was she to get Eva to stand still long enough to be bound? Eva was bouncing on the balls of her feet to walk further into the maze and explore Paradise.

Already knowing she would come up empty, Lucinda searched her jeans pockets for a feather. How easy it would be to simply cast a mind spell!

That thought gave her pause.

Yes, how easy it would be to use compulsion. What temptation magic held, especially Mental magic. No wonder Herminia distrusted it.

Her vacant eyes staring at the imaginary future, Eva began walking, pushing Lucinda backwards with zombie-like force, and Lucinda didn't know how to stop her. They were nearly matched in size and strength, but Eva had mindless relentlessness on her side. She just kept stepping forward, eyes a-gleam, an increasingly vacant smile tugging the corners of her mouth upward.

"Mateo, help me hold her!" Lucinda begged.

Mateo yawned. "What for? I'm bored."

What can I do? thought Lucinda. *What do I have...?*

The crystals: Spirit magic rules the Beyond.

Now holding Eva back like a linebacker, Lucinda dug her heels into the ground and, with difficulty, inched her hands down, down into Eva's pocket. Step by step she lost ground. Soon they'd be beyond the statue, what she knew was the point of no return. She hadn't time to remove the baggie of crystals from Eva's tight jeans; she had to do it right now....

Wiggling a finger inside the bag, Lucinda pressed it to one of the crystals and said, "Statue, Cherub, keep Eva here." And then, as the statue became supple, and the wings reached out, she added, "No hurting her!"

The statue sprang forward; the wings knocked Lucinda aside, wrapped around Eva, and squeezed, forming a sort of golden-feather cocoon. Eva struggled single-mindedly to walk forward, to reach her version of Paradise. But there was no moving that statue.

The pocket of Eva's jeans was just visible under the golden feathers of the cherub wing. With a bit of prying and tearing of the jeans fabric, Lucinda managed to free the baggie of crystals.

"Don't go anywhere until I come back for you," Lucinda told Eva, trying to hug her through the cold metal of the cherub (and swinging wide of the creepy ox face). "Understood?"

Eva's eyes filled with tears. "Just a little more; just let me walk a little more."

Lucinda had to turn away so as to not start crying herself. She held out her hand. "Come on, Mateo. Time is short."

"I'm bored," he said.

"And hungry. I know."

Lucinda was grateful to leave that body behind, and worried that she'd condemned Eva to a long death. With that spell, if Lucinda never came back, the cherub might just hold her friend there until she died of dehydration.

The hedges soared out of sight. Although wide enough for two to walk abreast, the maze began to make Lucinda feel claustrophobic. Mateo hesitated at the first intersection, no longer sure of the way without Eva's blind eyes to guide him, so Lucinda took charge, choosing whatever direction seemed to lead nearer the middle.

"I'm scared," Mateo confided. His palm had become sweaty.

Lucinda reminded herself the person next to her had the fears of a child. He needed to be reassured. "I will take care of you."

"I hear voices," Mateo said.

"Then we slow down. When you begin to see things, let me know. Like a body, or weird golden statues."

It didn't surprise her when, a couple of hours and a million complaints later, they found the body of El Brujo's second apprentice. The only difference was that rather than a grin, the man's lips curled back in terror. The cherub statue was also present.

Mateo took half a step beyond the corpse, dropped to the grass and writhed as if a thousand red ants covered his body. Lucinda tensed up, ready to go rescue her friend, but hesitated. The body of El Brujo's second apprentice didn't look swollen or damaged in any way, just terrified. With difficulty, she made herself stay there and watch Mateo.

It was frightening and painful to watch, and made her feel like a complete heel for not jumping forward and helping. But this maze required patience and thought. The sort of skills a brujo developed through training.

Although Mateo writhed and groaned, nothing appeared to be physically hurting him. So, Lucinda concluded, it was all in his mind. That made sense, being as Mateo's magic was Mental. And he'd heard murmuring voices along the path, a sign of Mental magic.

Lucinda waited until he writhed close, near enough to reach. She stretched out her fingertips....

Nothing doing. He was just beyond her grasp. Unless—

By holding onto the cherub statue's eagle face (its narrow shape made a nice handhold) she could stretch out and grasp Mateo's pant leg. Being careful not to touch his flesh, afraid that doing so would transfer that imaginary pain, or fear, or whatever it was, pulling each time

Mateo's own rolling movements seemed likely to help, Lucinda jimmied him back across the imaginary line of the statue.

Her hands, forearms, and back ached from the effort.

Incapable of describing what he saw, Mateo kept crying "Colonet" and "Mamá" and "Help, help."

"You know the drill," Lucinda said, and used another crystal to turn the cherub statue into a fancy set of manacles.

She squared herself for the final leg of the journey.

Is this the same path El Brujo took? Lucinda wondered. *I am no different from El Brujo. He went to reverse original sin. I go to remake it. Both of us have used people as fodder along the way.* As a gentle turn in the hedge path cut off the last view of Mateo, she said softly, "I will come back for you, friends. I promise."

In that, at least, I can do better than El Brujo.

I will do better.

I am better.

I am.

After a few more turns, each time expecting to be assailed by some sort of vision, Lucinda came to a large clearing. On the far side of the clearing, another path led out. Here in the center was the Tree of Knowledge. She had no doubt it was the real thing. Its rounded shape, the twisted bark of its trunk, and the light green leaves gave it a striking resemblance to an olive tree. It was of normal size, though the trunk had grown fat with age. Amber pitch dotted the bark where it had cracked, though overall, the tree appeared healthy.

Lucinda approached. The Null Wind reached down and stroked her face, her hair, her blue tee. She circled and circled the olive-like tree until she was no longer sure which of the two paths she had entered on. Dizziness assailed her. There was the Wind, the dust, the hedge.

No fruit.

No fruit on any branch.

No flowers, no buds, and no fruit.

Even the ground, which Lucinda searched on hands and knees, was clear of ground culls.

There was only the Wind.

The Wind.

Lucinda didn't, couldn't know the rules of Paradise. The most logical thing, she reasoned, was that the Tree of Knowledge only had one fruit at a time. The serpent didn't need to tempt Adam and Eve with buckets of fruit, it needed only a single one. In fact, if there were only one, it would seem so much more valuable than if the tree shed fruit like morning dew. Now that El Brujo had taken that single fruit, the tree wouldn't produce any more. What El Brujo had done must be undone before the tree would bear fruit again.

That was one theory.

Or maybe it had had lots of fruit and El Brujo had taken them all. Lucinda didn't like that idea one bit ... though it meant that somewhere in the mundane world, a storehouse of Knowledge fruit might be reclaimed....

Talk about a lousy Plan B.

Or maybe the tree only bore fruit once a millennium!

Heck, she thought, standing and brushing off the knees of her jeans, if it bore fruit once a year like a normal tree it would still take WAY too long. Lucinda and her friends would starve long before that happened.

Stupid tree!

Whatever the truth, the plan had failed: she couldn't recreate Adam's original sin and separate all men from their allies a second time.

Remembering her Mamá's exhortation, Lucinda bowed her head. "I don't know what you want from me, God. I don't know my place in all this ... but I'm yours to command. Thank you for healing Abuelita. Now, tell me what to do. Please tell me. Or show me. Not my will, but yours be done, Father.

"And I'm sorry for calling your tree 'stupid.' Amen."

Something in that prayer triggered a memory of the spells Herminia had cast to try to free El Jaguar from the Spirit bonds. Liquid stone had managed to sever the threads temporarily, though they reformed right after the passing of the blade. Ultimately, it had been the knife of Spirit power that had severed the Spirit bonds.

Hmm. Having used the last crystal, Lucinda no longer had Spirit power.

What if—? The Tree of Knowledge was certainly unique material, uniquely suited to sever, well, if it could cleave mankind from his allies, it could sever just about anything. Lucinda didn't have a fruit, but she had the tree, and just maybe if the tree's DNA lived in its wood as much as in the fruit, then some of the "cleaving" power would be contained in the wood as well.

She didn't like the idea of harming the Tree of Knowledge, and so instead of breaking a branch, Lucinda peeled off a forearm-length strip of bark. She didn't have any more Spirit-charged crystals, but she had something better. Something that she knew from experience could sever allies from brujos.

The Null Wind.

Using one of the maize kernels, Lucinda formed a knife and handle from these three things: bark from the Tree of Knowledge, desolation from the Null Wind, and Physical magic.

Suddenly sure which of the two hedge openings led to the exit, Lucinda turned not that way but back the way she had come. In less than a minute, she nearly ran face-first into Mateo and Eva, whose cherub statues held them not five feet from one another. As soon as Lucinda arrived, the statues reverted to their normal shape, and Eva and Mateo collapsed to the grass, panting.

The knife worked perfectly. As soon as Lucinda had severed the threads on eyes, ears and mouth, the maze dissolved. The Null Wind blew away.

The three friends were on a knoll overlooking El Diablo's house.

Thirty-Four

El Diablo's ruined foundation was about five hundred feet away. Beside it, a gaping hole from this world into the Beyond rebuilt itself. Sealed itself. Sphinctered open and closed every few seconds. A couple of rabbit allies squeeze through. A whole menagerie of squawking, roaring, twittering, and cackling creatures pushed against the far side, eager to come through to the mundane world.

Come through to find their respective humans, no doubt.

El Brujo, dressed in a blue schoolboy uniform, swung on a swing set with a silly grin on his face. Three crows perched on the top bar cawed furiously. Weirdly, the legs of the swing set were anchored in the two fireplace chimneys.

From different directions, Abuelita and Faustino advanced. They held their hands at the ready, as if expecting an attack at any moment.

El Brujo hopped off the swing and fell face forward, laughing.

"This is bad, isn't it?" Eva said.

"I'm not sure," Lucinda answered.

It was impossible to know which type of magic prevailed. Voices murmured in their ears like a thousand overheard phone calls; cinnamon filled their nostrils like a churro factory; if Lucinda's hackles stood any higher, she'd be a she-wolf.

Magic was everywhere.

The knoll gave them a 360-degree view, and Lucinda took a second to look around. Overcast gave everything a world-ending gloom. Toward the Pacific Ocean, perched on the derelict ships, the metal husks stranded on the beach, were many flying allies. Loch Ness-like monsters swam out to sea, surfacing in graceful arcs. In the distance, a cruise ship billowed smoke and flame. Lucinda could only imagine the terror of the passengers, and hoped they would be able to drop their lifeboats in time.

Overhead, a monstrous funnel cloud spiraled up and up — the Null Wind — like a slow-turning tornado that touched down here at El Diablo's foundation.

Toward the east, visible only as a rooftop quilt, the town of Punta Colonet appeared calm except for occasional crackles of lightning.

"He's had the gap open a long time," said Eva. "A lot of allies have come through."

"Hmm. Maybe not so many considering there are billions of people on earth," Lucinda said. "We could absorb a few hundred more brujos without overthrowing our current system ... I hope. Come on, we can't do anything from this far away."

Scrambling from bush to bush, Lucinda, Eva, and Mateo moved closer to the foundation, close enough that Lucinda could see blood pouring from Abuelita's eyebrow.

"They might have handled this. They just might," Lucinda said.

"They've been fighting," Eva commented.

Abuelita's left eye blinked furiously in an attempt to see past the blood. The back of her shirt was ripped, the end of her skirt dirty and ragged.

With a hiss, the hole into the Beyond sealed completely. The gap closed and the noise stopped ... all noise except the constant murmur that indicated Mental magic was being used in a big way. The lightning over Punta Colonet came less frequently. The three crows perched on the swing set fell silent. The funnel cloud overhead thinned.

"Can we go home now?" Mateo asked.

"No, come on. They need our help." Lucinda urged her friends forward. She didn't trust anything, in particular with regards to victory over El Brujo. Bush to bush they crept on.

El Brujo lifted his head. "Is recess over?"

The beavertail cactus that had been growing from one of the chimneys ripped free, flew, and wrapped itself around Faustino.

Faustino howled from the pain of the cactus needles.

"I am the teacher here," El Brujo rumbled, pushing himself to his feet. The school uniform melted away to reveal slacks and a button-down shirt. The swing set vanished, except for an iron bar, which El Brujo sent flying like a spear at Abuelita.

Transforming her arm to stone, Abuelita knocked it to the side.

Eva kept brushing her shoulders and hair as they crawled.

"What are you doing?" Lucinda asked.

"Checking for ticks." Eva held her hands to the side. "Lyme's disease, chica? You should be more careful. Mateo didn't just eat a pill bug, did he?"

Lucinda ignored that and kept crawling.

El Brujo's three allies, the crows, separated. Between them, a triangular breach opened, and once again, the Beyond began roaring across; Null Wind, magic, and more. The first allies through were about three dozen stampeding house kitties.

"Ahhhhh," Eva cooed, "All I got was a lousy Gila woodpecker."

"Better than a mole lizard," Lucinda said. "Keep crawling."

Abuelita reached Faustino, who whimpered and shook in pain. With her stone arm, the old woman began ripping the cactus to pieces. The sailfish zoomed in from the Pacific and skewered one of the crows with its horn. The crow turned into a badger and clawed back. It looked like a battle of two shape-shifting immortals.

The hole into the Beyond shrank but did not close.

The three friends stopped at the final stand of chaparral. A thirty-foot open area separated them from El Brujo and the battle.

"Do you think the gap will close if we kill El Brujo?" Eva whispered.

Lucinda did not reply.

"Lucy? We have to consider it. We might have to kill him."

Lucinda was steeling herself for just that. She didn't want to kill anybody. She didn't relish the idea of even hurting someone ... but El Brujo was an evil man. He had murdered children. He had lied to her, to

Mateo, to all of them. He had tricked Lucinda into becoming his apprentice.

He wanted to murder her grandmother!

Lucinda checked her grip on the knife she had made from the Tree of Knowledge, the Null Wind, and Physical magic. This had to work. It had to!

From the cover of the chaparral she dashed, determined to strike El Brujo down.

"So nice of you to come calling," El Brujo said casually, flicking his wrist. He didn't even bother to glance in her direction.

Lucinda was thrown sideways by a blow of solid air. She landed in sandy ground near the edge of the hole into the Beyond. It happened so fast she felt more shock than pain, like tripping pell-mell into a sand dune.

She lifted her torso gingerly on her forearms, just in case. Nope, nothing broken. From this close, Lucinda remarked that El Brujo looked so healthy, so physically strong, that she hardly recognized him from the wasted old man she'd met in Mulegé.

Of course, she thought. *He's bonded with both Physical and Mental allies since that time. He's become nearly invincible.*

"Ah yes," El Brujo smiled, "you see the hopelessness of your situation, my young apprentice. You could have been like my granddaughter if things had turned out differently ... but you have no allies, and no time. The days that humans must live like animals are over. The days of single-ally brujos are also over — unfortunately for your grandmother and her boyfriend Faustino." He cocked his head at the other two, who were still struggling against the beavertail cactus. "It is good to be able to see one's mistakes, Lucinda. That is the beginning of wisdom. And I see now that I have made one big mistake over the years. I have terrible taste in apprentices." He laughed as if this were a great joke. "They have all turned on me! Except for the two you must have met in the Garden of Eden. Those two had the bad taste to perish."

With that, he twisted his hands, and the beavertail cactus began writhing against Faustino, causing the poor man to shriek anew.

Lucinda tuned out El Brujo. Tuned out Faustino's cries. Tuned out all sound, lest she become paralyzed with despair. She had fallen near the triangular gap into the Beyond, but also near one of El Brujo's crow allies. It seemed like the three allies held open the gap as three hands might hold open a gigantic trash bag.

She guessed that Abuelita's sailfish ally had been trying to kill the crow in order to close that gap. Maybe Abuelita had ordered it to the attack, or maybe the sailfish had acted on instinct....

Following its lead, Lucinda lunged at the crow, stabbed it with the knife.

The crow's feathers deflected the worst of the blow. These weren't like normal feathers, more like something Iron Man would have created. Tumbling once, the crow righted itself with a look more of surprise than of pain.

Surprise — no. Not surprise.

Elation!

Something had changed. The magic contained in Lucinda's knife had severed the bond between ally and brujo.

The gap into the Beyond wobbled.

The crow looked around, cawed, and flapped through the gap.

The cactus resumed its normal shape and dropped away from Faustino.

El Brujo roared in frustration as his form became old again, withered, sun-damaged and splotched, but still standing. "You have taken my Physical ally! No, nothing I haven't been through before. I learned to eat with broken teeth." He cackled, spittle dripping down his chin. "The bullies forced me to eat rocks, you see. Eat rocks until my teeth shattered. They couldn't believe I would not cry. But I would not! I learned to eat with broken teeth; I can learn to live as a handicap with only two allies."

Mateo pelted El Brujo in the side with a rock. He gave Lucinda a thumbs up. Eva pulled Mateo back into the cover of the brush as the brujo turned in their direction, a look of fury distorting his face.

Lucinda sprinted toward the second crow. This crow opened its beak and spat as a camel spits, a disgusting blob square in Lucinda's eye. She stumbled. She tried to wipe the goop from her eye with the back of her hand, but this only smeared it across her face. It was as sticky as a spider web!

The crow attacked Lucinda's knife hand with claw and beak, its pecks piercing skin and muscle. Surprised and hurting, Lucinda dropped the knife.

The knife disappeared.

Lucinda told herself it was some Mental trick — objects don't just disappear. Not in this world, anyway. Still defending herself from the crow, she felt around on the ground as best she could, but she could neither see or feel it. The knife was gone.

By now, Herminia had helped Faustino to a sitting position. She wrapped her arms around him from behind, else he would surely have collapsed back to the ground.

"I can make you happy again," offered Faustino to El Brujo in an unsteady rasp. "I've learned much about Mental magic."

"A schoolboy on a swing set? Pathetic. No, my apprentices, my revenge on the bullies was commensurate with the humiliation they gave me. Yours will be equally painful — someday. For now, it looks like I will have to keep you two around a while longer until I can find more amenable helpers. I have need of the Physical power I draw from Herminia ... and your own Mental powers are not insignificant. However, of Lucinda, I have no use...."

"Oh, Lucinda didn't tell you? Herminia's granddaughter is my apprentice, too. How ironic, Herminia, I will just use your own Physical strength to kill your granddaughter."

Abuelita blinked in surprise. "Why would you kill Lucinda if she is your apprentice?"

"She has passed through the Null Wind. They all have." El Brujo's gesture encompassed Eva and Mateo also. "There is no place for them in the new world."

The struggle seemed to be over. Without her knife, Lucinda was out of the fight. Wounded terribly, so was Faustino. Mateo was useless, and Eva had neither objects of power nor an ally. El Brujo's two remaining crows tugged the breach open again, and the Beyond continued to leach through into this world. The allies were just the most obvious travelers, but other things crossed into the mundane world as well as well. Icy blasts, dry moans and humid, cloud-like figures without solidity; deep growls and high-pitched yips from invisible beings that made the hairs on her neck stand up; fiends that floated overhead and others that burrowed like moles — El Brujo himself probably had no idea what all he was allowing through.

Lucinda stood slowly, a desperate plan forming. Where the crow's spittle had struck, Lucinda's eye still didn't function properly, and so she walked toward Abuelita without much depth perception. Still, she walked. She could not fight El Brujo, but if she could trick him into losing his Physical apprentice, his great age might do for him.

"You won't begrudge us one final embrace, will you?" she asked El Brujo, swallowing against her fear. "Please? For the sake of your three apprentices?"

She was counting on El Brujo's nature to override his vindictiveness: he liked a good riddle. He'd be wondering what her plan was; he'd want to figure it out before killing her.

El Brujo frowned, but he didn't stop her.

Lucinda *did* have two charged maize kernels in a baggie in her pocket, their last objects of power, but she didn't intend to use them. She didn't think they would do much against El Brujo anyway. But given how weak the old man had become....

He'd lost his Mulegé apprentices. He'd lost his Physical ally. He'd lost Lucinda. The only thing keeping him alive was the trickle of power he borrowed from Abuelita. She hoped.

Ironic was indeed the proper word.

Keeping her back to El Brujo, hiding her actions as best she could, Lucinda knelt down and put her hand on Abuelita's ankle where the old woman always kept the diving knife. Slipping her hand inside the skirt Lucinda drew the blade up half an inch — just enough to slice open her thumb. She couldn't help flinching.

"Abuelita," she whispered, revealing her bloodied thumb, "what would happen if you apprentice to me?"

"I— I believe ... I am not sure."

"Can an apprentice serve more than one master?"

"I do not think so. I think it would break..." Abuelita trailed off as the implication hit her.

"Will you?"

Abuelita nodded and smeared her own thumb in the wounded mess of her eyebrow. "Of course, Little Chicken. We'll use Faustino's back — he makes a good table."

Hooved allies galloped past, blasting through chaparral and throwing up sand: goats, borregos, horses, and mule deer in a chaotic herd. Other living things crossed the barrier as well, things which would not be alive in the mundane world: Vibrations, sounds. Living light also, mulberry, sapphire, burnt tile, honey, tea, streaks of light of every hue that twisted, twined, folded, and quested, denizens of a kaleidoscope gone rogue. A murder of these living colors turned, Lucinda could only think of it as turning, and raced toward the ocean. She tried to ignore this, but it was so wrong. A pack of rainbow wolves on the hunt.

For what?

For what?

"Little Chicken? Help me with Faustino."

"Yes."

"Quickly, before El Brujo loses interest."

Gently the two women lay Faustino down and rolled him onto his stomach. Abuelita lifted his shirt, and together Lucinda and Herminia mingled their bloody thumb prints on Faustino's lower back.

El Brujo watched all this with his arms crossed, his expression smug. Incredibly, he seemed to float a few inches above the ground.

Your arrogance will kill you, thought Lucinda.

"Will you take me as your apprentice, Abuelita?"

"Yes, yes, but nothing is happening," Abuelita said with growing urgency. "There should be a ... a wave of force which descends over us, like electricity. Where is the wave of force?"

"I don't know," Lucinda answered. "I don't feel it either."

The groan of a hundred tons of tortured metal seemed to answer them. From the sea, carried by those kaleidoscope demons, one of the derelict ships levitated above the cliffs. Buckets of saltwater poured from its tortured hull.

Both women gasped.

Higher than the chimney the hull rose. As it stalked forward over the chaparral, Eva and Mateo darted out from under its shadow. They did a side-by-side baseball slide under another clump of brush to El

Brujo's rear. Mateo picked up a small rock and executed a decent over-hand throw at El Brujo but missed.

The witch ignored them.

"Where is the wave of force? Where is the wave of force?" taunted El Brujo in his high-pitched lisp. "Your granddaughter lost her allies in the Null Wind. She is of no use to you or to anyone else."

Lucinda's eyes were wide as the full moon. "He is so strong! How is this possible?"

Rivet's groaned from ship's side, pelting the ground.

"You know I am not wasteful, apprentice, and what could be more wasteful than a walking, talking piece of raw meat. Burning oxygen that could go to a true brujo…"

The women shared a glance of alarm. Panic, even.

"Run!" shouted Herminia.

The ship shuddered, and then rushed them.

"Here!" Lucinda waved both hands over her head, hoping to draw the attack away from Abuelita. She then sprinted towards the chimney, thinking to shelter behind its protective stone. It seemed that El Brujo could not accelerate so much mass quickly, for before the ship arrived, Lucinda threw herself sideways towards the hearth, covered her head in her hands, prayed and whimpered and made frightened animal noises. Metal met stone with a metallic peal as the girder skeleton smashed through the chimney. Stone rained down, and pain exploded from Lucinda's side and elbow. The ground buckled as the ship buried itself right behind her, right where Herminia and Faustino had been.

Each breath sent stabbing pain into her body, as if a clumsy surgeon had sewn a scalpel beneath her ribs, and a clumsy farrier kept missing the horseshoe and instead pounded his hammer on Lucinda's arm. A bone protruded from her right forearm like an alien trying to escape her own body. Every tiny movement made her useless arm slide down her side, and every slide hurt more than the last. She wished the falling stones had knocked her unconscious. She did not want to hurt so bad. She did not want to see her friends, her lovely Abuelita, murdered by this monster.

'Kill me! Kill me now!' she wanted to scream, and only just managed to keep her teeth pressed together. Only just. For spite.

For about thirty seconds, nothing happened at all.

Long enough for Lucinda to stop whimpering and try to rally her courage.

I will not go down without a fight. I am going to lose; I am going to die. But no one will ever say that Lucinda Eco went down without a fight. I will not shame my Abuelita that way. I will not.

Awkwardly, with as little movement as humanly possible, she reached across her jeans with her left hand for right pocket. Just this small movement nearly made her pass out from the broken ribs stabbing her guts. Her forehead crinkled; a vessel in her temple throbbed until it must burst.

Between her middle and third finger, she pinched the baggie containing the maize kernels. She tugged, tugged again. It didn't want to come free. Curled in this position, the pocket was too tightly compressed against her thigh.

Reluctantly, movement by painful movement, Lucinda hollowed her torso, straightened her leg. Her broken arm flopped sideways, and she shrieked ... which wrenched the broken ribs at her side.

El Brujo cackled at her shriek, giggled at her sobs. He relished her suffering.

"When did you become so cruel?" she whispered.

Each ragged breath, each sob hurt like a punch to the ribs. She managed to roll back to face Abuelita and Faustino, buried beneath the shipwreck. To her astonishment, the ship had not squashed the two of them. The prow had flowered open, creating a sort of hollow, and the wreckage imprisoned the pair within several tons of rusted metal.

He's keeping them alive so he can draw power through the apprentice bond. He needs them alive.

A brief thought, rejected immediately: If she killed Abuelita and Faustino, El Brujo might die. He just might ... but she could never, never do that to Abuelita. She hated herself for even thinking it.

The air seemed to warp, and in a blink El Brujo had crossed the distance to the ship. He peered through a rent in the hull and grinned his broken-tooth grin. Male and female groans came from within, echoing.

"I have never been cruel," El Brujo said. "With even one ally, in a world full of animals, I could have indulged my every whim, but instead, my whole life, I have worked for the good of humanity. I have sacrificed everything to turn animals into humans." His head swung toward Lucinda; his tongue licked his ugly lips. "But a cat cannot be blamed for toying with mice, can it?"

She tried to sit up straighter while keeping her face smooth. Each grimace felt like a victory for the evil witch, and she would not give that to him. *Give him nothing, nothing, no satisfaction,* a stubborn voice said inside her head. At the same time, with the fingers of her one hand, she tried to open the sealed baggie. *Abuelita would not give up. I will not give up.*

"A toy?" El Brujo said, presumably to himself. "I like the sound of that. One thing you learn with age, a little part of every man has never grown up. Within me is my ten-year-old self, my twenty-year-old self, my thirty-year-old, and so on." He stepped toward Lucinda, steadying himself against the ship.

"Abuelita, can you hear me?" No telling how badly Abuelita had been hurt by that ship.

He hardly has the strength to stand; how could he have picked up that ship from clear over on the beach?

"This is why old men are attracted to young girls; they do not see them from an old man's eyes. Or rather they do and they don't, both together." He chuckled at her look of horror. "But don't worry, Lucinda, I do not have my Master's tastes ... nor El Jaguar's. There are other ways to make a man or woman suffer without compromising your own dignity. I have much practice." All over the field, knives appeared, two or three dozen lying on their sides, any of which could be Lucinda's magical dagger. She resisted the urge to lung at them. She was in the thrall of El Brujo's Mental power and could trust nothing.

"You freed one of my allies with that knife of yours, Lucinda. I must study that, discover how it works. More importantly, I must make you suffer commensurately to my own loss. Thanks to your dagger, I will be a weakling, a two-ally witch. How much suffering do you think an ally is worth, Lucinda? How much torture?"

How had he picked up that ship?

Spiritual power. Of course, the power that controls the Beyond. So much of the Beyond has come through that El Brujo can control reality itself.

We are lost.

"An animal's mindless quest to survive has always fascinated me, Lucinda. Tell me, would you rather die quickly, or suffer ... and live a while longer? I give you the choice." He giggled. "I might even respect it. Do you hear her, Herminia? Listen to your granddaughter make her final choice."

Lucinda's fingers finally succeeded in opening the baggie. She reached in. Touched both maize kernels.

"Abuelita, can you hear?"

"Yes. Yes, Little Chicken. I am so sorry."

"I know why we failed. I lost my ally in the Null Wind."

A pause.

"Do not beg him, child. Do not give the evil man anything he asks."

Lucinda reached in. Touched both maize kernels at once. She could only hope that Abuelita understood. Lucinda had failed because she had lost her allies.

Not so, Faustino.

"I won't beg, Abuelita. I promise."

She wished. Screaming pain mended her forearm and ribs as it twisted her skeleton — into a massive, two-maize puma of a prehistoric size. Their last objects of power became dust.

El Brujo might have stopped her then, might have bent reality with his Spiritual power and torn her to pieces, but at that moment Eva thumped him from behind with one of the fake daggers. It wasn't the real one, of course. The illusion disappeared the moment the 'dagger' met El Brujo's skull. But it *was* a partially-burned stick. At the same time, Mateo wrapped his arms around the witch's legs and tried to pull him to the ground. El Brujo staggered under the dual assault.

Lucinda's senses sharpened. She could smell brine and drying barnacles on the ship's underbelly; blended sweat and perfume behind Eva's ears; fear-stink on Mateo's armpits, nopales breath on El Brujo. Her hearing improved also: El Brujo's gums smacked dryly; sand moved beneath the trios as they struggled; a mourning dove fluttered, pretending to be injured; the two humans shifted within the ship's wreckage...

All of these sensations and more in an instant. She became so hale, so alive.

With her feline ears laid back, with her tail twitching, Lucinda gathered her legs and sprang. One leap, that's all she needed. A good fifteen feet through the air, a wonderous, liberating, triumphant leap. Her leading claw bloodied El Brujo's cheek...

...and that pack of color demons slammed into her side. Knocked her off-target, and her failing limps took Eva down as well.

The color demons stabbed at Lucinda's face, tried to blind her, to force their way into her throat, to burrow into her nostrils. One made it halfway down her throat before she severed it with a bite. Another, rebounding against the lens of her left eye, began to wiggle between socket and eyeball. Her eyeball bulged and watered from the pressure. These snakes of living light had the cohesiveness of gummies, if the gummies were fifteen-feet-long and demon possessed. They could not harden or sharpen, thank goodness, but they could thicken, stretch, or shrink, and had the agility of eels.

Lucinda fought wildly, clawing, biting, roaring, twisting. Spinning over the ground seemed to work best. Dust flew. One by one she twisted the color demons around herself until they held still long enough for a claw or bite to sever them. Once cut in two, the two pieces thrashed for a few moments before losing cohesion and melting. Her fur became a sticky, muddy mess.

She caught sight of Mateo and Eva. The boy crawled onto her belly and was trying to strangle her. They writhed like maniacs, like lucha libre wrestlers crossed with ferrets. Their hair mingled, blond and black, slick with desperate sweat. Eva's fingernails scraped deep red rents on Mateo's cheeks, while Mateo's hands tightened on Eva's throat. He turned his face away, unwilling to look at what his hands were doing.

Mateo's eyes, watery and self-loathing, caught Lucinda's. "I don't want to ... play ... this way ... I'm not having fun."

"What a diversion!" El Brujo announced, nearly bent double with mirth.

And then Lucinda realized her mistake: she had been twisting the color-demons around her own body in order to restrict their movement so that she could claw and bite them more easily, and they had let her do it. Let her ball herself up like a fool, like a cat twisting itself inside the ball of string. Now, snake-like, the surviving demons squeezed. The air rushed from her lungs. The demons pinned three of her legs to her body. Now, with their flexible necks, they stabbed at her face in earnest. Although they were neither sharp nor hard, each stab landed on a pre-existing bruise. It was as if a dozen fingers poked her over and over, each time smarting more, each time threatening to burrow inside an orifice. She had to keep bobbing and twisting her head, moving, turning, biting or they would invade her mouth or nostrils and strangle her from the inside.

Little by little, Eva's struggle slowed. Mateo's crying became a howl of despair.

Little by little, the demons drew tighter around Lucinda's chest, her belly, her legs. Purple blobs spackled her vision. The throbbing in her temple became louder. Louder.

One of the color demons found an ear. It snaked inside and poked her eardrum. Lucinda-the-puma roared in agony.

"Faustino? Faustino?" Herminia's voice.

"Yes. I ... am ... alive."

Only the two-maize puma could have heard them outside the metal prison.

Both people sounded tortured, hardly able to articulate. For some reason, Lucinda's mind flew back to the final of final words from the cross:

It is finished!

The color demon slammed against her eardrum again. She nearly blacked out.

"Will you take me," Herminia croaked, "as your apprentice?"

The color demons stopped stabbing. Mateo's strangle-hold released a tad. The triumphant grin on El Brujo's face slipped to one side. Lucinda could see his attention turn from the three friends to Herminia and Faustino inside the metal prison, see him realize the danger closing in. He began to close a fist.

In response, the ship groaned anew. Rivets popped.

El Brujo prepared to crush his enemies ... and then paused.

He must have recalled that if Herminia died, he would lose access to her Physical power. Of course, he could do anything he wanted to Faustino, but he would have to separate them first. He had to be certain he did not kill Herminia.

Lucinda took advantage of the distraction to bite a color demon in two.

"It is ... my ... ah," Faustino rasped, "my honor ... mi amor."

With her puma's senses, Lucinda felt the wave of power as it descended over Herminia and Faustino, creating a new apprentice bond between the two, and severing the old between Herminia and El Brujo.

You cannot serve two masters, Lucinda thought.

But El Brujo did not die.

He sagged against the ship's hull, breathing heavily, weakened. But he did not die.

Mateo sat atop Eva, looking confused as to how he got there. Eva rubbed the hurt from her neck with both hands. Her beautiful, blond hair had never been such a mess of sand, sweat, twigs, and knots. In a croak, she said, "Now, Lucy. It's up to you. Go."

Lucinda flexed her giant feline back, bursting several color demons. Her roar vibrated the ship's hull like the mother of gongs. In response, El Brujo began to warp reality again using Spirit Magic, but he wasn't fast enough. Lucinda flung herself at him with all four paws forward. Her rear claws took him in the belly, her forepaws in the chest. He doubled over, and her jaw clamped over the back of his neck. El Brujo's threat ended with a bloody taste and the snap of vertebrae.

When the twitching stopped, the two crows, El Brujo's Spiritual and Mental allies, dissolved into feathers, the feathers into nothing. The gap into the Beyond closed.

After a few breaths, a dozen, Lucinda shape-shifted back to her human form. She was naked and did not care. She lay on her side, head turned away from the corpse of El Brujo, panting, savoring the air that pumped in-and-out of her lungs. Puny, human lungs inside a battered body.

A heavy, knowing silence descended on them. El Brujo, dead. The gap into the Beyond, closed. They would have to deal with the consequences of all those ... things ... entering the mundane world. But for now, for now they could rest.

The sun imparted delicious, wholesome energy to her exposed skin. Lucinda could have lain here forever, until—

"Off of me, tonto." Eva spoke from nearby. Free of Mateo's weight, she crawled over knee by shuffling knee. Lucinda felt her friend's arm across her back. "Nod if you can hear me."

Lucinda tried to lift her head but it dropped immediately. She managed to nod with her ear pressed to the ground.

"You did it," Eva said. "You killed El Brujo."

"We," Lucinda managed. "We did it."

"*We* saved the world," Eva agreed. "But *you* have the perfect excuse to go shopping. Your clothes are shredded."

Lucinda managed to chuckle, and, to her amazement, sharp pieces of rib did not attack her belly. Could it be...?

"Help me up."

With some awkward pulling and lifting ... and embarrassingly little help from Lucinda's core ... Eva managed to get Lucinda sitting. Lucinda twisted experimentally. Yes, her bones felt whole again; apparently the transformation to puma and back imparted that lasting benefit, but every one of her bones felt bruised, every muscle smashed, every nerve plucked.

A rock banged against the metal hull — from the inside.

From the inside.

That should be telling her something.

"Abuelita?"

"Little Chicken!"

"Are you? Is Faustino?"

"Fine. We are fine."

Lucinda's clothes seemed a mile away. Eva offered her shirt, but Lucinda declined. With tremendous will, she retrieved shirt, pants, and underthings, and managed to cover herself reasonably well. She'd seen worse on the Grammy Awards.

And then, from El Brujo's corpse, the bones started to creak. There was a nasty, fleshy sound that no one would ever want to hear outside of a butcher shop. El Brujo's chest heaved.

"Get a rock," Lucinda said, stumbling towards the broken chimney, hoping to find something to smash El Brujo with before he rose again. "Get anything. Move, now!" She imagined El Brujo reviving as a zombie and attacking anew. Who knew what could happen now, with the two worlds merged?

"What is it?" Abuelita asked, her pitch rising with panic. "Tell me, what is happening?" The little rock began banging the hull urgently.

El Brujo's body cracked open, his shirt split down the middle.

"Santa Madre—" began Eva.

A gnarled form emerged from El Brujo's chest cavity. It grew rapidly, almost as if unfurling rather than growing. It could have been an iguana tongue, but it was too stiff and too beautiful. At about a foot tall, its growth ceased. Buds pushed from the trunk, and from the buds extended little branches. They sprouted leaves.

"A tree," Lucinda said, for Abuelita's benefit. "A tree has sprouted from El Brujo's corpse."

Mateo clapped.

THIRTY-FIVE
PRESENT DAY, PUNTA COLONET, BAJA CALIFORNIA NORTH

Although a day and a half had passed since the battle at El Diablo's house, the cruise ship still smoldered offshore, now belching white smoke instead of black. It was one of those days when the onshore winds peppered your ankles with sand and tousled your hair, and threw eight-foot waves into the iron shell of the derelict boat on the beach off Punta Colonet, causing it to wail in a deep, resonant voice that reminded Lucinda of a gigantic singing bowl, a voice that recalled all too vividly that she had lost her allies forever. She felt the kind of ache you have when you are far from home and all alone, and she wondered if she would ever get over it. A part of her had been found, and joined, and now was lost. Forever.

Lucinda swung her gaze from the meditative ocean onshore. A row of cars and trucks were parked on the road leading to El Diablo's foundation, and twenty or so people stood around waiting for Lucinda to start the service. Lucinda had asked them all to come, though they had only a vague idea of the purpose. To their rear, the nascent tree had grown to about the height of her shins. El Brujo's body, from which it had grown, had disappeared, or become so much sand, or had fallen into the Beyond. Lucinda didn't know for sure, and didn't care to know.

Abuelita stood next to Lucinda.

"Remind me why we are here?" Abuelita asked, looking around the battleground with distaste. "And why you bother all these good people to rattle their behinds two miles on a bumpy road to see … this."

"Because," Lucinda replied, pulling her black sweater tighter around her shoulders, "the Punta Colonet cemetery is where El Jaguar is buried, so we cannot do it there. This is the most appropriate place I could think of to hold a funeral for Santiago."

"They are the same person," Abuelita said.

"No, they most certainly are not. You, of all people, should know this."

Grandmother Herminia sniffed in disapproval but said no more. She hadn't bothered with black, though she *had* dressed formally: a pleated white dress with red hem, some gold jewelry she hadn't worn in ages, and her hair done up in a bun. With Faustino as her guest, wearing a vaquero's leather vest and bolo tie, Herminia looked regal enough for the occasion.

Faustino still appeared haggard from the battle with El Brujo, but he did his best to stand erect.

Lucinda wore a black mourning dress, on loan from a friend.

Nearly everyone had come: Mamá, Papá, the Rattlesnake Thespians (seven members, including Eva), Abuelita and Faustino, the Fat Man, and a couple of people Lucinda couldn't name, all waiting respectfully around the burned-out foundation for whatever-it-was Lucinda had planned. They all shared that in common: both the guests and Lucinda wondered *what* she was going to do next. Bringing them all together was as far as she'd got, and now she hoped against hope that the proper words would come.

Everyone pointedly avoided looking at the shipwreck in the sand. Ever since the fire department had come with the Jaws of Life to free Abuelita and Faustino, the townsfolk did their best to pretend the metal skeleton did not exist. It was too strange, too great a reminder that a celestial rug had been pulled from under humanity's feet.

No one had asked Lucinda how it got there, not even the fire department.

A plume of dust indicated a car approaching. The Mercedes sedan pulled up, the rear door opened, and Mateo sprinted over. The car then turned around and waited at the front of the queue headed out, engine running. The driver, Mrs. Morales, clearly wasn't planning on joining them.

"Whoa, slow down!" Eva said, and threw herself in front of Mateo. He knocked her back several steps.

"Where's the kitty? Where's the kitty?" Mateo asked, in a giddy, child-like voice. He was taller than Eva, but Lucinda couldn't help wondering if he'd ridden over in a car seat. Wearing diapers. The vertical furrows Eva's fingernails had made on his checks stood out in sharp contrast to his childlike innocence.

And she realized that Eva could have escaped strangulation by scratching out Mateo's eyes, and she had refused.

"Kitty?" Eva asked, laughing. "What kitty?"

"He means El Jaguar," Lucinda guessed.

"Jaguar, Jaguar!" Mateo enthused. "Big kitty here, killed the bad man."

The other guests shuffled their feet. Some, like the blue-haired Thespian known as Maru, tended to grin. Others, like Lucinda's parents, tended to groan. They couldn't have known what happened to Mateo, but it was clear *something* had happened. Since all kinds of strange things had transpired these last few days — they would chalk it up as yet another freak occurrence.

But Lucinda knew exactly what had happened to Mateo's mind, and it triggered a touch of guilt.

"It's not a real kitty, silly," Eva said. "We're just pretending."

"Pretend?"

"Yeah. We're going to talk to the pretend kitty and then go home."

Mateo's chin dropped, the twinkle in his eyes fizzled, and he plopped next to the new olive-like tree. If it could even be called a tree. It was only about ten inches tall and sported about two dozen leaves. Mateo picked out a crow feather that had become wedged between the twigs and began scratching in the dirt with the quill, muttering something about wanting his tablet.

Lucinda was sure that it was a feather from one of Don Esteban's allies; probably one she had knocked free with her stone knife. Her face had flushed with all the warring emotions. Remembering their desperate battle. Recalling that she would never have access to her red cardinal again, never soar with the golden eagles, nor travel with her friends into the Beyond. And finally, remembering why her friend chose to have the mind of a child. A happy child — but a child nonetheless.

Could she ever forgive him completely?

How would Mateo ever catch up in school?

How would he ever live it down if he did attend school?

"We really botched it, didn't we?" Lucinda asked Eva.

"What? No! We did everything we could, and we ended up on top. El Brujo is gone. The world will adjust. Look at it this way, with all these brujos running around it will be a lot easier to get your warts cured."

"My what—?"

"Not *yours* yours, but warts in general. Is that what this is about?"

"I don't have warts!"

"Not warts, *tonta*, your ally. We were not witches before and we are not witches now, agreed? We still have each other. And baby-brain."

"Yeah, but do you miss it?"

Eva sighed. "Sure I do. It's like I missed a phone call."

"You value your phone a lot more than I do."

"Like a very important phone call. Like the announcement that I won the Oscars, but since I missed the call, they are going to give the Oscar to someone else, okay? Is that strong enough for you?"

Lucinda tried to thrust her hands in her pockets, but her black dress didn't have pockets. "I guess so."

They watched Mateo scratching around in the dirt.

Eva asked, "You?"

Lucinda squeezed her friend's arm. She tried to smell Eva's almond oil shampoo, but without the red cardinal, the smell was too faint. "Like I won the Oscars, but then I lost it. No one even remembers that I had it — except me. And I can't prove that I ever had it."

"That's harsh."

"Yeah."

"Lucy, look," Eva pointed, as Mateo continued to scratch out his drawings. "Do you see that?"

"Not skulls," Lucinda said.

"What do you suppose—?"

They peered intently over Mateo's shoulder.

"Puppies," Lucinda observed. "He's drawing puppies."

Little Rottweiler's, no doubt.

The girls smiled at each other, and Lucinda relaxed a little bit. Maybe this would turn out okay.

"No time like the present," Eva said, taking advantage of the happy mood. "It's time for your big number. But not here." And she steered Lucinda inside the wreckage of El Diablo's foundation in front of everyone.

And then she left Lucinda standing there.

All alone.

With everyone watching.

Lucinda waved urgently at her grandmother to join her. Reluctantly, she did. "I hope you know what you're doing," Abuelita whispered before turning around to face the crowd. Now their backs were to the Pacific and they faced the people, beyond whom in the distance lay Punta Colonet.

Faustino gave the two women a salute.

"Thank you all for coming," Lucinda told the crowd. "I, uh, I'm not good at speeches, so I'm going to let my grandmother do all the talking."

"What?!" Abuelita stomped her foot.

"Yes. I don't have nearly as much to say as you, grandmother."

"Well, that isn't a lot since I have nothing to say!"

Stubborn, just like Patti, Lucinda thought. "My grandmother," Lucinda raised her voice to drown out Abuelita's grumbling, "is the most wonderful person I have ever met." Lucinda smiled at her mother and father to show that no disrespect was intended, and they nodded back. "Abuelita, whom you know as Herminia García, has sacrificed more than you can imagine for us to be here today. I will tell you some ... but not all, of the story.

"Many years ago, my grandmother rescued a boy from an ... an orphanage. Sort of. He had no parents. He could not speak. He was mute, and angry, and hurt. The person responsible for hurting this boy is the same person who caused the cars to wreck on the Transpeninsular Highway yesterday, and the ships to burn, and the lightning to flash. My

Abuelita rescued this boy and adopted him as her son. That boy was named Santiago."

Eva's eyes were like saucers. Eva knew Lucinda wanted to conduct some sort of memorial, but didn't have any of the details.

"This boy you all know, but under a different name. For he was reborn later as El Jaguar."

Now she had their attention. Everyone here knew that Grandmother Herminia had killed El Jaguar. To imagine that he was also ... her adopted son?

"Kitty?" Mateo asked, looking around.

"Santiago Carrillo, who might have been my uncle if things had turned out differently, was not the wicked man he became. Under my grandmother's love he developed into a kind, caring boy, who gave much to save the world. He gave up his hearing and his voice. He gave up his freedom. He even gave up something that I would never ever be willing to give up." And now the emotion struck, and Lucinda couldn't keep the hitch from her voice. "He gave up his family." She tried and failed to clear her throat. She reached out and gripped Abuelita's arm. It helped her stay on her feet. "Abuelita?"

It took a moment for Abuelita to gather herself. "Yes, my granddaughter is very wicked to bring this up; some things are better left unsaid, but since the cat is out of the bag:

"Many years ago, I adopted a boy without parents. I gave him my surname, Carrillo, and called him Santiago. I loved him as my own, though at first it wasn't easy. He was a difficult child, having been rendered deaf and mute by that evil man who brought the chaos to this place, to my town." She looked at her sandals and gathered her thoughts. "You all know, if you watch the news, that there are now witches in the world, strange magic and powers that are tearing the world apart."

Faustino shouted out, "*La revolución!*" and pumped his fist in the air.

"Call it what you like," Abuelita said, clearly not pleased with the interruption. "This is real, and it is not going away soon. The man who did this to us we called El Brujo. I will not name him now, or ever. He does not deserve that.

"Many years another martyr gave her life to save Punta Colonet, in much the same circumstances. We celebrate her life each year at the Parade of Heroes."

"Marisol Sisson," shouted Maru, and the other Thespians repeated her name in a rolling chant which built and faded like a wave.

"Yes, Maru," Abuelita said, as the chant died. At this, she gestured to the smoldering cruise ship behind her back. Everyone contemplated that for a few seconds. "When I was young, and Santiago was younger still, only six years of age, he forestalled the coming of witches through his own bravery. He kept an evil man from becoming a demon, and he kept magic from invading our world. As Marisol Sisson saved the people of Punta Colonet, Santiago Carrillo saved far more. For a short time, he saved the world. But I—" her voice hitched, "—I failed to protect him. The evil man who did this to our world — El Brujo — caught up to us. He nearly killed us, and I saw no way out but to erase all that had been done. Erase Santiago's memories, and the healing we had done together, and everything. And so, when Santiago was ten, I abandoned him again — alone, broken, without memory, at the orphanage here in Punta Colonet."

"El Brujo did this," Faustino said. "Not you. Do not blame yourself."

Lucinda said, "Sí, El Brujo did this. Not you, Abuelita, not any of this."

Abuelita shrugged. "Bueno. El Brujo caused my adopted son, Santiago Carrillo, to be reborn into something sinister. Into El Jaguar. El Jaguar the man was a thug and a gangster. Santiago Carrillo, the boy, died at ten years old." Tears began to brim Abuelita's eyes. Faustino looked terribly awkward standing there, no doubt reflecting on his role in deleting Santiago's memories. "Little Santiago died on the day that all that was taken away from him. On that day, he died and became this ... this beast that you all know and feared, the beast known as El Jaguar."

No one muttered. No one turned away or scuffled their shoes.

"Kitty?" Mateo asked again.

It seemed that was all Abuelita had to say. Which was more than she should have had to say without warning, Lucinda granted. Now they both were crying. "So, this is a sort of funeral," Lucinda said. "Or, let's call it a little Parade of Heroes, forty-some years late. Today, we remember an innocent boy and the sacrifice he made to keep us all safe."

Lucinda bent down and took a handful of loose earth that had blown into the home's burned-out foundation. She picked it up and let it rain slowly through her fingers. "This is just dirt," she said, apologetically, "but I'm going to wash my hands anyway like it was ashes. Symbolic, you know?"

Although they couldn't have known exactly what they were doing, or what had happened so long ago, Lucinda and Abuelita's passion had clearly moved the listeners. Reverently, they bent down, picked up a handful of earth, and let it cascade through spread fingers.

"To the martyr, Santiago Carrillo!" Maru shouted.

"To the martyr!" everyone repeated.

Lucinda and Abuelita walked side by side to the edge of the foundation, then over the retaining wall. Each step seemed to take a thousand years. A great weight lifted from Lucinda's heart.

The Rattlesnake Thespians were the first to gather. As always, Eva's parents dressed in frank homage to macaws.

"How much did you rehearse that?" Eva's dad asked. He was shorter than his wife, and his bald head gleamed in the morning sun.

"Um, not at all," Lucinda said. "I kept thinking about who would show up, and how to get my mom to come, and Mateo, and everyone, so I didn't have time to think of what I was going to say. Which may have been the point about thinking about everything else, so that I didn't have to think of what I was going to say. Anyway, Abuelita said most of it."

"Brilliant," Eva's dad said. He and his wife hugged.

"Tell her," Eva said.

The blue-haired woman known as Maru took a step forward. "You didn't know it Lucinda, but this little oratory was your audition. And we Rattlesnake Thespians would like you to know, by unanimous decision, you passed! We have made you an honorary member of the Rattlesnake Thespians."

"Wait," said Lucinda, "I can't join ... my mother...."

Maru removed a necklace of wooden beads and placed it reverently around Lucinda's neck. "You have already joined. Past tense."

"That's very nice," Lucinda's mother said, formally. "Thank you."

"You're welcome," Maru said. "Practice starts this Wednesday at seven."

"What?!" Mamá exclaimed.

Papá chuckled and looked away, and Lucinda knew there was at least a chance. "Please, Mamá, can I?" she begged.

"Absolutely not."

"We promise we will finish and get Lucinda home before her bedtime," Eva's dad, Mister Navarro, said before Mamá opened her mouth again. "Rehearsal takes place in our home and we don't allow any funny business. There is no drinking or smoking from any of us.
"

"And no swearing," Eva added.

"Absolutely not," said Mamá.

"After all, Lucinda did just save the world," Abuelita put in.

"*We* saved the world," Lucinda said.

At that moment a gray whale surfaced in the Pacific, blowing up a gigantic plume.

Mamá seemed to deflate. Perhaps she thought the whale a sign from God. "Well, since you just saved the world. But she has to be back before nine. And if I even get a whiff of alcohol or cigarettes, even on her clothes—!"

"Yes, of course," Eva's dad said. "We have very strict rules."

Mrs. Navarro, Eva's mom, steered Mamá away. She was probably trying to reassure Mamá, but those peacock clothes would only make her more nervous. Still, Mamá allowed herself to be led. She must have accepted that Lucinda was more adult than child these days.

"That went well," Maru said, lighting a cigarette.

Eva and Lucinda squealed and hugged. "We're doing *The Mikado*, a musical comedy," Eva said. "You'll love it. You will have to do a reading, of course, but I know, just know, you will get the part of Yum-Yum."

Lucinda said, "Um, okay?"

Maru blew smoke over her own face and past her forehead. "Yeah, we'll see. I had to work spots the first two years."

"That's because you're lame," Eva said. "Oh, my dad's signaling. I have to go. Bye." She and Lucinda hugged again. Arm in arm, Eva and

Maru walked away, continuing to bicker good-naturedly. Eva gave Lucinda a thumbs up over her shoulder and mouthed "Yum-Yum."

The people began to depart, two to three to a car. Lucinda felt more and more anxious, especially when Papá fired up his truck and drove off with Mamá. "Um, Abuelita, are you sure we didn't want a ride?" She was not looking forward to walking back home, and wasn't sure Abuelita could even make it that far. Well, yes, of course she could. She's awesome Abuelita, but without water—

"What use of cars for a bruja?" Abuelita asked, waving at the final departure. "You forget, I don't have Don Esteban staring over my shoulder anymore. I need to work my lazy sailfish. I already told your mother: things are changing around here. Come, Little Chicken, there is something we need to do."

With a magical reality-wobble, they transported to the Beyond. It looked just like where they had been standing, but it felt different ... and the sky was stark purple. Offshore, a sailfish leapt impossibly high. Now Lucinda felt the huge emptiness of not having an ally. It felt like the loss of a dear friend, one who moved away and was never coming back. Or died suddenly. Left without the possibility of saying goodbye or grieving.

That, combined with the feeling of intrinsic weakness, a knowledge that if you jumped as hard as you could your heels would barely leave the ground; if you sprinted you would get winded after only two steps. Any race that you ran you would lose; any game that you played you would fail at....

Weakness. Emptiness. Yes, those were the words.

"Do you think I will ever get my ally back?" Lucinda asked, gulping back her emotion.

"I do not know. Brujos have always believed — at least according to Don Esteban — that once you lost your ally to the Null Wind it was gone for good, and you could never be a brujo again. Who knows if this is true? Yet here you are in the Beyond again, and you are still my granddaughter. That makes you a witch in my book. A good witch." Abuelita's matter-of-fact tone helped Lucinda feel better.

A tiny bit better.

"Can you feel Faustino through the apprentice bond?"

"No. The apprentice cannot track his master, and the master cannot feel his apprentice unless and until she uses her powers. Thank goodness, or Don Esteban would have tracked me decades ago."

Abuelita knelt. At her feet grew the little tree. "Mi hija, is this the same as the Tree of Knowledge?"

Lucinda knelt beside the old woman. "I think so. It sure looks like it. The leaves feel similar. The bark is different, younger. But still, it wraps around the trunk like the larger tree, and it folds...." She touched a tiny golden sparkle in a seam; the droplet tingled against her finger, as if emitting a teensy electric current. "Yes, there, the sap. I am sure this is a little Tree of Knowledge." The import of that nearly floored her. The Tree of Knowledge, here, on Earth.

What did it mean?

"You feel nothing from it?"

"I cannot sense the Tree, if that is what you mean. But the sap feels funny on my finger. It's kind of like an electric tingle — or the apprentice bond when it first takes."

Abuelita nodded. "The Tree is such a small, fragile thing. I want very much to dig it up and hide it. Too much has happened at El Diablo's foundation; others will come looking. And ... and Faustino knows where this is. What will he decide to do with the knowledge? He is still bent on his *revolución*." While she was talking, Abuelita began to fashion a knife of Physical power and stone. "I tried channeling Physical magic into the Tree of Knowledge back while we were standing around, to see if I could make it grow faster, or change shape, or even shake its leaves, but the Tree seems immune to what I can offer. I do not know if this is a good sign or not. I am even afraid to do this—" she nicked the little trunk with the stone knife, and as amber pitch oozed forth, she dipped the knife in it, "—though I believe the Tree is more robust than it appears. Your roots go deep, eh? Or so I hope. What would happen if the Tree of Knowledge were to die?"

The amber pitch spread perfectly over the knife, probably urged there by Abuelita's Physical magic.

Abuelita is so strong! Lucinda noted. *And I — I am empty.*

"This is what you did in the Garden of Eden, eh Little Chicken?"

"Yes, and I added the Null Wind."

"*Bueno.*" Abuelita stood and held the amber-covered knife above her head. Soon a brown haze blew in, wisp by wisp, and when it had become substantial enough, Abuelita gathered the Null Wind into the knife, crafting another blade like the one Lucinda had brought back from Paradise. "I wish I had a hundred of these," Abuelita said. "A thousand. When this tree is big enough, I will craft more. Arrowheads. Bullets even. But I am afraid to scar the Tree too much now."

"Why? What for?"

"Revolution rarely ends well," Abuelita said, testing the knife against her thumb. A thin red line appeared immediately, and she smiled grimly. "Revolution without God's values to guide it; sorcery without mentors to teach it; brujos who feel they are better than average folks: the worst atrocities are always committed by people who are convinced of their own moral justification. Mankind is a wicked beast without God to temper his excesses. Men and women, good as well as evil, will suddenly bond — and have power beyond what they ever imagined. Witches will need to be sundered from their allies. Lord knows, maybe a lot of them."

And then Abuelita did the most surprising thing of all. Handle-first, she offered the knife to Lucinda, saying, "Here, you have earned this."

Lucinda reached for it reverently. The knife felt heavier than the one she had crafted in the Garden of Eden, and yet better balanced. A pleasing, easy weight. "Why me? Why do I need this weapon?" Of course, she knew the answer: because Lucinda had lost her allies. As had Eva and Mateo. They were helpless babes in a world of brujos. But with this weapon, perhaps not so helpless.

"I am too old to race around the country seeking villains," Abuelita said.

"And I am too young!"

Abuelita laughed. "We always feel too young when responsibility falls upon us. Besides, I don't think you will have to do more than wait. Trouble will come to visit soon enough." She put her arm around Lucinda, and Lucinda noticed for the first time that, during the previous few months, she had grown taller than her grandmother by at least an inch. "Come on, Little Chicken, let's go home. Lunch is almost ready."

The Beyond wobbled, and they emerged inside the main room of their little house.

"About time," Mamá said, with tongs picking fried masa boats out of a pan of hot grease. She didn't seem surprised in the least that they had popped into her living room. "I'm making sopes."

Papá looked up from his armchair and said, "Leave your shoes outside. They're dusty."

Lucinda and Abuelita shared a grin.

END

Acknowledgments

Many, many people have gone into shaping me as a writer, and this manuscript in particular. Here are just a few:

First off, the tremendous bestselling author Lauren Kate, who mentored this project from beginning to end through Stanford's Online Novel Writing Workshop.

John Robinson, thank you for master class in method acting. I couldn't have written El Brujo without your help.

Next, Robert Enstrom, who inspired me with the SF novels *Encounter Program* and *Beta Colony*, and whose role as a mentor from our early *D&D* days cannot be understated. Also our mutual friend Rick Fowler, for the same reason.

To Jeanne Cavelos and the *Odyssey Fantasy Writing Workshop* for taking my writing to the next level.

To David Farland, Kevin J. Anderson, and Allyson Longueira for friendship and guidance in my writing career, and the same to all the folks at the *L. Ron Hubbard Presents Writers of the Future Award*.

Kristine Kathryn Rusch and Dean Wesley Smith, thank you for your workshops and unflinching honesty.

Robert McKee's *Story* and *Genre* workshops deserve mention, as I have taken over 120 hours of them in person and as many online.

To my editors at *NewMyths* magazine who, through sixteen years and counting, have helped me in so many ways, especially the stalwart Susan Shell Winston, who has kept *NewMyths* running all these years.

Barbara Ross King, my very first editor, thank you for showing me how to be a character psychologist.

To my kids, who inspire me with love; may I be the role model that you deserve; and to my wife, thank you keeping me on track, grounded, and well-fed.

Mom and Dad, despite not having any appreciation for SF & F whatsoever, you have encouraged and influenced my writing more than anyone else.

And to God, to whom I owe all.

About the Author

Scott T. Barnes won the L. Ron Hubbard Presents Writers of the Future Award for his short story "Insect Sculpture." He has published short stories in venues ranging from *Space Opera Mashup* to *History and Horror, Oh My!*

Western Americana is in Scott's bones and blood and it often finds its way into his stories. Both sides of his family have been farming and ranching in Southern California for several generations. Scott grew up on a farm (specializing in apples, pears, and cut flowers) in the small town of Julian, and later wrangled cows on his family ranches in Northern California and Oregon, where Scott spent many happy days breathing dust and learning the colorful turns of phrase of the cowboys.

Learn more about Scott and his upcoming projects at www.scotttbarnes.com

New Myths Publishing
Crafting Wonder Through Stories in Time

New Myths Publishing specializes in the publication of written works of fantasy, science fiction, and the Old West.

We pride ourselves on bringing our readers high-quality stories that will transport them through time and genres.

www.newmythspublishing.com

www.ingramcontent.com/pod-product-compliance
Lightning Source LLC
Chambersburg PA
CBHW040513170726
48295CB00012B/183